Finding Anna

By D. Emily Smith

This book is lovingly dedicated to …

Mrs. Hannah, Mrs. Erbe, Mrs. Peterkin & Mrs. Rogers: *Librarians are often the first heroes in a child's life. You ladies were mine at various chapters of my story. Thank you for not only opening up a world of reading to me, but encouraging my silly stories and giving me a safe space to grow.*

To all of the First Responders that helped me with the research for this book: *You will always have my utmost respect and admiration for all you do for your communities. May God give you safety and protection as you keep us all safe.*

1

Anna Munson stuck her earbuds in and set out at a steady pace down the street leaving her apartment far behind her. The pounding music vibrated off of her eardrums and matched the thudding of her heart in her chest. Anna inhaled deeply the scent of the recent early spring rains. Only an hour before, lightning coursed through the dark skies. The thunder roared and rattled her apartment's windows. Yet as Anna started her run, late afternoon rays of sunlight broke through the remaining clouds, offering hope that better times lay ahead. Anna wanted to believe the exercise would do the same for her mood.

Her favorite angsty song began and she turned the volume up. With each angry beat of the music, her footfall landed in perfect timing. Her ringtone interrupted her rhythm, causing her ire to rise. Anna swiped the tiny screen on her smart watch sending the call to voicemail without even looking at the name of the caller. She had a suspicion she knew who it was… and she did not want to talk.

Often when life got the best of her and she felt the need to run off steam, she would pray. She would tell God all about her hurts and stresses. But just like the person Anna sent to voicemail, she didn't want to talk to God either. Not yet anyway. Maybe after her rage subsided and she could see the sun beams through the clouds again. Until then … she would run.

Approximately three and a half miles out she saw the shoreline of the St. Lawrence River. She slowed her gait until she came to an easy walk along the water's edge. The breeze played with one of the loose amber colored curls that had come free from her headband. Anna allowed herself the comfort of standing with her face in the wind as it dried the beads of sweat on her forehead.

Why God? The simple prayer Anna uttered in disillusionment felt as if it returned to her unheard. She had never questioned God before, at least, not to that level. Even when her mother succumbed to cancer she had still trusted God. Hadn't she lived her life to be the *good girl* of their family? The Pastor's daughter... the one who lived above reproach while the other partied and spiraled out of control.

Anna felt her chest heaving with the emotions that – up till that moment - she had managed to keep at bay. Subconsciously, she went to twist the engagement ring on her left hand only to find her finger empty... except for the indentation where a gold band with a two carat diamond once existed. Her eyes slid shut as she rehearsed the events of that day over in her mind.

Traffic had been unusually heavy for a Thursday evening as Anna navigated the stretch of road to Jonathan's favorite restaurant. She'd been nagging him for weeks to discuss some of the details of their upcoming June nuptials. When he had called earlier that day and said he wanted to talk about the wedding over dinner, she had asked her boss if she could get off early. She left work to go home and grab her special planning binder before meeting him.

The closest parking spot was a block away, but she didn't mind. Armed with her binder chock full of visions and dreams for the big day she made her way to the restaurant. Anna spotted him right away. He was sitting under an umbrella at an outdoor table in the courtyard. Why he didn't opt for an indoor table, Anna didn't know. Ominous clouds gathered above, warning of a potential deluge. He was already sipping on his drink and glancing at his phone when she approached.

"Hey, Handsome." Anna leaned down and kissed his cheek as he casually placed his phone on the table face down.

"Hey, Annalise. I was wondering when you were going to show up. I already ordered for us." Jonathan looked agitated.

"I'm sorry I made you wait. Traffic is crazy and I needed to go home to get *this*..." Anna presented the binder as if it was a great thrill to behold.

"Oh, yes. The binder," he said dispassionately.

A waitress approached with a tray of food. Anna couldn't wait to eat. She had forgotten to pack a lunch that day and her breakfast had only consisted of a protein shake. Well... half of a protein shake. Most of it had spilled onto her boss when she ran into him while reading a rough draft at the same time as walking the corridor leading to the news room. This was probably why she was given the flower show to cover instead of the more ambitious story idea she had suggested.

The server put a kale and strawberry salad down in front of her.

"Oh, I'm sorry... I can't..." Anna tried to catch the server before she left but the woman didn't hear her calls.

"What's the matter?" Jonathan asked.

"I can't have strawberries, remember? I'm allergic."

"Can't you just eat around them?"

Anna laughed. "No. Not unless you want to run back to my car for my epi-pen."

"Is there anything you're *not* allergic to, Annalise?"

"It's not *that* much. Just bees and strawberries." Anna didn't like the feeling of defensiveness creeping up within her.

Jonathan Conrad was good for her. He helped her develop a thicker skin. She had always been too sensitive, most likely resulting from the constant teasing she received as a kid for her weight. Jonathan had a great sense of humor to get her to laugh at herself. After her gastric bypass surgery a couple of years prior, he had been her fitness coach. It was Jonathan who introduced her to the love of running. He kept her grounded.

"So you're not going to eat then?" he asked pointing to her salad, asking permission to take it and eat it himself.

"It's okay. I'm not that hungry anyway." Anna lied, watching him pull the plate away. She ignored the growl of her stomach.

"So, where shall we begin?" Anna asked.

"*Begin?*" he echoed in confusion.

She held up the binder again with an exaggerated cheesy smile trying to get him to laugh. "Do you want to start with seating plans or the menu?"

"Oh… uh…" Jonathan looked uncomfortable until his eyes locked onto something behind her and his face relaxed dramatically. Anna turned to see what he was looking at. Then she realized the *what* was a *who*.

Kirstyn. Anna furrowed her brow as she watched her best friend approaching. *This is odd timing.*

"Hi, Anna." Kirstyn's tone sounded different... almost sympathetic. "Is this seat open?"

Her friend didn't wait for an invitation. She sat in the chair between her and Jonathan at the small circular bistro table.

"Well... I guess it's yours." Anna tried to laugh off the odd behavior, but the smile on her face faded when she noticed the exchanged glances between Kirstyn and Jonathan. "What's going on? I'm getting the feeling you're not here to talk dress fittings."

There it was again. A stolen glance between two of the most treasured people in Anna's life.

"Did you start yet?" Kirstyn asked quietly to Jonathan.

"No, I said I was going to wait for you," he responded.

Anna felt her chest grow tight. "Start *what*? Will someone please tell me what is going on? Kirstyn, why are you here?"

Her friend reached across the table and took hold of her hand. Tears started forming in Kirstyn's brown eyes.

"Anna, you have to know that I never wanted to hurt you. I *love* you. You're my best friend. And I need you to promise me that you'll just listen. Hear us out. Promise?"

Anna did not say a word, nor did she nod in agreement. In truth, she sat motionless as she braced for whatever words were about to come from their lips. "We wanted to tell you together and ask you for forgiveness. I haven't been able to eat or sleep for days." Kirstyn cried openly now and Jonathan placed a hand over hers. "Somewhere along the way... we ... Jon and I..."

"We fell in love. There. It's out. I love Kirstyn, Annalise," Jonathan said abruptly. His face looked pained, but not as remorseful as Kirstyn's. "I'm so sorry. I never wanted to hurt you. I had every intention of going through with the wedding, but I'd be lying to you and to myself if I did. I let my guard down. She and I started texting and found out how much we have in common. You were so busy with your writing all the time. I got lonely."

"Anna…" Kirstyn's hand on hers felt as if it were burning through skin and flesh straight down to the bone. Anna pulled away.

Thunder grumbled somewhere off in the distance.

"Annalise, please don't make a…" Jonathan's tone warned.

"*Don't*!" Anna spoke out loudly as she got to her feet, catching the attention of a few patrons who were quickly gathering their food to take cover indoors as heavy drops of rain fell. "Don't tell me what to do, Jonathan. You have *no* right."

The man put his head in his hands and Kirstyn started sobbing. Anna aggressively tugged at the ring on her finger.

She looked down at it one last time. The day Jonathan took her to pick it out had been the happiest day of her life. As a younger girl- heavy and awkward - she never thought she'd get married. When Jonathan proposed, she thought she had found someone who knew her and loved her despite her quirks. Yet, in that moment Anna realized he had tried to change everything about her. Her writing. Her sense of humor. Her appearance. Had he ever even loved her?

"I suppose you want this back?" Anna held up the ring just as a flash of lightning illuminated the sky.

Jonathan and Kirstyn both got to their feet and he held his hand out to receive the ring. The words her father spoke to her when she was a child came flooding into her mind. *I swear your temper is as fiery as your hair is red, Anna Banana.* And he was right.

It all happened so quickly. One minute the ring was safely grasped between her index finger and thumb. The next minute, as rage built up and bubbled over, it was flying from her hand towards the street. There was some gratification to see the shock on Jonathan's face and to hear Kirstyn scream as the golden ring rolled its way under a parked Fiat a few feet away.

Anna spun on her heels, leaving the precious binder in the pouring rain on the chair she had just vacated. The loud crack of thunder was oddly satisfying as she walked in the pouring rain in the direction of her Jeep.

Behind her, she heard Jonathan yell, "Are you kidding me right now? Do you know how much that ring cost?"

She *did* know. She didn't care.

A seagull called out, bringing her back to the present. Daylight was quickly fading and Anna knew she needed to finish her run and head home. She started jogging before gradually increasing her speed to a full run. She stayed on the trail alongside the water's edge for a bit before turning towards home, passing cars and people living their lives as if the hurt she had just experienced hadn't happened at all.

Tiredness set in as she approached her street. Hopefully, the run would make her tired enough to sleep soundly instead of staying up all night thinking about what she should've said or done. Anna moved over to the side of the road that overlooked an embankment. The railings were helpful to use for her post-run stretches.

It was while she was extending her knee on the bottom rung of the railing that she heard something behind her. She turned just as a man came barreling towards her with a frantic look in his eyes. Anna quickly tried to right herself in time as he came crashing into her, knocking her off balance.

"Call Jake... Call Jake Cory. Make sure he gets it!"

"Excuse me," Anna pushed the man off of her as he clung to her arm with a death grip. She easily recognized the look of a man drugged out of his mind. Her sister, Alexis, gave her a good crash course in recognizing those signs. This man was on something.

He stumbled away from her then and began running towards the railing, going over it. The strange man slid down the embankment to the next street below on his rear end before getting up and disappearing into an alleyway.

Anna looked around to see if anyone else saw what had just happened. No one. She shook her head. It was no secret among her friends and family that if something *could* happen... it *would* happen to Anna. Her mother used to refer to it as *Anna's Law*.

Just as Anna decided to finish stretching inside, she heard tires screeching. She jumped back just as an SUV took the corner on two wheels. The vehicle slowed down as it passed her. Anna's brow furrowed as her eyes met those of the man in the passenger seat. He looked as if he were scanning the area for something... or *someone*. He gave a slight nod before the SUV took off like rocket fire once again.

Maybe she should seriously consider moving back to Deer Creek like her father had asked her to before she met Jonathan. She thought the move to Skennan Cove would help her discover herself. It turned out that moving two counties and several towns away only showed Anna that men lied, writing for a newspaper wasn't as exciting as she had thought it would be, and the effects of drugs were everywhere.

Finally, back in her apartment, Anna slid out of her warmup jacket leaving it in front of the washing machine. *I'll take care of it tomorrow. I just don't care right now.* Anna left a trail of clothing leading to the bathroom and started the shower.

Loneliness crept in. She wished her mother was still alive. Mary Munson was always a phone call away with the right words to encourage her daughter. Now she had no one. No Jonathan. No Kirstyn.

You could pray. You still have God. The thought hit her and she could've sworn it was whispered in her mother's voice inside her head. Anna shook her head vigorously.

"No. I'm not ready to talk to you yet, God." She looked up at the ceiling as if she could see past the plaster into the heavens. "I mean... what are You doing to me? Haven't I done everything You want? Why are You doing this to me?"

Anna caught a glimpse of herself in the mirror above the sink. Her red curls were unruly. Her freckles that ran across the bridge of her nose seemed more prominent in that lighting. Her cheeks were flushed and her green-gray eyes looked red from the tears she let fall to the ground unhindered.

For a split second as she stared at herself, she saw the chubby book nerd that used to hide in the school library. She blinked and she was back to the woman she had grown into. Slim, but still just as insecure.

Another tear slipped down her cheek. "What if he was my last chance, God? Who's going to love me now? I'm alone."

*****

"Why did you do that, Rob?" The man in the black hoodie jumped out of the SUV. His partner stood over the lifeless body of the man they had hunted all evening. "The orders were to bring him *back* to the warehouse so we could question him. Davidson is going to kill you."

The other man reached down and grabbed a handful of leaves from a pile of debris. He remained silent as he wiped the blood off the blade of his knife before returning it to its sheath. Finally, as if sensing the frustration of his friend he looked up and smiled.

"We did Davidson a favor, Keith. We stopped this guy from getting back to his police buddies. That's all that matters." He nudged the dead man with the toe of his boot to emphasize his point.

"Is it? I don't want to die for your mistake."

Rob laughed as he snapped a picture of the dead man with his phone. "So dramatic. Get in the car before we *do* have something to worry about. I didn't like the way that lady was looking at us."

"Should we go back to find her?" Keith asked as he took his seat behind the wheel.

"No. We have to report back to Davidson before his meeting tomorrow." Rob stared at the picture of their target before sending it to his boss. The thrill of the kill never got old. As they drove back up the roads they had come from, Rob looked for the woman, hoping he made the right decision to spare her life.

2

Anna muttered under her breath as she kept dropping the keys to her apartment. If she didn't hurry she'd be late for work *and* the flower show she was supposed to cover at the arena. When her alarm went off that morning at 4 AM she almost rolled over and went back to sleep instead of going to the gym as was her normal routine.

Jonathan wouldn't be checking in anymore so it wasn't as if she had anyone to be accountable to. Yet, the gym was therapy for Anna so she pushed herself to get out of bed. She had gotten so engrossed in her workout regimen that she lost track of time.

Finally, she got the door unlocked and stumbled over the running clothes she had shed the previous night. She refused to let the events of the day before turn her into a slob. Scooping the clothes in her arms, she went right to the washing machine and noticed her warmup jacket on the floor. Throwing the few items into the open washer, she reached down for her jacket. Something made a noise as it fell onto the tile at her feet.

That's odd. Anna reached down to the small silver USB drive and looked at it in her hands. She didn't use drives like that for work. With a furrowed brow she put it on the counter and went about getting ready for the day. She packed her lunch, brewed the coffee, showered, and dressed quickly.

It was while she was sipping on a steaming mug of coffee her eyes landed on the mysterious USB once more. She tucked it into her laptop bag and decided to look at it at work when she had more time. As she was headed out the door, her eyes landed on a picture of her and Jonathan at the last 5k she had run. He had his arm around her proudly. A moment of pain constricted her heart, but she grabbed the frame and put it face down on the table before leaving.

She made it to work a few minutes late and slipped into the staff meeting as it began. Seeing an empty seat next to her friend Lewis, she tried to casually glide into the chair without drawing attention.

"So nice of you to join us today, Munson," Mr. Price said, not even looking up from the agenda he held in his hands.

"Sorry I'm late," Anna apologized and grabbed her notepad from her bag.

"As I was saying," Harold Price began. "Here are the assignments for today. Sparks and Munson are heading to the flower show, where you will also interview Representative Scott after he opens the festivities. He wants to announce a new push to crack down on crime. It's also an election year, so…"

"An interview with State Representative Scott?" That made the assignment a little more appealing.

"Yes. It just so happens the timing worked out for a quick interview. You're welcome."

Anna shot Lewis an excited smile but quickly schooled her features in case Mr. Price decided she was *too* eager and took it away again.

"Smith and Collins, you have a breaking story. The body of a man was found overnight near Hudson Street…" Mr. Price stopped and looked right at Anna in surprise. "Isn't that near you, Munson?"

Anna lifted her head and tried to rewind what she had just heard. A dead body near her apartment? All of a sudden the events of the night before flashed into her mind. Could it have been the man who had knocked into her? The neighborhood wasn't the nicest, but dead bodies didn't just pop up willy-nilly either.

"What time did they find him? Is there a description of the victim? How did he die?" she asked.

"Well, I don't know, Munson," Mr. Price asked clearly irritated. "That's why I'm sending out reporters. Do *you* know something?"

"There was a guy last night, but…" Anna stopped mid-sentence. "Sir, could I switch with Collins and Smith to cover this piece? I mean, it is in my neck of the woods. I would kind of like to know what happened."

"And you'll read it like the rest of us after Collins writes it." Mr. Price dropped his gaze back down to his agenda. "Anyway, I already have your credentials for the flower show. It's too late to switch out journalists. Representative Scott is expecting you."

Anna glanced over at Sherry Collins and resisted the urge to scowl when the other reporter shrugged her shoulders with an arrogant smile. In the time Anna had written for the *Skennan Gazette*, she had attempted to submit stories worthy of the front page. Yet, she never seemed to land a solid piece. At least she was granted an interview with the State Representative. Maybe it was a first step to something bigger.

Lewis and Anna grabbed their press badges to the flower show at the arena and left. It was while they drove that Anna filled him in when he questioned the absence of her engagement ring.

"He broke up with you for your best friend? What a loser! Honestly, Anna…" Lewis shook his head emphatically. "I don't know how you tolerated him this long. I think you dodged a bullet. I never liked that idiot."

"Wow, Lew. Tell me how you *really* feel." In truth, Anna wasn't overly shocked by Lewis' words. Jonathan did have a way of coming off as… *harsh* … to those who didn't know him.

"Didn't you say your mother even had reservations about the guy?"

Anna sighed. "She didn't know him well."

Lewis laughed sardonically. "Actually… it sounds like she *did*."

"He's not my favorite person right now, but he was still the best thing to happen to me." Anna looked out the passenger window to hide the tears forming in her eyes.

The grunt that came from Lewis made it clear he disagreed. Anna needed to change the subject before she felt even worse about her current life situation.

"So… I had something strange happen," she began. "I was finishing up my run last night and this guy came out of nowhere and fell into me. He said something about finding a guy named Jake Cory and took off down the hill."

"Do you think he was the dead body they found?"

"I hope not, but my guess is… if it *is* the same fellow… he died of an overdose. His pupils were dilated."

"Poor guy." Lewis shook his head as he pulled into the congested parking lot.

"Yeah, well that is not the end of it. I was throwing my clothes from last night into the wash and a USB dropped out of my pocket. I've never seen this thing before in my life. I think *he* put it there."

Lewis turned his full attention to her after they parked in a spot. "Did you see what was on it?"
"No. I was running late. And what if it's a virus? I don't need my laptop contaminated by some weird ransomware."
"Munson, you know we need to look at it, right? Who knows what could be on it." Lewis grinned. "If it has something to do with that dead body they found... you could outscoop Collins."

Anna smirked. "I was going to use the computer at work to check it out. It has better virus software than my laptop."
"Good thinking." Lewis grabbed his camera bag and got out of the car.

The two walked through the glass doors into a floral fantasy. Instantly Anna wished she had thought to take her allergy medicine that morning. With the theme of *Fairytale Dreams*, it felt like stepping into one of her favorite childhood stories. Above them were countless of Kokedama tulip arrangements hanging upside down in a brilliant array of colors from yellow to deep pink. Breathtaking.

Achoo. Anna sniffed and stifled another sneeze while Lewis started taking shots of the entryway.
"Where do you want to start? We have an hour before Scott is set to give the welcome," Lewis pointed out as he took pictures of an elaborate display depicting a woodland path with borders of daffodils and various types of greenery.

Anna spotted a group of people pointing and pulling at various displays. One person in particular caught her attention due to the badge hanging around her neck. "I will see if I can get an interview with the director. Why don't you go get shots of that life-size wicker cottage and rose display," Anna instructed as she beelined it to the director when she saw an opportunity to squeeze her way into the group.

Moments later, her head swam with information about forcing blooms, warming mats, and cold storage. The flower show was a bit more involved than she had anticipated with over a thousand volunteers and artisans. The flora world was foreign to her as she had always killed... albeit unintentionally ... every house plant that she attempted to care for.

Anna looked for Lewis amid the brightly colored displays and found him talking to a few of the gardeners as they did last minute arranging and watering. She took the moment to wander and take in the sights around her.

Pulling out her cell phone she started taking pictures for her own benefit. Her mother would've loved the experience she was having. If only she could show her the peonies in various shades of pink. Those were Mary Munson's favorites.

It was while she was snapping a selfie in front of a castle made of carnations that she noticed two men in her image. Anna turned to see them standing on the other side of the floral structure. One was wearing a nice suit. Anna was fairly certain people weren't supposed to stand in between the displays and the outer walls of the arena unless they were maintaining the exhibitions. The one handed off something to the man in the suit and quickly hurried away after receiving an envelope. Another man joined him seconds later, dressed in a hoodie and jeans.

It was while she was leaning over to sniff a rose that the man in the hoodie looked over and noticed her presence. He gave her a look of familiarity and ... *fear*? Anna looked around to see if he could be looking at someone else but saw no one behind her. She turned back to the man and noticed he began whispering to the man in the suit. The two disappeared briskly walking the edge of the perimeter wall behind the displays. *Strange.*

"Look at the wedding display! I want all of these at my wedding next year." A cheerful woman gushed to her friend as she walked by Anna.

They walked down another aisle marked with a sign that read *Fantasy Wedding*. Her binder had images similar to the very displays that Anna now found herself gazing at. She should've known better than following the woman and her friends down that path. Looking at the twinkling fairy lights and whimsical topiaries caused the wound to reopen.

"The butterfly house is now open," a woman announced, coming from a mesh walled structure full of wildflowers.

"Butterflies?" Anna questioned as she moved closer.

"Yes, would you like to come in?"

Anna nodded. The butterflies were certainly more appealing than going down the aisle she stood in… a path that only led to sadness and misery. Stepping inside the tent Anna was surrounded by fluttering varieties of magical butterflies. They flew from flower to flower in such a joyful dance.

"Over here you'll see caterpillars in various stages of their transition. Look, one of our chrysalises opened and the little guy is trying to get out," the guide pointed out with quiet excitement.

Anna walked over to see the chrysalis and a wrinkled little insect trying to wriggle its way free of its confines.

"He doesn't look like he's doing so good. Can't you open it wider for him?" Anna asked in concern.

"Goodness, no. If I did that he would die. It looks like he's struggling, but if he doesn't go through this process, his wings won't dry. It's in this struggle that his wings will develop the strength needed to fly."

Something about the statement hit Anna right where it hurt. If her father were there undoubtedly he would have said, "*That will preach*!" Maybe God was using her struggle, as horrible as it seemed, to help her build muscles to soar, too. *Or maybe I'm just doomed to be grounded and alone like a crippled butterfly*.

"Anna, it's time for the opening remarks," Lewis called to her from the other side of the mesh wall.

Anna thanked the butterfly enthusiast and headed to the tent opening. Lewis was already a few steps ahead and forged a path for her to get to the front of a growing crowd. He often teased that he was the brawn and she was the brain. Lewis was the big brother and closest person she had to family in Skennan Cove.

Representative Scott stood behind the podium and sported a wide, white toothy smile. Anna pondered on how much he spent on whitening as he began his spiel. "What an honor it is to host the *Annual Northern New York Flower Show* once again! I want to personally welcome you to our wonderful area and…"

Anna scribbled down a few key things, but nothing he said stood out as earth shaking.

"In recent years we have seen an increase in crime and drug-related incidents. I want to take this moment to reaffirm that I have and always will stand behind our officers who fight crime tirelessly…"

Lewis gave Anna a side glance and smirk, while the man spoke many words yet said nothing significant or new. As he concluded, Anna grabbed Lewis' arm and tried to pull him in the direction of Rep. Scott.

"You go on ahead. I have to find the bathroom. Those three cups of coffee are catching up to me," Lewis said.

It was after her friend left that she realized he took the camera with him. Using her phone, Anna attempted to take candid shots of the representative greeting those around him hoping Lewis would hurry up and get better pictures for their piece. As she approached, she cleared her throat to alert him of her presence.

"Representative Scott? I'm Anna Munson from the *Skennan Gazette*. I believe Mr. Price contacted you about an interview."

The man standing next to the state representative looked an awful lot like the man she had seen behind the carnation castle display. He flashed Anna a winsome smile that probably made most women swoon and he reached out, touching her hair.

"You have a hitchhiker," he said as he showed Anna a butterfly that had gotten caught in her curls.

"Oh no. I was just in the butterfly house."

"Well, now he is free thanks to you. What was your name again? Munson?" Something in the man's tone and expression felt off though she couldn't put her finger on it.

Rep. Scott cut in abruptly addressing the man in the suit. "It was nice to meet you. Enjoy the rest of your day."

Odd. They looked very deep in conversation right before Anna approached. They didn't give off the appearance that they were previously strangers. The man in the suit smiled at Anna one last time, taking the butterfly with him as it perched on his hand.

She followed him with her eyes as two other men joined him—the man in the hoodie and another person. The second man turned to look back at her and Anna could've sworn she recognized him. Familiarity registered on his face as well, but he turned around and continued to walk discreetly behind the man in the suit. "I'm sorry, Miss Munson, can we please make this a quick interview? There are many other people I need to visit with before I leave." The politician not only sounded annoyed, but he looked it as well.

Anna hastily asked the questions she needed for her piece. Mr. Scott didn't offer any type of goodbye when she thanked him for taking the time to speak with her. He headed down a different aisle with his assistant. Rep. Scott had always come off as fake when she listened to his past speeches, but he never gave Anna the impression that he was rude. However, that encounter seemed rude.

Lewis joined her again. "Ready to go?"
"Yes." Anna followed her friend towards the exit but turned around to see where the man in the suit had gone. There was no sign of him or the other two men

that accompanied him. "Lewis, did you see the man that Rep. Scott was talking to right after the speech?"
"You mean Lance Davidson? Yeah, I've seen him on the news. He's a pretty prominent businessman. He's always doing some kind of charity event or another. That guy is rolling in it." Lewis turned to her with a smile. "Why? Are you looking for someone to replace Jonathan already? I tell you what, that guy would definitely be a step in the right direction for once."

Anna ignored the rest of Lewis' teasing and tried to brush off the unsettled feeling in her gut. Something about those two men that accompanied Mr. Davidson was agitating her. An image floated in her head of the SUV that slowly passed her and the man that smirked at her from the window. Could it have been the same man? Why would he be at the flower show? And what did they have to do with Representative Scott?

*****

"So now you're telling me, that *that* woman... a *reporter* of all things... might have recognized you from last night?" Davidson's voice was not loud, but the steely tone was unmistakenly dangerous as the three walked to the black sedan. The butterfly that had been resting on his finger was now scrunched into a ball in his palm. Davidson wiped his hand on Keith's hoodie.
"She doesn't know anything. I swear." Rob assured his boss.
"Oh really? You want me to trust *your* assessment of this, Rob? Now, does that sound like something I would do?"

Rob didn't respond and Keith wisely kept silent as he stared down at the butterfly guts smeared on his sleeve.

"Find out about her. I want to know *everything*," Davidson ordered. "I'll have Scott give Mr. Price a call to fix the mess you two imbeciles made. Now get going."

The two men wasted no time in obeying, knowing full well that the next time they made a mistake they may not get out of it alive.

3

"Are you almost done with that piece?" Lewis sounded like an impatient child.

When the two returned to the office, he wanted to see what was on the USB drive in Anna's bag. She did as well. However, she also wanted to get her work done and submit it to her boss in case he happened to catch her doing something other than what he had assigned to Anna.

"You're worse than my two-year-old niece," Anna smirked as she stared at her friend over her black framed glasses. As wonderful as those flowers had been, they aggravated her allergies bad enough that she had to take out her contacts.

"You know… I can pull it up on my computer while you finish that up," Lewis offered innocently.

"Are you *that* bored?" Anna reached down into her laptop bag and threw the USB to her friend.

"I prefer to think of it as multitasking," was his cheesy reply.

Anna turned her attention back to her article. She tried to include more of Rep. Scott's speech than the flowers at the event. She was given a fluff piece, but maybe she could give Mr. Price back a genuine news article.

Admittedly, writing for the small paper was not her dream job. Anna loved writing and she would be content with whatever allowed her to do that, but her passion was storytelling. Anna had several outlines for novels stored away on her computer. Unfortunately, that didn't pay the bills and, according to Jonathan, it was a waste of time.

"So? Do you see anything worthwhile on the USB?" Anna asked after her friend had remained quiet for too long.

"Nah. Looks like a bunch of nonsense to me." Lewis got to his feet then. "I'm hungry. Do you want anything?"

"I have a banana here. I'm good until later. Thanks anyway," Anna said not taking her eyes off her computer screen.

Moments after Lewis left, Mr. Price came out of his office and called out to her.

"Anna, could I see you for a moment please."

"Sure." Anna got to her feet and smiled at her boss. "I think you will be pleasantly surprised with my piece."

Mr. Price closed the door of his office after she entered and motioned for her to take a seat.

"Anna…" He sat back down at his desk and just stared at her for a moment.

"Yes?" Anna attempted another smile as she waited for her boss to gather his thoughts. The silence made her uncomfortable.

"I've been put in a very unpleasant position. I just received a call telling me that I need to let someone go." Mr. Price looked pained.

"Oh, no. That's horrible. Who are you …" Then reality hit. *Anna's Law* struck again. "*Me*?"

"I'm sorry, Anna. As you know, money has been tight. We've already had to cut back significantly… even going from a daily paper to a weekly."

Anna sat in shocked silence.

"This is not a reflection on your abilities or talents. Please don't take it as that," Mr. Price stated kindly. It was *too* kind… uncharacteristically so. "It's just that you're the newest on staff. The other writers are already well established with our readership."

"I'm not *that* new. Please, Mr. Price. I think you'll like the piece I am finishing up. I feel I covered the speech today in a way that…"

"Anna. Anna. Stop." He put his hands up to interrupt her sentence. "This is hard enough as it is. We're prepared to offer you severance pay. Email your finished piece, but you don't need to report to work tomorrow."

"Wait. You're not even giving me notice."

"I'm sorry, Anna. Best of luck with your upcoming wedding." Mr. Price moved to the door and held it open for her even though she still sat motionless in her seat.

Slowly, Anna stood. Mr. Price kept his eyes on his shoes and refused to make eye contact with her as she left.

"There are empty boxes in the printing room. You can take one of those to empty out your desk," he said quietly before he closed his door.

Anna couldn't believe what had just happened. She watched the shadow on the other side of the frosted glass window on his door move back towards the desk. What was she going to do now? How long would it take for severance pay to hit her account? She had never been let go before.

Anna slowly moved back to her desk, ignoring the curious expressions on the faces of her coworkers. It felt much like the time the teacher had called her to the front of the class to explain why she was drenched in water.

Gianna, one of the most popular girls in the seventh grade, ran up to Anna who was sitting contentedly on the bench reading her book.

"Anna, you'll never believe it," the girl said excitedly.

"You're probably right. I won't believe it. So leave me alone please." Anna stated without raising her eyes from her book. For added effect, she shifted her body to give Gianna her back.

"Michael Tyler likes you!"

Anna's heart fluttered. Michael Tyler was adorable with his chocolate brown eyes and dimples. For a moment, she wanted to believe it. Then she remembered she dwarfed the other girls at school by a solid fifty pounds. Anna smelled a lie.

"Go away, Gianna."

"Look, he's waiting right over there."

Against her better judgment, Anna lifted her head and saw Michael standing not too far away. He gave her an awkward smile and a slight wave. She smiled in return. The two attended the same church and were a part of the same youth group. Outside of school, they had an easygoing friendship that Anna enjoyed.

Anna ignored Gianna behind her and got to her feet to go talk to Michael. She didn't trust Gianna, but Anna did trust Michael. He looked up at something above her with a look she couldn't read.

Whoosh. All of a sudden a torrent of icy water fell over her, taking her breath away. Her eyes were clenched shut, but when she finally opened them she saw Michael had run away leaving her standing in a puddle with ice cubes at her feet. She looked around and found Stephen Turner with an empty bucket in his *hands, laughing with a group of other boys from an open window on the second story of their school.*

Just then, the bell rang. Anna figured she had two choices. She could cry and run away. Or she could pretend as if it didn't bother her and go to class. She chose the latter. It was when the teacher had entered the room that she noticed Anna dripping in her seat. "Miss Munson, please come here."

Anna stood with her chin raised ever so slightly and passed Michael Tyler's desk. As she moved by him, she made sure to shake her hair to get the homework on his desk wet. She heard him whisper something to her, but she didn't listen. As far as she was concerned, they were no longer friends.

As she approached the safety of her desk, Anna pulled herself from the troubling memory. Sometimes those recollections popped up at the most inopportune times. This being one of them. Maybe it was because she could hear people whispering. Maybe it was because she could feel the stares on her back as she sat down at her desk and began emptying it of the few items she kept there.

Where was Lewis? Of all the times she needed a friend, it was now. She closed her laptop and put it in her work bag. It was then that she noticed the USB was still sticking out of Lewis' computer. Without thinking she reached over and tugged it free, throwing it into her bag with the rest of her possessions.

A few people attempted to say goodbye as she left and she did her best to behave the way she had been taught. Smile. Be polite even when you want to scream. Make a graceful exit. It was while she was heading to the elevator that the doors opened and Lewis came out.

"Where are you going?" he asked.

"Mr. Price fired me."

"*What*? Why?"

Anna felt the emotions she had attempted to keep bottled up threaten to surface. She needed to get out of there. "I'll call you later, Lewis."

"Lewis, can I see you for a moment?" Mr. Price called from his office door.

Anna and Lewis exchanged perplexed looks as her friend slowly headed to the editor-in-chief's office. She stood still a moment as she watched the door close behind him. What was happening? In the span of one day, Anna lost her fiancé, best friend, and her job. How had her life been reduced to a sad country song in a mere twenty-four hours?

*****

Lewis Sparks paced back and forth in his living room and stared down at the phone in his hands. He debated whether to call Anna. Guilt kept him from finding relief in the fact that he still had a job to report to the next morning. When Mr. Price told him that all he had to do to keep his job was to hand over the camera they used to capture pictures that day at the flower show, he was eager to comply.

He stared at his laptop displaying the files he had secretly downloaded from the USB Anna had let him look at. Could Davidson's name staring back at him connect the USB to Anna's mysterious firing? When he returned from making a few inquiries regarding the name *Jake Cory*, he saw the USB was no longer inserted in his computer. Had Anna taken the USB from his desk or had Mr. Price? If Anna had taken it back was she aware that she could be in more trouble than just losing her job?

Lewis pulled up Anna's contact information on his phone screen but hesitated before putting the call through. What was he going to tell her? That he had lied to her about what he found on the USB? Maybe she had looked at it for herself and already knew. What if she tried to write an exposé on Davidson's dealings before *he* managed to?

He put his phone away and sat back down in front of his laptop. Lewis had one shot to get beyond *Skennan Gazette* and this was it. Pushing aside his troubled conscience, he started composing the article that would take him from sidekick to professional journalist.

*****

Anna crawled into bed, placing a wet washcloth over her swollen eyes. Since coming home from work, she cried for a solid two hours. It didn't help to see that Kirstyn had stopped by and left a card taped to her door. As soon as Anna opened the envelope and saw her ex-friend's name at the bottom, she crumpled it up and threw it into the trash.

At 7 PM Anna's cell phone rang and she remembered it was Friday. Every Friday her father would call and she would tell her nieces and nephew a story before bed. How was she going to muster the strength to get through this call?

"Hi, Anna Banana." Her father's voice was like a soothing balm.

"Hi, Daddy."

"Uh oh, what's wrong?"

"How do you do that? How do you know when I'm a mess?" Anna smirked despite the tear that slipped down her cheek.

"For starters, you called me *daddy*. That's normally reserved for extreme situations. What's going on, Sweetie?"

In the background, Anna could hear the kids milling around… probably waiting for the next installment of "*Princess Anna and the Magical Pen*". As if sensing her hesitation, her father called to the kids.

"Hey, guys. Instead of story time tonight how about ice cream?"

A resounding cheer went up from baby Livi and Sam.

"Ellie, will you please take your sister and brother into the kitchen for ice cream?" Tim Munson addressed his twelve-year-old granddaughter.

"Ugh, why do I have to do everything? Can't Sam do it himself? He's a big boy," Ellie whined.

"Because you know very well that Sam will take the whole carton if you let him," Tim reasoned. "Can you please just do it without arguing?"

It sounded like Ellie made some type of sassy comment, but soon the background was quiet.

"Why does Ellie sound like a grown up woman?" Anna asked, putting off telling her father the inevitable truth about her current situation.

"I'm sure she *thinks* she is a grown up woman." Then Anna noticed it. Her father sounded weary.

Tim Munson was a pastor of a thriving church and, at the same time, trying to parent his three grandchildren. Anna's older sister, Alexis, was in and out of different rehab facilities while her ex-husband, Jared Hadley, was in and out of prison. Five years prior the Munson family remained hopeful Alexis would benefit from the first rehabilitation program she entered. Ellie and Sam had come to live with Anna's parents then. However, Alexis only made it a few weeks before getting kicked out.

When Alexis found out she was pregnant, she moved home with her parents and appeared to be on a good path again. She managed to stay off drugs during the pregnancy for the baby's sake. Yet soon after Olivia was born, she slipped back into her old ways and left home in the middle of the night to follow some guy. Legal guardianship of all three kids was granted to Tim and Mary. Soon after, Mary succumbed to the cancer she had been battling off and on, leaving Tim as sole guardian.

"Okay, Annalise. Out with it. What's going on?" he asked when the silence had gone on long enough.

"I don't know where to start." Anna stifled a sob.

"Start with what hurts the most."

"Jonathan left me for Kirstyn. The wedding is off," Anna cried. "Then today I lost my job. Oh, Daddy, what do I do now? I think God has left me."

Tim sighed. "What a *jerk*."

"Dad? Did you just call…"

"Yes. Yes, I did. Jon's a jerk. A *big* one." Anna couldn't remember her father ever calling anyone a jerk. "Jonathan left you, Sweetie. *God* didn't. There's a huge difference."

"What do I do? I have nothing left."

"Yes, you do. You have a God who loves you and has a plan for you even when you can't see what He's doing. You have a family that adores you. You have talent that doesn't require you to live in Skennan Cove. Use it here, Anna."

"I'll need a job. I can't just live there mooching off you like I did when I was a kid."

"Do you remember Mrs. Erbe?"

"Of course I do." Anna had precious images in her mind of the sweet librarian at Deer Creek Elementary. "I hear Mrs. Erbe is looking for an assistant. I can't think of a better person to do that than the very first ever *Student Assistant Librarian*."

The head librarian came up with the title for Anna to appease the principal when Anna didn't want to go eat lunch in the crowded cafeteria with the kids who were bullying her. Mrs. Hannah Erbe harbored the girl in the library, putting her to work by doing various library tasks that felt more like a reward than a job. Every day she'd eat lunch with Mrs. Erbe in that library… her sanctuary.

"But where will I live? You've got a full house."

"Never too full for you. Do you have any idea how much I miss you?"

"I have to admit it's tempting," Anna said quietly, looking at the box of stuff that she had packed earlier that night... all the things that reminded her of Jonathan. "I know I don't want to stay here anymore."

"Then it's settled," Tim concluded gently. "It's time to come home, Anna."

4

Anna said goodbye to the church friends who showed up at her apartment to help her load the rental trailer hitched to the back of her Jeep. She had been hoping to see Lewis before she left Skennan Cove, but he had been oddly hard to reach. In their last conversation, she had told him she was leaving and he didn't seem to care one way or the other.

His response seemed rather flippant. "It's probably a good idea. There's not much here for you anyway, right? Just go and don't look back."

And that was what she was doing. Putting her Jeep in drive, Anna pulled away from the curb and headed in the direction of Deer Creek, New York. One of her church friends, being well-intentioned, put a copy of the *Skennan Gazette* on her passenger seat. Anna glared at it out of the corner of her eye.

She had every intention of throwing it out when she stopped for lunch. However, as she munched on a chicken Caesar wrap she couldn't resist the urge to leaf through the pages to see if her final piece was published. She landed on one of Lewis' pictures and saw the headline. *Northern New York Annual Flower Show a Success.*

"Pfft. They changed my title." Anna furrowed her brow as her eyes scanned the content of her article.

There was no mention of the state representative or his speech nor were there any pictures of his appearance. The article had been condensed to nothing but drivel. *Why bother even putting my name on it? It's barely even the piece I wrote.* In a fit of anger, she threw it to the floor of the passenger seat.

She took a long sip of water to calm her, but her eyes glanced back at the paper noticing the headline of a different story. *Body Found on Residential Street.* Curiosity got the better of her and she reached back down and grabbed the paper. She read Connor's article on the man that they found near her block and Anna wondered if this article had been mutilated as well.

"Sherry Collins writes better than this," Anna muttered under her breath as she read the small piece that stated a homeless man was found dead due to unknown circumstances.

Homeless? The man Anna had encountered looked high, but not homeless. His clothes were clean and he smelled of cologne. He looked to have been in his mid-twenties and clean shaven. There was nothing stating that officials awaited a toxicology report or that the man had been identified. Maybe the weird stranger wasn't the deceased body they found after all. Yet, something was off. Anna's street wasn't the best but there wasn't a homeless population there either.

Anna glanced over her shoulder at her laptop bag that contained the USB that Lewis said contained nothing. Maybe *his* idea of nothing differed from *her* idea. Just as she was about to reach for the bag, her phone dinged and she saw her father's text.

"*Looking forward to seeing you! The door is unlocked. I'll see you after I get the kids from school.*"

If Anna wanted to get settled before the kids came home, she had to hurry and get to the house. When they saw her there would be wrestling and nonstop chatter. The USB mystery would have to wait until after they went to bed. So, she gathered her trash, threw it away, and headed home.

It didn't take long to pass the sign that said, "*Welcome to Deer Creek*". The steeple of the church was visible from the street she drove on. Next to the church was the only home she had ever known. She swallowed hard as she braced herself for the onslaught of emotions. To her shame, it had been quite a while since she had been back to her hometown. She couldn't bring herself to visit after her mother passed away.

"Well, I'd better get over it quickly," she whispered to herself as she pulled into the parking lot of Deer Creek Community Church. "There's no going back now."

*****

Michael Tyler wiped his feet before entering the church after mowing the grass. His brother was humming from his office and a smile crept across Michael's face. Sean Tyler, for the most part, had always been an upbeat person. There was a spell in high school when he went off the rails for a bit, but God used it to get Sean's attention. Now as a husband, soon-to-be daddy, and an assistant pastor… there were very few times Michael didn't see his brother with a smile on his face.

"Hey, Boss. I finished the mowing. Can we go eat now like you promised?" Michael came into Sean's office plopping into an upholstered chair.

"Yes! I'm starved, too." Sean said grabbing his jacket from a hook on the wall. "Tessa hasn't been very hungry lately and I don't want to eat in front of her."

"Morning sickness still bad?"

"I had no idea pregnancy would be like this. Kate and Dan made it look easy." Sean's eyes grew large and Michael suppressed a smirk. "Tessa can't even stand the smell of coffee right now. She *loves* coffee."

"Don't worry. Give it a couple of weeks and Tessa will be eating the same crazy stuff Kate does."

"I don't know, Mike." Sean shook his head. "All I did was *mention* tacos and she ran to the bathroom."

Michael followed his brother out of the church with a smile. Both of his brothers had become domesticated over the past five years... something he refused to do. Dan and Kate were cooking baby number two while Sean and Tessa were just starting their family. Michael was content being the fun uncle. His baby sister Jen was even going to marry before him. Ben had asked their father for permission just the other week.

Poor people. Michael shook his head at it all. He had his life just where he wanted it. If he wanted to go rock climbing with the guys, he could. If he wanted to go eat a burger at ten at night, he didn't have to ask anyone. He finally had the apartment that he and Sean had shared as bachelors all to himself. He played his music loudly. Michael got to watch the football games that he had missed while working his shift at the fire station any time he wanted... sometimes even after midnight. And no one stopped him or complained. Life was great!

"What the..." Sean stopped abruptly and Michael bumped into him. "Who is blocking the parking lot entrance?"

Michael looked past his brother to see what he was talking about and saw a Jeep with a trailer hitched to the back. He laughed as he watched the Jeep repeatedly reverse, begin to jackknife, and then try to pull forward to right itself.

After the fifth attempt Michael asked, "Do you think we should help?"

"I guess so... or I won't see my wife until sometime tomorrow." Sean laughed as he locked the church door and walked in the direction of the Jeep.

"By the time they get that thing unstuck, your kid will be in college," Michael teased.

As they neared the Jeep and trailer, which was now wedged precariously between a culvert drop off and the parsonage mailbox, Michael noticed a flume of red curls hanging out of the window as the driver tried to see where her tires were.

"Who is that?" he asked.

"I don't..." Sean paused and let out a sigh. "*Anna*. I totally forgot Tim said she was arriving today."

"Anna? As in *Annalise Munson*?" Michael squinted at the woman in the driver's seat. She looked very different than he remembered.

Sean nodded. "She's moving back to help Tim with the kids. I know he was very happy the other day that she was coming home."

"I thought she was getting married or something," Michael said as he watched her hit the steering wheel in anger.

"I guess they called it off." Sean tugged on his brother's arm. "Come on... before that trailer lands in the culvert."

Michael laughed as he heard her yell through the open window, "Come on, you idiot trailer! Piece of junk!"

"Do you think they broke up because she has anger issues?" he chuckled.

Sean glared at him and pointed a finger straight at his brother's chest. "You... behave."

"What?" Michael feigned an innocent face and put his hands up in the air as if he were a perfect angel.

Moving closer to the Jeep, Sean waved his hands until Anna put the Jeep in park and leaned her head out of the window.

"Welcome home, Anna," Sean said cheerfully. "Can we help?"

"Hey, Sean. No. I've got this," Anna said as she blew a loose curl from her eyes. "Thanks anyway."

"Are you sure about that?" Michael piped up, clearly amused.

Then he saw it. It was like a flash of lightning in her eyes and for a moment he was on the receiving end of her fire.

"Like I said... I've got this," she reiterated. The Jeep shifted back into gear and she leaned back out the window. "You may want to back up."

The men obeyed, albeit reluctantly. She appeared to set her jaw and pulled forward just enough to pull the trailer back into position, but she hit the mailbox with her bumper, causing it to lean backward. Still, she persisted.

"Determined, isn't she?" Sean asked under his breath to his brother.

"More like stubborn," Michael muttered under his breath. It was when the back tire of the trailer started dipping dangerously close to the culvert drop off Michael moved to take charge. "Enough already."

Michael went to the mailbox to examine how firmly planted it was into the dirt. Content that the last nudging of the Jeep loosened it good enough, he motioned for his brother to join him in pulling it from the ground. Anna watched from her seat with wide eyes, but he just shook his head and ignored her. Michael came to her side of the Jeep and pulled the door open.

"I'm sorry! What are…" Anna started to protest, but Michael reached in, undid her seat belt, and pulled her out gently by the hand.

"I forgive you," he smiled broadly. "Now go wait over there before we have to tow this trailer out of the ditch."

Sean, seeing Michael had commandeered the driver's seat, quickly went to Anna's side to stand by her… and to potentially aid in damage control depending on how angry she was. Her mouth gaped open in shock, but Michael paid little attention. In just a few maneuvers, he backed the trailer up the driveway to the parsonage with her Jeep facing out.

By the time he walked back to where the two stood, Anna's mouth was no longer gaping open. No. Her mouth was clenched shut and her eyes shot out sparks. Maybe he should've handled things differently. His stomach growled then, reminding him that if they had waited for her to get out of her predicament he would've passed out from hunger.

"Your keys, Milady." Michael flashed Anna his most winsome smile... the one that got him out of almost every scrape in the past.

She snatched them with a less than enamored expression and replied in a sarcastic tone, "My hero. Whatever would I have done without you?"

"Anna, can we help you unload?" Sean asked, clearly trying to smooth over his brother's audacity.

Anna spun to face Sean and completely turned her back to Michael. Since she was making such a point of excluding him, Michael took that moment to put the mailbox back into the hole they had pulled it from. Later, he'd return to make sure it was more secure as it still leaned to the side.

"I appreciate the offer, Pastor Sean, but I think I can manage from here." Her tone was as sweet as honey and friendly. "I hear you and your wife are expecting a baby. Congratulations."

"Yes. A little girl. She's due in September."

"That's wonderful. I look forward to meeting Tessa. I've heard wonderful things from my father."

"Welcome home, Anna. Let us know if you need anything."

With that, Anna nodded and began walking up the drive. She did, however, send Michael one last scowl.

"What did you do to her? Anna was the nicer of the two Munson girls," Sean laughed as they headed towards their respective vehicles.

"I have no clue." Michael caught himself staring after her. Not many women disliked him. In fact, he couldn't name one.

Sean was chuckling to himself as he unlocked his car.

"What is it? What are you laughing at?" Michael questioned.

"I just never thought I would see the day that Michael Tyler would be disliked by a woman. That's gotta be humbling."

Michael snorted at his brother's words. "Give her time. She just got here."

"You could use a little humbling, Mike." Sean shook his head before changing the subject to food. "Follow me to Woody's?"

"If you're still paying," Michael smiled at his brother but turned his attention back toward the parsonage before climbing up into his truck cab.

Why did Anna's chilly response bother him? The Annalise he remembered was always so nice and sweet. Had he really offended her by helping back in the trailer? Michael determined he would find a way to make it up to her somehow. Before long, they would be friends again.

*****

Anna let herself in the side entrance of the house and the familiar scent of her childhood home filled her nostrils. She could almost imagine seeing her mother sitting at her sewing machine in the living room whirring away at some new project. Yet, as Anna walked further into the house, the corner where Mary's sewing machine once sat was now occupied by stacks of books.

The sight brought both sadness and a twinge of amusement. Her mother once said if anything should happen to her, Anna's father would turn every available corner of their home into a church library. Tim Munson undeniably did not have the decorating skills that his wife possessed.

A rustling sound came from down the hall and a friendly fluff ball that she knew as Bentley came quickly towards her, his tail swooshing back and forth excitedly.

"Bentley!" Anna gushed getting down on the golden retriever's level as he came to her for kisses. "Look at you, Old Man! You're still the cutest fur baby in the world."

Bentley's tail moved faster at her loving tone and he licked her face aggressively almost knocking her over.

"Okay, enough of that. I already had a shower this morning."

Anna moved quietly through the house with Bentley at her side, looking over every piece of furniture, allowing the memories to flood her. She could see Alexis and herself running down the hallway to the Christmas tree on Christmas morning while their mother got the camera ready. Near the back sliding glass door was the old desk that Anna used to type her first stories on. The computer had been upgraded since then, but the chair and desk hadn't changed.

For a moment she felt ten years old all over again as she moved down the hallway of the ranch house to the bedrooms. She opened the door to the room that used to be hers. It now had a crib. Several dolls, some of which used to belong to her and Alex, stared back at her from little doll-sized chairs.

The sound of the front door swinging open followed by a cacophony of voices made Anna back out of the room and close the door silently behind her. Bentley barked a greeting and ran to welcome his family home. "Anna! Anna!" It was Sam's voice calling.

"I'm back here." She called out as the eight year old boy came barreling towards her, knocking her into the wall. "Whoa, Sammy! Take it easy on me."

His arms circled her waist and she gladly wrapped him in her arms. His red hair matched her own, only without the curls.

"Abba! You here!" a high pitched voice came from her legs. Livi sucked on her pacifier and tugged on Anna's jeans.

Reaching down to the toddler, Anna picked her up and brought her to eye level. "Well, hello there, Olivia Jean! Look how big you're getting!"

The cutie pie smiled.

"And where is Ms. Ellie?" Anna called down the hall. No answer came so, with Sam at her feet and Livi in her arms, Anna walked back into the main part of the house to see a very grown looking preteen wearing ripped jeans and a hoodie. "Are you too cool to hug your Aunt Anna?"

The girl let a smirk slip through her defenses and allowed Anna to put an arm around her.

"Hello, Anna Banana," Tim Munson said standing off to the side of the room enjoying the scene playing out in his living room.

Her father looked older than she remembered. Tired. Yet, his eyes were every bit as loving as they ever were. Seeing the tenderness there was her undoing. Putting Livi down on her own feet, Anna walked into her father's open arms and buried her face into his shirt.

"Oh, Daddy," she whispered as she let the tears fall.

His arms encircled her.

"It's okay now, Annalise. You're just starting a new chapter, that's all. Just like in your stories you used to write," his voice soothed. How did he always know the right thing to say?

Then he cleared his throat.

"So... I couldn't help but notice my mailbox is now tilting." His tone changed slightly and Anna could hear the knowing smile in his voice. "Did you by some chance have an issue getting the trailer up the drive?"

Anna smiled. "Shh. Let's just hug."

5

Lewis Sparks pulled into his parking space in front of his townhome. For a man who just handed in a top notch exposé piece, he should've been celebrating. Instead, he was racked with guilt... and indecision. Had Anna ever realized the goldmine she had on that USB? His head still reeled from the extent of corruption and depravity he uncovered in those files. Financial records, call logs, and audio files of conversations... as well as images of some disturbing actions.

A lot of prominent people were mentioned in what appeared to be a variety of shady deals in everything from drugs to underage prostitution. Would someone on drugs, such as the man who ran into Anna, have the wherewithal to put such evidence together? Was he just a delivery boy or was he more than what he appeared?

It was still unclear as to whether the body that had been discovered the next day was the man Anna described. Collins' description of the man in her piece didn't fit what Anna relayed to him. Lewis had questioned Sherry Collins about what she found while doing her article and she was oddly silent on the subject. Even the news on the television had neglected to cover it. It wasn't like Collins' normal arrogant manner to downplay her work.

Yet all she said was, "The guy was just a dead homeless man. Nothing suspicious."

Come to think of it, Lewis thought to himself, Sherry acted very uncomfortable when talking to him and kept glancing towards Mr. Price's office. Anna's piece had been picked apart and edited of all mention of Rep. Scott, whose name showed up several times in the documents on the flash drive.

If Sherry's piece had been censored as well, what would Price do to *his*? Mr. Price's name didn't show in any of the documents on the USB, but could he be protecting his job by covering up a name on one of those lists?

Reaching into his pocket, Lewis pulled out a piece of paper that he had hastily scribbled some information on. After some calls and poking around, he found the man named Jake Cory. *Detective* Jake Cory to be exact. He had put off the call long enough. He dialed the number but it went right to voice mail.

"Hello. My name is Lewis Sparks. I'm a reporter with the *Skennan Gazette*. I think I have information that you need. I just finished an exposé piece on Lance Davidson, implicating several other important people doing some less than stellar things. My source was given a USB and was told to contact you directly. Please call me back immediately and I will connect you to my source."

He hung up and stared at his phone, hoping the detective would call him back quickly, but he did not. Anna had to be made aware of what was going on. She needed to get that USB to the police. He'd call her as soon as he got inside. Grabbing his laptop case, Lewis got out of his car and unlocked his front door.

Putting his laptop bag down and kicking off his shoes, he pulled his phone out once again to call Anna. A lamp clicked on in his living room, and his breath caught in his throat as he saw Lance Davidson sitting in his recliner.

"Hello, Mr. Sparks."

Lewis reached behind his back and put his hand on the doorknob but noticed two other men moving out of the shadows both pointing guns at his head.

"I don't think you want to do anything stupid. My friends tend to be... *jumpy*."

"Move." One of the men pointed into the living room with the barrel of his gun.

Reluctantly, Lewis complied.

"Have a seat. Let's get to know one another, shall we?" Davidson smiled and motioned for Lewis to sit in a chair that had been brought in from his dining room. This was not going to end well.

*****

Anna's eyes flew open in the dark and she tried to acclimatize herself to her surroundings. A weird scraping noise woke her. Groggily, she sat up on her air mattress and looked around the room she was in. Her father's study. The door had been pushed open and a glow from the nightlight in the guest bathroom across the hall illuminated just enough to cast creepy shadows. A furry mountain moved towards her, dragging something along the floor.

"Bentley. Not now." Anna fell backward onto the air mattress with a thud as she recognized the scraping sound was just Bentley's leash.

The dog must've taken Anna's acknowledgment as permission to persist because he attempted to jump up onto the mattress bouncing Anna alert.

"Stop it, Goofball. You're going to pop my mattress with those claws." Anna tried not to laugh as Bentley kept trying to get to her in the center of the bed.

She reached over and grabbed her cell phone. The time was just before six o'clock in the morning. Anna's interview with the school principal and Mrs. Erbe was at eight o'clock. She figured she might as well get up and maybe go for a small run. With a groan, Anna gently pushed Bentley back and tried to get to her feet.

The urge to use the bathroom hit and she rushed across the room, forgetting that her niece and nephew had placed her boxes from the trailer haphazardly in the room. Her big toe made contact with one of the boxes. By the way her foot smarted, Anna presumed it was a box of books.

Trying to shake the pain off, she moved to the open doorway but forgot to grab her glasses. She ran straight into the door jam. Her nose took the brunt of that mishap. Whimpering, she finally made it into the bathroom but felt the warm trickle of blood flow from her nose down onto her favorite nightshirt.
"Really?"

Anna packed her nose with toilet paper and tried to remember the rule about nose bleeds. Was it put your head forward to keep it from going down your throat? Or was it put your head back to stop the bleeding? After washing the sink quickly, she felt her way to the study and her glasses. When she could see, she looked online for the answer.
"Pinch. Pinch your nose and lean forward," Anna read out loud as she leaned forward, pinching the bridge of her nose.

It was then that the hall light flashed on and her father stood there in shock. "What in the world, Annalise?"

"Whoa. You look like a scary movie," Sam said coming up behind his grandfather in morbid curiosity.

"Sam, scoot. Go get breakfast," Tim ordered and ushered the young boy away from the study.

"I'm sorry if I woke everyone," Anna said, still leaning and pinching.

"You didn't. The kids have school." Her father smiled gently at his wounded daughter.

"Oh. What time do they need to be there? I have to go in for my interview. I may as well take them," Anna offered in a nasal voice. "I don't think running is an option this morning."

Her father looked at her a second as if he were trying to ascertain whether the kids would be safe in her company.

Finally, he said, "Are you sure? It's a big day for you with the interview and the kids can be... high strung."

"I can handle a couple of kids, Dad." Anna blew out a laugh causing the toilet paper in her nose to lift in the breeze.

Tim shook his head and stifled a laugh. "Suit yourself. I can get Livi to the sitter and drop off your trailer at the rental return."

"That sounds like a fair trade." Anna smiled at her dad proudly. "Look at us... we're dividing and conquering."

Her father gave her one more amused look before alerting the kids that their aunt would take them to school that day and to be on their best behavior. A whimper from the corner caught her ear and Anna looked over to see Bentley. The leash still hung from his mouth and a puddle slowly made its way across the hardwood in her direction.

Shoulders slumped, Anna let out a heavy sigh and got to her feet. Thankfully, her nose appeared to have stopped bleeding. Throwing her bloody tissues into the trash in the kitchen, Anna grabbed the roll of paper towels off the counter.

"Ellie, can you take Bentley out please?" she asked her niece as the young girl entered the kitchen smelling as if she had just spent an hour in a perfumery.

"Why do I have to..." Ellie looked up and finally caught sight of her aunt's bloody shirt. "Eww. Gross."

"Bentley is in the study. Take him out... *now*."

"Geesh. Someone is cranky in the mornings." Ellie rolled her eyes and went to find the dog.

Anna was about to warn her niece that Bentley had peed when a loud shriek came from the room.

"Eww. I stepped in it! Now I have to go wash."

"*After* you take him out."

Ellie leaned out of the study and looked at her aunt as if she had misheard her. "But..."

"I said what I said." Anna put her hands on her hips the way her mother used to. "Do it, Eleanor Carter."

Her father smiled a weary, but appreciative smile at his daughter. How did he do this all on his own? He made sure everyone ate breakfast, got dressed, and had everything they needed before dropping them off at school... *daily*. Anna felt overwhelmed already.

An hour later, Anna was showered and dressed. Even her red nose had returned to a reasonable shade. The kids dashed around grabbing everything they needed and Anna waited patiently at the kitchen island, sipping on her coffee when her father came in from the garage.

"You may want to get air in your back passenger tire, Anna Banana. It's looking low."

"I will. That tire has a slow leak. I've been babying it until I can put a new one on," Anna told her father.

"Are you sure you don't want me to drive you all to school?" Tim Munson asked. "I can go get your tire looked at when I return the trailer."

"No. Don't be silly. You just unhitched the trailer and put it on your truck," Anna reassured him. "I've got this, Dad. No worries. Just get Livi to the sitter."

Tim paused a moment as if deliberating, but he finally reached down and picked up Livi to take her out to his truck. "Everyone have a good day. I'll see you after school."

"Bye, Grandpa," Sam called from the other end of the house.

Ellie gave an uninterested wave and grunt.

Anna waited for her father to pull down the driveway with the trailer in tow before calling the kids to attention.

"Okay… this crazy train is heading out. I have to stop at the gas station on the way. Let's move."

"Can I get an energy drink if we're stopping at the one with the minimart?" Ellie all of a sudden sported a smile.

"An energy drink? Does my dad know you drink those?"

Ellie shrugged but her smile grew bigger and hopeful.

"No energy drinks…"

"But…" Ellie started to argue.

"*However*… you both can grab one thing that won't give you a premature heart attack," Anna smiled at the look of satisfaction on the kids' faces. "Now move."

"Yes! You're the best, Aunt Anna," Sam yelled and ran out to the Jeep.

"Can I get *two* things?" Ellie pushed with that cheesy angelic smile again.

"*Ellie.*"

"Just kidding."

Anna stood in the silence of the house for a moment while her niece and nephew fought over the front seat in the driveway. What had she gotten herself into? It wasn't even seven thirty and she was already exhausted.

"Be good while we're gone, Bentley. No more accidents, okay?" Anna bent over the dog and kissed the top of his furry forehead.

She watched with some envy as the dog went to his cushion and plopped down to sleep. Maybe when she came home, she'd find time for a nap… and that run she didn't get to take.

Sam yelled something at Ellie and Anna knew she had to go. They stopped and got air for the tire, a coffee for Auntie Anna, and the kids' respective treats. Once parked in the school parking lot, the children ran to their respective buildings: Sam to Deer Creek Elementary and Ellie to the Jr. High School. Anna wasn't ready for the feelings that emerged when she saw the old familiar buildings.

For a moment, Anna stood still in the parking lot as people passed by her as she stared at the building. Some of her best memories happened there, but also some of her worst. Michael had acted as if nothing had ever happened the day before. Could he so easily forget how his betrayal hurt her? Anna shook her head free from the thoughts. She was a grown woman. There was no room for the thoughts of a twelve year old girl.

"Oh, my word! Annalise? Is that you?" a voice came from behind her. "I'd recognize those beautiful curls anywhere."

Anna turned to see an older woman coming towards her. Mrs. Hannah Erbe. She wasn't gray anymore. Her hair was snowy white. There were more wrinkles at the crooks of her eyes and the corners of her mouth than Anna remembered. Evidence that she smiled and laughed much in her lifetime. Anna relaxed in her mentor's presence.

"Mrs. Erbe, I'm so glad to see you."

"When I heard your father say you put in your resume to be my assistant, I about did a cartwheel!" Mrs. Erbe embraced her. "Welcome home, Anna."

6

"Make yourself at home and catch up with some old friends while I get Mrs. Peterkin." Mrs. Erbe showed Anna to the new and improved library before heading back down the hall to let the principal know Anna was ready for the interview.

Her old friends. Anna knew very well Mrs. Erbe referred to the rows and rows of books. Some of the titles may have changed over the years, but the classics were still there. Anna pulled out a few books one by one to read the back covers before gently returning them to their slots. Every new story was a friend waiting to be discovered. They were children's books mostly, but she looked forward to reading each one if she was given the position.

The hallway bustled with activity as kids walked in lines alongside their teachers. Anna heard her name and looked out the door to see Sam waving wildly at his aunt as he passed by with his class. Her heart burst at the sight and she waved back. Ellie's classes were in the other building, but she probably would never wave and call to her as Sam had just done. She was too cool to do that.

Wandering around the library reminiscing, Anna smiled when she spotted the old media closet. It was called a closet, but it was in actuality a small room that stored various types of video cameras and DVD players. Well, at least back in *her* day that was what it held.

She opened the door and smiled. There weren't DVD players anymore, but there was a green screen and a camera set up. Anna had memories of she and a handful of her friends recording videos in that room. How many *interviews* had she conducted with her friends and fellow classmates, discussing life and school?

What happened to those old videos? There were several recordings of her reading stories she had written for her friends. Looking over her shoulder she spotted the table where she had written those very stories. It still sat in the farthest corner of the library away from everything else, partially hidden behind the old encyclopedias no one ever used. Reverently, Anna ran a hand over the wood and smiled.

"What are you doing way over here?" Michael Tyler had asked her once. "Aren't you coming out to play kickball with the class?"

"No. Mrs. Erbe is letting me stay here to use a laptop to write," Anna said excitedly. Laptops were tools fancy writers used. It wasn't every day a fifth grader had that privilege.

"Will you write one for me?"

"For you?"

"Yeah... Carie said you wrote one for her. I want one, too."

Anna laughed at her friend. "Well, what do you want it to be about? Carie wanted to be a princess. I doubt you want to be a prince."

"Make me a superhero. You know, a guy that always saves people."

"Like with a cape?" Anna laughed and Michael pulled the chair out to sit down.

"Yeah! A cape that is bulletproof! And I want to be invisible, too."

"No superhero has all of the super abilities. That's why they have friends with different superhero talents."

"Fine. What superhero thing do you want to have?"

"Me?"

"Yeah... do you want to shoot lasers from your eyes?"

Anna thought for a moment. "I want to run fast. Faster than all the bad guys."

"But that's not enough to keep you safe. You need to shoot lasers, too."

"Okay. I'll run fast and shoot lasers. You can have a bulletproof cape and ... what else?"

"I'll fly next to you while you run fast," Michael said excitedly.

"You'll need a damsel in distress."

"A what?"

Anna leveled him with a look. "A damsel is a girl you save from danger. What do you want her name to be?"

"Petunia," Michael offered and Anna burst into giggles at the silly name choice.

All of the sudden, Michael's face contorted and he asked, "I don't have to kiss her, do I? That's just gross."

Anna opened the laptop and started tapping away with Michael offering suggestions as the story began taking shape. The two laughed and joked about their characters all the way up to the time their class came back from recess.

Stupid Michael Tyler. Why couldn't he just stay as sweet as he had been when they were kids? Why did he have to let Stephen Turner make him into a jerk? And why, of all of the memories she had in the library, was it *that* memory that popped into her mind? Maybe because she saw him the day before in all of his arrogant glory.

"That's the desk where we put our kids that come in for lunch detention." A voice startled Anna from her reverie. She turned to find that Mrs. Erbe, the principal, and another woman had entered the library.

"Well, back in Anna's day that was the desk where she wrote some pretty entertaining stories." Mrs. Erbe smiled warmly. "Anna, this is Mrs. Peterkin, our fearless principal. This is Mrs. Rogers, the assistant superintendent of the school district."

"You used to write stories, Miss Munson?" the principal asked with a raised eyebrow.

"I think she still does. Don't you, Anna? Please tell me you haven't stopped writing."

Anna moved away from the corner table to join Mrs. Peterkin, Mrs. Erbe, and Mrs. Rogers.

"I still write. Not as much as I'd like. Though lately, my writing has focused on journalism, not superheroes or magical castles."

"Aww. I loved your stories. Maybe you can pick it up again."

"Maybe." Anna blushed and smiled awkwardly.

"Well, shall we sit over here at the big table to chat?" Mrs. Peterkin motioned to a large round table and pulled a copy of Anna's resume from a manilla folder that she had brought into the library with her.

About an hour later, Anna walked out of the school with her mind swimming. The interview seemed to go well, but she didn't want to get her hopes up. They promised to call her within the week.

As she pulled out of the parking lot onto the street, Anna felt a surge of energy. Maybe she would go for that run when she got home after all. Her thoughts were racing and running was a good time to think and pray.

She turned down a country road and out of nowhere a horrible flapping noise came from the back of her Jeep. She struggled to steer straight and when she looked in the passenger side mirror she saw why. The tire she had put air in just that morning flapped against the gravel road. Flat... deflated... like her mood was quickly turning.

Pulling off to the side of the road, she got out to look at the tire.

"Oh, come on!" Anna threw her hands up in the air in frustration. "I just put air in you! You stupid..."

Resisting the urge to kick the other rear tire in anger, she returned to the driver's seat and tried calling her father on her cell phone. Her calls went to voice mail.

"Please answer your phone, Dad," she whined in frustration.

She sat for a few moments in silence waiting for a lightning bolt idea to strike her. Other than her father, she had no one to call. All of her good friends from high school had long since moved away. Once again, Anna was reminded how lonely her existence had become.

About five minutes into her pity party, she decided to walk home the remaining three miles. She could run that little bit in her sleep. Walking should be fine. At least she chose to wear her flats and not her heels. She put her blinkers on, grabbed her purse, and stepped out onto the gravel road.

Muttering under her breath about the stone in her shoe, she did not hear the truck approach. Out of the corner of her eye, she saw a red mass slowly pull alongside her. The sound of an electric window going down finally caused her to turn her head.

"Well, hello again." Michael Tyler smiled that cheesy smile.

Why, God? Why of all people does it have to be him to stop? Anna nodded, but kept walking.

"Flat tire?"

She stopped, turned, and glared into his truck. "No, I just thought my Jeep needed a rest."

At first, he looked shocked at her response, then a slow smile spread across his face. "Hop in. I'll take you home."

"No, thank you. I like the exercise."

"Well then at least let me look at your tire. Maybe I can fix it so you can drive home."

Anna paused and contemplated the offer. She didn't want to get blisters on her feet from walking home in her dress shoes.

"Okay. That will be fine. Thank you," she conceded with a nod.

"Great. Get in."

"I can walk it."

It appeared as if Michael was about to say something, but he snapped his mouth shut and rolled his eyes. His truck went into reverse and pulled back the distance to where her Jeep sat. A few moments later, she joined him where he waited, arms crossed and leaning impatiently against her Jeep.

"Unlock the back and I'll grab your spare," he instructed.

"Spare?" Anna repeated absently and dreaded the next part of their conversation.

"Please tell me you have a spare."

"Of course I do."

Michael pushed away from the Jeep and moved to the back hatch waiting for her to open it. "Well? Where do you keep the spare? Your tire carrier is empty."

Anna pursed her lips.

"Please tell me you have one inside. Maybe in the back compartment?"

"That *was* my spare."

"Of course it was," Michael muttered before softening his expression. "Well, my offer still stands. Hop in the truck and I'll take you home."

"Do you have an air compressor? Maybe we can just refill it?"

"Have you looked at it, Anna? There's a visible hole and the treads are worn completely thin."

"Fine." Anna unlocked her Jeep and started to climb back in.

"What are you doing?"

"I'm going to wait here until my father answers his phone. Or I'll call a garage or something."

"Then I'll wait with you. If you want to be stubborn I can be stubborn, too."

"You don't need to stay. You may go now." Anna waved her hand as if she were the queen dismissing a royal subject.

"If that's how you want it." Michael turned and walked towards his truck.

Anna watched him in the rearview mirror wondering why she was mad that he was doing exactly what she had told him to do. Then she realized, he *wasn't*. Michael opened his truck pulled something out and started walking back to her Jeep.

Leaning out her window, she asked, "What are you doing?"

"You left me no choice, Anna. I'm calling my mother."

Anna laughed. "What? Why?"

"So you can explain to her why her son ... who she raised to be a gentleman... would leave the pastor's daughter on the side of the road broken down."

"Oh, for heaven's sake! You're so dramatic." Anna laughed in aggravation. "You're not *really* calling your mom... are you?"

Michael held up his phone and showed her his mother's contact info queued and ready to go. His finger lingered over the call button.

"Don't be ridiculous, Michael."

His smile grew as he pressed down and the phone started calling Colleen Tyler.

"Okay. Stop it, Michael. I'm serious!" Anna said getting out of the Jeep.

"Hey, Mom. I just wanted to let you know I'm running late to help Dad. I found an old friend on the side of the road who needed a lift to their house."

Michael motioned for her to get in the passenger side of his truck and she begrudgingly complied. "Could you please keep Anna company while I get the tire off of her Jeep, Mom?" Michael then handed Anna the phone with a smug smile as he grabbed a jack and a tool bag from behind his seat and proceeded to work her tire free from the hub.

"Hello, Anna! Welcome home! I know your father is delighted to have you back in town," Colleen Tyler gushed in her usual sweet maternal way.

"Hi… Mrs. Tyler. Yes, it's good to be back."

Anna tried to make polite small talk while watching Michael remove her tire in record time. Every so often he would glance over at her with that absurd smile. She tried her best to return it with a glare, but she had to admit it was getting harder to stay stoic. Finally, he hefted her tire onto his flatbed and got back into the truck, taking his phone back.

"Thanks, Mom. I'll probably be home a little after lunch. Bye." Then he had the audacity to wink at her as he pulled away from the side of the road.

Anna shook her head and turned away towards the window to hide the smile that threatened to undermine the stern look she sported.

"You're ridiculous," Anna muttered.

"I know. You're welcome." She could hear the smile in his voice.

She shook her head.

"You know, we used to be good friends. Don't you remember?" He asked out of nowhere. "What did I do to make you act so cold to me?"

Her head snapped around and leveled him with her glare.

"*Really*? You don't remember?"

"Should I?"

Anna laughed sardonically. "Yes. You *should*."

"Well then remind me, Anna. Because all I know is that we went from hanging out as kids to you glaring at me and not wanting me to give you a ride home when you're *clearly* in need."

"How can you *not* remember?" Anna stared at him incredulously, but he looked perplexed. "Do you remember the bucket of ice water?"

Silence. Then recognition dawned. "In seventh grade?"

Anna nodded silently.

"That's what this is about? A stupid prank from seventh grade?" Michael laughed. "I was an idiot kid, Anna. *And* I distinctly remember apologizing for that."

"Uh… no you didn't."

"I did. I remember it well because we were all brought into the principal's office. I was terrified."

Anna paused as the memory came into focus. Michael might have actually apologized now that she was thinking about it. All Anna remembered was Stephen Turner saying, *"I'm so sorry, Anna"* in a sickeningly sweet tone with an undercurrent of an unrepentant smile. Had she assumed Michael's apology was contrived as well?

"Clearly it still bothers you. So please…" Michael stopped the truck in the middle of the road, turning to her. "I *am* sorry, Anna. It was dumb. *I* was dumb."

Tears threatened to surface. Anna had been perfectly content never to have this confrontation with Michael Tyler, but here it was. Everything was going to be out on the table.

"And do you remember telling Stephen in eighth grade that I was nothing but a fat cow wearing lipstick and a dress?"

Michael looked shocked. "No… I definitely *don't* remember that."

Anna gulped. "It happened in the library. I was shelving books and you boys were hanging out in the reference section, probably thinking you were being sneaky."

"Anna, I…"

"Do you know that every time I looked in the mirror I *saw* a cow with lipstick?"

"Anna, that wasn't me. After the water bucket incident - and a few other stupid things I did with Stephen - my parents made me stop associating with him. In eighth grade I was mostly hanging around with Rick Smith."

Anna stopped as his words sunk in. Did she believe him? She could've sworn it was Michael's voice that she had heard. After all of the obsessing and ruminating she had done in the past fifteen years, had she actually gotten it all wrong? Now that she forced herself to think about it, she vaguely remembered Rick and Michael started a geeky friendship centered around science fiction novels.

"Is that why you left mid-year?" Michael asked all of a sudden.

Anna nodded. "Partly. And because of what was going on with Alexis at the time. I think my parents hoped putting me in a Christian school would keep me from going down the same path as her."

"I just assumed we stopped talking because you had made different friends," Michael said quietly.

The truck stayed silent, awkwardly so. Then both tried to talk at the same time.

"Anna…"

"Michael…"

Neither got a chance to speak. Michael's phone rang. As soon as he saw the name on his car's display, he said, "I'm sorry, Anna. I have to take this. It's important, but I do want to continue…"

"Just answer it, Michael."

There was no way Michael could've known that Anna's flippant response wasn't a result of their uncomfortable conversation. No, she sat in stunned silence as an oddly familiar name appeared on Michael's phone screen. *Jake Cory.*

7

Michael began driving as Anna sat as still as a statue in his passenger seat. Guilt racked him as he was reminded of what a jerk he had been in Jr. High. When he apologized for helping Stephen Turner prank Anna with the ice water bucket, Michael meant it. Anna had always been such a sweet friend.

He had no idea what was said about her in the library that day, but he could imagine how those words had lived with her all this time. His sister Jenna had bullies in school as well and she *still* rehearsed past hurts they had said about her tomboy appearance. Jenna was grown up and about to graduate college, but it still affected her.

Just as he was about to apologize again, his phone rang. There was no such thing as good timing for Jake's call under the circumstances. Michael didn't have a choice but to answer the phone. He took the call off of the truck's speaker system and put the phone to his ear for privacy.

He glanced over at Anna and his heart wrenched. She looked unnerved. Would she ever forgive him?
"Hey, Cory? How are you holding up?" Michael asked his friend.
"Not good. I'm sorry I didn't get back to you right away after you called."
"Hey, don't apologize. I can't even imagine what you're going through right now."
"Thompson was a good cop. He didn't deserve this. The way we've been told to handle his death is ridiculous." Jake Cory sounded as if he had just woken

up, but Michael knew he probably hadn't slept at all since the news of his friend's death.

"What's the latest? Anything you can share?"

Jake's caustic laugh was answer enough.

"They're supposed to make some type of statement tonight about J.T.'s death on the news. But they're leaving out *how* he died." Jake was seething. "The toxicology reports don't make sense. The way his death is being reported doesn't make sense. *Nothing* makes sense, Tyler."

The anger his friend vented, however, made perfect sense. Michael wasn't a cop like his friend, but he knew what it meant to be part of a close knit team that risked their lives alongside one another. Michael shared a similar bond with his fellow fire men and women he worked with day in and day out.

"I'm sorry. I just wanted to let you know the details of his memorial," Jake sniffed. "The family wants to wait until they can get his grandparents here. We're probably looking at another week or two for his service. Do you think you can get your guys at the Deer Creek station to attend? I think that would mean a lot to J.T."

"Of course. Let me see what I can do. I know a lot of them will remember you both from your time here."

"We want to have the streets lined. He deserves that honor."

Michael sat quietly as he listened to his friend trying to get himself together on the other end of the phone. Both John Thompson -J.T. to his friends- and Jake Cory had served with the Deer Creek police. By the time Michael came on as an EMT at the fire station, J.T. had already taken a position with the major crimes unit a few counties over. A few years later, Jake followed his friend when the opportunity opened up.

"Jake, is there anything else I can do for you?" Michael asked quietly, glancing over at Anna. Her face remained frozen in the same expression.

"Just pray. First I lose Beth… now J.T. It's hard to feel God's presence right now. Does that make sense?"

"Yeah… that makes sense. God hasn't left you. Things are just dark right now." Michael didn't have words that would adequately comfort his friend. Jake was only thirty two and a widower after losing his wife to Leukemia. Then he lost his best friend so violently. Michael said the only thing he knew to say. "I'm praying for you, Cory."

The call ended as they pulled up the church parsonage driveway. Michael imagined Anna would jump out and slam the door behind her without looking back, but she didn't move. She didn't even blink. Then all of a sudden she spoke.

"Jake… Is he from *my* area? Does he live near Skennan Cove?"

"Yeah." Michael looked over at her surprised. "Do you know Jake?"

"He's a … *police officer*?" Her tone sounded odd to his ears.

"A detective actually. He used to be an officer here in Deer Creek. Why?"

"No reason. The name just sounded familiar," Anna said quickly. "Thanks for the ride home."

She opened the door of the truck and slid down.

"Anna… wait," Michael called out to her. "Don't you think we should finish our conversation?"

She turned around but didn't look him in the eyes. "It's okay. Let's just forget it."

"It's not okay. Not if it's bothered you all these years." He waited until she finally looked at him. "I'm sorry, Anna. I was just a punk kid trying to fit in. Please forgive me. And for what those guys said... they were just jerks."

Anna pursed her lips tightly but eventually gave a slight nod. "Okay. I forgive you. I really need to go now. Thanks again for the lift."

Michael jumped out of the truck to guarantee closure of the matter as she started walking up the sidewalk to the house. "So we're friends again?"

She stopped abruptly and looked over her shoulder. There was a hint of a smirk there that he had to admit intrigued him slightly.

"I didn't say that," she smiled.

"Didn't say what?" Pastor Munson called out as he stepped out of the garage. He emerged wiping his hands on his pants as though he had been working on something.

Anna jumped.

"Hey, Pastor Munson. Anna's Jeep had a flat tire and I saw her on my way home." Michael all of a sudden felt nervous in front of his pastor… as if he had been caught flirting with his daughter. "So I gave her a lift."

Pastor Munson's eyebrows rose as he looked down at his daughter. "The tire that I *specifically* warned you about this morning?"

Michael resisted the urge to laugh when Anna flashed her father the same angelic smile he had seen his sister Jenna give their father on many occasions. Oddly enough, it had the same effect on Pastor Munson as it did on John Tyler.

"Well, I'm just glad you're safe," the man leaned down and pressed a kiss to her head.

"If you give me your keys," Michael spoke up, "I can get your car fixed and bring it back to you later tonight. If you trust me, that is."

He challenged Anna with both his tone and expression. Just when she opened her mouth to protest, her father took the keys from her hand and walked them to where Michael stood.

"That's very kind of you, Michael. Isn't it, Annalise?"

She grunted.

"It's my pleasure." Michael smiled as he got back into the truck.

He watched as Anna and her father walked into the house together before backing back down the drive. He hoped they could put the past behind them especially if she was going to be living in Deer Creek. And Michael was willing to do whatever he needed to do to make things right again.

*****

Anna made a mad dash for her father's study. Her mission: find that flash drive. She didn't believe in coincidences. What was the likelihood that Michael Tyler had a friend named Jake Cory... who happened to be a detective in the area where she had lived? And what were the chances the man who ran into her was looking for *this* Jake Cory? How many people in her area were named Jake Cory?

"Whoa. Where's the fire, Anna?" Her father moved to stand in front of the hallway that led to his study.

"I'm sorry, Dad. There's something I need to look for in my things. It's kind of important." Anna did not hear Jake's side of the conversation, but from what she could pick up someone had died. Could it have been the man she encountered? The only death from Skennan Cove that made the news was the body of the homeless man. She had to call Lewis and see what he knew.

"Well, before you go in there," Tim began, "Promise you won't get mad."

Anna's heart thudded. "Why? What happened?"

"It's not bad. At least *I* don't think it is."

Her father was stalling. His face held that expression he used to give when he had a surprise he was dying to tell her but was trying to draw it out for suspense. Normally it was cute. At that moment, it was not.

Anna sighed. "Okay. What have you been up to while I was gone today?"

"I just got to thinking that you really need your own dedicated space. I feel bad that since you came home you can't even have your old bedroom because your niece is living in it."

Tim paused and smiled, really drawing out the suspense. "So I did a little rearranging in my study. It's not finished, mind you. And I still plan on getting you a real bed instead of that air mattress."

"Wow, Dad. That's so thoughtful." Anna winced and hoped she sounded convincing. "I hope you didn't hurt yourself. You didn't move my things, did you?"

"How about we have a look?" His smile was ginormous.

Anna nodded and moved to the door.

"First, you have to close your eyes," her father insisted.

Scrunching her eyes shut tightly she said, "Okay. I'm ready."

Anna felt her father move her to stand just inside the door of his study. "Okay. Ready? Open them."

Her eyes flew open and frantically scanned the room.

"Remember… it's a work in progress," Tim reiterated.

Anna gulped as she took in the room before her. Her father had emptied most of the room's contents, including all of his possessions. All that was left were a few pieces of furniture and her air mattress. She tried to even her breathing before reacting poorly in front of her father. He had meant it as a loving gesture. "And… where are *my* things?" Anna asked weakly.

"In the garage. I figured instead of tripping over things in the night, you can pull things back in as you unpack them." Tim smiled warmly at his daughter. "What do you think?"

Her father's face melted her heart. Had he always been this precious and unselfish? Anna looked back into the room. All of his books were gone. This room had been his haven when she was a child. Tim would disappear into the study to prepare for his sermons or Bible studies. If she and Alexis were too loud, he'd shut the door and drown them out. Now he was offering his inner sanctum to her as a gift… so she could have her own place.

"But where will you do your sermon preparation? What about all your books?"

"Ever since we added that new wing to the church I have a fancy office over there. I've been meaning to move my things over for a while." Tim smiled. "This just gave me a push to actually do it."

Anna's eyes landed on an old dresser. Above it rested a familiar painting. She felt her previous frustration fade. "Is that…"

"I moved your mother's dresser in here so you'd have a place for your clothes. It needs a good dusting still."

A lump rose in Anna's throat as she looked up into her father's face and saw a faraway look. The grief was still fresh. She wrapped an arm around her father's waist and gave him a tight side hug.

"Do you recognize the painting?" he asked.

Anna moved to stand directly in front of the watercolor peonies. Her mother had been so talented. Painting had been another of her mother's outlets.

"I recognize it," Anna said softly. "Everything mom touched turned beautiful."

Tim laughed quietly. "I thought your mother was the most creative and talented woman in the world."

"She was," Anna nodded emphatically.

"But then we had you and I saw right away you possess that same gift."

Spinning on her heels to look at her father, Anna gave him a skeptical glare. "No. Not like Mom. Not at all. Have you ever seen my drawings?"

"Not through your drawings… through your writing."

Anna shook her head. "I got fired, Dad."

"Anna, I remember listening in at your bedroom door as you read your stories to Alex."

"I was just a kid… writing childish stories."

"And what about the stories you tell Sam and Livi? Even Ellie enjoys them. You paint pictures with words. You capture people's imaginations."

His words made her want to cry.

"I'm hoping maybe you'll have the freedom to write again. You were always happiest when you wrote your stories." Tim moved to the desk. "You can put a computer here and look out the window when you write."

"Maybe."

"Anna, look at me." Her father came to stand in front of her. He waited until she brought her tear filled eyes to his. "I know you're hurting. Jonathan hurt you. Losing your job hurt you. But let this new chapter be a time you rediscover who you are. It's time to find Anna again. Not the Anna that Jon wanted you to be. Not the Anna that forced herself to write pieces she hated. Find the *joyful* Anna that I know and love."

Anna hiccupped as a sob escaped. She let her dad pull her into an embrace. "I think that Anna is gone, Dad."

"No, she's not. She's just hidden right now and we're going to pray that God helps you find her again." His words were spoken over her so assuredly.

He backed away and gave her a tender smile before smirking, "So are you going to tell me about Michael?"

"Eww, no. Let's not ruin this moment."

Tim laughed. "He's not the same person you used to know. Michael Tyler is a goofball, but he's a Godly young man."

"Dad…" Anna gave her father a warning look.

"What? I'm not telling you to date the guy. Just be nicer, okay?"

"We'll see."

Tim laughed. "How about you let your dad buy you some lunch before we go get the kids? You can tell me how the interview went."

Anna did a final look around the room with a sigh. She'd have to look for the laptop bag later. "Is there a healthy place to eat in Deer Creek? All I remember are diners and fast food places."

"Healthy… as in a salad?" Her father's twisted face told her everything she needed to know about her father's eating habits.

"Oh, Dad. Something tells me I'm going to need to put you on a better eating plan."

It was later in the evening after Anna prepared a nutritious meal- a meal no one liked except for herself- that she stood overwhelmed in the garage. She repeatedly reminded herself that her father's intentions were sweet. However, looking at the mix of her boxes combined with his stacks of books waiting to get moved to his office, Anna wanted to scream.

Then she saw it. Her laptop bag was above her head on top of the mountain of boxes and books. Glancing around for a stepstool and not finding one, Anna let out an exasperated sigh. She put her foot on a pile of books, testing to see if it would hold her weight. It did, so she climbed a little higher. Her fingertips were just within reach of the black leather strap that dangled above her when all of a sudden a male voice said, "What are you doing?"

The books under her feet started shifting and her arms began flailing as she lost her balance. She felt hands on her sides as she was lifted from the teetering mountain and placed firmly on the concrete.

She spun in defiance to look straight into Michael Tyler's chest.

"Hasn't anyone ever told you not to sneak up on people? Sheesh!" Anna hissed.

The pleasant scent of his cologne disarmed her and she backed away quickly. She scowled at him as she tried to purge the temptation to take another sniff at the air.

"Hasn't anyone ever told you not to climb up a pile of books? That's not exactly safe, you know." He returned her scowl. "Do I need to tell you how many falls I have had to respond to?"

She looked at him confused for a moment until she remembered her father had mentioned over lunch that Michael was an EMT and had recently become a fulltime firefighter.

"Now, Miss Munson…" he said patronizingly. "What was it you were after?"

She crossed her arms over her chest. "I don't need your help, *Mr. Tyler.*"

"Of course not. You don't ever need help." His smirk was obnoxious as he turned and looked at the mound she had climbed. "Was it this?"

He pointed to her laptop bag and she pursed her lips which gave herself away. Grabbing it from the side, Michael brought it down and handed it to her.

"Why are you here exactly?" Anna asked annoyed.

He pulled out a pair of keys and handed them to her. "Your Jeep is all better."

"They were able to fix the tire? That's great!" Anna's demeanor changed instantly as she went to go look at her car.

"Not quite. Your tire was a hot mess."

"But how…" Anna looked from Michael to the Jeep. There was a brand new tire on her rear passenger side. Then her stomach sank. "How much do I owe you?"

"Nothing."

Anna rolled her eyes. "Seriously, Michael. How much?"

"How about we call it even now?" he asked with a contrite look.

"What do you mean?"

"You forgive my pre-teen foolishness and I'll cover the tires."

"*Tires*? Plural?" Anna ran to the other side of the Jeep with her mouth gaping.

"Yeah… it's not good to change just one. They always recommend you do both at the same time." Michael said slightly awkwardly, which Anna found momentarily endearing. "Your front two are going to need to be replaced soon, too, but I'm not a millionaire so…"

"I don't know what to say."

"You don't have to say anything. Just know that people grow up and change, Anna." Michael finally looked at her.

Anna nodded slowly as his words registered.

"I guess I'll be seeing you around," Michael smiled as he started walking down her drive.

"Wait…" Anna watched him turn around. "How are you going to get home? I mean, you drove my Jeep here. Do you need a lift?"

He smiled a large grin and nodded his head over to a car waiting off to the side with a beautiful blonde in the driver's seat. "I'm good."

Anna rolled her eyes as the girl flashed him her doe eyes as he got in the passenger seat. *Apparently, not everything changes.* Michael Tyler was still the heartthrob of Deer Creek.

8

Jake Cory flashed his credentials at the officer guarding the front of the townhouse. The pit in his stomach grew as he took in the scene upon entering the house. Just the day before the man that lived in that home had called him and left a cryptic message. And now he was dead.

"Hey, Cory. It appears to be suicide." Fellow detective Nick Spencer filled him in as he entered the dining room. A man lay face down on the table while sitting in a dining room chair. His wrist dangled to the side, a deep gash right over the artery.

"Is there a note?" Jake asked as he took in the insane amount of empty vodka and tequila bottles scattered across the table and floor.

"No note. However, his boss... Mr. Harold Price of the *Skennan Gazette*... called when Sparks didn't come into work this morning," Spencer said. "He was concerned because yesterday Mr. Sparks was given notice that layoffs were imminent. Price said Mr. Sparks left in an emotional state."

Jake looked away. If he had answered his phone would this man still be alive? "Who found him?"

"Mr. Price had the local police do a well check. They saw Mr. Sparks through the window and the door was unlocked."

"Seems straightforward." Jake didn't like it.

"He was losing his job. Had too much to drink. Figured this was his best way out." Spencer shrugged nonchalantly. "It wouldn't be the first time someone panicked at the idea of losing their job."

Sighing to himself as he walked into the adjacent living room, Jake spotted something under the couch. He bent down and used the pen from his pocket to move it out from under the upholstery. It appeared to be a piece of crumpled duct tape.

"Tanner, bag this," Jake called to a crime scene technician. "Add a note to check for fingerprints or fibers on the adhesive."

As the technician complied, Jake moved back to the body of Lewis Sparks. He took in every inch of the scene, looking for any abnormality. He would keep the voicemail Lewis left for him under wraps for now, as Spencer … and most of the department … had no idea about the secret investigation launched weeks prior. The investigation that got J.T. killed.

Spencer went out to talk to one of the officers outside and Jake took one of the rubber gloves from one of the techs. He ran his hand up and down the back of Lewis' chair until something sticky caused the glove to catch. *Adhesive residue maybe?*

"I want this chair taken in as well."

The tech looked curious and Jake pointed out what he had discovered on the back.

"Yes, Sir."

"Has anyone seen an office or a desk anywhere in this house? He was a reporter. I imagine he'd have a laptop," Jake pointed out.

"Nothing that we saw."

"That's odd. Was his car checked?"

"Yes. Nothing of interest."

Jake moved through the rest of the house. A reporter is always working on something. What reporter didn't keep a laptop or computer at home? He made a mental note to check the items at the *Gazette* office. In the voicemail, Mr. Sparks mentioned having information. He mentioned a USB and his source. Whomever this source was, they needed to be made aware that they had better keep a low profile. If this death was connected to what J.T. had been working on, whoever was responsible for Lewis Spark's death would likely kill again.

*****

Davidson stared at the information accumulated on Sparks' laptop about private dealings that even his closest associates weren't aware of. Decades of hard work were about to unravel if this information went public. It took him forever to earn the reputation and nickname of *The Broker* and it would all disintegrate in a matter of minutes should those details get out.

His clients trusted him and paid him well to secure all types of *exotic* goods curated from some of the scariest and shadiest people around the world. If he were exposed the names of politicians, celebrities, and the wealthy of the northeast would be leaked. The fallout would be catastrophic.

He cursed the day he allowed J.T. to work for him. Davidson always prided himself on his ability to pick good people… trustworthy people … people he could intimidate into keeping quiet… to join him. His right-hand man had brought J.T. on, promising he would be a great fit. Now both were dead. One died a traitor, the other an undercover cop.

"Lance, I'm hungry. When are we going? We're going to miss our reservation if we don't hurry," Kyra, his current girlfriend, whined as she walked into the room.

"You go on ahead, Love. I have some work to catch up on."

"You promised we'd have time tonight since you were gone so much the last couple of days."

Lance Davidson looked at her and sighed. "Give me five more minutes and I will be down."

That seemed to appease Kyra for the moment. She'd be back six minutes later if he didn't materialize at the car. She didn't know the duress he was under. If she knew… well, she *couldn't* know. Kyra lived in ignorant bliss of where his wealth came from. All she knew was that Lance was a financial advisor. Which was true … at times.

Lance's mind went back to the interrogation of the reporter. In any other situation and any other time, Davidson may have considered hiring Lewis Sparks in some capacity, but the man knew too much. His zeal to get to the top, in this case, worked against him.

When asked who else knew about the details that he had written about in his article he stayed quiet, even when Rob thrust the pins under the fingernails of his duct-taped hands. When the name of his friend came up, his face gave him away.

"She doesn't know. I'm telling you the truth. *I* stole the USB from her before she could see what was on it."

"Then where is the USB, Mr. Sparks?"

His eyes diverted and that was when Davidson knew Sparks wasn't being completely truthful.

"Does Anna have it, Lewis?" he had asked him.

"No. I... I threw it away."

"Sure, you did." Lance shook his head and turned to his men. "Rob, let's change our approach. Maybe our friend here would like a drink to calm his nerves. Did I see a bar in the dining room, Lewis?"

Lance Davidson waited patiently as Rob forced the liquor down the man's throat. When he seemed as though impairment was setting in, he tried his questions again.

"Anna is gone. Moved far away. She doesn't know anything. I swear," Lewis slurred.

"I'm getting bored of this," Davidson said getting to his feet. "Finish him. Make it look like a suicide. I'll give Price a call and see if he knows where Miss Munson has gone."

The car horn beeped outside bringing him back to the present. Lance sighed. As he rose to his feet, he felt his cell phone vibrate. The name on the screen caused his heart to stop beating. If he didn't answer, he'd get a visit the next day... something he didn't want.

"Hello, Sir! Always a pleasure to see your name pop up," he lied as he addressed one of the biggest drug ring bosses in the North East whom he simply knew as Damon.

"I've been hearing rumors, Broker. Tell me you're taking care of it."

"Yes... yes, Sir. Don't worry. It's being handled."

"Because you don't want me to send my people to help you figure this out, do you?"

"There's no need, I promise. You have nothing to worry about." Davidson swallowed hard.

He hoped the man didn't sense his fear. In their line of business, weakness of any kind could sign his death certificate. Davidson was a killer shark, but he wasn't the biggest in the tank.

*****

Anna sat clutching the phone in her hands with glee. Hannah Erbe had called to give her the good news that she had gotten the position. Doing a little dance around the room, Anna emerged from her father's study to find the house empty. The kids had already been dropped off at their respective places. Her father had mentioned something about a meeting with other local pastors in the community. Apparently, he had already left.

With a sigh, she went back into her room. Earlier that day, she had pulled the USB out and had gotten settled at the desk with the intention of finally looking at the contents when Mrs. Erbe had called. She had tried the night before, but things had gotten busy with the kids. Sam needed help with his homework and Livi... well, she was a toddler. Anna was going to look at the information on the flash drive during the day while the kids were in school when she could devote her full attention to it.

She had time now, but there was so much pent up excitement at getting the library assistant position that she really wanted to share it with someone.

"I need friends," Anna said to the empty house. Bentley wagged his tail from his bed.

"No offense, Pup. I need *human* friends."

She paced excitedly with her phone in her hands wondering who she could call to tell her good news to. The familiar feeling of loneliness set in. Jonathan and Kirstyn would've been her first calls. Then her father. If her mother had still been alive she'd have been at the top of that list.

Who did she have now? She may have grown up in Deer Creek, but Anna didn't know anyone anymore. Those whom she would've considered old friends had moved on. Those who remained local had lives of their own and so much time had passed.

Anna looked up at the painting of the peonies her mother had painted years ago. Her mother would've been so happy to know she had gotten a job in a library. She would've been thrilled to know her husband wasn't left to raise their grandchildren alone and that Anna had come home.

Mary Munson would've made a fun dinner to revel in Anna's good news and she would've pulled out the celebration plate. The memory of the celebration plate caused a faint smile to creep onto Anna's face. It came out at birthdays or if Alexis or Anna made honor roll. If her father had something special happen at church or even for half-birthdays, her mother would pull out that plate and someone would get made much of.

"I really miss you, Mom. The world is so different without you here," Anna said quietly. "No one understands me like you did. No one makes things special like you did."

The silence in the house was deafening.

All of a sudden, she felt the need to be near her mother. Her mother had been gone a couple of years and Anna had not visited her grave since the day they laid her to rest. Her parents had always said not to worry about visiting or putting flowers on their resting places because they would be with the Lord. Yet, Anna felt propelled to go.

Grabbing her keys, she drove to the memorial park just outside of town. The grounds were expansive just as she remembered. Anna had done a good job blocking out most of the day of her mother's funeral from her mind.

She remembered Alexis crying on her shoulder. She remembered her father being strong for everyone except for himself. She remembered Jonathan holding her hand and drawing strength from his presence. Everything else became a vague blur.

The driveway wove through a well-maintained park with the deceased's placards sunken into the ground to enable mowers to keep the appearance neat. Following the drive up the hill, she came to a stop at a mausoleum.

A smile touched her lips as she remembered the day her parents came to pick her up for spring break in her sophomore year at college.

"I hope you don't mind taking a detour. We have a surprise to show you," her mother had said excitedly.

Anna assumed it was a meal at their favorite restaurant that happened to be on the road they were driving, but instead, they pulled up to the Deer Creek Memorial Gardens. Her father gave her a mischievous look in the rearview mirror.

"Guess what we bought?" he asked with an amused tone.

"Please tell me you're kidding. This is just plain old creepy, Guys." Anna furrowed her brow as they drove

up to the mausoleum.

"Come on. Let's go look," Mary chuckled.

"Really? Should we be going in there?" Anna watched as her mother got out of the car and headed to the door of an elaborate glass and marble building.

For a place to hold dead people, it was quite elegant. They walked through the glass doors into what looked like a chapel. A small pulpit stood at the far end of the building against a wall of glass looking out onto a wooded backdrop.

Above them were several crystal chandeliers casting a beautiful glow onto the marble floors below. The walls on either side were covered in orderly, engraved markers.

"Here we are. We're going to be filed under M for Munson," her father teased as he pointed out their spot and referred to it as their "filing cabinet". "Your mother and I met with someone to help us plan for the inevitable. We don't want it landing on you to worry about these things when we're gone. Everything is already pre-paid and planned."

"That's very... thoughtful," Anna murmured, trying not to crush the obvious joy her parents seemed to derive from the arrangement. "Can we go now? This is disturbing."

Their names were already inscribed on the slab about two graves high off the ground. Anna shuddered. For a kid not far into her twenties, death was not even on her radar yet... let alone, her parents' deaths. Little had they known at the time, Mary would get a cancer diagnosis a couple of years later.

Now at the age of twenty six, she stood inside the building staring at the etched stone with her mother's birth date and date of death. Reverently, she ran her hand over the numbers.

"I'm here, Mom. I know you're dancing in heaven right now having a great time with Jesus. I'm so happy for you, but I'm so devastated for me."

Anna paused and sighed before continuing.

"So, you were right about Jon," she spoke conversationally into the air. "I guess I didn't see in him the things you did. That's why I really need you here. Apparently, I miss important things like that."

The room was silent. Eerily so.

"The kids are doing okay. Though, what is up with Ellie? Where did our cutie go? She's turned into a brattier diva than Alexis ever was," Anna chuckled. "And I'm home now. I know that would probably bring you comfort to know Dad isn't raising those crazies on his own. I'll make sure to pull out the celebration plate and read to them like you did."

Silence.

"You may be wondering *why* I'm home," Anna continued. "Well, you know how I always wanted to work for a newspaper? I got that job… then I got fired. So maybe I'm not all that great after all. But I do have good news. Remember Mrs. Erbe? I'm going to be her assistant in the library. This time I'll be paid… unlike how it was when I was a kid."

Anna paused and stood transfixed at her mother's name glaring back at her.

"I miss you so much. It hurts, Momma."

Psssttt.

The odd whisper soft noise made Anna stand up straight.

"Momma?" Anna asked into the air. Of course, she didn't believe in ghosts.

Psssttt.

The scent of gardenias wafted into the air. Anna turned slowly in the direction from where the sound came. Then it happened again.

Psssttt.

Above the other wall of grave markers was a time-released air freshener. Anna sighed in relief and laughed. Her laughter blended into a mix of laughter and tears until she sobbed quietly. She rested her head on her mother's stone.

"How am I supposed to make it without you?"

John 14:18 floated into her mind. *"I will not leave you as orphans... I will come to you"*.

Anna sighed.

She'd felt herself distancing from God since that night Jonathan broke up with her... then after she had lost her job. It was as if she could hear her mother say, "God never left you. You don't need *me*. You need *Him*." It sounded like something her mother would've said.

Anna walked back to her car slowly and began driving home. As she did, she prayed seriously for the first time in weeks. "I don't know what You're doing, God. To be honest, I don't know what I'm doing either. But I know if I am going to make it, I need You. Please help me figure out who and what I am supposed to be."

9

Saturday morning dawned bright and early with sunlight streaming through the slats of the blinds on the study windows. With her eyes closed Anna could feel the light playing on her eyelids. She smiled and gradually opened her eyes as she realized she felt … *enclosed*. The sides of the collapsing air mattress engulfed her as if she were a tightly wrapped burrito. "Drat," she muttered.

She tried to sit up, but every time she moved the air mattress felt like a waterbed rocking her and bouncing her back to where she started. Anna flailed around ungracefully trying to free herself from her deflating confines.

The night prior, she had found baby Livi wrestling Bentley on her bed. The two were having a great time bouncing and prancing. It must have caused a hole to form somewhere in the heavy vinyl. Did she want to spend her Saturday trying to locate the hole where the air was escaping? Maybe she just needed to commit to buying a real bed. Her back would be grateful.

Anna rolled to her right until she landed partially on the floor – her behind stuck in the air – as Bentley came and covered her face in wet slobbery kisses.

"Well, that's attractive," Ellie muttered walking by Anna's half opened door on her way into the bathroom, a towel wrapped around her frame.

Anna shot her a disgruntled look before questioning her niece. "Why are you up so early on a Saturday? And why are you going into that bathroom instead of the one down your hall?"

Ellie rolled her eyes as Anna was becoming accustomed to. "It's the third Saturday of the month. So, we have to go through the motions of going to see Dad... just in case he shows up this time. And my little hot water hog of a brother is in the other shower."

Anna just blinked as the information sank in and Ellie disappeared behind the door of the bathroom. Soon, music started playing loudly and the shower turned on. Anna had assumed the kids had little to no contact with Jared since his last release from prison. A pit in her stomach formed.

She scrambled to her feet and saw her father feeding baby Livi her breakfast at the kitchen table.

"Good morning, Sunshine," he smiled faintly.

"Good morning. I hear the kids are visiting with Jared today?" Anna scrutinized her father's face as he kept his attention on the baby.

"You heard correctly."

"I guess I thought he wasn't in the picture anymore."

Tim grunted with a smirk. "Technically, he's still not. We go to these court-appointed meetings once a month just in case he decides to show up one of these days. He hasn't come to a visitation since the judge implemented them after he got out of prison this last time. There's always an excuse. Transportation. Illness. Trying to get work. Who knows if any of it is true. We still have to go in case *he* does."

Anna looked down the hall where a happy little boy sang in the bathroom and her heart hurt. She didn't know what she wanted more for the kids... a life free of being hurt by their father or for Jared to show up for them that day.

"Do you want me to take Livi while you take care of Sam and Ellie?" Anna asked. Jared wasn't Ellie's father and Anna imagined her presence would just reignite Jared's rage.

"No. That's all right. You were going to go to the gym."

"It can wait, Dad."

Her father smiled. "You still try to save the world from pain, don't you, Sweetheart? You've only been home a week. Let yourself adjust before you jump into this craziness."

"I came to help."

"And you are. Believe me. You being home has made a huge difference already." Tim got to his feet and pulled his daughter into a hug. "I'm used to this stuff. I've got it under control."

Anna nodded against his chest, wishing she could alleviate the stress of this task from him.

"Anyway, Livi-Boo and I have a standing playdate at the indoor play area at the library. The library in Glenhaven is larger than the one we have here."

"You have to drive all the way out there? That's close to where I lived."

"It's a halfway point for both Jared and me. There's a center there that specializes in these types of visits with a trained social worker that watches over everything."

"Okay. Let's get this over with. I have homework to do." Ellie groused as she came out of the bathroom fully dressed and her hair twisted up in a clip at the back of her head.

"I'm ready." Sam ran down the hallway, after clearly hastily dressing himself. "Wait! I need to grab the comic book I made for Dad."

Anna tried to stifle the smile. The purple shorts and brown t-shirt he wore couldn't clash more if he tried. "Hey, Buddy. Let's find you something that goes together, okay?"

"Why? It doesn't matter. It's not like he's actually going to see Dad. The only person that will be there is that mean Mrs. Clardy."

"Ellie." Tim's tone held a hint of warning.

"Come on, Sam. I think I saw you wearing a shirt the other day that will match these shorts perfectly."

"I like green and brown." The cute eight year old asserted.

"How about you choose *which* of those colors you want to wear today."

Anna prayed for the kids after they left with her father. At first, she struggled with what to pray for. Should she pray that Jared showed up? What would be the lasting effects of seeing him if he did come? Or should she pray that he didn't show? Ellie's anger would grow and Sam at some point would begin to take on the same bitterness as his sister. Anna just prayed God would insulate the kids from hurt and that she would be the best auntie she could be.

Less than an hour later, Anna walked into the gym and was delighted to find it fairly empty. She waved politely at the lady behind the counter, stuffed her things into a locker, and found an empty treadmill. She did a few stretches and put her earbuds in. Soon she was in her zone. Anna had been training for a 10k before Jonathan had broken up with her. She was angry that she allowed herself to slack off as long as she had. Anna had some ground to take back.

She ran at a medium pace for some time when all of a sudden someone got on the treadmill next to hers. She didn't think anything of it until she thought she heard someone talking over the music piped into her ears. Glancing over, Anna caught sight of Michael Tyler. *When did he get muscles?*

With a groan, she reduced her speed slightly and took the earbud out.

"There are literally five other treadmills open..." she pointed out.

"Hello to you, too. I thought we were going to be friends now. Why the sass?" He smiled as he bumped his speed to match hers. It irritated her so she increased her incline *and* speed.

His eyebrows shot up and a look of admiration mixed with *challenge accepted* crossed his face.

"This isn't sass. I just don't like people dripping sweat on me," Anna sputtered through heavy breaths.

"I'll try to keep my sweat to myself."

She was about to put her earbud back in when Michael spoke up again. "How long have you been running?"

"A couple of years."

"I'm impressed."

Anna smiled politely and tried to keep her eyes on her own monitor. Michael ran effortlessly as he kept increasing his incline. His arms were bulging out from under his t-shirt and Anna scolded herself for sneaking a curious look over at the man.

"I hear you got the job at the school," Michael said out of nowhere.

"How did you..."

"Your dad told Sean. Sean told me. We've all been praying for you."

Anna shook her head. Her father must have had the entire church praying.

"You're going to be great there. You're like Mrs. Erbe 2.0." Michael laughed.

"No. There's only one Mrs. Erbe." Anna reduced her speed as she entered her cool down.

"When do you start?"

"Monday." Anna smiled wide.

"I'm sure Sam and Ellie will be happy to have you there."

Anna laughed out loud. "Maybe Sam. I don't think Ellie is happy about much these days."

"Pre-teens."

Anna laughed at Michael. "And what do you know of pre-teens?"

"I help lead the youth group at church."

Anna came to a stop and turned to look at Michael in surprise.

"You?"

"Yes… me. I told you people change, Anna." He laughed and a bead of sweat dripped down the side of his face. "Between being boy crazy and moody, Ellie seems normal enough. She'll grow out of it."

"*Boy crazy*? My Ellie?"

Michael laughed louder. "Every Sunday night I get an earful from across the youth room about who's cute and who's gross. I get to work with the poor smelly Jr. High boys who still think the way to a girl's heart is by aggravating them."

"Ha. And do you boys ever grow out of that one?"

Michael shot her a side glance. "Are you implying something?"

"Not *implying* anything."

Anna started gathering her water bottle and phone, but her mind was on Ellie and how little she seemed to know her niece. She wasn't the adorable large-eyed little girl who liked to play with Anna's hair anymore. "You know…" Michael's voice brought her from her thoughts. "We need another female youth worker. You interested?"

"Me?" Anna was shocked at the thought. She was great in the library, but youth groups were…. *foreign*… to her to say the least. "I don't think I would be a good fit for that."

"I was just thinking it might give you and Ellie something in common. Tessa is struggling with this pregnancy and she's been talking about stepping away until after the baby is born," Michael said as he continued reducing his speed. "Think about it. Text me if you change your mind."

"I don't have your number." Anna regretted the words as soon as they were out of her mouth. Did that sound forward? "I can get it from my father … if I ever need it. Which I probably won't… because I don't think I'd be a good youth leader."

Michael smiled and motioned at the phone clenched in her hand. "May I?"

"You want my phone? Why?"

He held out his hand and she gave it to him. She watched as he typed something in and handed it back. An odd feeling rushed through her. It reminded her of all the times she had handed Michael her yearbooks for him to sign before school let out for the summer.

"Now you have my number." He smiled and grabbed the towel he had draped on the side of the treadmill to wipe his face.

"Okay. Thanks." Anna said absently and turned quickly to leave, forgetting she was still standing on the treadmill. She tripped and his hand shot out to steady her. "I'm fine. I need to get going. Have a good day, Michael."

Anna retreated to the women's bathroom to shower before leaving. All the while, she berated herself for acting ridiculously in front of the man. It was after she had gotten dressed and left the locker room that she found herself scanning the gym for Michael on her way out. She spotted him chatting up a guy as the two lifted weights in the far corner. He looked up and smiled at her and she quickly looked away, pushing through the glass doors to the outside.

What was wrong with her? She had no right to get flustered. Jonathan had just broken things off with her a few weeks prior. And this was Michael Tyler. He was probably the *last* person she should ever allow herself to get rattled over. Every woman in Deer Creek probably clamored for his attention. She didn't want to be one of them.

Anna drove a few parking lots over to the mattress store. There were more important things to think about at the moment. Such as getting a decent night's sleep so she didn't keep waking up with a kink in her back. An overwhelming feeling hit as soon as she walked through the door. She wanted a simple bed… an affordable bed… that wouldn't hurt her back. How would she find the right one when the store contained over a hundred mattresses?

A salesperson approached and showed Anna what was in her budget.

"If you want to save money, you could skip delivery. That is… if you have a truck," the woman suggested.

"How much will that bring down the cost?"

"If you shop our clearance section, it could reduce the price by at least $100."

"Show me the way to clearance, please." Anna smiled.

The saleswoman looked less than thrilled but obliged Anna, nonetheless. How would she get a queen-sized bed into her Jeep? The answer was simple. She *wouldn't*. Anna paused a moment and looked down at her phone. Would it be wrong to impose herself on Michael after acting so insolent? She looked for him in her contacts and smiled at the name he gave himself, *The Ex-Jerk Michael Tyler*. "Cute," Anna whispered to herself.

"What did you say?" the saleswoman asked.

"Nothing. Could I have a moment please? I'm seeing if I can find a truck."

The woman walked away and Anna sighed as she gave in and texted Michael Tyler. "Are you still at the gym by any chance?"

A second later her phone rang.

"Did you miss me?" He snickered into the phone.

"Pfft. Not even close." Anna realized she'd better tone down her sauciness if she wanted his help. "But… I was wondering if you'd be willing to help a friend out."

"Maybe… what's up?"

"I'm at the mattress store trying to find a way to get a bed back to my father's house." Anna bit her lip as she looked at the plastic wrapped mattress.

"Give me five minutes."

"*Really?*" Anna asked surprised into the phone.

"Yes, really." He laughed and disconnected the call.

He pulled into the parking lot and entered the store with a wide smile.

"Thank you so much, Michael." Anna smiled back sheepishly.

"Hey, I'm just glad you thought to call me. Maybe if I help with this you'll consider helping with the youth group?"

"I'll think about it, okay?"

"Maybe you'll come Wednesday night to meet the kids?"

"You're pushing it… but maybe." Anna smiled. Then she remembered the blonde in the car from the other day. "Your girlfriend won't be upset with you helping me, will she? I don't want to get you in trouble for being nice."

Michael guffawed. "*Girlfriend?* Are you spreading rumors about me, Anna Munson?"

Anna furrowed her brow.

"I don't have a girlfriend." Michael laughed. "That's the best part of staying single. I don't have to report back to anyone."

"But the pretty blonde from the other day…"

"*Kate?* She's my sister-in-law. Dan's wife. Haven't you met Kate yet?"

Anna felt foolish. She had known of Kate and had seen her from a distance growing up but didn't remember enough of what she looked like to make the connection. *Well, I assessed that whole scenario wrong,* Anna silently berated herself.

After loading the mattress onto the truck with the help of a warehouse worker, Michael followed Anna as they drove to the parsonage. Every so often she would glance into the rear view mirror. Michael Tyler was an enigma to her. He wanted to stay single. Isn't that what he had said? The Michael she remembered dated everyone in town. Maybe he finally maxed out the female population?

"Stop it, Anna," she scolded herself with a wry smile.

Her phone rang and ceased any further thought of Michael Tyler's love life.

"Hi, Anna." Her father's voice sounded wearied.

"Hey! How did the visit go?"

"Just as expected. I'm taking them for ice cream and stepped away to call you." Tim lowered his voice. "I just didn't want to talk about it when we got home in front of them. Ellie is being Ellie. She's angry and bitter, but acting indifferent. Sam is crushed."

"Maybe I can take them out. I've been wanting to go hiking. Do you think they'd like that?"

"I don't know. Normally Ellie goes into her room and locks the door after these trips. But maybe if it's you asking…"

Anna finished talking to her father and hung up as she pulled into the driveway. Her face must've said it all because as soon as Michael jumped down from his truck he looked at her and said, "Whoa. What's the matter?"

"Nothing."

"It's clearly something. But if you don't want to tell me…" He turned to go to the back of his truck and undo the tailgate.

"The kids' father missed another visit with them and they are upset… which makes me upset," Anna blurted out.

Why she felt so inclined to share this with him, she did not know. One thing Anna *did* know was that she was lonely and missed having friends. Kirstyn would've grabbed a bunch of snacks and sat down with her to solve the world's problems. Kirstyn and Jonathan were probably giving each other loving glances over lunch at that very moment.

"I'm sorry to hear that. I can't imagine what that must be like for them." Michael's face seemed to mirror her own disgust.

"Sammy had been so excited to see him. He had written a comic book for his dad. And Ellie… I don't think she can handle any more disappointment." Anna shook her head and tried not to let her anger surface.

"Why don't you go on ahead of me and unlock the door? I'll start unloading the mattress."

"Oh. Yeah. Okay. I'm sorry. Let me go do that." Anna turned on her heels and chastised herself for being so quick to overshare.

After Anna had unlocked the door to the house and made sure there was a clear path to the study for her new bed, she returned to find Michael ending a conversation on his phone.

"So, I just realized the kids haven't been to the farm in a while," he stated as Anna approached. "I hope you don't mind, but I asked my parents if they'd be okay with a few extra people at the house today. We're having a family cook out since Jenna is home for Spring break."

Anna didn't say a word and just stared at the him.

"Before you shut me down…" Michael began with a smile. "Sam likes the sheep we got in last year. And I *did* promise him a hayride a while back, but winter hit and I couldn't carry through with my promise."

Before Anna could respond, her father pulled up the driveway. Anna watched Ellie's sullen face in the front seat turn from angry to curious when she spotted Michael.

"Hello again, Michael," her father said as he got out of the car with a grin aimed at his daughter. "I've been seeing you a lot lately."

Anna cleared her throat to give her father a warning. "Michael helped me bring home the bed I bought. I saved money on delivery fees."

"Let me get Livi and I will help you get the mattress inside," Pastor Tim said going into the back of his car to get the sleeping toddler free from her car seat.

"I'll get her, Dad. I didn't get my Livi snuggles today." Anna moved to Livi's side of the car and paused when she heard Michael speak.

"I wanted to extend an invitation from my family to yours. We're grilling out and playing some games outside tonight since Jenna is home from college. Ben is also home on leave."

Anna watched as Ellie looked at her grandfather to see what he would say. Sammy jumped out of the car and ran to Michael to play wrestle, leaving his comic book crumpled on the seat he had just vacated. Grabbing the papers in one hand and lifting Livi into her arms, Anna joined them as Tim mulled over the offer.

"Can we please, Grandpa?" Sam asked excitedly.

"Do you want to go, Ellie?" Tim asked.

The teen shrugged her shoulders, but Anna caught the hint of a smile forming on her lips.

"It *has* been a while since I had Colleen's cooking," her father said wistfully. "Nothing beats her cooking."

"Hey. What's wrong with *my* cooking?" Anna asked stifling a laugh.

"Nothing at all. It's very… healthy."

"Then shall I tell Mom you're coming?" Michael asked with a smile.

"What do you say, Anna? I know you said you had a project you wanted to get to." Of course, Anna's father would put the decision on her.

Ahh, yes. The project. The infamous flash drive. With every passing day that she put it off, the importance seemed to wane. Lewis hadn't returned her calls. If it had been important, surely he would've called her. As she looked at the faces of Sam and Ellie, Anna figured she could wait a little longer to check out the USB.

"What can we bring? We can't come empty handed when we're adding five extra mouths to feed."

Michael's expression was surprisingly sweet.

"I like healthy. Mom isn't big on making salads. If you wanted to bring one I'd eat it." His smile grew.

And Anna smiled right back.

10

Anna pulled her Jeep behind her father's car in the Tylers' driveway. They decided it would be best to take two cars in case Tim needed to get Livi home before everyone else was ready to leave. With it being a Saturday, Anna also anticipated her father would want to go home and rest up for his Sunday activities.

Neither she nor Ellie made much of an effort to move from the Jeep at first. They watched Tim and Sam exit the car and then take the baby out.

"Are you feeling shy?" Anna asked her niece, who had spoken very little but seemed content to dominate the music they listened to on the way to the Tyler Farm.

"Are you?"

"I asked you first." Anna smiled.

"I didn't realize there would be so many people," Ellie said looking out over the vast front yard.

Anna nodded in understanding. She watched as Michael welcomed her father and Sammy, who had run straight to a swing set off to the side of the house. Anna saw Sean helping a beautiful brunette to a yard chair in the shade of the tree. She imagined that was his wife, Tessa.

Then Anna spotted the woman she had mistakenly assumed was Michael's girlfriend. Kate stood next to Dan Tyler with a little boy pulling on her arm for attention as she chatted with a pretty younger woman that Anna recognized instantly as Jenna Tyler. Mr. Tyler stood behind a grill and Colleen buzzed around the tables that had been set up with all different types of food.

"They have a big family, huh?" Anna said absently.

Out of the corner of her eye, Anna saw Ellie nod.

Michael walked to the car and tapped Anna's window.

"Are you going to join us or are you just going to eat your salad in here?" He smiled down at her.

Ellie chuckled.

Michael opened the door for Anna and when she got out of the car, he took the salad bowl from her.

"It's not heavy. I can carry it."

"Of course it's not heavy, but have you met my mother? I'd hear about it later for not being a gentleman." His smile was playful and Anna forced herself to look away from the deep set dimples in his cheeks.

"So, I'm helping you save face then?" Anna attempted to sound neutral.

"Exactly. Now you're catching on."

Anna walked beside Michael and took in the farm in wonder. "I remember that you lived on a farm, but I don't remember it being like this."

The sign at the front of their property advertised the Tyler Farm as a family fun spot with corn mazes, a petting farm, and pick-your-own produce.

"Kate really helped my parents get this place to the next level. They're opening up for the season next week."

"I'm impressed."

"You'll have to come pick some strawberries when they ripen. *I* planted those." Michael pointed to a field a distance away.

"No strawberries for me. I'm allergic," Anna said. A flashback to that fateful lunch date with Jonathan popped into her head but she pushed it away.

"Really? Well, there will be other things. How about blackberries? Blueberries?"

"I love blueberries."

"They'll be ready *hopefully* in mid to late July." Michael chatted on. "But you don't have to wait that long to visit."

Anna caught sight of Ellie in the corner of her eye with a huge smile on her face. She sent her a warning nudge, but it only made the young girl smile larger.

"Anna! I'm so glad you could join us!" Colleen Tyler said with a warm and welcoming tone. "Hello, Miss Ellie."

"It's nice to see you again, Mrs. Tyler." Anna smiled at the woman who, at one point, was her Sunday school teacher. "Thank you for letting us come. I brought salad."

Colleen smiled again and took the bowl from her son, placing it on the table with the other food.

"Have you met Kate and Tessa, Anna?"

"Not really. I mean… I kind of remember seeing Kate around school and church. I don't think I've met Tessa, though I've heard wonderful things." Anna hated how self-conscious she felt. Hopefully, no one else noticed.

"Well come on over and meet them. Jenna, Kate, and Tessa… say hello to Anna," Colleen said leading her to where the Tyler women were conversing before turning to Ellie. "Would you help me grab a few more things from the house, Dear?"

Ellie nodded and disappeared with Mrs. Tyler.

Suddenly alone, Anna looked over her shoulder at Michael's location, oddly wishing that he had followed behind them. He had gotten pulled away by Sam to the goat and sheep pens. Anna sat in an open lawn chair uneasily.

"It's good to see you again, Anna. I almost didn't recognize you," Kate said with a brilliant smile.

This was not surprising. The last time Kate would've seen her, Anna would've been a hundred pounds heavier.

"Yes. I lost weight." Anna fumbled with her fingers awkwardly.

"I may be coming to you for guidance after this little one is born. I hear you are quite the runner now. I've always wanted to get into running." Kate smiled warmly.

"I'm still learning myself. I was training for a 10k before I moved back, but I don't know if and when I'll enter a race."

"What got you started in running, Anna? If you don't mind my asking." This came from Tessa. Anna liked the softness she saw on her face and decided these were people she could talk freely with.

"My fiancé... ex-fiancé... and I were big into fitness. He was training me and encouraged me to try a small race." Anna winced internally at the memory of Jonathan. "I finished pretty high in my age group and wanted to push myself further. So, I kept on running and training. I know a lot of people think I'm crazy for it."

"I am impressed. That takes a lot of dedication and hard work," Tessa affirmed.

Anna felt her cheeks flame. "Tell me about what's new here in Deer Creek. It's been so long since I've been home. It's like stepping into a new world."

Kate started telling Anna all about the events and evolution of the Tyler farm. Tessa spoke on the future plans to turn the old Richards' mansion on the outskirts of town into a home for women of domestic abuse.

"What happened to Mrs. Richards?" Anna asked suddenly.

"Evelyn passed away a few years back. She left Sean and I her house to use for ministry." Tessa looked sad and Anna imagined there must've been a relationship between the women for such a bequeathment.

"I'm sorry to hear that. I remember her being quite entertaining." Anna smiled at the memory of the town's best dressed woman.

"She was. Judging by the way little Evie is kicking right now, I bet she'll be living up to the name." Tessa shifted in her seat to find a more comfortable position.

"And how have you been, Jen?" Anna smiled at the younger woman sitting cross legged on a blanket on the grass. "I hear that you're home on Spring break."

Jenna smiled a dimpled smile and Anna couldn't help but notice the Tyler family similarities.

"Yes, and I am *so* thrilled."

"What are you studying?" Anna asked, half distracted by the arrival of another car pulling into the driveway.

"Nursing." Jenna turned her head towards the car that arrived and a wide smile spread across her face. "Excuse me. Ben is here."

With very little effort, Jen jumped to her feet and took off on a mad dash up the incline of the driveway to a young man with a close-shaved haircut.

"Ugh. To be able to bounce up like that," Kate said wistfully and Tessa laughed.

"I suspect something is up with those two," Tessa said conspiratorially.

"I think that has been pretty obvious for a while." Kate rolled her eyes.

"No. I mean… I think something is up *imminently*."

Anna's eyes went to the young couple and watched as Ben lifted Jen and twirled her before putting her back on solid ground. The two whispered and walked back side by side, holding hands. Anna had always been happy for others' joy, but this time there was a tinge of hurt.

"Dinner! Come and get it!" John Tyler called out from his place at the grill. His smile grew as he watched Ben approach. "Well, look who showed up just in time to eat."

Everyone gathered around and Mr. Tyler turned to Tim. "Since we have the Pastor here… maybe he'll bless the food?"

Tim smiled and everyone bowed their heads as he prayed a prayer asking God to not only bless the food but also the entire growing Tyler family. The whole thing was very picturesque. If her mother had lived longer, Anna wondered if they'd be the ones hosting the picnics.

Get out of your head, Anna. Anna scolded herself and moved quickly to help the younger kids put their plates together. Sam had eyes bigger than his stomach so Anna had to step in before he put two burgers and a hot dog on his plate. A smaller boy named Eli, Kate and Dan's son, followed right behind him laughing and trying to keep up with Sam.

"Come here, Livi," Anna called to her niece who chased a butterfly too far from the table. "Come eat. Do you want chips?"

Instantly, the little head poked up and looked at her aunt with a broad smile.

"Tips. I want tips, Na-Na," Livi exclaimed.

Behind her Kate and Tessa cooed at the sweet baby talk.

"She's adorable," Kate gushed.

"She's something all right," Anna said as she reached down to the little one who now held her arms up to be lifted.

Anna was not a parent. She stared at the food laid out on the table and felt an instant sense of panic. What do toddlers eat… other than chips? The healthy food she had tried to introduce since she arrived home had been met with pursed lips and violent head shaking.

"Livi, point at what you want," Anna instructed.

Livi pointed at the big cake at the end of the table. Kate chuckled behind her.

"I'm new to this. What do two year olds eat?" Anna quietly asked Kate.

Kate smiled gently and turned to her husband. "Will you get Eli a plate please, Sweetheart?"

"Of course," Dan smiled and kissed her forehead before calling his son over. "Eli, food!"

"I know with Eli, he likes a hamburger patty cut into bite sized pieces. Maybe a piece of cheese. Here. Let's try that to start with," Kate said as she began getting a plate assembled for Livi. "Oh, and we can't forget Miss Livi's chips. How about a carrot to try? Maybe she'll like dipping it in some ranch dressing."

"Thank you. This is very new to me," Anna whispered.

"I'm glad to help anytime you need me. What you're doing... helping your father with the kids... it's admirable," Kate said softly.

Anna blushed and took the plate Kate offered to Livi. "Thank you. They've not really enjoyed my cooking so far."

"My family doesn't really enjoy mine either," Kate laughed.

Michael, who had apparently been listening in, couldn't resist piping up from his place in line behind them. "At least you're past the crispy tuna casserole days."

Dan's amused smile earned him a punch from his wife.

"What? I didn't say anything." The oldest Tyler son feigned an innocent face, but his smile lurked just below the surface.

The scene was wholesome and wonderful. Anna hardly classified herself as a spinster at the age of twenty six, but she wondered if she would ever get to enjoy such playful affection someday.

Anna settled Livi on the blanket in front of the chair she had been sitting in. Her father sat at the picnic table with Mr. and Mrs. Tyler and seemed to genuinely enjoy their conversation. Ellie brought her plate and sat next to Anna. Soon, Sam followed suit. Michael plopped down in between him and Eli on the grass and tussled his hair.

"So, Anna," Michael began. "Have you given anymore thought to helping with youth group?"

Tessa's head popped up with a look of excitement.

"Uh… not really." Anna wanted to send a warning glare at Michael so badly, but all eyes were on her.

"I really wish you would," Tessa smiled. "For purely selfish reasons, of course. I haven't been able to do much of anything lately and Sean's been saying if we don't find another female volunteer, we'll have to cancel the retreat to the beach this year."

Ellie's head spun around and looked at her aunt with an expression Anna had yet to see on her niece.

"Aunt Anna, please! I'm really looking forward to this. We're going to a *real* beach! The ocean."

Michael cleared his throat and gave her a sly smile. "Ellie, you don't want me hanging around you and your friends, do you? I'm not very cool," Anna pointed out.

"You're cool enough. As long as we can go to the beach."

Anna snorted a laugh. "Gee, thanks."

"Why don't you come to one of the youth group meetings and see how you feel about it? You may just fall in love with the group," Tessa suggested. "We have some great kids."

"Please! Please! Please!" Ellie begged and even went as far as laying her head against Anna.

"Yeah. Okay. I guess I can give it a try."

Happy cheers went up and the conversation turned to Ben's experiences in the Army. Anna was content to fade into the background as she processed what she had just committed to. It was definitely out of her comfort zone, but maybe that wasn't a bad thing. After all, she was trying to re-find herself. Part of that involved stepping out into the unknown, right?

"This summer is my first time PCSing," Ben told the group, but was looking down into Jen's face.

"What does that mean? PCSing?" Anna asked, rejoining the conversation.

"It stands for *Permanent Change of Station*. It means I'm being sent to a different base soon to start new training." Ben squeezed Jen's hand. The two seemed to communicate with their eyes and facial expressions for a moment and Ben laughed. "What? *Now*? Are you sure?"

Jen laughed and nodded.

"Okay. If you're positive." Ben grinned like a fool and got to his feet, motioning for Jenna to join him. "Everyone, can I have your attention? We have a very special announcement to make. Last night, I asked Jen to be my wife and she said yes. We wanted to wait to announce it until everyone was gathered in one spot."

Ben smiled a huge cheesy smile as Jenna reached into her pocket and pulled out the ring she had been hiding. Anna felt her eyes growing big and tried to act normally. She glanced at the faces of the people around her to see how they all were responding.

Colleen gushed. John smiled proudly as he patted Ben on the back and hugged his daughter. Dan looked uncertain and glanced back at his wife to see if this was really happening. She smiled and got to her feet to hug her sister-in-law, pulling her husband reluctantly behind her. Jenna was the baby, after all. Sean and Tess smiled and hugged the new couple.

Anna remained in her seat uncertain of what to do. She looked at Michael who was still sitting on the blanket. He shook his head slightly with a small smile.

"Here it comes in 3… 2… 1…" He whispered quietly to Anna.

"Here comes *what*?" Anna asked, also in a whisper.

"Michael… that leaves you, Bro," Dan said with his arms crossed at his chest.

Michael laughed out loud. "I already told you. I'll leave the wedded bliss to you all."

A few people chuckled at Michael's hold out, but the attention quickly returned to the giddy couple.

"Here's to singleness," Anna said as she held up her cup of lemonade in solidarity to her friend. Michael gave her an appreciative smile, clinking his can of soda to her glass.

Hayrides, games of corn hole, and dessert followed as the Tyler family continued their celebration. Anna's father grew tired and decided to take Livi home to get her to bed at a reasonable time. Ellie helped Colleen take food items into the house and seemed genuinely pleased to do so. Sam played with little Eli on the swings.

Anna spotted a trail and her curiosity piqued. A quiet walk seemed appealing as she wrestled with the emotions inside of her. How long would it take for the sting of her broken engagement to subside? She wrestled with being happy for the young couple and feeling bitter at Jonathan at the same time.

A bird chirped and chittered away from a branch above her as she wandered down the little dirt path. She made it to what looked like a cabin off to the side of the walkway when she heard footfall behind her. She turned to see Michael.

"Where are you off to? You were supposed to be my partner in corn hole and we're up next."

"I was just enjoying the quiet for a moment," Anna said as she breathed in the scent of pine.

"Yeah… I get that." Michael smiled and dropped his head before looking back up at her. "This is probably raw for you. Your father mentioned …"

"Jonathan dumping me? Of course he did." Anna grimaced. "It's fine. He was a jerk… Jonathan, that is. Not my father."

"I figured that's who you meant." Michael grinned, but his smile faded as he considered Anna. "It sounds like he was definitely a loser."

His eyes on her made her feel jittery so she tried to shift the focus.

"So, what's your story? I mean, I'm jaded from a breakup, but you… You don't seem to be brokenhearted. Why are you so adamant about staying single?" Anna questioned.

"I have watched my two normally rational brothers turn into mushy piles of goo thanks to those two women," Michael spoke emphatically.

Anna couldn't help but chuckle.

"Don't get me wrong. I love Kate and Tess. I even *encouraged* my brothers to marry them. I did not know how severely limited they would be after those rings were on their fingers though."

"The proverbial ball and chain?"

"Here's an example. I wanted to go for a hike before we go on the youth retreat. They had to *ask* permission… like they were kids again. And now… get this… Kate and Tess want to come along, too." Michael stared at Anna with an incredulous face. "Six years ago, if the three of us wanted to go hiking. Guess what? We just went hiking."

"What trail?" Anna asked absently. Hiking sounded wonderful.

Michael cocked an eyebrow. "Water Run State Park. Why? Do you want to come?"

"I don't want to invite myself."

"I just invited you, Anna," Michael laughed.

"But I'd probably have Ellie and Sam…"

"The more the merrier at this point." Michael smiled wryly.

Anna's phone rang. She still had a smile on her face when she pulled it from her pocket, but her smile quickly faded as she saw the name on her screen.

"What's wrong? Who is it?"

"My… boss."

"Mrs. Erbe?" Michael laughed.

Anna shook her no and answered the call. "Mr. Price?"

"Hello, Anna." The familiar voice of the editor took her by surprise. "I wasn't sure if anyone else had reached out to you. Have you heard the news?"

"What news?"

"Lewis Sparks passed away. I know the two of you were close. His funeral is Tuesday and I wanted to make sure you knew about it. I knew you'd want to come."

"Lewis …" Anna gasped. "How?"

"Who is it? What's going on?" Michael questioned her but Anna couldn't hear him.

"He… he killed himself, Anna." Mr. Price's voice broke. "I feel responsible. It's these layoffs. He didn't take it well. None of us are taking them well, but I never thought he'd… you know."

"No… he wouldn't have… This can't be real." Anna fell against a tree for support and Michael reached out to steady her. Mr. Price told her where the funeral would be held and offered her his condolences before he said goodbye.

Anna stood frozen. This wasn't right. *Not Lewis. Lewis would never have done that. He was the most upbeat and determined person I know. Losing his job wouldn't drive him to that. Say it's a mistake, God.*

"I have to go." Anna pushed away from the tree and ran back up the trail with Michael on her heels.

"Anna, what's going on?" Michael asked from her side as he tried to keep up.

"My friend… died."

"Anna, I'm so…"

"I'm sorry, Michael. Thank you for inviting us, but I need to go home."

"Of course. Will I see you tomorrow?"

Anna nodded and tried her best to hold the tears at bay. She stopped long enough to attempt a normal goodbye to the rest of the Tyler family. The kids chatted obliviously in the car all the way home, but Anna heard nothing… just Mr. Price's words echoing over and over in her mind. *Lewis Sparks is dead.*

*****

"Are you sure she'll show up?"

"I'm positive, Sir. Anna and Lewis were good friends. She'll be there." Mr. Price assured.

Was the money he was promised worth the feeling of guilt that was going to keep him up that night? Would they do the same to Anna that they did to Lewis?

"I'm positive Anna doesn't know anything, Mr. Davidson. Believe me when I say... if she did, she would've said something by now."

"That may be true, Price, but I don't like taking chances."

"But... but... you're not going to *hurt* her, right? Wouldn't that draw more attention? Wouldn't that be too coincidental... so soon after Lewis?"

"I don't pay you for advice, Price. Mind yourself."

The phone call dropped and the editor sat in his office with his head in his hands, staring at the piece Lewis had submitted for publication on his computer screen. A small part of him wanted to hide it in a secret folder on his laptop in case he needed leverage, but he knew he was as good as dead if Davidson ever found out. He clicked delete and the file disappeared ... just like he would if he dared cross The Broker again.

11

Anna sat in the back pew at church the next morning. Being the first time back at her home church in years, several of the older members greeted her with hugs and welcoming words. In Skennan Cove, Anna attended a large congregation which made absorbing into the crowd easier. Deer Creek Community Church was smaller. It didn't help that she was the Pastor's daughter.

She couldn't help but picture her mother sitting in the front pew singing with all her heart. It hurt to sit there without the scent of her mother's perfume or to see her greet people as they entered the sanctuary. Quite likely, the tears threatening to fall were also because Lewis was gone. *Gone.* How was that even possible?

As soon as she had brought the kids home from the Tylers' farm the previous night, Anna beelined it to her room and did what she had been putting off. The only light in her room came from her illuminated laptop screen as she scrolled through documents and files of what appeared to be ledgers.

At first, the numbers and spread sheets made no sense to her. Then she came to a file that drove an icy spike into her chest. Pictures of young girls holding signs with what Anna assumed were made up names and prices for their *services*. The youngest couldn't have been much older than Ellie.

"Do you mind if we join you, Anna?"

Anna jumped at Jenna's voice and tried to quickly recover. "Yes, please. Sit."

"You left so quickly last night. Was everything okay?" Jenna asked as Ben took a seat on the other side of his fiancé. "Did Michael say something to upset you? That stuff about staying single... I'm sure he doesn't mean it."

"No, no, no. He was fine." Anna tried to come up with the right words. She all but choked on them. "I received a call that a friend passed away. I didn't want to bring the party down."

Jenna's eyes filled with compassion. "Oh, Anna. I'm so sorry. Is there anything I can do for you?"

"Prayers are always appreciated." Anna knew she sounded trite, but truly only prayers were going to help Anna at that moment. And maybe a nap.

"Is this where the cool people sit?" Michael's voice came out of nowhere and he nudged Anna until she, Jenna, and Ben scooted down to accommodate him on the end of the pew next to Anna.

"Dork." Jenna smirked at her brother.

He ignored his little sister completely and leaned in to Anna. "Are you doing okay?"

"Not really, but I'm holding it together."

He gave a quick nod.

"After church the young adults are going to go to the barbecue place for lunch. Want to come?"

"I don't know. There's something I need to work on after church."

"It's Sunday. It's supposed to be a day of rest." Michael smiled slightly. "Think about it at least. My treat."

"I appreciate the offer. I'll think about it." Anna smiled graciously. She was thinking about several things as the music began and her father took his place at the front of the church.

Her mind could not focus on much. Her thoughts went to Lewis. His funeral was Tuesday. She was supposed to start work Monday. How could she start her employment at the school by calling off? Then her mind drifted to more serious questions. Had he seen everything on the flash drive? If so, why had he said there was nothing on it? Was it possible that he hid the information from her and it got him killed? Or maybe he really did kill himself. But that didn't feel right at all.

The entire service passed and Anna still tried to figure out mysteries she didn't have answers for. As people started dispersing following the closing hymn, Anna politely excused herself from the pew and headed towards the parsonage. Her Father's voice stopped her before her foot even hit the parking lot.

"Anna, I invited a young married couple over for lunch. They were new visitors today."

"*Today*? Do we have enough roast in the crock pot for two more mouths?" Anna knew she probably sounded like a brat.

"Four mouths actually. They have two kids. And, yes, I believe we do." His smile was sympathetic, but stern, nonetheless. "This is ministry life, Anna. Did you forget?"

Her father still had no idea about the call she received the day before and Anna knew if she told him he would probably reschedule with the church guests. However, she didn't have it in her to tell him.

Anna sighed. "I was invited to go out to lunch with the young adults. Maybe I should go."

Tim's face lightened. "That's a great idea. I was praying you'd find a group of friends. This is a good start."

"But what about you? Having company and trying to keep the kids under control doesn't sound very restful."

"Don't worry about me. Their kids are similar in age to Livi and Sam. Ellie will most likely disappear into her room regardless of who is over anyway," Tim quipped. "Go on. Go make friends."

Anna groused under her breath as she turned on her heels, hoping she could locate Michael. She found him easily enough. There was a group of young women surrounding him.

It reminded Anna of feeding time at an aquarium. The gaggle of ladies stared up into his face, hanging on every word he said. They burst into a chorus of lilting giggles when he said something slightly humorous. Anna rolled her eyes at the spectacle. He spotted her and a look akin to relief flooded his face.

"Hey, Anna! Everybody, you remember Anna, don't you?" He slipped through a gap between two ladies as he came to stand near her. He put his arm around her and pulled her close, whispering "Help me", into her ear. Anna chastised herself for almost leaning into the warmth she felt next to him.

"Really, Mike?" she muttered for his ears only.

"Did you change your mind about coming?" He looked hopeful.

"Dad has company joining him at the house today. I guess that means I'm coming."

Michael beamed. "Great!"

"Not to be greedy, but you're still treating, right? My purse is at the house." Anna asked quietly with her back to the group.

"I got you, Girl." He smiled and then addressed the people waiting near by. "So where are all the guys? I feel seriously outnumbered here. Ben, go see who wants to come so I know a head count. Anna and I will go ahead of everyone and get in line at the restaurant to get a table. Text me the number of people."

Ben nodded and started moving through the remaining groups of people at the church inviting them to come along. Michael tugged on Anna's arm and motioned her to follow him to his truck.

"You know, people are going to think we're *together*," Anna warned.

"I'm okay with that." He laughed. "As long as it keeps *that* from happening again."

Anna shook her head. "Is that not a normal occurrence for you on a Sunday?"

Michael looked chagrined. "Jenna has gotten it into her head that I need her assistance in finding a significant other."

"You're not asking me to pretend to be your girlfriend, are you? Because I really don't think that would…"

"Of course not. Though now I know where I stand with you. Sheesh, Anna." Michael gave her a humorous side glance. "Don't worry. About half of those girls will be back at college working towards their *MRS* degrees by this time next week and you won't have to protect me anymore."

Anna guffawed. "You know, they are probably attending college for an *actual* degree… not to find a man. That was chauvinistic, Michael. It's not like you're the best thing to happen to woman-kind."

Michael's eyes grew big and he blew out a large gust of air. "Ouch, Anna."

"I'm sorry." She rubbed her temples. An outing was not what she wanted. "I'm tired. I get snappy when I'm tired."

"Do you honestly think I think those things about myself?"

"Don't you?" She turned to look at him.

"I wouldn't say I'm the *best* thing…" He smiled a cocky smile.

Anna laughed despite the turmoil she felt. Michael was a good distraction if nothing else. She wished she could unload on him all the horrible information she had taken in the night before, but she couldn't.

"Someday a *Petunia* is going to pop onto the scene and you're going to have to eat your words about staying single," Anna said as they walked into the restaurant.

Michael looked at her like she had two heads as he held open the door for her.

"You don't remember? In our story… you were Super Mike with the bulletproof cape and you rescued Petunia… your beautiful damsel in distress... from Mr. Bad – the bad guy."

A light dawned on Michael's face and he laughed out loud. "Ahh yes. Petunia. Why did we name her that?"

"Who knows? We were hyped up on Pixie Sticks and in fifth grade." Anna shrugged with a wry smile.

"We made you a superhero, too. Didn't we give you the guy equivalent of Petunia?"

"No. It was a story for you, not me," Anna pointed out.

"That doesn't seem fair."

They put in Michael's name with the hostess and waited for a block of tables to open up for their group that had started to arrive. Talk of their superhero alter egos halted. The buzzing of multiple conversations allowed Anna to fade into the background. She zoned out watching the television that hung on the wall in the area designated for waiting patrons.

While she stared absently at the TV a familiar face flashed up on the screen. At first it didn't dawn on her who she was seeing. There was something about his eye shape... his nose structure.... the curvature of his mouth. Anna stared into the eyes of the man who had run into her that fateful night. The headline above his picture read, "*Memorial Planned for Slain Officer*".

Anna grabbed Michael's arm. "He's a cop."

Michael looked up at the screen to see what Anna was talking about and a sadness crossed his countenance. "Yeah. That was J.T. Great guy."

"You knew him?"

"A little. He was a close friend of my buddy Jake's."

"Jake Cory." Anna gasped.

Michael turned to face Anna. He appeared to be trying to read her face. "Yes. Jake Cory. What is going on, Anna. Why do you look like that?"

She was still grasping his arm as she looked up into Michael's face. "I think I have something that belongs to him."

*****

Day one of the library was in the books. Anna felt overwhelmed by the time the final bell rang. She drove the kids home and disappeared into her room to change into running clothes.

"There's my girl." Her father smiled as she came out of her room. "Am I going to get to hear how your day went? I know this morning was hard."

Anna had finally told her father about Lewis over coffee during breakfast, though she held back information that would cause him concern… like a flash drive implicating several important people in shady criminal dealings.

"It was a good day. I trained on the computer and refreshed myself on shelving books. Nothing earth shattering."

"And what about tomorrow? Did you decide what you are going to do about your friend's funeral?"

Anna sighed.

"Not yet. I'm hoping to get some clarity while I run. Mrs. Erbe said to call her as soon as I decide. She and Mrs. Peterkin were understanding when I explained the situation."

"Be careful if you're running the roads. They're doing work on several streets today," Tim advised.

"I'll run at the P-A-R-K." Anna spelled the word over Livi's head so she wouldn't get excited. "The trails would be pretty right now."

"Take your epi-pen."

Anna patted the running bag affixed to her waist and smiled at her father. "Not my first run, Dad."

Anna drove herself to the park, grateful that the rain predicted by the weatherman had held off. As she parked, her phone rang and she saw Michael's name pop up. He was becoming a common fixture on her phone. That morning, he texted her, *"Happy first day of school."*

"Hello, Mike. I'm getting ready to run. What's up?"

"Where are you running? Maybe we can meet up?" he suggested.

"I'm just running the trails at the park. It's probably not the best day to get together."

"We'll catch up another time. I want to hear how your first day went."

"Sounds good." Anna smiled as she hung up. If anyone had told her Michael Tyler would be the closest thing she had to a good friend a couple of weeks prior, she would've laughed at them. Yet, there he was... being a good friend.

Anna pulled her hair into a ponytail and put on her headband before sliding her earbuds in and setting her playlist up. Then she was off. She hadn't run these trails before. When she had left home for college, she hadn't been fitness minded and – back then - the park was for kids only in her opinion. She was appreciative of the people that decided the trails needed proper attention.

The path was heavily tree lined and secluded with varied inclines and hills. Anna liked the newness and scenery of the path and soon was at her full pace. She was so engrossed that she didn't see the man leaning against her car as she finished her run. He looked to be in his early thirties, kind of gruff looking, and seemingly waiting for someone.

Then, he looked directly at *her*. She stopped dead in her tracks as he smiled a smile of familiarity, making Anna uneasy. He waved and pushed off from her car, heading in her direction. She took a few steps back towards the opening of the trail. She quickly calculated her possibilities. If she ran up the trail, she'd be isolated and out of sight from help. Running the other way would take her to the playground area, though it wasn't heavily populated at the moment.

"Anna?" he finally asked.

She didn't respond.

"We have a mutual friend. He told me I'd find you here," he said keeping his hands where she could see them as if sensing her distrust.

"And who would that be?" Anna demanded.

"Michael Tyler." He must've been fairly confident that she wasn't going to run now as he took a few steps closer to bridge the distance between them. "Please don't bolt. Something tells me you could very easily leave me in the dust. I'm not here to scare you. Just talk. I have information on your friend Lewis."

Anna furrowed her brow at the man. "Do you have a name?"

He smiled slightly. "Jake Cory."

Anna felt her pulse quicken, but she tried not to show it. She motioned with her head to a nearby picnic table towards the playground. He nodded and let her lead the way. She quickly scanned the man, concluding he was not what she had imagined. He didn't wear a black suit or sunglasses like she had always pictured a detective would wear. Jake sported a pair of jeans and a Syracuse University sweatshirt.

She took a seat at the picnic table and watched cautiously as he sat across from her.

"What do you know about Lewis?" Anna cut to the chase.

"Okay. I guess we'll cut out the formalities..." He smirked. "Tyler said it might take you a while to warm up."

Anna sat up straighter and leveled the man with a look. "Is that right?"

"Whoa, I'm a friend. I promise." Jake put his hand up.

Anna looked skeptical. The man sighed and pulled out his cellphone. Lewis' voice filled the air as the detective played the voicemail.

"Hello. My name is Lewis Sparks. I'm a reporter with the Skennan Gazette. I think I have information that you need. I just finished an exposé piece on Lance Davidson implicating several important people. My source was given a USB and was told to contact you directly. Please call me back immediately and I will connect you to my source."

Anna gulped. Lewis had betrayed her. For what? To outscoop her? "What a liar!"

"It's a real voicemail. You can look at it if you want." Jake offered her his phone.

"I'm not talking about you. *Lewis* told me the flash drive was empty," Anna muttered more to herself than to the man who listened intently across from her. "I didn't see a piece published in the *Gazette* by Lewis though. I would've noticed it."

"It didn't get published."

"But that would've been headline news. Why didn't Price..." Then Anna stopped and thought of the implications. "Lew didn't kill himself, did he?"

"That's what the coroner is content with," Jake said softly, but his steely blue eyes gave him away.

"But you don't think he did either..."

"No, I don't." Jake leaned in across the table to make sure Anna was paying attention. "And I think that you need to be very careful what you do from here on out, Anna Munson."

12

The parsonage made weird noises at night. Why had Anna never noticed that while growing up? Every click or bump of the kitchen appliances startled her. Outside, a dog barked somewhere down the street. Was it a normal dog bark or was it alerting its humans to potential threats?

Anna lay on her back staring at the ceiling fan spinning above, waiting for sleep to claim her. When she last looked at her smart watch, it was after 3 A.M. She debated whether she should just get up and start her day. Every time she dozed off she had bad dreams.

Jake Cory had asked for the flash drive, but of course she didn't have it on her while running the night before. Anna hadn't felt comfortable bringing him to the parsonage. He didn't seem overly thrilled at the delay, but Anna didn't care. She didn't even know if this man could be trusted. Lewis died after leaving him a message.

The detective invited her to an all-night fast food joint for coffee at six in the morning to make the hand off before she had to get the kids and herself to school. Jake put enough fear into her about going to the funeral that she concluded it would be unwise to attend. And to be honest, Anna struggled with the knowledge that Lewis had lied to her about what he had seen on the USB... just to get a story. Did he not know she would eventually look for herself? Was their friendship not as important as the potential story he could write?

Not for the first time since coming back to Deer Creek, Anna questioned her judgement. First, there was Jonathan. She thought he had loved her. Yet, as she evaluated their relationship since being away from him, Anna concluded that Jonathan viewed her as a trophy more than anything. He took the fat girl and turned her into a butterfly. She was nothing more than his project.

Then there was Kirstyn. Looking back over their friendship Anna could pinpoint times that her friend had been overly flirtatious with Jonathan, but Anna hadn't wanted to confront her because what if she was wrong? What if she hurt Kirstyn's feelings?

"And how did that work out for you, Anna?" She scolded herself as she turned onto her side and stared at the wall.

And Lewis... It wasn't as if Anna and Lewis got together and hung out in their spare time, but they worked closely together. They had been a good team, or so she thought. At least with Lewis, Anna recognized the pressure they were under as journalists. It was easy to see how he could succumb to the temptation, but it didn't make it hurt less.

And how was she to trust her judgement moving forward? What about Michael? What if he ended up being the jerk she used to *think* him to be?

"Is there anyone left on this planet I can trust, God?" Anna whispered.

Trust me. I don't change. Anna felt God speaking deep into her spirit. She looked at her Bible on a shelf. Her father preached many a sermon on how to know the difference between what was right and wrong. Every sermon urged people to read the Scriptures.

At first, Anna thought maybe she should get up and grab her Bible. Instead, she sighed, rolled over the other way, and grabbed her phone. Distraction felt easier than reading God's Word. She looked over the texts exchanged with Michael before she had gone to bed.

"What did you do to Jake? He's moping." He had texted. "You said you had something that belonged to him and now you're not giving it to him?"

"Is he trustworthy?"

He had sent her a frustrated emoji with "YES" in all caps. "I wouldn't have sent him to talk to you if he wasn't."

Anna contemplated texting him. She knew he'd be up. Michael was working an overnight shift at the firehouse. Thinking better of it, she decided to get up and get on with her day since it was already now after 4 A.M. She went on a small run, came home and showered, and grabbed the flash drive.

Her father wandered out of his room looking confused as to why his daughter was already dressed and ready to go before six o'clock in the morning.

"Was that you I heard moving around? What's got you riled up, Anna Banana?" he asked with a concerned, but sleepy expression.

"I'm sorry if I woke you. I went for an early run. I couldn't sleep."

"Is it because of the friend that passed away?"

"Not completely. I feel right in not going to the funeral."

"You've been acting differently the last couple of days. Are you going to tell me about it eventually?"

Anna smiled gently. "I'm fine. I promise."

"Don't go getting involved in any relationships too soon, Anna. I know Jonathan hurt you. That can leave you vulnerable."

She couldn't contain the laughter. "What in God's green earth are you talking about, Dad?"

"Michael. You two have been interacting quite a lot since you came home."

Anna chuckled at the thought. "He's a friend. That surprises me too, but that's all he is."

"Don't get me wrong, I think he's a great guy... I just don't want to see you rushing into anything too soon."

Anna hugged her father. "No worries there. I think he enjoys being the last Tyler holdout as far as relationships go. Can't say that I blame him."

"Well, hold on there. I don't want you throwing the baby out with the bathwater. Don't give up on relationships permanently," Tim said giving Anna a squeeze before letting her go.

Anna looked at the time and moved away. "I have to go. I'll be back to grab the kids for school."

"Where in the world..."

"I'm meeting a friend for coffee... and, no, it's not Michael." Anna smirked as she grabbed her keys and wallet before heading out the door, leaving her father looking bewildered.

The sun was rising as she pulled into the parking lot of the small eatery. The lights were on inside the diner but there looked to be very few patrons. One truck was parked in the lot and she assumed it belonged to Jake Cory. Anna had a moment of uneasiness as she felt in her pocket for the flash drive. Was she being a fool trusting this person?

There were employees inside moving around so thankfully they were not alone in the event that he turned out to be a bad guy. Maybe it was her writer's mind at work, but she imagined sitting across from the man and hearing him release the safety of a gun pointed at her under the table. And what did she have to protect herself with? An epi-pen?

She walked into the building and scanned the tables and booths until she spotted him in a far back corner booth. She tried not to laugh at the sight. He hardly looked like an assassin- or even a detective for that matter- all ruffled and groggy looking with his head leaning up against the wall.

"Not a morning person?" she asked as she approached and he startled.

He looked displeased.

"You know, we could've handled this in a way that would've been much easier for us both," he groused as he took a sip of his coffee. "I assume you trust me now?"

"You assume wrong." Anna slid into the booth.

Jake brought his hands up and rubbed his face in aggravation. It was then that Anna noticed the gold band on his left ring finger. She hadn't noticed it there the day before, but then again she was a little caught off guard by his visit and she didn't make a habit looking to see if a man was married or not.

"Is your wife okay with you meeting strange women this early in the morning?" Anna asked.

"What?" Jake looked confused at first but then noticed his ring. He dropped his hand back to his lap. "Oh. I sometimes forget that I have it on."

What was he? Some kind of a creep? He must've read her thoughts because he let out a sigh and explained.

"My wife passed away last summer. Her name was Beth and considering she cared about J.T. as much as I do, I doubt she would mind us meeting so I can get the evidence I need to prove his death was Davidson's doing."

Anna scrutinized the man. His words sounded painful to say. Jake's blue eyes looked incredibly sad. Overall, he seemed more like a man who was heartbroken rather than a threat.

"I'm sorry to hear that," Anna said softly.

Jake cleared his throat as if shutting down that part of the conversation. "Do you mind telling me how you got the flash drive?"

"He gave it me."

"J.T.? You knew him?"

"No. He fell on me while I was stretching."

The confusion on Jake's face was evident so Anna explained the events of that fateful night in detail, including that he was high on something.

"Tell me what he looked like? Was he in distress?"

"I know what people look like when they're amped up on something. My sister is a meth addict. His pupils were dilated and he was antsy."

"He wasn't a user. He was undercover as one of Davidson's men," Jake defended his friend. "They probably shot him up with something before he got away. I'm still waiting on the tox results."

"The newspapers reported the death of a homeless man on my street. Was that really J.T.? If so, why are the news outlets saying your friend died at a traffic stop gone wrong?" Anna questioned.

She was met with a derisive laugh. "Because people are hiding things. You don't trust me… well, I don't trust very many people right now myself. I think someone gave J.T. away."

"As in another cop?" Anna's mouth dropped open.

Jake gave a curt nod. Anna digested everything that he had said and reached into her pocket, pulled out the flash drive, and scooted it across the table to him.

"Did you look at the contents on this? Did you see any of the names Davidson has dealings with?"

Anna wasn't sure she wanted to divulge what she knew, but she finally nodded.

"There are a lot of important people who could get in pretty big trouble," she stated quietly.

Anna thought back to Mr. Price editing her piece on the State Representative at the flower show. He had been talking with Davidson and acted agitated at being interrupted. Or was he agitated at being caught talking to the man? Things were starting to make sense. Was Mr. Price involved as well? She shuddered as she recalled their conversation Saturday. Was he banking on her attending Lewis' funeral that day? And what would happen to her if she did go?

"Lewis' funeral… is that why you told me to stay back? Am I in danger?" Anna asked suddenly.

Jake's expression softened.

"I'm sorry that you had to get involved in this, Anna. I'm grateful that J.T. was able to trust you with this."

Jake leaned in closer commanding her full attention. "I will say this… it would be a good idea to rethink running isolated trails alone like you were doing the other day. Be alert. Call me if you think something feels off."

"So, I *am* in danger…" Anna felt sick to her stomach. "I hope not. Hopefully, Davidson believes that Lewis was the only one with the information. Keep a low profile and don't go back to Skennan Cove. I'll be keeping an ear out."

"And what about you? What will happen if they find out you have that flash drive?"

Jake gave a hint of a smile. "You're worried about me now?"

"Well, if Michael trusts you…"

Jake let out a pleasant sounding laugh. "Tyler is a good guy. I've filled him in a little so don't be surprised if he…"

"Oh great. He'll go superhero on me," Anna muttered.

"What?"

"Nothing. Did you have to drive all the way from Skennan Cove this morning?" Anna asked as if she just realized how truly inconvenient the early morning meeting must've been for the man.

"I crashed at Tyler's place last night. I need to get back to Skennan Cove for the funeral."

Anna's head shot up. "*You're* going?"

"I want to see who shows up," Jake stated. "I told you, I'll keep my eyes and ears open. You should be safe here. Call me if you need me."

He slid a card across the table to Anna and started getting up. With that he was gone and Anna was left wondering what exactly she had managed to get herself into.

*****

The funeral was well attended. Jake blended in well with the crowd, but he tried not to appear obvious as he scanned the myriad of faces. He didn't have the luxury of a partner to help scope out the mourners. Technically, he was not there as a detective at all. This mission was personal and off the books. He used a couple of his vacation days to accommodate skittish Anna and to attend the funeral. Hopefully, there wasn't anyone at the funeral who would recognize him as a cop.

The eulogy was lacking. Jake couldn't help but reflect on his precious wife's funeral. Their pastor had done a wonderful job celebrating her short life and incorporating the good news of Jesus Christ. Lewis' funeral seemed sad and despairing. No hope. Jake's heart broke for Lewis' mother who wept openly in the front row, mere feet from her son's closed casket. Did she believe her son had killed himself?

A man sat in the row behind the family and kept looking back behind him as though he were looking for someone. Jake recognized him as the editor of the *Skennan Gazette*, Mr. Price. Price's eyes locked with another man sitting in a section on the other side of the aisle. He was a younger man in his twenties, sporting a smug expression on his face.

Was that fear on Price's face? Jake had done right to tell Anna to stay back. There was no way of knowing if Lewis had divulged to Davidson's men that Anna held the flash drive. For now, Anna was safe and he was determined to keep it that way.

*****

"You said she'd be here," Rob muttered quietly over a tray of cold cuts at the luncheon in the church's basement following the funeral.

"I thought she would come. They were close friends," Harold Price defended himself quietly as he prepared a plate, trying not to make eye contact with the other man. "She made it sound as if she would."

"Do you think she suspects something?"

"Anna? No, she's not that astute," Harold chuckled. "I still don't think she is even aware of what she saw that day. Trust me, she's not involved in this."

"Call her and find out where she is." Rob's words were not a suggestion.

"If I keep calling her, then she *will* get suspicious. I never talked to her this much when she worked for me... and I left three messages on her voicemail already."

"Do it. If you can't get her to come here, we'll have to go to her... wherever that is."

"I don't know where she went. I tried to help by looking up land records to see where her family lived, but there is nothing."

"Keep looking."

Harold watched as Rob slinked away with a plate piled high of food. Instead of walking to a table, he slid out a side door to the outside. Glancing around the room, he felt very exposed and alone. This was not what he had wanted. At first, helping Davidson gloss over indiscretions that could've made the news was lucrative. Then Davidson started using Harold's family as pawns in his sick game to ensure allegiance.

A text came through on his phone and he reluctantly pulled it out. An anonymous number sent an image. He swallowed hard. He knew it came from Davidson. He opened the picture and his heart nearly stopped beating in his chest. It was a picture of his daughter sitting at a café with her roommates having coffee.

Shawna appeared oblivious that she had been captured in a picture. Indeed, she was carefree and happy. The picture should have brought him joy, but it only reminded him of what was on the line. It was Anna or his daughter and to Harold there was no contest. He had to keep his Shawna safe.

13

A couple of days passed and Anna started feeling comfortable that all was well. Jake had not reached out to her to say anything was amiss and Michael hadn't mentioned anything either. Maybe she could finally rest. The first couple of nights since Anna first encountered Jake Cory had been sleepless. Wednesday night Anna finally got a full night's sleep and woke up Thursday refreshed and ready to conquer the day.

That day was to be Anna's first day of interacting with the students. Up till that point, Mrs. Erbe had been the one to read to the kids and help them check out books at the end of their class's designated time in the library. Anna had finally reached the point in her training that Mrs. Erbe was content to let Anna broaden her responsibilities beyond reshelving books.

The first grade class came in and sat on the brightly colored carpet, waiting for her to start their story. Anna had picked an old favorite from her childhood and at first the kids groaned.

"The pictures are ugly," one little girl said.

"That's an old book." Another child piped up.

"I want you to try to hear the story and see if you can picture what is happening in your mind. Everyone, close your eyes," Anna instructed as she sat on the floor with the them. She closed her eyes too and the kids giggled.

One little girl tucked her arm through Anna's and closed her eyes as instructed. Then Anna began storytelling. She read the story from the pages, but a lot of it was improvisation. The class erupted into laughter when Anna's voice changed to suit the character she had become. Off to the side, Mrs. Erbe laughed as well and occasionally nodded Anna on in approval.

"The end," Anna concluded.

"Can we read that again?" a little boy asked.

"It's time to pick out books. I want to make sure you have time to find a good story to take home." Anna smiled at the feeling of contentment she experienced at that moment.

"Can I take home *that* book?" asked the same little boy who just moments before rejected the old book.

"No. *I* want to take that book out," a little girl called out followed by a few others.

Anna held up her hands and the kids quieted to see who would be the chosen child.

"I need to keep this book here to read to the next class, but it will be here to take out tomorrow. Whoever gets here first thing tomorrow morning can take out the book. How does that sound?"

There were a few complaints, but most of them seemed content to find a new book as Mrs. Erbe called them up one by one to look for a new treasure. After every child had been called and was busily looking at the shelves, Mrs. Erbe sidled up next to Anna with a broad smile.

"I see not much has changed. Remember when I would let you read to the younger grades? You've always had a way of drawing people in."

"It doesn't feel like it was that long ago."

After a few more classes of the doing the same thing, Anna concluded that *indeed* it had been a long time ago. She didn't remember ever feeling so tired and drained. Her throat hurt from all the talking and speaking in weird voices. She was happy when the last class concluded before lunch time. Mrs. Erbe put the closed sign on the library door and the two pulled out their lunches.

The conversation was pleasant and enjoyable when all of a sudden there was a tiny knock on the library door. It opened a crack and a little head poked in wearing a construction paper crown that read, "It's My Birthday" across it.

"Come on in, Zach," Mrs. Erbe encouraged. "What do you have there?"

"I brought cupcakes." Zach was a cute little boy from the first class Anna had read to that day. "Do you want one, Miss Munson?"

"For me? Don't you want to give them to your friends?" Anna questioned as she looked down into his precious eyes.

"You can be my friend... if you want to be," Zach said shyly and held out a bright blue icing-covered cupcake.

"Well, thank you. I would love a cupcake and I would definitely love to be your friend."

Anna's words brought a huge smile to the boy's face and he headed to Mrs. Erbe to offer her a cupcake as well before bounding out of the library.

"And this..." Mrs. Erbe held up the cupcake with a large smile, "... is one of my favorite parts of working with kids."

Anna sat back at her desk and enjoyed her cupcake when a knock sounded on the door once again.

"How many birthday cupcakes do you get in a day, Mrs. Erbe?" Anna laughed. "I'm going to have to run a little extra tonight if this is the norm."

"Oh, it's not another cupcake. That's our after lunch activity for Mrs. Henry's class," Mrs. Erbe walked to the door and opened it.

How did Anna miss that on the schedule? She looked down at the desk calendar and saw it written in pencil. *Fire Department at 1 PM – Mrs. Henry's Class*.

"The fire department?" Anna asked as she brought her head back up just as Michael Tyler entered the library in full gear.

He looked at her and burst out laughing. "Do I need to go get the oxygen from the truck, Miss Munson?"

"What?" Anna looked at him confused.

Mrs. Erbe seemed amused as well as she motioned for Anna to wipe her lips. Anna grabbed a tissue and wiped her mouth. An ocean blue smear stood out against the white tissue.

"Did I get it all?" Anna asked and Michael just smiled bigger. She scrubbed at her lips with another tissue before looking at Mrs. Erbe's normal colored lips and asking, "How did yours not turn blue?"

The older woman smiled and held up a fork. "That's a newbie mistake, Anna," Mrs. Erbe chuckled.

"Why didn't you tell me you were coming by the school today?" Anna asked Michael after she was content her lips were back to a normal hue.

"I assumed you knew considering you *work* in here." Michael smirked as he grabbed another tissue and got a spot on her chin that she had missed.

Anna's face felt warm all of a sudden and she swatted his hand away. She turned to Mrs. Erbe for more explanation and to get her eyes off of Michael in his gear. She didn't like how distracted he made her feel at that moment.

"Since we're getting to the end of the school year, it's not uncommon for the teachers to ask us to put together activities for the kids. We try to do a Fire Safety event in October and then one near the end of the school year." Mrs. Erbe smiled at Michael. "It's always a treat when I get to see my former students at work."

Mrs. Erbe gave Michael some instructions before the kids were due to enter the room. While they discussed the agenda, Anna ran to the small bathroom off the side of the library to check the mirror. What was in that icing? Why were her lips still tinted blue? She tried applying a coat of tinted lip gloss to mute the color. It turned to a nice shade of purple. Anna gave up.

Mrs. Henry's class filed into the library excitedly and sat on the floor facing Mrs. Erbe and Michael. Anna caught sight of Sam sitting close to the front. His head tilted back as far as it could go to look up at his favorite fireman with wonder. It was endearing to hear Michael address the kids in such a welcoming, nonthreatening tone.

She smiled as he got to know the kids a little and asked them questions about what they would do if they saw a fire in their home. He gave his little talk and when he was done, Anna joined the kids in applauding him.

"Now, I have a treat for you all." Michael smiled at the kids. "I heard from your teacher that you all have been very good. Is that true?"

The kids yelled a collective, "Yes."

"Well, we like to let the kids who have been really good see a real fire engine. Would you like to see our truck?"

A resounding cheer went up, especially from Anna's nephew.

"Follow your teacher's instructions and I will see you all outside." Michael headed to the door and Anna caught up to him.

"Well done, Super Mike." She smiled referencing his super hero alter ego from their story.

"Thank you."

She moved to sit at her desk when Michael cleared his throat.

"And what do you think you're doing?" he asked with a mischievous gleam in his eyes.

"Working. That's what us commoners do if we don't have cool jobs like yours."

"Nuh uh. You need to come outside with the rest. See even Mrs. Erbe is coming out."

"I'm not a fan of fire engines."

"What now? That's crazy talk." Michael's expression of feigned hurt amused her.

"They're loud and obnoxious if I'm being completely honest."

Michael's mouth gaped open before snapping it shut. Then he let out a maniacal laugh. "Just for that I'm making you my volunteer."

"I've got books to process, Mike. You run along now."

Anna laughed as he caught her hand in his and began pulling her with him towards the door.

"Super Anna isn't scared of fire trucks. Unless you're a Petunia… the damsel in distress." The challenge in his eyes caused her to raise her chin a tad.

"I am not a *Petunia*."

"Prove it."

"Come on, Aunt Anna! Come with me," Sam called from his place in line with his class.

Michael smiled at Anna. "You'd have to be absolutely heartless to tell that face no."

Anna sighed snagging her hand back from him and joining her nephew. They exited out a side door that led to the parking lot where a big yellow fire engine waited. Another fireman jumped down as soon as he saw the large group approach. He and Michael exchanged a few words and Michael addressed the kids once more.

"So, what kinds of things do you think we have to wear when we go to fight a fire?" he asked the group.

There were many answers, some silly and some valid.

"I need a volunteer to help me model everything that we take with us into an active fire." Michael pretended to look over the group for the perfect volunteer. Then his eyes shot up to Anna's.

She immediately looked away and to the side of the building as if something caught her interest.

"Why don't we get Miss Munson up here to help us out." Michael motioned for her to come join him by the fire engine.

"No, that's okay. Why don't we let one of the kids give it a try," Anna said through gritted teeth.

"Turnout gear can weigh up to forty-five pounds, kids. Some of you don't even weigh that," Michael pointed out as he waited for Anna to comply.

"Go on, Anna. This will be fun," Mrs. Erbe chuckled.

Anna forced a smile on her face. As soon as she got within earshot of Michael she hissed, "You're dead to me."

He laughed and called to his friend.

"Scooter, bring out the first item." Michael turned back to the kids and explained how the gear went on overtop of the clothes they wore.

The man he had called Scooter, brought a pair of heavy looking pants with suspenders. He held them out for Anna to step into. Michael offered her his arm as she tried to get into the oversized getup. Begrudgingly, she took a hold of his arm as she almost fell down.

Once both legs were in Scooter helped her pull the pants up and she slipped the suspenders over her shoulders, though they were very loose on her.

"Next is the jacket. These have three very thick distinct layers that help keep us safe when we are in a fire. They also protect us against sharp objects." Michael informed the kids as he placed a very heavy coat on Anna. She couldn't even find her hands through the sleeve openings.

He helped her fasten the front and gave her a wink.

"I can't move," Anna complained, but he ignored her.

"What do you think comes next kids?" he asked the group. "Right! Boots! You can't go in regular shoes. They'd melt."

Scooter reappeared with boots that clearly were too large for Anna. He helped pull up the legs of the pants so she could step inside. She probably could've fit both feet in one boot. She glared at Michael as he continued his spiel.

"The helmet is very important. We never know if there will be debris falling around us," Michael said as he placed the massive helmet with a visor over her head.

The claustrophobia she was feeling was real. She reached out for Michael's arm and held on for dear life. At any moment, she felt as if she could fall over.

"In addition to what Miss Munson is wearing, we also would take in a radio to help us talk to one another and a breathing apparatus so we can breathe clean oxygen. We won't make Miss Munson wear the tank." Michael knocked on the helmet and asked Anna, "How are you feeling in there, Miss Munson?"

He did not want her to answer that. Anna squeezed his arm as tightly as she could to express her displeasure. She heard the smile in his voice as he asked the next question. "Who would like a turn wearing the helmet? Maybe Miss Munson will let you have a turn now."

The helmet was lifted from her head and Anna quickly forced a smile again for the children's benefit. She turned to the other fireman on her other side.

"Scooter…" Anna called to the stranger and he turned around at the sound of his name. "Could you help me out of this please?"

His smile was huge as he came forward to rescue her from the heavy gear while Michael placed the helmet on the heads of the excited kids.

"Thank you for your help," Anna said while casting a glare in Michael's direction.

The man nodded and opened up the truck to let the kids see the inside.

"Who wants to hear the siren?" Scooter called out.

Anna put her hands over her ears and several of the more timid kids followed suit and stuck by their teacher's side. Scooter flipped switches and pushed buttons resulting in the loudest noise Anna had ever heard accompanied by flashing lights on top of the truck. Once the noise ceased, kids started climbing all over the truck like little ants.

"Wasn't that fun?" Mrs. Erbe said gleefully.

"Oh, yes. So much fun," Anna said wryly as her boss chuckled.

"You were a good sport, Anna. I'm so glad I got pictures on my phone! We can put them on our bulletin board."

After a little while, the teacher called her students to attention and lined them up to reenter the school. Everyone said a loud thank you to the firemen and applauded them before going back inside. Anna was just about to go through the door when she felt a tug on her arm. She turned to see Michael smiling at her.

"You're not *really* mad at me, are you? It was for the kids, Anna."

"No, I'm not mad. But next time can I have a little warning please?" Anna smirked.

"*Next time…* that sounds like I have a willing victim for when we get called back."

Anna rolled her eyes and headed back into the school, leaving Michael to stare after her with his obnoxious smile.

14

Sunday came around again and church had just let out. It had been a tough week. Lewis hadn't been far from Anna's thoughts. Her father's message had been on being heartsick and how Jesus Christ can heal the hurts. Deep down, Anna thought she still believed that. However, the hurtful things just kept coming and coming.

She knew it was a stupid thing to do, but Anna got on her old social media page to see if Kirstyn and Jonathan were still together. Of course, they were. And they looked happy… which made her miserable. She wanted to see some type of remorse. Any sign that things wouldn't work out for them. Yet, her old friend's smile was enormous and irritating to behold. In one picture, Jonathan had his arms wrapped around her while they appeared to be on the same hiking trail he used to take Anna on.

Sam excitedly ran past his aunt and out the door to cross the parking lot to the parsonage. Anna snapped out of her funk.

"Sam, watch out for cars! Walk!" she called out.

"See? You're a natural for working with young people," Michael said appearing at her side as she walked into the warm sunlight.

"I think there's a little more involved than that."

He chuckled and continued walking alongside her towards the parsonage. She stopped finally and turned to him.

"Are you looking for a lunch invite or something, Michael? I guarantee whatever your mom is making will be better than the vegetable soup in my crockpot."

"I like vegetable soup." He shrugged.

"What's on your mind, Tyler?"

"*Tyler*?" He laughed. "Feeling sassy today?"

"Spit it out already."

"Remember how you committed to volunteering with the youth group? Well, I think maybe you should sit in tonight. You know, get to know the kids and all."

"You took that seriously, huh?"

"I think the Bible says something about letting your yes be yes and your no…"

"Don't quote scripture at me," Anna growled.

Michael's smile was downright cheeky.

"Come on. The kids will love you."

"And what makes you think that? I think Ellie's exact words were: *You're cool enough*. I don't think that means they'll love me." Anna started walking and Michael began tagging along once more.

"What's not to love about you? You're funny…" He paused as if trying to think of more things off the top of his head. "Oh, and you're a fast runner."

Anna stopped and faced him again.

"Is it really that hard to think of things that make me loveable? I'm funny and fast? *Really*?"

For a moment, Michael's expression softened and he opened his mouth as if he were about to say something, but then…

"Aunt Anna! The door is locked." Sam called from the parsonage followed by the sound of Bentley barking from the doggy door.

Anna forced her focus towards the house and away from Michael's chocolate colored eyes. Whatever he was going to say was lost and he looked away appearing rather flustered.

"You *did* promise, you know," he said under his breath lest she forget what they had been talking about.

"For heaven's sake! Fine!" Anna threw her hands up in defeat. "What do I need to do?"

"Just show up tonight at youth group and hang out. Get to know the kids."

She sighed. It honestly didn't sound all that bad. "That's it?"

"That's it." He smiled. "So, I'll see you tonight then?"

"I guess so." He had stopped following her and she paused to look at him. "Aren't you coming in for vegetable soup?"

His smile was downright irksome. "I can't. Mom is making a pretty wicked roast. See you tonight."

Later that evening, Anna carefully snuck into the youth room and, not for the first time, questioned what she was doing there. The music was loud. Teen boys hit one another with what looked like homemade duct tape swords while the girls sat off to the side staring at each other's cellphones.

Ellie sat in the midst of that group. She looked up at her aunt and gave her a look as if saying *if only I could have a cell phone like the cool girls*. Anna tried to smile at her but Ellie just looked back at the screen on her friend's phone.

"Anna, I'm so happy you're here!"

A pleasant voice came from behind her and Anna turned to see Tessa.

"Don't be happy yet. I feel like I'm a little out of my element," Anna admitted. Indeed, she was having flashbacks to her own awkward experiences in youth group as a teen.

"I'm sure they'll love you," Tessa smiled warmly.

"So Michael keeps telling me. How are you feeling today?" Anna asked as she noticed Tessa put a hand to her stomach.

Tessa grinned and said, "I didn't expect pregnancy to make me so sick. I miss eating food and actually enjoying it."

"That bad, huh?"

"The only thing I hold down is ice cream. It doesn't make any sense. I thought morning sickness was only for the first trimester."

Anna chuckled. "I can't offer any input on this one."

"I'm honestly concerned the store is going to run out of chocolate caramel swirl ice cream. Right now, I'm living on it."

Michael called the youth to attention and everyone took their seats.

"In case you haven't met her yet, this is Anna Munson," he motioned for Anna to stand, which she did hesitantly. "She is Pastor Tim's daughter. She will be volunteering in youth and coming along on our retreat. Don't make her want to run away or I'll duct tape you to the wall and let everyone use you as a Nerf target."

A few snickered with laughter. A few actually volunteered to be duct taped to the wall. Anna forced a smile and quickly sat back down next to Tessa.

"You know, he's pretty happy you agreed to volunteer," Tessa whispered to Anna with a smile.

"Hmm. He's pretty persistent."

"He talks very positively about you." There was a gleam in Tessa's eyes.

Anna wanted to stop her line of thought right there, but Sean took over the group and began praying. Conversation ceased, but Anna's mind kept turning. People were going to get the wrong opinion of her and Michael's relationship.

Maybe Anna should try to distance herself more. It made sense to do so, but at the same time the idea made her... sad. Anna enjoyed Michael's friendship. Yes, he annoyed her. But he was also funny and helpful. *And crazy good looking.*

As soon as that thought hit, Anna sat up straight in her chair as if she had been stung by a bee.

"Are you okay?" Tessa asked quietly.

"I'm fine." Anna nodded and pretended to pay attention to Sean as he began the lesson.

What was wrong with her? These intrusive thoughts had to stop. He wasn't *that* good looking, Anna reasoned. His constant teasing diminished any attractiveness Michael possessed. That ridiculous half grin that turned into a full on cheesy smile was rather dorky now that she thought of it. And his hair was messy quite often. Not well kept like Jonathan's had been. Anna liked men neat and tidy. Not wild and ... and... with stubble.

The lesson came to a close after a while and Anna tried to find a safe place to observe the kids. They were taking chairs and moving them to the side, which meant one thing. She remembered the activity and game time of youth group well. Some of her most embarrassing moments happened during those rowdy times... unless they played dodgeball. Anna seemed to have a knack for that game.

"There you are!" Michael said as he came close. "It's a tradition that we welcome all new people with a game of dodgeball."

Sean and Tessa shook their heads at the preposterous notion. Yet they didn't shut it down either. In fact, Sean started putting people on teams and the kids ran to their respective walls to line up.

"Anna, you're on this team. Michael you're on the other," Sean instructed as he and Tessa started putting rubber balls in a line at the center of the room.

"No, that's okay. Really. I'll just watch," Anna tried to object.

"What's the matter, *Petunia*? Scared of a little friendly game?" Michael taunted.

"I am *not* a Petunia." Anna asserted forcefully, poking a finger into his chest. Who did he think he was? Did he not remember the summer before their junior year? Anna was a beast at dodgeball. She took off her earrings and stuck them in her pockets. "Okay, Tyler. You wanna play?"

Michael leaned in a little too close and said, "Bring it!"

Then all chaos ensued. Teens yelled in frustration as ball after ball hit their targets. Teams diminished. The smell of rubber and sweat filled the room as the aggressive players dove to catch balls in midair.

A few of the kids played it smart, hiding behind the more aggressive ones until they had a clear shot to pelt their friends on the opposite team. Cries of victory and defeat echoed until only a small handful remained. Both sides were even.

"Make a hole!" Anna called out to a boy she had heard others refer to as Seth.

"What? What does even that mean?" he asked in confusion.

"Don't stand so close to me. It makes us easier targets," Anna stated emphatically, apparently amusing Michael who stood at the line repeatedly throwing the ball up into the air and catching it.

"You don't intimidate me, Tyler," Anna called out. "I think you're forgetting who won the dodgeball tournament three years straight."

His smile broadened. Without even looking away from Anna, Michael threw the ball hitting Seth in the shins.

"Out!" Sean called with a laugh. "Anna, it's just you and Macy against Michael and Holly."

Michael whispered something to his teammate and handed her a ball. Anna pulled Macy over and suggested a few maneuvers. Then it was on again. Michael and Holly threw balls as if they were pitching machines stuck on high speed. Macy tried to catch a ball but dropped it.

"You're out, Macy!" Sean yelled. "It's two against one."

The entire group surrounded the playing area. Even Ellie stood with a proud smile on her face as she took in the spectacle. Anna felt a twinge of pleasure when her niece called out, "Stick it to them, Aunt Anna!"

Michael nodded to his teammate as if they had some special code and he went to one end of their side while Holly went to the opposite. *I see what you're trying to do. You're going to try to ambush me,* Anna concluded.

Once again the two went into fast throw mode and Anna jumped over, dodged, and side stepped every ball. All of the balls came to a stop on Anna's side of the dividing line… except for the ball in Holly's hands. Holly gave a good throw and Anna caught it with ease. "Holly, you're out. It's Michael and Anna left."

The cheers began and the girls started chanting her name. "Anna! Anna! Anna!"

Michael dropped his head in a moment of amusement and Anna took her shot. The ball flew through the air and almost struck his head. He reached for it, but it accidentally bumped against his watch and bounced away from his grasp.

"You're out!" Sean exclaimed laughing. "Anna is the winner!"

The kids rallied around Anna and Michael fell to the floor in a dramatic heap of defeat.

"Well done, Anna!" Sean smiled widely. "Only one other person has ever beaten Michael at dodgeball. He tends to be ruthless."

Anna smiled as she looked over at her friend sitting up from his place on the floor with a appreciative smile on his face.

"Who was the other person?" Anna asked Sean.

"Yours truly." Sean smirked and gave a regal bow.

"I let you both win," Michael said finally joining them.

"Is that right?" Anna's chin rose. "Rematch?"

"You've got it… but not tonight."

Anna laughed out loud. "That's what I thought, Tyler."

"What? I have a shift tomorrow. I need to be at peak performance… you know in case I need to be the hero."

"Excuses, excuses. Just admit, Tyler. I'm too much for you."

There was something in his expression… a serene smile. He sighed deeply. "You might just be, Petunia."

15

"So, what's the deal with you and that librarian?" Scooter asked joining Michael at the table in the firehouse during a lull.

Michael looked up from the pictures of Anna in full turnout gear that Mrs. Erbe texted him from the previous week. His amused grin faded quickly as he looked up at Scooter. "What do you mean?"

"*What do you mean*?" Scooter mimicked Michael with a smile. "What do you *think* I mean? Are you two dating or what?"

Michael laughed. "No. We're just friends. We go all the way back to grade school."

"Really? Because I could've sworn you were flirting with her that day we visited the school."

The smirk on his friend's face was highly unnecessary, Michael concluded.

"I was *not* flirting. It's Anna. She's like the friend you want to hang around and laugh with... she's not the dating type." Michael felt like the conversation was disrespectful of his friend. This was Anna. He didn't want to talk about Anna with Scooter... not in *that* way.

"Well, I'm glad to hear *you* think that because *I* think she's adorable."

Sitting up straighter in his chair, Michael leveled Scooter with a disgusted glare. "What did you just say to me?"

"She might not be your type, but funny and adorable happens to be my type," Scooter said. "That hair! And those green eyes! Do you think you can set me up? Or give her my number?"

"Absolutely not."

Scooter looked shocked. "But why? If you're not interested…"

"Because some jerk just broke her heart and I happen to know that she is not interested in dating *anyone* right now."

"Come on, Mike." Scooter was normally one of Michael's closer friends at the firehouse, but at that moment his face annoyed him. "Maybe she just needs a little Scooter in her life."

Michael opened his mouth to say something to shut his friend down when a call came over the radio. A car accident on I-81 needing medical attention. Much to Michael's relief, the conversation was dropped as they jumped into action and headed to the scene. *If Scooter knows what's good for him he won't bring Anna up again.*

Later that night, Michael found himself frustrated. Kate and Tessa went out to a women's event, leaving Dan and Sean free for some brother bonding time with Michael. Little Eli was with Aunt Jenna and his future Uncle Ben. For the first time in months, Michael had his brothers to himself and they decided to shoot skeet. Yet, his mind was still running over the conversation with Scooter.

"Mike, you're a better shot than that. What's wrong with you tonight?" Dan laughed after he pulled a third clay pigeon from the thrower and his brother missed miserably.

"Nothing. It's windy."

Dan laughed, licking his finger and sticking it in the air. "Do you feel any wind, Sean?"

"Nope. The smoke from the grill is going straight up."

Michael emptied the rifle of ammo and clicked the safety in place. "It's just an off night, I guess."

"What's on your mind, Man? You've been wanting time together and we have it... now you're acting all grumpy," Sean pointed out as he put a steak on a plate and handed it to his younger brother.

"Did you see something upsetting at work during your shift?" Dan asked coming alongside of Michael. Michael had seen some pretty sad and troubling things over his years of being an EMT and then in the fire department.

"Nah. It's nothing." Michael attempted a smile.

"You're a horrible liar," Dan stated. "What's wrong?"

"Do you guys think I..." Michael snapped his mouth shut as he thought better of what he was about to ask.

"Out with it," Sean prodded as he joined his brothers at the picnic table in Dan and Kate's back yard with his and Dan's plates of steak.

"Do I flirt too much?"

Sean and Dan looked at each other and then both burst out laughing.

"Stop it. I'm serious. Do I flirt too much?"

Dan cleared his throat as he tried to control his amusement. "I think we all know that you do. What's this really about?"

"Scooter made this stupid comment. He thought I was flirting with Anna. Isn't that stupid?" Michael asked forcing a laugh.

"Anna is pretty great. If you *did* have feelings for her..." Sean tried to tread gently, but was immediately halted.

"She and I are just friends. Why do people think there's more than that? Can't a guy and a girl just be buddies?"

"The best relationships start as friends. Look at Tess and me." Sean smiled. "She was… and still is… my best friend."

"It's okay if you're starting to feel something for Anna, Mike. She's sweet." Dan added his two cents.

"I don't have feelings for Anna. I keep telling everyone… I have no intention of getting saddled with a wife like you two. No offense."

Both Sean and Dan howled in laughter.

"Yeah, we have such a sorrowful existence, don't we, Sean?"

"It's horrible. I can't believe that Tessa actually insists on kissing me every morning. Ugh. And she's always wanting to spend time with me… *Why*?" Sean said in an overly dramatic tone.

Michael rolled his eyes.

"I know what you mean. Get this… Kate not only laughs at my jokes, but she even enjoys listening to me talk about my day. What's wrong with her?" Dan shook his head. "That little sicko."

"Knock it off, Guys," Michael muttered but he couldn't hide his smile over his brothers' horrible acting.

"How did we get into this mess, Dan?" Sean asked with mock horror on his face.

"Don't even get me started on how horrible it is to have a little person that has Kate's eyes, running around calling me *Daddy*." Dan sat back smugly, arms crossed at his chest.

"Alright. Fine. I get it. It's great being married," Michael chuckled. "It's just not what *I* want. I don't know if I will ever want that. I like my freedom. I'm happy."

"You look it, Mike." Sean grinned and Dan laughed.

"You don't even know what's got me upset. You're *assuming* it's because I have feelings for Anna." The words were even hard for Michael to say out loud.

"Okay. Okay. We're sorry," Sean said attempting to really hear his brother. "What is it then?"

"Scooter wants Anna's number. Like that's what she needs right now coming off that horrible break up."

Michael looked to his brothers waiting for them to be understanding and irritated at Scooter as well. Instead, they looked like they were biting their cheeks and lips to keep from laughing. Eventually the dam burst and they guffawed at his expense. Michael got up from the table agitated.

"I shouldn't have even told you two."

"We're sorry," Dan said as he tried to compose himself. "But why does that bother you? You don't have feelings for her."

"Because... he's ... she..." Michael ran a hand through his hair as he tried to figure out what he was trying to say. "She doesn't want a relationship either. And I don't want him pushing her into one."

Dan looked at his brother compassionately. "What if she changes her mind? It happens. Believe me. You're the one who used to tease me about staying a bachelor until I was too old to get married. Remember?"

"I remember." Michael felt worse at the thought that Anna could possibly change her mind.

What if she wanted a relationship eventually? What if she wanted a relationship ... *with him*? Then, he'd lose a friend just like he lost his brothers. What if she mistook his friendship for flirting? Anna had been hurt already by one jerk. Michael couldn't let himself add to it. Maybe it was time to back away.

*****

Late Saturday morning, Anna parked her Jeep where she saw Michael's truck. Judging by the number of vehicles parked there, the hike he had once hoped to be just he and his brothers had blossomed into a churchwide event. *Poor guy. All he wanted was brother time now it's a huge production. And yet, here I am... with my nephew and niece.*
"Jaden from youth group is here," Ellie said excitedly. "And Bryden!" Sam pointed out.
Anna was happy that they had friends to enjoy the day with. "Well, let's not keep them waiting then."
Opening the back hatch, Anna stared down confused at the three identical backpacks she had picked up for their day trip to Water Run State Park. The price overruled the aesthetic factor and Anna bought three of the same style and color.
"This one is mine," Ellie said after unzipping one and peeking inside. She grabbed it and headed towards the sounds of revelry. Anna handed Sam his and they followed behind Ellie.
Anna looked around for Michael. Days earlier he had said he'd meet her at the entrance when she got there. Yet, as of the last text she had received that morning, he just said to follow the path. He hadn't

been as talkative lately. Anna went over in her mind if she had said anything hurtful, but she couldn't think of anything.

Surely, he wasn't so prideful as to get bent out of shape over her dodgeball victory. No, Michael was better than that. She concluded Michael was probably put out by his trip with his brothers getting commandeered by a whole bunch of people and nothing more.

Everyone greeted Anna and the kids as they joined the group at the picnic pavilion.

"Where's your dad and Livi?" someone asked just as Anna spotted Michael laughing with a few other guys. "Livi doesn't do well without a solid nap so Dad thought it best to keep her home. He had some last minute sermon preparations for tomorrow anyway," Anna said politely.

Michael finally looked up and saw her. She waved and started to head towards him, but he looked away quickly. He started a conversation with someone else and turned his back to her. Anna stopped short. Had she imagined that? Or did he just snub her? Was she being too sensitive?

Anna diverted to an available picnic table and put her things down. She started rifling through her backpack to make sure she had her epi-pen. She already knew it was inside, but it gave her something to preoccupy her thoughts.

"Aunt Anna, are you going to take us hiking? Jaden said she wants to go, but her parents said only if we have an adult with us." Ellie spoke more in that moment than she had all day.

Anna smiled at her niece and pulled out the trail map from her bag before zipping it back up. "Yes, but find Sam first. He wanted to come, too."

It didn't take long for her nephew to come barreling towards them throwing his backpack onto the table next to hers with an excited expression. "Can Bryden come?"

"If his mom says it's okay." Sam and Bryden nodded and ran to go ask his parents.

Anna caught Michael looking at her before glancing away again. What was his problem? She was about to go over and ask him just that when she was assailed by two rambunctious eight year olds.

"His mom said yes!" Sam called out.

"Okay. Anyone else want to come before we head out?" Anna asked loud enough to extend the invite to a certain elusive friend of hers, but she was only met with several polite *no thank you*'s from those within earshot.

"Are we going to see bears?" Sam asked excitedly.

"No, Dork. Bears hide from people... unless they're going to eat them."

"Eat them?" Sam looked nervous.

"Knock it off, Ellie. No bears are going to eat you, Sam," Anna promised.

She grabbed the backpack from the table and slid her arms through the straps. Anna started toward the opening of the trail with four chatty kids following behind her. With a sigh she opened the trail map and forged ahead up an incline where the overlook trail sign pointed.

The sunshine felt amazing on her face and Anna was grateful that she could bask in it. The kids were happily preoccupied with their friends, leaving her to her own thoughts.

Every so often Anna slowed to allow the kids a moment to catch up. They hadn't been hiking more than ten minutes when Ellie voiced her complaint.

"Why … are we … going so fast?"

"I'm sorry. I'll try to slow down." Anna smiled as the four, who were talking less than they had been when they set out, caught up to her location. Anna had been lost in her thoughts and hadn't realized she was walking briskly.

"Can we sit for a minute?" Sam asked, finding a log.

"I guess. Just for a minute though. And make sure there aren't any bugs there, Sammy."

"You almost killed us with bug repellent before we left. I don't think any bugs will get us, Aunt Anna," Ellie teased.

Anna looked at the trail ahead, but when she turned her head back to the kids she saw at least a dozen bees swirling above her nephew and Bryden. It was then that Anna noticed the hive near the log Sam had sat on.

"Sam… move carefully towards me… slowly."

"What?" he asked shrugging, not seeing what she saw.

Ellie noticed right away and her friend Jaden gasped.

"Stay calm. They don't sting if they aren't provoked," Anna instructed the kids.

Bryden rushed to Anna's side, but Sam started swatting at the bees.

"Sam, stop!" Ellie yelled. "Didn't you hear Aunt Anna?"

"I don't want it to get me! Make it go away, Aunt Anna." Sam panicked.

Anna pulled Sam away from the log and checked him over. "You're okay, Little Dude."

Just then Anna felt something on her face.

"It's on you!" Sam screamed and before she could stop him, his hand swatted at the insect. Anna thought he was aiming for the one on her face but instead he smacked one on her arm.

A small pinprick of pain resonated on her skin.

"I got it. He's dead!" Sam said proudly as the bee fell to the ground. "There's another one on your face!"

Without thinking, Sam flicked the bee and Anna felt the second sting. Her thoughts went wild. If she were to have a reaction, she needed to get the kids back to the group ... and fast.

"I think that's enough hiking. Anyone hungry?" She tried to sound as normal as possible as she redirected the kids back down the trail they had just come from.

Keep calm. Don't panic. Anna started sliding her backpack off her shoulders so she could access her epi-pen as she felt her throat starting to feel funny. *Mind over matter. Don't create symptoms that aren't there just because you're scared.*

Anna tried to clear her throat. "Hey, Kids. Hang on a minute, please."

They were quite a few steps ahead of her this time as she stopped and unzipped the backpack.

"Are you okay, Aunt Anna?" Ellie asked from down the path.

"Yes. I just need to get my medicine…" Anna's heart stopped beating as she reached into the backpack and pulled out a toy dinosaur that let out an electronic roar.

"Hey, that's *my* backpack," Sammy laughed as he ran forward and took it from her.

Anna muttered a few choice words in her head before calling to her niece, "Ellie, can you… come…"

Ellie looked concerned. Anna desperately needed her to be level headed, not terrified.

"I need you… to take the kids. Get my …"

"Oh no. Aunt Anna, what's wrong?"

"Calm… down. Just go. Get my bag… *quickly.*"

"Sam, stay here with…" Ellie started to call out.

"No!" Anna's voice was stronger and louder than she had intended. "Take them all."

"I can't just leave you…" Ellie's eyes were wide and fearful. "You're turning really pink and puffy."

"I'm… good. I promise." Anna lied. "Go on. Hurry. Please."

"Come on, Guys. Let's run." Ellie said pulling her brother and Bryden with her down the hill.

"Aunt Anna?" Anna heard Sam call out as she eased herself down onto the trail, praying help would come quickly.

*****

Michael felt guilty. There had to be a happy medium between ignoring Anna completely and acting flirtatious. He saw the confusion in her eyes earlier. He didn't want to hurt her. At the time he thought distancing would be a lesser hurt than her developing feelings for him and finding out he still didn't want a relationship.

Well, that sounds plain old arrogant. You're assuming she wants that with you. Maybe you're not even on her radar in that way. Michael's inner voice chastised him. Was he willing to lose a decent friend? Anna made him laugh and he didn't feel pressure from her like he did with other women.

He got to his feet with the intent of trying to catch up with her on the trail when he saw four people scrambling down the incline. *There were five that went up. Where's Anna?*

"Help! Someone, please help!" Ellie ran towards the tables out of breath.

Michael caught up to her at the table as she grabbed the bag and started back.

"Ellie, stop. What's going on?" Michael held her shoulders and turned her to face him, but Ellie struggled to get free.

"She can't breathe. She needs her epi… epi…"

"Epi-pen?" Michael filled in. He pointed to the backpack in her hands. "Is it in here?"

Ellie nodded as tears started pooling in her eyes. Michael grabbed it and started running up the incline. To Dan he yelled, "Call 911."

He rummaged through the bag as he took two steps at a time. He found two epi-pens and threw the bag to the ground as he continued to run. *Please, God. Keep her airways open. Please let her be okay.*

It felt like forever until he saw her gasping for breath, leaning against a rock. Her face and neck were swollen badly and her skin was blotchy. His heart dropped at the sight. He tried to normalize his breath and tone before speaking so as not to give away how afraid he was at that moment.

"Hey, Petunia. What trouble did you get yourself into this time?"

"Not… Pet… Pet…" she tried to speak.

"Right. Not Petunia." He smirked as he bit the lid off her epi-pen. "Hold still."

He jabbed her thigh and held the needle in place for a few seconds before pulling it out.

"You're okay. Just breathe, Anna." She labored for a bit but eventually she started regulating her breath.

"Sam…"

"He's okay. I'm sure he's taking this opportunity to eat five chocolate chip cookies." A siren cried through the air. "Your chariot is approaching."

Anna started struggling to get up. "No. I'm fine now. Thank you."

"There's no arguing with me on this, Anna. In about ten minutes you're going to need this second dose. Do you want me to bore you with all the reasons why we make people go to the ER after getting epi-pen injections?"

"Shut… up, please." Anna breathed out and he smiled.

"Good to see your sass is still there." Michael sighed in relief. "Where did the little booger get you?"

Anna motioned to her arm and face. Michael rolled her sleeve up to find the sting and inspected the area right under her eye.

"What's this? I thought it was your day off?" One of Michael's coworkers teased as he approached carrying a backboard.

"You know how much I love my job." Michael smiled and looked down at his watch. "I administered her epi about ten minutes ago. I have a second here."

Connors knelt in front of Anna. "Hey there. What's your name?"

"Anna… Munson."

"Raspy breathing," Connors muttered to Michael who nodded in agreement. "Anna, do you feel like you can walk?"

"I … can try." Anna struggled to get up and Connors put a hand on her shoulders to keep her where she was after seeing she was weak.

"That's okay. We have a really fun ride for you to take down the hill." Connors turned to his partner and a man appeared with a backboard.

Anna moaned and shook her head. "No. I'm… good."

"Yeah, you're great. Hold still for round two, Anna," Michael said as he gave her the second epi-pen.

"Is she a friend of yours?" Connors asked.

"Yes." Michael winked at Anna who glared up at him as she was eased onto the backboard and secured.

"I assume that means you're going to want to come with us?"

"You assume right." Michael grabbed a hold of one of the handles. "You good, Petunia?"

"Jerk," Anna uttered out and Michael smiled. That word had never sounded so good.

16

Anna's Law struck again. After the hospital felt she was safe to go home Saturday evening, Anna woke up Sunday with hives and her eye was swollen shut from the sting.

"Good morning, Quasimodo," Anna said to her reflection in the mirror.

Her curls were in a tangled mess. She wore one of her mother's old baggy night gowns because her own clothes were too form fitting. It irritated the itchy bumps to have fabric rubbing against her skin. One eye was open and the other closed. But she was alive.

"Oh wow!" Ellie said as Anna walked out of the bathroom. "Are you going to church like that?"

"Uh, no. I'll watch the live steam online," Anna sighed.

"And school tomorrow?"

"Probably not, Ellie." Anna walked past her niece, who was still staring at her with large eyes, and went into the kitchen.

"How are you holding up, Anna Banana?" Tim asked as he paused his sip of coffee when she entered the room.

Anna whimpered and rested her forehead against her dad's chest. He put an arm around her and she wriggled free when she realized the hug bothered the hives on her body.

"Maybe you should go to urgent care?"

"No. I'll be okay. I'll call my doctor tomorrow if it doesn't calm down," Anna said as little Livi wandered into the room.

The toddler looked at Anna as if she were a monster. Livi backed up and shook her head "no" when Anna tried to hand her a sippy cup of juice. Sam was off to the side watching his Aunt with concern.

"I'm okay, Little Dude. It looks worse than it is," she tried to comfort her nephew.

"I'm sorry, Aunt Anna. I didn't know the bee would hurt you." His eyes started filling up with tears.

Anna, despite the fact her skin stretched uncomfortably, bent down in front of him. "Buddy, you were trying to be my protector. It's okay. Do you need a hug?"

He nodded slightly and she held him for a moment until he was himself again.

"You know, it was kind of romantic," Ellie said coming out of the bathroom with a toothbrush dangling from her mouth.

Both Tim and Anna looked up at the same time and asked, "What?"

"It was cute how concerned Michael was. I think he likes you, Aunt Anna."

Anna shook her head with a laugh. "No, Ellie. That's his *job*. He saves people for a living. That's all."

Ellie rolled her eyes.

"And I don't want you saying anything like that in public, you hear me? That's how rumors get started."

"Fine. I still think it was romantic," Ellie muttered as she went back into the bathroom to finish brushing her teeth.

"You're twelve. Stop thinking about romance." Anna sounded stern even to her own ears. "When I was twelve…"

"When you were twelve you wrote fairy tales about princes saving princesses," Tim smirked.

Anna harrumphed.

"Okay, everyone out the door for church," Tim called out to the kids before turning a softer response to his daughter. "Except for you, Dear. You go rest."

She watched her father lead the kids across the parking lot to the church through their kitchen window. Tim waved at church members with his free hand and held Livi's hand in his other. Ellie carried his Bible for him and Sam appeared to chat and run circles around them the entire way until they disappeared into the building. The sight was endearing.

All of a sudden, the front doorbell rang causing her to nearly jump out of her skin. Instead of heading towards the door she ran to her bedroom. Surely, whoever it was would go away. Eventually, they'd realize her father had already headed over to the church and make their way over as well.

The doorbell rang again and Anna saw her phone light up with a call from Michael Tyler.

"Answer the door. We know you're in there," he said after she answered the call.

"Nope. Not doing it. I look horrible," Anna said emphatically and then paused. "Wait… we?"

"I brought mom with me for propriety's sake." Anna could hear the smile in his voice. "I just want to check to make sure you're okay. Any side effects from yesterday?"

Anna laughed out loud. *Any side effects?*

"A few."

"Such as…"

"I look like Quasimodo."

"Quasi… Open the door, Annalise Munson."

"Get to church. You'll be late for Sunday school."

"I can be just as stubborn as you. If you're still having reactions from yesterday you need to be seen by a doctor."

She walked stealthily against the walls into the living room. The window adjacent to the door would give her a good view of him if she could just peek while still staying out of sight.

"Come on, Petunia. You're making my mom late for church," Michael teased.

"Who's Petunia?" Anna heard Colleen ask.

With a sigh, Anna hung up and opened the door a crack. Then she realized that the side that opened to Michael and Colleen revealed her swollen eye.

"Whoa!" Michael said without thinking.

"Nice. Thank you for that. I feel much better about things now," Anna glowered.

"Oh, Anna. You poor girl. Is … is that all over you, Dear?" Colleen asked in a maternal way that caused Anna to ache for her own mom.

"So it seems."

"Anna, you need to…" Michael started in his professional EMT tone and Anna opened the door a little further so he could see the full disgruntled glare she was giving him.

"I know. I know, Dr. Mike. I'm calling my doctor tomorrow morning."

"Take an antihistamine. Do you have some?" He asked as he scrutinized her.

"Yeah. I think so."

"Anna, I have some lavender oatmeal bath. It should help relieve your hives." Colleen smiled gently. "Can I bring some over later?"

Michael smiled at her, daring her to reject his sweet hearted mother.

"That would be great, Mrs. Tyler. Thank you."

He nodded with an approving smile.

"Call if you need anything, Anna. I'm serious. Don't let this get worse." He waited for her to agree before he and Colleen turned to leave.

Anna closed the door and realized she was smiling. *Ellie needs to stop putting silly notions in my head.* The last thing Anna needed was to think about Michael in any way other than a good friend. Michael Tyler could attract any woman in town. Anna looked down at the huge nightdress she wore and her blotched arms.

A familiar feeling of discontent rose up inside of her. Even when she was with Jonathan, she was always made to feel like there was something more she needed to change. Straighten her hair. No, that didn't fix it. Go curly. Maybe a different color. Lose more weight. Try wearing makeup. And then it turned out that *nothing* she could've done would have been enough because his eyes were on another woman.

Michael had the right idea. Staying single was a good choice. She'd try to feel whole on her own. Maybe eventually she'd be able to figure out for herself who she was and what she wanted to be instead of conforming to what someone else wanted of her. And her heart would never break again.

*****

Anna's father was her hero. Monday he took the kids to school, picked up her prescription from the pharmacy, and grabbed *sick-day* snacks to keep her happy as she convalesced. Thankfully, Mrs. Peterkin and Mrs. Erbe understood why she had to take off from work. Still, it bothered Anna to have to do so after such a short time on staff.

Fresh from a lavender oatmeal bath - courtesy of Colleen Tyler - Anna wrapped herself in a blanket on the couch with Bentley taking his place on her feet. She turned on the television and saw that the local news covered the memorial for J.T. His picture flashed on the screen and Anna felt sorrowful. Was there anything she could've done differently that night? Could she have done something to save J.T.?

"What a turn out to celebrate the life of Detective John Thompson! Units from other cities as well as various emergency personnel have gathered to line the roads as the ashes of Detective Thompson make their way to his final resting place," the reporter said solemnly. "We're going to observe a moment of silence now as we continue coverage of the memorial. Our thoughts and prayers go out to his family and friends."

Somewhere in the sea of flashing lights, firetrucks, ambulances, and squad cars were Michael and Jake. As the black car holding J.T.'s remains traveled down the road, men and women stood along the roadside, saluting the fallen officer. The scene was so heart wrenching that Anna couldn't help but cry.

Reaching for her phone, she sent a quick text to Michael to let him know she was praying for him. Funerals were never easy, especially when the circumstances around the death were in question. Anna's mind turned to Lewis. Even if he had made a disloyal decision, they had shared several pleasant memories together.

Anna started going through her pictures on her cellphone hoping to catch a glimpse of her old friend's face once more. It hadn't been uncommon for him to photo bomb her selfies when they covered stories together. She scrolled back to the opening of an amusement park they had written on. They took a selfie on a roller coaster with crazy expressions. It brought a smile to her face, then tears.

"This is why I need to be at work. I think too much when I am alone," Anna said to the empty room as she swiped at her tears.

Then a picture on her phone caught her attention. It was from the flower show. She had taken a picture of Lewis in front of a display. His face was comical and she smiled despite the great feeling of loss. She scrolled through a few pictures of the displays she had captured until her eyes landed on one in particular.

The picture of the carnation castle Anna had taken had people in the background. She zoomed in and saw the man in the suit… Davidson. What had Jake called him? The Broker? And then there was another stranger holding an envelope. The next pictures contained both Davidson and the man in the hoodie. Anna zoomed in to his face and got chills. Did he kill her friend? Was she staring into the eyes of a killer? She needed to get the pictures to Jake, but the quality was not the best. Anna wondered if the digital arts teacher at school would be able to help.

Anna was about to text Jake, but her father came home with a fast food bag full of lunch for the two of them.

"How's my little sicky?" he asked as he handed her a bottled water.

"I'm much better." Anna smiled. "You didn't have to do this. You left me enough snacks today to last into the next year."

"Those were snacks. This ..." he held up the bag with grease stains on the bottom. "...is lunch."

She didn't have the heart to tell him that the snacks he left were probably healthier than whatever caused those greasy stains. He handed her a wrapped cheeseburger and a French fry carton before sitting in his chair with his food.

"You know, Mom would have a fit if she knew we were eating junk food in the living room."

Tim chuckled with a nod. "She definitely would have words for me. But, if I remember correctly, it didn't stop us from time to time, did it?"

"What do you mean?"

"Remember the weekend she went to the ladies conference with the church women? Alex, you, and I made forts, watched movies, and binged on pizza for two days straight."

Anna had forgotten about that. A smile tugged at her lips. Alexis must've been around Ellie's age. Anna would've been nine or ten years old. Things were happier then. Carefree. Church business wasn't mentioned. Tim didn't have anything to distract him from his daughters. They giggled and watched movies all night and slept in sleeping bags.

"That was a good memory," Anna said wistfully.

"I'm sorry there weren't more of those types of memories."

Anna's eyes shot up to her father's. A familiar sadness emerged there in his brown eyes.

"We had a lot of them, Dad. Why would you say it like that?"

"I've heard from Alex."

Anna let the words register. Alex had been off grid for a while. If she was reaching out it meant she needed something or that she was in trouble.

"What does she want now? Money?" Anna knew her tone sounded bitter.

"She's going into a new rehab facility. She says she's serious this time." Tim's voice sounded tired as he pulled out the letter. "Everything in me wants to believe her."

Shaking her head Anna mindlessly munched on a french-fry... then another... until they were all gone. Her insides felt heavy and she chastised herself. Old habits die hard. She'd have to run extra miles to account for them.

"I blame myself still. Even after all of these years. I keep thinking if I had insulated you and Alex better from the church drama... if I had paid you both more attention... Maybe I didn't set the example I should've." Tim's voice trailed off.

"Dad!" Anna threw the blanket off her lap, startling Bentley. "Stop saying that. Alex *chose* this."

"You both were so scrutinized. Pastors' kids have it rough… and I know I didn't make it any easier on you."

"Yes, but we also *choose* what we do with the stuff we go through. We're adults now. Not little kids running up and down a church aisle."

Anna remembered each hurtful comment she had been told or overheard from the people in the congregation she grew up in. *You're getting chunky, Annalise. Don't your parents ever take you outside to play?* Anna decided to have extreme surgery to lose her weight and still people talked.

She blocked out those voices and focused on what she needed to do to be healthy. Meanwhile, Alex chose to get lost in her addiction… and to add to their father's stress. Alex could've charted a different path for herself, but she didn't. It was hard to sympathize with someone who chose destruction.

"She's asking for you specifically. She wants to know if you'll come see her." Her father stated the words as he read them from the letter he held, but there was also something in his tone… his expression.

"I assume you want me to?" Anna sat up a little bit straighter. And Anna would most likely do it if he said he wanted her to… because that is what Anna did. She pleased others.

"I think it would be helpful to you both if you could just talk to each other. You carry a lot of anger, Anna. At one time, you had mercy towards your sister."

Anna harumphed. "Was that after her third overdose or her fifth? I can't seem to keep count of them all."

"I'll leave this letter on top of the refrigerator if you want to reach out to her. She wrote her cell number down. I don't want to mention this in front of the kids until we know she's doing better," Tim said as he quietly got up and slid the envelope onto the top of the refrigerator. "I have work to do and then I'll go get the kids. Get rest, Sweetheart."

Great. I'm the bad guy now.

Anna took a huge bite out of the burger that now felt cool rather than warm and chomped mindlessly. Bentley looked up with longing eyes at her sandwich. "Am I wrong for feeling this way?" Anna asked the dog which resulted in tail wagging. "You remember... How many times did I end up taking up the slack for Alex? When she made mom cry who was the one to try to alleviate it? Who tried to redeem the family name at school and in the community after she OD'd after prom?"

Bentley snorted and turned in circles a few times before laying down with his back to Anna.

"Fine. Be that way," Anna muttered. Honestly, she didn't blame Bentley or her father for looking at her with sadness. Where had all this bitterness come from? Jonathan and Kirstyn's betrayal? Lewis' death? No. Anna realized she'd been angry for a lot longer than those two events. Who was she becoming? She didn't like this version of herself.

The empty burger wrapper sat open in her lap and she realized she hadn't even tasted the food. *Is your addiction less offensive than Alexis'? Are you somehow better because you figured out how to work out to counteract the side effects of your drug?*

"Stop it, God." Anna knew very well what the chastising voice of the Holy Spirit felt like… and that was it.

Couldn't He see she was hurting? Where was *His* merciful side? So, she did the only thing she felt comfortable doing at that moment. She snatched her pillow and blanket, stumbled into her room, fell onto the bed, and took a long nap.

*****

"Here you are. You said a bench near the south corner. Do you know how many benches there are in the south corner of this park, Cory?" A voice snapped Jake to attention.

Sergeant Terry Branson took a seat next to him on the bench and sighed. "Rough day. How are you holding up, Jake?"

"I've been better, Sir. Did you get my message?" Jake got right to the point.

There wasn't time to chat. He needed to know who he could trust and this conversation would either backfire miserably or his gut would be proven true. The Sergeant had a reputation for his stellar integrity. He attended the same church though they rarely had occasion to interact. Jake was banking on the rumors of Branson's moral character being accurate.

"I did." Branson let out a slow whistle. "I wish I hadn't. That's a hornet's nest I'd rather not have to touch."

"But are you?"

"Can't ignore it now, can I?" The older man shook his head. "Do you have the flash drive?"

Jake sighed and looked at the man directly, reading his expression and the look in his eyes. Jake recognized genuine concern and maybe even a little trepidation. Casually he slipped the copy of the drive into the man's hand that rested on the bench next to him.

"Very few people knew of J.T.'s assignment. It's hard to say who or how many of them worked to expose him. Did I hear you're going on vacation, Cory?"

"Yes, Sir. I'll be off grid for the next several weeks."

"Good. Don't tell anyone where you're going, just go. Call me on this number if you find yourself in a situation." Branson handed Jake a slip of paper. "Are there any other people aware of this?"

"Yes."

"I'll need names."

"With all due respect, Sir, I need to know I can trust *you* before I give any of that information. I can't even trust my own partner in this."

Branson looked Jake square in the eye. It felt like an eternity, but to Jake's shock the man relented with a nod. "Whoever it is, we'll need access to them at some point. I know you know that, Cory."

"Yes. I'm aware."

"Check in with me daily. I have your number if I need to get in touch with you. Get going." Branson got up and walked away as if nothing had just transpired.

Jake felt exposed and opened up. He calmly got to his feet and walked to his truck, scanning the perimeter casually so as not to draw attention. He owned a few rental properties he could alternate staying at, but he knew he'd have to keep his eyes open and keep moving.

Lord, trust has never been something I'm good at. But I don't have a choice right now. If I just gave the wrong person that information... both Anna and I are as good as dead.

17

"How was your first day back?" Tim kissed his daughter on the forehead as she put down her keys and purse on the kitchen table.

"Good. I don't like myself a great deal when I've had too much time to think… and I had way too much time to get in my head while I was off. It's good to be back in a routine."

Her father laughed out loud at her words. "You definitely get pensive when you're not active."

"Thankfully my blotches are finally gone." Anna rolled up her sleeves to inspect them for the tenth time that day.

"Good. Stay away from bees from now on please," Tim smiled as he grabbed his keys off a hook near the door. "Livi came home early from the sitter's with a belly ache so she's napping. I need to go to my office and get some work done."

"Of course. You go be productive. I'm going to make us a yummy vegetable stir fry for dinner."

Her father paused at the door and turned around with a comical expression. "With meat though, right?"

"You need vegetables, Dad. So do these ridiculous yahoos." Anna pointed to her nephew who was grabbing a cookie from a container in the pantry closet.

Tim didn't look won over by her argument.

He was about to leave when he stopped and said, "By the way, I will be sending Sean and Michael over here in a little bit to grab a few of my book boxes from the garage. One of the deacons put up the new book shelves in my office today."

"Oh boy! I bet it feels like Christmas." Anna laughed at the excitement in her father's eyes.

Having his books boxed and not easily accessible had been challenging for him since she arrived. She was glad to see the deacons were looking out for her father.

"They'll probably come over within the hour. Can you make sure you let them into the garage?"

"Sammy, remind me, okay?"

"Okay," the little boy said with a mouthful of cookie.

After her father left, Anna turned to her nephew and asked, "What vegetables do you like to eat?"

His face scrunch spoke volumes.

"Come on. Surely you like at least one vegetable. Green beans? Peas?"

He made a gagging noise with each suggestion and Anna knew she had her work cut out for her getting them to eat healthier. A cry sounded from the other room and Anna sighed. She had hoped Livi would sleep a bit longer.

"I think I have Livi's tummy bug. Ugh. I don't think I can eat dinner." Sammy held his midsection and rolled on the floor.

"Nice try, Kid." Anna reached down and tickled him until he giggled before entering Livi's room to get her from her crib.

She opened the door to find Livi standing up with her arms raised towards her aunt, her little face was flushed pink.

"What's this I hear about you having a sick belly?" Anna scooped her up, but Livi twisted to reach back for something in her crib.

"Paci... Paci!"

That was another thing Anna was determined to change. Kate Tyler said that Eli had given up his pacifier at two years old. She didn't want Livi to become dependent on a pacifier. She had read an article online about it and had settled the matter in her mind. By the end of summer, she would have Livi pacifier free *and* potty trained. Her mother would be so proud.

"My *paci*! *PACI*!" Livi screamed at the top of her lungs as she contorted and twisted into a squirming little fiend.

"Livi, stop. You're being too loud." Anna tried to reason with the toddler over her tantrum. When that didn't work she called out the door to her niece. "Ellie... come help."

Ellie's door opened and the pre-teen sauntered casually into the room, just staring at her aunt. "What? I was doing my homework."

"Take your sister while I look for this pacifier," Anna said as she passed the little one off to Ellie, immediately opting for giving in rather than enforcing the no pacifier idea. Livi had a pair of lungs that wouldn't quit.

The toddler continued to scream and cry while Anna lifted up every piece of bedding... no pacifier.

"Where is it?" Anna gripped the edge of the crib in frustration. "It couldn't just have disappeared."

"Didn't you put the spare in the dishwasher this morning in that weird little plastic cage thing?" Ellie asked as she tried to get her sister to calm down by holding her close.

"Yes! Yes, I did!" Anna felt a moment of relief as she walked briskly to the kitchen. Ellie followed with the distraught toddler wailing in her sister's arms.

Opening the dishwasher, Anna noticed that the basket she had placed the pacifier and sippy cup stoppers in had fallen over. She spotted the hot pink pacifier in the very far rear corner. With a sigh, she pulled out the loaded bottom drawer of clean dishes as far as she could while still being able to fit her torso in to reach the much needed mouth plug.

Leave it to her parents to get the biggest dishwasher unit available in the appliance store. Anna reached in a little further, feeling her hair snagging on something. Thankfully, Anna didn't hear any blood curdling screams anymore. Either Anna had gone deaf or Livi was finally calmed down.

"I think I almost have it... *Ouch*!" Anna called out.

Then she realized what was pulling the curls from the messy bun on top of her head.

"Wee... Wee..." Livi said with a giggle as she spun the spray arms.

"No, Livi. Stop." With each rotation, Anna felt her hair being pulled a little tighter. "*Ouch*! Livi..."

Livi giggled. Then all of the sudden, there was the horrible sound of retching.

"Oh please ...no! Livi, please don't throw..." Anna didn't get the words out when she felt the splash of warmth somewhere near her right ankle.

"Eww. Gross!" Sammy yelled. "Uh, I'm going to be sick."

Anna sighed and rolled her eyes. "Breathe, Sam. It's mind over matter."

Clearly he didn't listen to her because Anna heard the sound of feet running down the hallway towards the bathroom.

"Ellie? Are you still there?"

"Uh… yup."

"Is Livi okay?"

"Yeah. She's curled up on the couch. Please don't ask me to clean this up."

"Can you try to untangle my hair from the spinning thing? Please."

"I'll try but I don't want to step in…"

Silence. Then came the sound of the kitchen door opening.

"Ellie? Where did you go? Come on. This is hurting my back... and my scalp."

"Oh, Petunia. What have you gotten yourself into now?"

*****

Michael had woken up that morning still feeling the solemnity of the funeral processional. There was a heaviness at the station when he left from his shift. Jake wasn't answering his texts, which concerned Michael. So when Sean asked, Michael was more than happy to volunteer to help his brother do a few tasks at the church to distract him from his thoughts. What he *hadn't* expected to see that day was Anna being eaten alive by a massive dishwasher.

"Who's throw up is this?" he asked as he moved closer to see what had his friend trapped inside.

"Livi's. She's sick." Ellie laughed as she pointed to a little sleeping angel on the sofa.

"Looks like she ate really neon colored cereal," Michael observed.

"Eww. That's so gross." Ellie giggled.

Anna cleared her throat. "Could someone kindly untangle my hair please? Or do you want to keep describing toddler vomit?"

"Testy today, are we?" Michael laughed as he bent low to see where Anna's head was.

Just then Sean appeared in the doorway.

"Mike, what is taking so long to get Anna to open the garage door? Oh... wow."

"Welcome to the party, Sean." Anna's tone was sardonic and Michael couldn't resist laughing. "Are you seriously laughing at me right now, Michael Tyler?"

"No. Not at all." He coughed to cover his laugh and looked up to Ellie who hovered nearby. "Ellie, would you be a hero and find some rubber gloves and paper towels to clean this up so I can try to free your Aunt Petunia?"

He saw Anna's back go rigid. "Call me Petunia one more time... I swear I'll..."

"I don't know where the gloves are. Do we have rubber gloves, Aunt Anna?" Ellie asked.

"In the bathroom under the sink. Grab the clear spray bottle of bleach water... oh, and the disinfectant spray, too."

"What can I do to help?" Sean asked his brother with a puzzled smile on his face.

"Got a pocket knife handy?"

"No! *No, Sir*! No one is cutting my hair!" Anna's body flailed as she attempted to pull herself free and quickly realized that was a bad idea. "*Ow*. Stupid pacifier!"

"Pacifier?" Michael asked as he leaned in again to get a good view of the spray arm that had Anna's hair coiled tightly around the center.

All of the sudden Anna reached her hand backwards towards Michael and revealed a bright pink pacifier clenched in her fist.

"You can wash those things in there?" Sean looked genuinely pleased. "That's good to know."

"Aunt Anna puts it in the cage thing. It's supposed to keep it from falling... normally," Ellie supplied as she scrunched her nose wiping up the mess on the floor.

"Is the throw up gone?" This came from Sam who finally reemerged.

"Yes, Twerp. Thanks for your help," Ellie rolled her eyes.

"So how exactly did your hair get wound on this thing?" Michael asked as he tried to gently pull a few of her amber colored strands free without much success.

"*Anna's Law*," Sam said with a smile.

"What's *Anna's Law*?" Sean asked.

"If it can happen to Aunt Anna... it does," Ellie answered taking off the gloves, throwing them into the trash can, and tying up the trash bag. She pulled it out and held it out to her brother. "Here, Twerp. Put this in the can outside."

"So *Anna's Law*, huh?" Michael asked Anna as he continued to try to work the puzzle that was Anna's hair.

She sighed. "Please don't cut my hair."

"I'm sorry, Anna. I don't see a way around it. It's wrapped a million times."

"Livi was spinning it while I was trying to reach the stupid pacifier."

Was Anna crying? Michael thought he heard a sniffle.

"The good news is I don't have to cut anything close to your scalp. Your little librarian bun saved you."

Another sniffle.

"It's just hair, Anna. It grows back." Michael tried to comfort her before motioning to his brother silently to hand him his pocket knife.

Sean looked nervous as he reached into his pocket and pulled out the folding utility knife.

"I like my hair." Anna whimpered. "It's the only thing I have going for me. Jon always liked my hair long."

Michael felt his heart constrict a bit. "Really? I mean... your hair is nice, but I always thought it was your amazing green eyes that stood out the most."

"You think my eyes are pretty?"

Her little voice was pitiful and all of the sudden Michael had the urge to pull her into his arms and reassure her. The realization caused him to hit his head on the top of the dishwasher.

"Hold still, Petunia." He said gruffly as he started cutting her free.

Moments later Michael closed the knife and handed it back to his brother, who still looked nervous. Michael got to his feet first and reached down to help Anna. "Sean, get her other arm. She's been in that position a while. She's probably stiff."

Anna tried to steady herself by holding onto Michael's arm.

"Whoa... that's some crazy hair, Aunt Anna," Sam said without thinking and Ellie hit him on the shoulder.

Anna instantly brought her hand to the chopped remains of a bun on her head. She ran to the bathroom mirror and groaned loudly. He saw her dart into the room across the hall and reemerge with a baseball cap on.

"Ellie, order a pizza. Here's cash. If you need something call Grandpa at the church. Sam, put this somewhere safe for Livi so we don't lose it." Anna handed her nephew the infamous pacifier before turning to Michael and Sean. "Gentlemen, thank you for your help. Please tell my father I'll be home as soon as I can."

"Where are you going?" Michael asked with a chuckle as he followed her outside.

"I'm going to see if some salon will fit me in before they all close for the night."

"Wait…"

Anna paused as she was getting into her Jeep. "What?"

"The garage… Your father wanted us to get his books."

Reaching up to her visor, Anna pressed a button and the garage door lifted. She waved goodbye and sped down the driveway.

Michael watched as she drove out of sight. Sean came to stand next to him with a slightly amused smile on his face.

"*I always thought it was your amazing green eyes that stood out the most.*" Sean repeated his brother's words in a saccharine sweet tone and batted his eyelashes at Michael, which earned him a solid punch in the arm.

*****

"Do you see him parked out there?" Jake asked his friend and tenant Brian Hamilton.

Jake was watching video feed from his laptop while he camped miles away from the duplex he lived in and owned. Both his porch camera and the surveillance camera he had set up on the side of the house caught the fuzzy image of a car parked alongside the road. The car drove up, but no one ever left the vehicle. When Jake noticed it, he alerted Brian who lived on the second floor.

"Yeah. I see him. Who else knew you gave Branson that drive?"

"No one, but if Branson is stirring up the dust it wouldn't take a genius to figure out I'm helping root out the mole. J.T. confided in me. I'm the one taking a vacation while it's going down."

"What if they're parked outside because they suspect it's *you*, Jake?" Brian asked honestly.

Jake sighed. "You know better than that."

"Of course, *I* do." Brian sighed in frustration before asking, "Should I tell Trip we have a watcher?"

"No. Not yet. I'm still not sure who I can trust with this and who I can't."

"You can trust Trip. He would never..." Brian sounded offended on behalf of their mutual friend.

Jake agreed. Trip Sullivan was a good guy and a good tenant. Jake was selective of who he rented his properties out to. He stuck to mostly law enforcement and their families. Trip was a single guy... a patrol cop for Skennan Cove. Up to that point, he didn't give Jake any bad feelings.

Brian Hamilton was a fellow detective. He occupied the middle floor of the property with his wife Helena and their baby girl. Brian and Jake went all the way back to the academy together. He was the closest thing Jake had to a blood brother. In fact, he was the one who led him to the Lord and introduced him to Beth.

"For now, just keep an eye open and an ear out. It would be dumb for them to do anything that would draw attention. They're probably just trying to see if I come home."

"I hope that's true, Cory. I have a family to protect."

"I know. Your family is *my* family. I'm watching. Believe me." Jake looked at his laptop to the split screens he had up. "Go to sleep, Brian. I'm not taking my eyes off this guy. If he even moves forward an inch, I'll call you."

"What about you? Are you safe?"

Jake laughed as he stuck a marshmallow on the end of a stick and put it close to the fire outside of the old hunting cabin. Goose, his German Shepherd, perked his head up and Jake threw him a marshmallow. "Yeah. I'm just enjoying my vacation time. Living the life. Give Stinkerbell a kiss for me."

"She misses Uncle Jake and Goose already. Stay safe."

Jake disconnected the call and stared into the flames. Since Beth's passing, he had become more reclusive. He liked being alone and the solitude had never bothered him. But this was different. Hiding wasn't his style. He would let his Sergeant handle the content on that flash drive, but Jake was determined to find out who outed J.T. Only a very few people knew of the operation he worked. All claimed to be loyal brothers. One of those brothers stood by and let J.T. get murdered.

He stared at the blurry image of the car on his screen. Whoever it was in that black car, they parked just far enough that their license plate couldn't be seen. Behind the pixelated windshield a dark shadow sat. An unknown enemy... who he suspected masqueraded during the day as a friend.

18

Anna checked her reflection in the bathroom mirror. Her hair bounced right above her shoulders. Too short to pull up nicely into a bun or pony tail, but long enough to fall on her face in a way that irritated her immensely. She had found a hair dresser willing to take her in right after the dishwasher faux pas but the woman had to cut her hair shorter than Anna had expected to make everything even.

Maybe it was vanity... okay, yes it was definitely vanity... but her hair had been her favorite asset. A little girl once told Anna that she had *princess hair*. When Jonathan complimented her it was always on her hair. Yes, it would grow back, but not fast enough. Now it was short, bouncy, and wild.

Michael's words from that day came back to her mind. He thought her eyes were her best quality. Why that caused her stomach to flip flop she didn't know. He was just trying to keep her calm and make her feel better about the inevitability of having to cut her hair free.

Her phone chimed.

"Are you coming?" Michael texted.

It was Friday morning of Memorial Day weekend. Outside the house in the church parking lot, Anna could hear the excited bantering of the youth kids as they waited to load into the vans for the long awaited youth retreat. Ellie had jumped on Anna's bed early that morning with an excitement she hadn't expected of her niece. She had paced back and forth in front of the bathroom door while Anna got ready, until she couldn't wait any longer.

"I'll see you out there, Aunt Anna. Don't keep everyone waiting."

Anna gave her reflection one last look before shaking her head, accepting reality. With a sigh, she grabbed her suitcase, her sleeping bag with her bedding tucked inside, and her favorite pillow to head out the door. It was then that she noticed the manilla envelope that the digital arts teacher handed her before leaving work Thursday. He had taken the pictures from Anna's phone and blew them up. Anna hadn't had a moment to look at them while getting ready for the retreat. She quickly shoved the envelope into her oversized purse, adding it to her pile of luggage, and left the house.

She was grateful to see parents still pulling into the parking lot with their kids. No one could blame her for holding up the crowd if others were still arriving as well. In the distance, Michael played around with a couple of the boys. Anna's father and Sean were discussing something while loading the mound of luggage into one of the vans. Sam was crawling over the seats in the van like the wild child he was. Ellie held Livi giving her occasional hugs and kisses. *So she does have a tender heart under that indifferent persona.*

As she got closer, Anna watched as Michael's playful smile faded from his face. Replacing it was a weird expression that she didn't know how to take.
"Your hair…" he blurted out.
"Yeah, Mike, I know. It's hideous. Thanks for pointing it out." If her hands hadn't been full of luggage, she might have reached up to touch her hair self-consciously.

"No. That's not it at all." Michael came closer, reached out, and pulled one of her curls down before letting it go, making it boing back into place. "I like it. It looks ... beautiful."

Anna gave him a disbelieving look.

"I have to say, my cutting skills are awesome." Michael smiled broadly.

"Um, I think the credit goes to Amanda at *Classy Cuts*, Sir. You and your primitive cutting made her have to take off way more than I wanted."

Michael smiled and took the sleeping bag and suitcase from her. Her eyes landed on his arms as he lifted her things to take them to the cargo van. His black t-shirt with the fire company's emblem and name showed off his muscular arms. It bothered her that she noticed. It also bothered her that the fact he liked her hair made her feel good. Anna shook her head as if clearing it of nonsense.

"Okay. I think we have everyone," Sean called out to the group. "Let's gather around. Pastor Tim is going to pray for our trip before we head out."

Anna's father wrangled Sam out of the van, holding him in place with a stern hand on his shoulder while he offered up a prayer for safe travels and lives to be changed through the various speakers. As soon as the *amen* was spoken, kids started to call dibs on which seats were theirs.

"Senior high in my van," Sean called out. "Jr. high in Michael's."

A total of five leaders and eighteen youth group kids said goodbye to their families before the mad dash ensued to claim the window seats before their friends.

Joy, a college aged volunteer, sat in the middle of the chaos in Michael's van. Anna noticed her pillow and purse were on the front seat already, though she had not put it there.

"Are you okay with being my co-pilot?" Michael asked her as he led her to the van.

"What does that involve?"

"Keep me awake. I've pulled quite a few shifts this week."

"That's comforting. Do we need to stop for coffee?" Anna took her seat and waved to her father, Livi, and Sam.

"Believe me, we will."

And they were off. Every so often, Anna would pull down the mirror on her visor to look behind her at the excited kids. Ellie chatted and laughed sitting in between her friends. Anna smiled at the sight.

"See? I told you," Michael said without taking his eyes off the road.

"What?"

"They're not so bad. A little loud, but overall… pretty great."

Before closing the visor Anna caught sight of Joy sitting two rows behind them staring at the back of Michael's head in nothing less than awestruck adoration. Anna sighed and closed the visor.

"Are we going to stop soon, Mike? The two cups of coffee I had this morning are catching up."

"Yeah, I could use a refill anyway."

The van pulled into the parking lot of a rundown gas station and minimart. The stretch of road they traveled offered very little variety of nice rest stops.

She resisted the urge to shudder and checked to make sure she had her hand sanitizer in her purse.

"Hey, listen up…" Michael addressed the van. "This is the last stop for a very long time. I highly recommend you go now. I'm not stopping again until lunch and we get into PA."

Several kids echoed Anna's thoughts.

"This place looks sketch," one said.

"It builds character. Everyone out." Michael smiled as he opened the side door.

"Should I call Sean to let him know we stopped? Is he going to wait for us up ahead?" Anna asked Michael, noticing the other van continued on.

"Nah. He needs to get there sooner to sign us in. Don't worry. I won't get us lost."

"I wasn't worried, but now that you mention it… I kinda am." Anna smirked.

He reached out and grabbed another curl like he had earlier. It bounced back into place as he released it and he grinned at her. Someone off to the side cleared their throat and Joy smiled waiting to be noticed.

"I took a head count. We have twelve kids. Five boys and seven girls," she announced proudly.

"Great! Thank you." Michael smiled as they all moved towards the minimart.

The line was quite lengthy for the restrooms and by the time Anna made it into the store, she was at the very end. The gas station attendant granted the female population permission to use the men's restroom while there weren't any male customers in the store.

Anna chuckled at the horrified looks of the Jr High girls at the mere notion of going into the *forbidden* men's bathroom. Many of them chose to stay in line and wait for the women's bathroom to open up. For a little while, so did Anna. However, watching the guys go into the other restroom and exiting in a timely manner proved to be too much of a temptation. Especially while she stood there cross legged at the end of the never ending girls' line.

"If no one cares, I'm just going to go on ahead and use the men's room," she said as the last boy left.

"Ew, Aunt Anna!" Ellie scowled.

"Desperate times, Ellie. Desperate times," Anna muttered as she opened the other bathroom door.

She heard a few girls snickering and commenting on the fact that it looked like a mess in there. At first, Anna did not care. After she experienced relief, she finally took notice of the facilities. A shudder crept up her spine. She didn't want to touch anything. Even the sink contained substances of unknown origins in the basin.

The flush valve was to the side of the toilet and stuck out enough that Anna was sure she could use her foot to push down with her shoe rather than using her hand. The less amount of skin-to-surface contact the better, in her opinion.

Balancing her large purse strap over her one shoulder, Anna raised her foot high. Just as she made contact with the lever, a loud knock sounded on the door startling her.

"Anyone in there?" A gruff male voice asked.

Anna teetered on her one leg and with the next knock of the door her leg came down… right into the unflushed toilet bowl.

"Anyone in there?" The man repeated.

"Yes. Yes. Someone is in here," Anna yelled back in anger as her body started convulsing in disgust.

The man on the other side of the door mumbled something but remained quiet. Anna pulled her soaked foot from the toilet and whimpered as she made her way to the sink. Using her elbow to turn the faucet on and off she hastily washed her hands and grabbed at least a dozen paper towels from the dispenser. Using the cluster of paper towels, she turned the door knob and exited, trying not to draw attention to the odd squishing noise her foot made on the linoleum.

Once outside, Michael looked up from where he stood next to the van with the kids and Joy. He had been on the phone, most likely with Sean, when he spotted her coming out of the store.

"Ah. Here she is. I'll talk to you at the next stop," he said. Judging by the way his expression changed from pleasure to confusion, he knew something was amiss.

She limped her way past the van to the dumpsters at the side of the parking lot and used the paper towels she still grasped to take off her offending shoe. Angrily she tossed it into the large trash receptacle. Realizing the other shoe didn't serve a purpose without its mate, Anna threw that one away as well. At least she packed another pair in her bag.

"What exactly are you doing?" Michael asked as he casually made his way to where she stood.

"Just … don't."

"Don't what?" An amused smirk started to form on his face.

"Don't ask. Please."

She began to walk barefoot back to the van.

"Hold it, Petunia. What are you thinking walking on this gravel without shoes?" His smile faded and he looked momentarily irritated. "There's broken glass." "I need to grab my other pair of shoes from my suitcase. Those," Anna motioned to the dumpster, "are *not* salvageable."

"You mean your suitcase that is currently twenty miles ahead of us in Sean's van?" His hands were on his hips.

What he said dawned on Anna. Her shoulders slumped, but she was tougher than that. With her chin raised ever so slightly, she looked Michael straight in the eye and stepped onto the gravel from the concrete slab that she had been standing on. In a swift and unexpected move he grabbed her and lifted Anna by her waist back onto the concrete slab. He stood in front of her and knelt lower, offering her his back.

"Put your arms around my neck, Petunia," he instructed.

"The kids are watching. No way."

"Really? You're going to make me carry you back to the van the other way?"

"What other way?" Anna asked a little taken aback.

"If you don't want to find out, put your arms around my neck."

Something in his tone said he was serious. Anna slid her arms around his neck and she felt his strong hands hold tightly to her forearms. He pulled on her arms and lifted her until they were almost cheek to cheek. Anna breathed in the woodsy scent of his cologne. With her feet dangling above the ground, he walked her back to the van.

The kids laughed and cheered at the spectacle as if this had been a planned amusement for their benefit. He backed up against the passenger side and she transitioned to her seat, refusing to make eye contact with her friend. Once she was sitting, he shut her door and mumbled as he walked to the driver's side. She thought she heard him utter the words, *"Anna's Law"*, but she could've been mistaken.

"I told you not to go into the men's room, Aunt Anna," Ellie said from somewhere behind her.

"Noted." Anna sighed and pulled out her pillow.

She laid her head against the window after bathing in hand sanitizer. Soon her embarrassment was forgotten as the movement of the van traveling down the highway lulled her to sleep.

*****

Michael drove in silence. They were well into Pennsylvania on the turnpike headed towards New Jersey. Everyone in the back of the van either slept or stared blankly out the windows in the quietness. Anna had been asleep for some time. Every so often he'd cast her a side glance and smile.

Anna's Law. It sure did seem like the weirdest things happened to her. Was she doing something on her own to bring about the odd occurrences or was she just a magnet for trouble? Maybe a combination of both. She fascinated Michael. Even at that very moment, a curl sprung free from its confines and clung to the corner of her open mouth as she snored softly. If she knew, she'd be embarrassed. Yet to him it was oddly endearing.

"Are we going to stop for lunch soon, Mike?" A voice from behind startled him from his thoughts.

Shifting ever so slightly, Michael saw Joy in his periphery leaning forward between the driver's and passenger's seat.

"It's a little after noon." Joy pointed out.

"Oh yes. There's a turnpike rest stop up ahead with a few fast food places. We should probably start waking up the sleepyheads." Michael smirked as he turned on the radio and pumped up the volume.

Some jolted awake, like Anna. Others grumbled and put pillows over their heads to drown out the music. Out of the corner of his eye, he saw Anna quickly pulling the strand of hair from her mouth and checking her reflection in the mirror.

"Sleep well?" he asked as she shut the mirror and sat back against the seat with a thud.

"How long was I asleep?"

"About an hour."

"I'm so sorry," Anna apologized with wide eyes. "I'm not being a good co-pilot."

Michael smiled at her. "It's all good. We're not lost yet."

The van turned off onto the winding exit that led to the restaurant and gas station.

"What would you like to eat? I'll go in and grab something for you since..." Michael motioned to her bare feet.

Anna looked down at the polished toe nails of her bare feet and sighed.

"Don't worry about me." She pulled out a banana and showed him. "Jonathan always said potassium is good for long trips if I'm going to be sitting for a long time."

"You like chicken wraps, right?" He asked giving her banana a disinterested glare.

"Yes, but…"

"Stay put, Cinderella." He smirked as he got out and rallied the kids into a semblance of an organized mob.

Once inside, Michael made sure that all of the kids got their food and made it back to the van safely before double checking bathrooms for any stragglers. Anna texted him from the van to assure him that she had the full group accounted for. Joy grabbed her lunch and Michael set about getting his and Anna's. He was about to leave the building when something caught his eye.

A moment later, he climbed back into his seat and handed Anna a chicken wrap and a bottled water.

"If you'd rather just eat the banana that's fine, but at least now you have options," he said.

"Thank you. How much do I…"

"Stop. It's a chicken wrap, not a filet mignon." He smirked before pulling out a brown paper bag and handing it to her. "Here. A little memento of our trip so far, Petunia."

Quizzically, she took the bag and looked inside. She burst out laughing, a beautiful sound.

"What is it, Aunt Anna?" Ellie asked from the back.

Anna pulled out a bright blue pair of flip flops decorated with the Pennsylvania state flag. A few from the back laughed as Anna put them on her feet.

"Nice. Thanks. I'll treasure them forever." Anna chuckled as she took a bite out of her chicken wrap.

19

It was late afternoon when the van pulled into the New Life Bible Conference and Retreat Center in the coastal region of New Jersey. As soon as Anna got out of the van and the humid salty air hit her face, she smiled. Though she couldn't see the ocean from the parking lot, she could hear and smell it.

"Glad you could make it." Sean grinned at his brother as he approached the group with an armful of materials. "These are wristbands and room assignments. Anna, here are the keys to the girls' dorms and their conference schedules. You may want to get their stuff unloaded into their rooms before the first meeting at seven. We'll meet in the cafeteria for dinner at five."

Anna looked at her watch and saw there wasn't a lot of time. She grabbed Joy and filled her in on the plan and rallied the teen girls to her side. Everyone grabbed their bags from the back of Sean's van and started to set out when Michael called out to the boys, "Where are the gentlemen?"

The teen guys begrudgingly started carrying the luggage towards the girls' building and Anna felt her suitcase lift from her grasp.

"Obviously we're not allowed inside, but we can at least get it to the common area," Michael commented as he led the charge.

After everything was inside, Michael turned to Anna.

"I guess I'll see you at dinner."

"Mike…"

He paused his departure and looked down at her.

"What if the girls don't like me? What if they don't listen to me?" Anna whispered, feeling highly insecure. "Who am I that they'd pay attention me?"

"Are you kidding? You're Super Anna." He pulled her curl one last time before leaving her staring after him.

She turned to find many sets of curious eyes on her and Anna rifled through the papers Sean had handed her to figure out where they needed to be.

"Joy, you have the senior high girls in your room. Here is your key. Everyone, I know it's tempting to want to relax and play around, but get your bedding onto the beds first in case the meeting goes late tonight," Anna suggested. "We'll meet right here at five o'clock and walk to the cafeteria together. Got it?"

Everyone agreed and Anna led her Jr. High girls to their room, next door to Joy's room. Anna had memories flood her from her own youth group experiences at that very same camp. The facilities had been updated since her youth days. The rooms were now air conditioned. The rickety old bunk beds were replaced with newer sturdier models. The rooms were still very bare as far as décor, but the point was to be out at the beach and enjoying the outdoors anyway.

"Look! You can see the ocean from our window," Ellie gushed. Her best friend Jaden came to her side and the two stood for a bit transfixed.

Anna cleared her throat and smiled at the girls before they got the hint and began unrolling their sleeping bags across the bare mattresses. When everyone was satisfied with their sleeping accommodations, Anna tried to herd them to the lounge to meet up with the older girls.

So far so good, she thought as everyone was accounted for in the common area. Anna felt some satisfaction that the girls followed her lead to the cafeteria without any issue. In fact, they beat their male counterparts. The girls made it through the food line and sat down to eat before the guys came barreling into the cafeteria.

Michael nodded at Anna with a smile as he ushered the guys alongside his brother through the line.

Anna mouthed the words, *"You're late"* with an irksome smile and he just shrugged with an equally playful smirk. Moments later the gentlemen squeezed into any available seats left in the room and wolfed down their food.

For the first time since arriving, Anna took in the whole scene. The cacophony of voices was deafening as teens from all over the northern states chatted, laughed, and goofed around. Her eyes landed on a girl in the center of the room who looked completely oblivious to all that was going on around her. She was reading a book while her group conversed nearby. The girl reminded Anna of herself many years prior.

"Anna... Anna." A voice pulled her from the notebook in her hand. Anna looked up and found her sister Alexis staring at her with a perturbed expression on her face.

"What?" Anna spat out.

"If Mom and Dad are forcing me to be here, you need to stop doing whatever you're doing and be with me."

"I'm editing my new story."

"Well, stop it. The only half decent person here is Sean and he's hanging with those losers." Alexis tilted her head in Sean Tyler's direction.

Anna glanced up and saw Sean mingling with a few of the younger guys. Michael laughed louder than them all and Anna rolled her eyes.

"Do you want to go to the beach with me during free time?" Alexis asked pulling the notebook from her sister's hands.

"I didn't bring my bathing suit." Anna said quietly.

"What? You knew we were coming to the beach... of all of the things to forget."

"You know I don't wear bathing suits in public," Anna said under her breath so as not to catch the attention of some guys at the table behind them.

"Go in your shorts." Alexis got to her feet dramatically, still holding Anna's notebook. "I'm not giving this back until you come to the beach with me."

"Alex..." Anna reached up and tried to grab it back but without success.

"You want to go to the beach? I'll go with you to the beach." One of the guys stood up and sauntered over to Alex.

Anna rolled her eyes. He looked as if he had been practicing his smolder in the mirror for days leading up to the retreat.

"I would love to." Alex flirted right back. "Maybe you can help me convince my dork of a sister to come with us?"

Anna wanted to disappear from sight as the guy looked her up and down. He let out an uncomfortable laugh.

"Let her stay if she's not the... athletic type. We can still have fun, right?"

The guy started pulling Alex with him and, despite a moment of hesitation, Alex returned his smile and threw the notebook back at Anna. "Right. Let's go. Enjoy writing your stupid story."

Anna stood awkwardly clutching the notebook that now had ripped and bent pages. Quickly sitting back down, she looked around to see if anyone noticed. Her eyes landed on Michael. He seemed oblivious to her. Good. He was basking in the attention of the crème de la crème of Jr. High girls. Gathering her notebook and pens, Anna quickly left the noisy cafeteria and sought out the solace of a table not far from the pier. With tears soaking the page, she kept writing.

"Hey, are you going to join the real world?" A voice pulled Anna from her memories. A guy hovered over the young girl that Anna had noticed earlier. She looked taken aback that anyone was talking to her at all.

"No thank you. I'll just keep reading," the girl said without looking up. The girl only glanced around after the boy left. Her eyes met Anna's.

With boldness Anna didn't really ever demonstrate before, she approached the girl at the other table and asked, "What are you reading?"

The girl shyly held up the book and let Anna read the title.

Anna smiled as recognition hit. It was a Christian suspense book that Anna had read and re-read many times over. In fact, she had just read it for the tenth time the week prior. "I love that series. It's very well written."

"It's a series?" The girl looked pleasantly surprised.

"Yes. That's the first book, but there are three more. How far are you into it? Can I sit down?" Anna asked.

The girl motioned to the empty seat at the empty table. "I'm almost done. I have one more chapter left. I don't want the story to end."

"Yeah, I know how that feels. She's one of my favorite writers, too." Anna smiled warmly at the girl. Then in an impulsive move, Anna went to her bag and pulled out a book. "This is book two."

The girl asked permission to look at it and held it almost reverently in her hands as she read the back cover. They discussed the plot and characters for a few minutes when Anna felt an overwhelming sense of camaraderie with the girl.

"How about you keep it?" Anna even surprised herself with the offer.

"No! I can't. What about you? Don't you want to read it?"

"I've read it several times... as you can tell by the condition of the book." Anna chuckled.

"Are you sure?"

"I'm sure, but there's one condition. Try to spend *some* time talking to your group. Build a memory or two apart from the reading... okay?"

The girl glanced over at the other table filled with chatty teens and she slowly nodded.

Anna's group started getting up and putting their trays away so she said goodbye to the girl and quickly joined her own group.

"I see you're making friends already," Michael said quietly as they walked out of the cafeteria into the ocean scented air.

She just smiled and wondered what she would do in her spare time now that she gave away her book. Ironically, Anna concluded that maybe she should follow her own advice. Interact with the others. Make a few memories.

"Whoa… those are some bright flip flops," Sean said coming up on Anna's other side with a grin.

Looking down at her feet, Anna realized she never changed into her other pair of shoes.

"They're actually very comfortable," she laughed as she walked between the two Tyler brothers wondering if young Anna would've ever believed that one day she'd be there with them again … enjoying their friendship.

*****

The first night of the conference was wonderful. After dinner, they attended a Bible session and finished the evening with a bonfire on the beach with s'mores. By the time they made it back to their room, everyone was tired. There was less giggling and chattiness than Anna thought there would be.

Waking up and getting everyone ready for the day was another story. Everyone groaned and moaned as Anna threw the curtains open, letting sunlight fill the room. Eventually, they made it to the cafeteria for breakfast although it was their turn to be late. Michael mouthed the words "*You're late*" just as she had and pointed at his watch with a look of mock disgust.

As they filled the chapel for the conference after breakfast, Anna wondered if she was ready for the high energy music and fun like they had had the night before. A band led them in various praise and worship songs and the mood shifted to her surprise. A speaker got up and started with the question: *What is your worth?*

"If you could put a price on your life what would it be? A million? Billion? Maybe for some of you, you don't think you have a great value at all."

Anna shifted uncomfortably and looked around her to see how the others reacted. Everyone gave the speaker their full attention as he shared his testimony about being the unpopular kid that no one liked. Anna's throat constricted.

"I tried to be what everyone wanted. Girls wanted the muscular guys so I spent hours in the gym. My academics weren't great so I worked hard and still was an average student. It wasn't until I found my identity in God… who He made me to be and for the purpose He made me… that I felt comfortable in my own skin."

Anna reflected on the past several years of her life as the man's words resonated with her. Anna had changed everything about herself. Her looks. Her likes and dislikes. Her motivations. Her passions. All for what? Where was Jonathan now? Where was Anna? *Who* was Anna now?

"Acts 17:28 says that it is in God alone that we have our being. Think about that for a moment. What *is* your being? It's your personality. It's your gifts and abilities. Did you know God gave you those? He designed you each unique with a purpose to use them."

Anna felt a stirring in her heart. For weeks she had been pushing away an urge to pull out her notebook and jot down a story idea that had been coming in and out of her mind. She assumed those dreams died long ago. Self-consciously she cast a side glance at Michael who sat a few rows away with the Jr. High boys from their group. He had encouraged her to take up her writing again.

"But listen to me... here's the kicker," the speaker said with a dramatic pause. "All of our gifts... all of the best things about us... if we're not using them *in Him* we're spinning our wheels. The verse doesn't say that we have our being *in ourselves*. The verse doesn't say we find our being in the approval, love, and acceptance of *others*. No. It's *in Him*. That means *for Him*. Our identity is never fully realized until we have a relationship... an ongoing healthy, loving relationship... with Jesus Christ."

It made sense now. Anna held her breath and released it slowly as the truth dawned on her. For so long, she tried and tried to please others and make everyone happy. She gave up the core essence of who she was for the people she loved, but it ultimately didn't matter. Her energies were not directed in the right places. She replaced God with those people. She replaced God with *herself*. Then in the process she lost herself.

The session ended and everyone was dismissed for several hours of free time. A plan was made for a group to go to the beach with Joy and Sean. The remainder wanted to stay and hang out around the game rooms and volleyball courts right there on the immediate property of the conference center.

Anna volunteered to position herself in a central place in case anyone needed anything. Michael took a group to play basketball. As she watched the rest of their group trail behind him, Anna went to see if her old table near the pier was still there. Her table was gone, but replacing it was a beautiful gazebo with benches inside, overlooking the water.

Sitting down, Anna stared out over the bay and prayed. *I'm sorry, Lord. I've made my life about everyone but You. You're the One who created me to write. You're the One who loved me when everyone else wanted to change the very essence of me. You only want to change the things that don't belong or that hurt me. Forgive me. Remind me of who I am. Remind me of the Anna You love.*

Reaching down into her bag, Anna pulled out her notebook. At first, she started jotting ideas and brainstorming possible chapter outlines. A few hours later, Anna stared down at the tentative book outline that she had been pushing aside for far too long. A few tears mixed with the ink and smudged the sheets, but she stared down at the scribbling with joy and a renewed feeling of purpose.

Someone cleared their throat off to the side and she jumped.

"I'm sorry. I didn't mean to scare you." Michael smiled from the opening of the gazebo. "Mind if I join you?"

"Sure." Anna smiled gently. "Where did the kids go?"

"They are celebrating their victories over ice cream at the snack shop."

"*Victories?*"

"Yeah. I thought it would be fun to play me against them. Guess who won?" Michael eased his way down onto the bench next to her.

Anna laughed. "You're not a teenager anymore, Michael."

"I guess I'm not." He grinned and then his eyes landed on her open notebook. "What's all this?"

"Nothing. It's nothing... yet."

"It looks like something." His smile grew. "Anna, is that what I think it is? Because it looks a lot like chapter headings."

"Stop." Anna swatted his hands away as he tried to reach for her notes. "I said it's nothing yet. We'll see what it becomes."

Michael looked into her face with an expression akin to admiration. "Anna, I'm proud of you."

A shudder ran through her and she had to look away. After a moment she realized he had his arm across the back of the bench and his body was still leaned in as he tried to look at her notes. His proximity caused an unusual feeling to rise up in her and she quickly jumped to her feet. In doing so, her bag fell to the ground dumping all of its contents onto the wooden floor of the gazebo.

The large manilla envelope that the digital arts teacher had handed her fell with everything else.

"Here, I'll help you pick this up," Michael said as he knelt and grabbed a variety of odds and ends.

Anna picked up the envelope from the wrong end and the pictures fell out. Reaching for one, Michael looked at it and his brow knit.

"Anna, what are these? Where are they from?" he asked.

"You know, you really are quite nosy." Anna chuckled as she reached for the picture in his hands. Then she noticed his expression. "What? What's wrong?"

He showed her the picture and pointed at the two men Anna had accidentally captured in her selfie at the flower show.

"Do you know who this is?" he asked.

"The man in the suit is Davidson. I know." Anna reached for it, but Michael didn't release his grip.

"This guy right here. Do you know *him*?" he asked with heightened tension in his voice.

"No. I was going to take these to Jake when we got back. Why? Who is it?"

"It's Nick. Nick Spencer. Jake's partner." Michael scowled and the reality hit Anna. "Why is he talking to the Broker?"

20

Nick Spencer sat in his car gathering his thoughts before he entered the back room of the club owned by the Broker. Whispers and rumors had been making their way to Nick that someone had information to put a lot of people away... himself included. Jake Cory mysteriously cashed in his vacation time. It didn't take a genius to put it all together. Especially after Jake's scrutiny at the Sparks crime scene. The Broker's men had been sloppy.

Nick's employer grew impatient with the wealthy business man. The Broker's ability to get goods to clients discreetly was helpful, but not required. The drug market wasn't hurting, that was for sure. But sloppy work on the part of those fools could definitely affect their bottom line. *Nick's* bottom line.

He had worked too hard to develop a flawless system. Nick had men positioned in evidence lockup, on street patrol... he even had an associate in the courts. When word got back to him that Davidson hired a new man, it was in Nick's best interest to find out about him. That's when he discovered the Broker's man was an undercover cop... J.T.

Maybe he would've tried to throw his old friend off his scent or even see if he'd be willing to earn a few extra bucks coming to work for he and Damon, but J.T. was too honest. When The Broker's men caught him accessing and downloading sensitive information from Davidson's private laptop, something had to be done.

For the most part the Broker and his men handled it quickly, but J.T. must've reached out to Jake with the information before they got to him. Important information had been leaked. Just that morning Sergeant Branson called an emergency meeting with some pretty high ranking individuals, but didn't feel the need to share with anyone what was going on.

An insider who sat in on that meeting informed him there was a USB that managed to make its way into Branson's hands. Nick felt like a noose was tightening around his neck. Damon decided that the Broker and his men needed to be taught a lesson for their sloppiness. And Nick was going to be their teacher.

He entered the bar through the employee entrance off the back alley. It was one of many establishments the Broker owned, but it was a given the two guys he was looking for were inside.

"Make sure that by the time you leave them, they know they're as good as dead if they make one more mistake. If the Broker can't get his men under control, *we* will." Damon's words floated into his mind as he approached the back hallway.

Nick was more than happy to work out some of his frustrations on those losers. Jake had vanished into thin air and Nick was sleep deprived from watching his house all hours of the night with the hope he returned. Nick patted the brass knuckles in his pocket as he walked past oblivious club personnel. They knew exactly who he was and they knew to leave him alone. "Rob and Keith … where are they?" Nick demanded of one of the security guards.

The man nodded to a shut door down a hall from the rest of the loud music and flashing strobe lights. Without a thought, Nick entered the room, finding several men around a table playing high stakes poker.

Nick singled out the men he did not need and simply said, "*Go*."

With no questions asked, they dispersed. A few paused to grab their respective monies on the table, but Nick cleared his throat and pulled out the brass knuckles from his jacket. The men must've thought better of their greed because they left in a hurry.

"Come on, Man," Rob smirked. "What's this about?"

"There's a lot of talk going around about a USB with some pretty damaging information on it. Hear anything about that?" Nick asked as he slipped the brass knuckles onto his fingers.

"Pfft. Yeah… we heard about it," Rob waved it off, trying to come off as cool and collected. "But that girl knows nothing. If she did, she'd be writing all kinds of stuff. It died with her friend, Man."

With a low, menacing laugh Nick shook his head and sighed. "You see… this is what makes Damon mad. Why is this the first time we're hearing about this… girl?"

"Because it's under control." Rob held his hands up to emphasize his point. Nick hated that smug smile on his face. He gripped his knuckles and tried to use restraint.

"Under control? If I am hearing about it … at the station… does that sound *under control* to you?"

Keith looked as if he were about to soil himself and for once Rob had the smarts to stay quiet.

"I take your silence as a no." Nick rushed forward and Rob put his arms up to protect himself from the imminent impact of Nick's fist on his jaw, but to no avail.

Rob fell to the ground and Nick stood still watching as the man scrambled back to his feet. He wasn't smiling anymore. Good.

"Now what else haven't you been telling us, Gentlemen? What is your boss doing to keep his suppliers safe?"

Rob spit a tooth out onto the floor. "That's Davidson's job... not ours. Take it up with him."

Nick gave the man no notice before hitting him several more times, reducing him to a pile on the floor again. Rob writhed in pain for a few moments and Nick leaned down to look in the man's face. "I don't like cocky attitudes."

Keith still stood in scared silence. Nick doubted the man had taken a breath once since he had entered the room.

"You're being awfully quiet, Keith. Do you have anything of value to add?"

"Price fired her after she saw Davidson and that state rep talking at the flower show."

"I'm listening. Keep going."

"We saw her the night that cop got away from Rob, but he let her go," Keith's voice trembled. Nick laughed at how easily the other man threw his friend under the bus. "I pointed her out to the boss, but they lost her. She left town. No one can find her."

Rob cussed Keith out from his spot on the floor.

"Is that true, Rob? You let both J.T. *and* a witness get away?" Nick laughed at the incompetence.

"J.T. didn't get away. We caught up to him the same night. And the girl... she disappeared." Rob groaned.

"Does she have a name, Keith?"

"Annalise Munson. Price tried to get her to come to Sparks' funeral but she didn't show. They had been close," Keith supplied. The kid was growing on Nick. "Today is your lucky day, Guys. I'm going to find out who this Annalise Munson is and where you can find her. Then *you* are going to kill her." Nick wiped the blood off of his brass knuckles onto Rob's shirt as he pulled him to his feet. "If you screw *this* up, you're both dead. Understand?"

Nick left the building and sought the solace of his own apartment. He pulled out his laptop and started doing what he did best. In a matter of hours, he found articles written by Annalise Munson. He knew what she looked like thanks to a blog she had written online a few years back. He knew she came from a small town a couple hours away and recently broke up with her fiancé according to a frightened Mr. Price at the *Gazette*.

What he could *not* find was a current address. Ms. Munson hadn't changed the address on her license. Without a warrant there was little more he could look for without drawing attention to himself.

While digging around, a past file popped up in his search that contained her name. An overdose occurred and Annalise Munson had called the police to help her sister. *So, she has a druggy sister. Interesting.* Nick scanned the information and names. A smile curled his lips. Turned out, Annalise Munson and his boss had a mutual friend.

Grabbing his phone Nick dialed his best chance of finding the missing link. "Hey, I've got a job for you. I need you to tell me everything you know about Annalise Munson."

The sun felt intense that Friday afternoon as Anna sat in her car in indecision. It was hard to believe that it had been a week since they left the church parking lot for the youth conference. Yet, an entire school week had passed.

Since coming back from the conference, Anna had started making changes. She pulled her Bible off the shelf and borrowed a devotional book from the church library that Tessa recommended highly. Her writing time became her favorite part of her day. It normally came after the kids were in bed and the house was quiet. Three chapters from her outline were complete.

Yet, in the back of her mind at all times was the name Nick Spencer. Since Michael pointed out Jake's current partner in her picture she had tried calling and texting Jake numerous times. She didn't send the picture or leave a message because she didn't know how deep the danger ran. What if Jake wasn't responding to his texts because he *couldn't*?

Her phone dinged as a text came through.

"Are you just going to sit there?"

A smile touched Anna's lips at Michael's text. She looked into the rearview mirror and saw him leaning against the opening of the fire station garage door, arms crossed and phone in hand. Slowly she got out and made her way to where he stood.

"Have you had any success in getting ahold of Jake?" Anna asked Michael.

"Hello to you as well, Anna Munson." His smile sobered. "And, no… no success."

Anna's shoulders slumped. "But he needs to know what we know."

"And what is that exactly? That Nick was talking to a *bad guy*?" Michael pushed off the wall and came a little closer. "There's a chance that Nick is undercover... like J.T. was... and we might blow it for him."

"Do you really think that?"

"I don't know what to think." Michael looked down at Anna. "What I *do* know is that he warned me not to let you leave this area or to let you put yourself in the center of this. I shouldn't have pointed Nick out to you."

"It's too late now, Super Mike. And I can't just let this be. What if I could've helped J.T. that night?"

"Anna..." Michael shook his head. "You're not a cop. Stay out of this."

"Is that what you're going to do? Stay out of this... let your friend get hurt?"

The two stared at each other for a few moments in a standoff. There was something in Michael's eyes. A slight wince.

"Oh... my... word, you already have a plan, don't you? And you weren't going to include me?" Anna accused.

Michael sighed and looked away in frustration.

"What? What is your plan, Mike?" She asked moving back into his line of sight.

"Has anyone every told you that you can be annoying at times?" he asked.

"Hmm. Fine. I don't need your help." Anna backed away, hoping he'd take the bait she just dropped.

"Anna..." His tone sounded pained. "Please drop it."

"The kids have a visit tomorrow with their father. It's close to Skennan Cove and I offered to take them to give dad a break. While they're safe at the center for a few hours, I'm going to swing into town and drop these off. Are you with me or not, Tyler?"

"And where exactly do you think you're going to drop them off at? Do you know where Jake is?" Michael asked clearly annoyed at her persistence.

"No, but I'm starting to think *you* do." Anna smiled coyly.

"I don't know for certain... it's a hunch. Nothing more."

"Well, that's better than nothing," Anna said. "Especially if it keeps Jake safe if his partner is in cahoots with the Broker."

Michael's face twitched before breaking into a smile. "*Cahoots*? Is that like some cop lingo you picked up, Petunia?"

Anna just glared at him before asking once and for all. "Are you coming with me or not?"

"Fine."

"Fine." Anna smiled proudly. "We leave tomorrow from my house at 8 AM. See you then, Super Mike."

*****

How was it possible to want to wring someone's neck in one moment and wrap them in a hug the next? This was what Michael pondered as he watched Anna walk back to her Jeep and drive off. She gave him a sassy wave for good measure.

"What's tomorrow at eight?" Scooter's voice asked from behind him.

Michael turned on his heels to find Scooter popping a chip into his mouth with a curious expression on his face.

"Don't do stuff like that, Man."

"What?"

"Don't be sneaking up on people and listening in."

"You two *are* dating, aren't you? That's why you won't give her my number." Scooter smirked as he followed Michael back inside.

"I thought I told you to reorganize Rescue Unit 3's supply cabinet. This doesn't look any different than it did this morning." Michael stood inside the emergency vehicle scrutinizing every inch.

"I'll get to it. Man, I thought being in a relationship would soften you up. You're like the complete opposite," Scooter groused.

Michael just shot him a warning look and moved to the locker room to grab his things. He was grateful his shift was done so he wouldn't have to listen to Scooter prying for more information on Anna. *But you didn't tell him you're not together this time.* The thought struck Michael on the drive home.

He needed a voice of reason. Between Anna, Scooter, and all of the feelings he was still unpacking from the youth retreat… Michael needed to hear from someone sane. He dialed his brother Dan.

"Hey, Dan. I know it's a long shot but what are your plans tonight? I was thinking maybe we could go try out the rock wall in the new fitness center."

"Uh…" That was not the response Michael was hoping to hear. "I can't. But neither can you."

"What do you mean? Why can't *I*?"

"You probably should get home as soon as possible."
Dan's tone sounded odd.

"What's the matter? Is Kate okay? Tessa?"

"Oh, yeah. They're fine. No new babies, but there's definitely a new member of the family."

"Quit with the cryptic stuff. Spit it out, Dan." Michael was getting irritated.

"Jen is home… with Ben."

"Okay… and?"

"Let me go outside so I can talk freely," Dan whispered. After a few seconds he came back and talked louder. "You know how Jen was supposed to come home from school and help Mom with the produce shop? Not going to happen. She and Ben eloped."

Michael slammed the brakes of his truck and pulled to the side of the road. "What did you just say?"

"You heard me. They said it was in case Ben deploys. There's been rumors he might have to. He wanted to make sure they were set up with on-base housing just in case he leaves… so she'd have community."

"Wait… does that mean she's *leaving* us?"

"They're here to get her stuff. She's moving with him to North Carolina… *next week*."

The news slowly started sinking in. The baby of the family was married… and leaving them.

"How is Mom handling this? I know she wanted to throw a big wedding for her only girl."

"As you could imagine. Trying to be happy for them, but one hair away from losing it," Dan sighed. "It's not like we didn't know it was coming… We just thought we had more time with her."

"I'm almost home. Give me five minutes."

As he ended the call and merged back onto the road, Michael once again felt the resentment that came with change. Jenna, his baby sister... was married and moving away. He could still see her hanging upside down from the tree rocking back and forth like a monkey in his mind. Or chasing after them down the trail to Kate's house yelling at them for not including her on their treasure hunts. Why did everything have to keep changing? And why couldn't friends just stay friends forever?

21

Jake woke up Saturday morning with a sore back and the beginnings of a cold. Hopefully his *vacation* could come to an end soon and he could go back to his life.

"Goose, come," Jake called to the German Shepherd playing at the edge of the pond. The dog looked up at the sound of his name and obeyed, falling in place next to Jake as he walked to his truck.

The cabin was wonderful, but it had no electricity. His cellphone was dead and his laptop was about to die. He started his truck and pulled cords from a bag on his front seat and started charging everything. He munched on a protein bar, breaking off a piece for Goose.

His phone came back to life and started chiming as all of his missed texts hit at once. Jake sighed and reluctantly looked at the names that popped up. Michael. Anna. And then Michael again. They were worried about him. Jake understood that. However, there was no way he could explain the situation without putting them at risk as well.

One text stood out above all the others. It was from Michael.

"We're heading your way Saturday. Are you at the cabin? We have info that you need to know."

Jake resisted texting what he really wanted to say. It would be less than Christlike. He took a moment to think things through before responding.

"Idiot! What part of *keep Anna away from here* are you not understanding?" he texted back. "Are you trying to get her killed?"

"She'd come with or without me. Have you met her?" was Michael's instant response.

Jake sighed in frustration and Goose laid his head on Jake's arm.

"I'm sending you an address. Meet me there at one but keep an eye on your rear view. If someone hangs on your tail too long take a detour."

Jake muttered a few words under his breath before repenting of his language to God. Goose nudged his hand and Jake scratched behind his ears. He had left Skennan Cove so quickly, he hadn't adequately packed for the dog. Maybe he could put Michael to good use after all. "Since you're here… if I give you a list can you stop at a grocery store?"

*****

Anna let Michael in the side door of the parsonage Saturday morning, noting his less than cheerful demeanor.

"Are you changing your mind about coming with me? You look… *put out*." She observed as her friend stood just inside the doorway.

"Is your dad here?" he asked.

"No. He's dropping Livi off. He decided to take the babysitter's offer to watch Livi so he could do a few things around the house. Why?"

Michael nodded and moved closer to Anna so he could speak for her ears only.

"Jen and Ben eloped. They're moving to North Carolina next week. We thought we'd have another year to adjust to the idea of her leaving us."

"Wow. I don't know what to say." Her father had helped many couples marry before deployments. They lived in a military town near an Army base. It wasn't uncommon. However, this was Michael's sister. "You *like* Ben, right? He's a good guy?"

"I'm not sure at the moment." Michael smirked before allowing his expression to relax. "Yeah... he's a good guy. But she'll be all alone in North Carolina. What if he deploys?"

"Jen makes friends easy, Mike. She's a Tyler." Anna put a hand on his arm and smiled gently.

"Now we have to find someone to take over her job at the farm. She can't help run the produce sales from North Carolina."

"Maybe I can help. I'll be out of school for the summer and don't have a job lined up yet." Anna smiled. "I heard a rumor once that you have blueberries in July."

"You mean I'd have to see you on a daily basis? I don't know about that." There was something in the way he said the words. His tone. His eyes. There was a tenderness that belied the teasing words.

"Mike! You're here!" Sam ran straight to Michael and started play fighting with him. "Why don't we just stay home and go to the farm instead?"

"I'd be okay with that!" Ellie called from the bathroom down the hall as she emerged with a toothbrush dangling from her mouth.

"Sammy, why don't you go find your comic book that you made for your dad. Maybe he'll be there today," Anna urged her nephew.

"Nah, he's not coming. Ellie is right. He doesn't care about us anymore."

"What am I right about?" Ellie asked, popping out of the bathroom again still with a toothbrush in her mouth.

"That dad doesn't care," Sam yelled back.

Something about the nonchalant way the little boy said the words broke Anna's heart. It was mirrored in Michael's eyes.

"You wrote a comic book? I'd love to read it. I love comics." Michael said enthusiastically.

"Why don't you get it and show Michael? You worked hard on that," Anna encouraged.

With a shrug Sam ran to his bedroom and reemerged with a crumpled pile of pages stapled together. Michael took them, smoothing them out on the kitchen counter. He read the little boy's work with an occasional head nod and chuckle before turning back to the boy with an expression of admiration.

"This is good stuff, Sam. Don't stop. I want to know what happens to your superhero next."

Sam beamed under Michael's praise.

"In fact…" Michael turned to Anna and tilted his head at her. "Maybe the two of you can write together. Do a collab."

"What's a *collab*?" Sam asked.

"That means we could work together on something," Anna supplied.

"No thanks!" Sam said adamantly. "You write kissing stories."

"*What*?" Anna asked loudly.

"Yeah… I heard you reading out loud last night while you were writing at your laptop."

At first the color drained from her face, but then the blood rushed back quickly flushing her cheeks. Out of the corner of her eye she saw Michael stifling his laughter.

"Go get your shoes on, Sam," Anna instructed quietly.

An amused Michael turned to Anna with a curious smile. "So when am I going to get to read this story, Anna?"

Rolling her eyes, Anna walked away to corral the kids out to the awaiting truck. Once they were on the road, Anna attempted to ask about their mutual, reclusive friend without getting the kids' attention in the backseat.

"Any word from Jake?" she said softly while Sam and Ellie laughed about something that had happened at school.

"He sent me quite the text."

"Oh? Do you mind if I...?" Anna gestured to Michael's phone and he nodded permission.

All of the sudden, Anna paused as she held his phone in her hand. If that had been Jonathan's phone, he would've had a fit. He'd most likely grab it back and yell at her for being nosy. Then another thought struck Anna. It was June. *If everything had stayed the same, in two weeks I would be marrying Jon.*

"What's the matter? Need my pin?" Michael asked sensing her hesitation. He spouted out the numbers needed to unlock his phone.

"You're very trusting with your phone," Anna said numbly as she unlocked the screen.

"Why shouldn't I be? Are you going to change my wallpaper or something?"

"Jonathan didn't like me going into his phone. I just assumed most guys..."

"I'm not most guys. There's nothing there to hide."

"Well, we're not dating either. There's a difference." Anna regretted the words as soon as she said them.

Michael opened his mouth to say something but snapped his mouth shut and remained quiet. Probably a safe move. Anna knew his feelings on starting a relationship. Their words at his family's farm months prior haunted her. She realized she craved being in a relationship again. What was even more distressing to Anna was she wondered what it would be like to be in a relationship with Michael. *Snap out of it. That's not a possibility. Keep focused.*

Opening the texts, Jake's popped up right away. *Are you trying to get Anna killed?* The words made her shudder.

"That's it?" Anna asked.

"Oh, I'm sure he'll have plenty more to say when we get there." Michael grimaced.

No more was said about Jake. The remainder of the conversation centered on the kids until they pulled into the parking lot of the center that facilitated the mandatory visitations.

"While you take the kids inside, I'll text our *friend* to let him know we're close by," Michael said softly and Anna nodded.

"Okay, Kids. How does this work? What does Grandpa do normally?" Anna asked as she walked the sullen kids towards the building.

"He signs us in and the social worker takes us to a room to wait until you come back," Ella groused.

"You just sit and wait?" Anna didn't like that one bit. Why did they keep jumping through hoops for Jared?

"They have toys and video games." Sam shrugged.

"I guess that's something." Anna scanned the front foyer.

"Ellie and Sam. How nice to see you again," a plump woman with short hair appeared to usher the kids into a room. "So far you're the first to show. Go ahead and make yourselves at home."

The woman turned to Anna. "You're their aunt? Mr. Munson had called to let us know you'd be bringing the kids today. Can I see your ID?"

"Oh, sure." Anna reached into her purse and grabbed her driver's license. "So how long do I leave them if he doesn't come?"

"An hour is reasonable. If he *does* come, he's allowed to visit with them up to three o'clock."

Anna watched as a meeting room door opened and a crying woman exited. She held tightly to a child only to pass the little girl off to a waiting social worker. Many tears followed. The child cried. The parent cried. It broke Anna's heart to witness. Yet, it was a different experience than her niece and nephew had every visit. Their father *never* showed. She tried to squelch the bitterness rising up in her as she walked out the doors back to the parking lot.

Her mind was so consumed with the children she almost ran head long into a man carrying giftbags and a bouquet of helium balloons.

"Oh, I'm so sorry. Excuse me," Anna said politely.

"*Red*? Is that you?" the man asked and Anna's head popped up. Only one person ever called her *Red*. She loathed it. Shock filled her.

"*Jared*?"

The man let out a long slow whistle.

"Look at you… wow!"

Anna heard Michael's truck door open and the footfall as he approached. Jared gave him a stoic side eye and turned his full attention back to her. To say it made her uncomfortable was an understatement.

"Where's the rest of you, Red?" He looked her up and down in a way that made her want to vomit. "Looking good. If I had known you were the one bringing the kids to these visits, I'd have come sooner."

Michael cleared his throat.

"Who's this guy?" Jared nodded at him with an amused expression on his face.

"This is Michael. He's a friend. Michael this is Jared. The kids' father." The words tasted like bile on her tongue as she said them.

"It's a pleasure." Michael held out his hand, but his tone betrayed the sentiment.

Jared made no effort. "Sorry. My hands are full."

"The kids are inside waiting. Just like they have every time they've come here expecting to see you," Anna tried to control the rage building up. She felt Michael's hand on her back.

Jared laughed and winked at her. "Still fiery, I see. Maybe even more fiery. I guess all that was left of your manners were stored in the fat you lost."

This time Anna had to put a hand on Michael's arm as she felt him lurch forward.

"We should go and let Jared see his kids. It's been a while. They should have a lot to catch up on."

Jared nodded with a smirk. "Always a pleasure, Red. Oh... where are my manners? How's my tweaker of an ex-wife been? Has she been frequenting any new gutters lately?"

Michael's hand covered hers and she felt him tug her toward the truck. Good thing he did. Anna was about to try out a few of her kickboxing moves on her ex-brother-in-law.

"Breathe." She heard Michael whisper as they got back to the truck. "In through your nose and out through your mouth."

Anna complied and felt her muscles relax as she watched Jared go into the visitation center. She didn't want to leave the kids. Maybe they should just stay in the parking lot... let Jake Cory find them there instead of them trying to hunt *him* down.

"I have to go be with the kids. He's going do more harm than good," Anna said as she started pulling her hand away.

"Anna, they have trained social workers in there and we have another purpose for this trip remember?"

Anna nodded and tried to calm down. "You're right. Did Jake respond to your text?"

"Yes," Michael said as he opened the door for her.

"Is he mad?"

"Yes." Michael sighed. "He has every right to be."

"It's not your fault. I would've come without you. Maybe next time he'll answer his texts."

Michael looked serious.

"What is it? Did he say something?"

"He gave me an address where to meet him... and a grocery list. How long do we have before we have to pick up the kids?"

"Three." Anna looked at him puzzled. "A grocery list?"

"Looks like we have some time to kill. Are you hungry? We can find a drive-thru and a secluded place to eat lunch. Then I'll run into a store and grab these things."

"Along the water's edge there are a few places. I used to run there. It'll be nice to smell the water again," Anna said wistfully.

"That might be more out in the open than what Jake wants you to be, Petunia."

As they pulled away, Anna glanced back at the center and prayed that whatever was going on inside that meeting room, her niece and nephew would exit unscathed.

22

Michael waited patiently as Anna called the visitation center to check on her niece and nephew. She insisted on calling, claiming she needed assurance that they were faring okay and not traumatized at their father's reappearance. Judging from the little he was able to hear, they were actually enjoying themselves. This caused a mixed emotional response from Anna.

Holding the bag containing two chicken wraps Michael had ordered from the small sandwich shop, he tried to give Anna space as she ended the call. They had parked on a fairly populated street and Michael replayed Jake's texts. They should probably go somewhere out of public sight. Just in case.

"I guess they're okay," Anna sighed.

"Of course they are."

"I'm sorry. I left you holding the bag... literally." Anna attempted a smile, but Michael could tell she was still unnerved at Jared's presence. "Can't we please go eat on the water walk, Michael? I see some benches out of the way. It's not terribly crowded."

Michael looked at the area she pointed out and weighed their options. Saturday in Skennan Cove was different than a Saturday in Deer Creek. Skennan Cove was probably the place everyone from his hometown traveled to spend the day on a beautiful Saturday. The call of the water was a draw for many in that area. Especially those who owned boats.

"I don't know, Anna. It's not a good idea. I'm sorry."

"Maybe just for a minute or two *after* we eat?"

Michael never fancied himself a sucker... until that moment.

"Three minutes. No more."

Anna seemed content with that and the two ate their food, keeping conversation light. When both had finished their lunch, Michael drove as far down the street as he could to a less populated area. The two got out and walked to the water's edge.

"I used to run the entire length of the water walk every morning before work," Anna said reflectively.

"You miss it here?"

"Sometimes. I miss the way things were before…" Anna stopped and snapped her mouth shut and forced a smile. "It had its good parts."

"I can see why people would want to live here," Michael said staring at the waves on the water. "Jake owns a house a little further down on that incline. He turned it into several apartments."

"Is that where he is now?"

Michael shook his head no as he noticed a man walking a little distance away that kept looking in their direction. At first, he looked as though he were walking towards them and then paused, stopping to look out on the water. Every so often, however, he would turn his head slightly and glance at them.

"Anna, do you recognize that man down the walk to your left? The one just standing there?" Michael leaned in close and spoke quietly yet loud enough for her to hear.

He watched her reaction as she turned her head to see the man in question. Anna's back stiffened and she let out a pitiful little moan before turning her head abruptly back to Michael.

"Can we just go? Please?" Anna asked frantically. Her eyes were large but they didn't hold fear. In fact, she looked close to tears.

"Who is it?" Michael asked.

Her breathing picked up almost as if she were getting ready to hyperventilate. Michael put a finger under her chin, lifting it to bring her attention to his face. Her eyes finally met his and not for the first time he got lost in the golden flecks that seemed to dance in her pools of green.

"Who is he?" He repeated.

"It's Jonathan. He was my fiancé."

*****

Anna struggled to catch her breath. What was she thinking coming back to Skennan Cove? First, Jared materialized and then Jonathan just so happened to be on the water walk less than twenty feet from where she stood. Michael held her arms tightly. She appreciated the support. Truly, she wasn't sure her legs were going to move without betraying her in some horrifically awful clumsy fiasco in front of Jonathan.

"Please tell me he didn't notice us," she whispered softly. She watched as Michael's eyes looked past her and she hissed, "Don't look. What are you doing?"

Michael rolled his eyes with a sigh. "How am I supposed to see if he saw you if I can't look?"

"Does it look like he recognized me?"

"He's walking over."

"No. No. No." Anna muttered under her breath.

"Hey," Michael got her to look up into his face. "Just follow my lead."

"What are you going to …"

"I'm returning the favor." He smiled down at her and she felt her knees turn to mush. His forehead lowered and rested against hers. "Can you *try* to act normal please? You look like you're going to throw up."

"That's not far from the truth," Anna wheezed.

That moment was anything but normal. Anna was keenly aware of Michael's hands on her arms and his face so close to hers. His soulful brown eyes gave her a place to stare, but she felt like she was getting lost in them.

"Remember… follow my lead. For all he knows, we're together," Michael whispered.

"I'm going to be sick."

"Nice. Thanks for that validation, Petunia."

She relaxed and rested her forehead against his and closed her eyes, trying to compose her racing thoughts.

"Annalise? Is that you?" Jonathan questioned from behind her.

Anna took a breath and turned slowly. Michael released her shoulders, but his one hand slid down and took her hand. His fingers intertwined with hers as they stood side by side facing the man Anna had been prepared to pledge herself to just months prior.

Mustering the strength, Anna managed to get out, "Hello, Jonathan."

"Wow… you look amazing." After the words were out, Jonathan looked flustered - similar to how he looked when they first started dating. "I never pictured you with shorter hair, but it works."

"Are you going to introduce me, Babe?" Michael spoke up and gave her hand a squeeze.

Something about him calling her *Babe* made her want to giggle despite the tenseness of that moment. "Jon, this is Michael. Michael, this is Jonathan."

"Ahh, yes. *Jonathan*. It's nice to meet you."

Jon gave Michael a curt nod but redirected his attention back to her. "I heard you had moved. What brings you back here?"

"I had some business to attend to."

"Someone came to my apartment looking for you after you left. They wanted to know where they could reach you. I didn't have an address to give them. And none of my texts or calls seemed to go through."

Because I blocked you, You Fool! Anna screamed inside her head.

"I tried to find you, but you kind of just disappeared into thin air." There was a hint of scolding in his expression and tone.

Anna let out a slight laugh. "There wasn't exactly anything keeping me here, was there?"

At first, Jonathan looked as if he had been slapped, but he recovered quickly. "Where are you living now?"

Michael cleared his throat as if sending her a warning. Anna did not need his reminder to keep her location secure.

"A few towns over. How is Kirstyn?" Anna tilted her head with a hint of nervy sass.

"Do you think we can talk in private, Anna? No offense to you... Mike, was it?" Jonathan looked at Michael and returned his gaze to Anna. "There's just a lot I want to say to you."

"I don't think that's a good idea," Anna said as she saw Michael puff out his chest next to her. She wanted to laugh at the demonstration of machismo.

"Can I call you? Please, Annalise."

"I don't think that's a good idea either." This came from Michael. Having him by her side felt right.

"I'm not talking to you," he bit out at Michael. "Anna, be reasonable."

"Reasonable?" Anna laughed out loud at the word.

"I... still love you. Kirstyn was a mistake. I miss you, Anna." His tone was pleading, almost heart wrenching.

Anna remained silent drawing strength from Michael's hand as it held hers tightly.

"Come on, Anna. Surely you think of me. You must feel something still." In a rare showing of emotion, he reached out for her other hand. "Our wedding date is just two weeks from today. Don't you think about what it would've been like?"

Recoiling her hand, Anna stood in stunned shock. Michael must've sensed her inner struggle because he leaned down and pressed a gentle kiss to her forehead, snapping her from her tortured thoughts.

"We should get going, Petunia." His expression was one of pure tenderness.

"Petunia? What in the…" Jonathan looked beside himself as if finally realizing he had lost his hold on her.

"Goodbye, Jonathan." Anna looked her ex-fiancé in the eyes before turning and walking to Michael's truck.

Micheal opened the door for her and she felt his scrutiny on her face as she climbed up.

"Are you okay? That was kind of…"

"Intense?" Anna supplied. "Yeah, I think I'm okay."

"Sorry if I went over the top." Michael smirked.

"I think we're even now. The girls at church have backed off and I doubt Jonathan would be stupid enough to try to reach out now," Anna concluded.

"So, you're saying no more pretend relationships then?"

"That's exactly what I am saying," Anna said thoughtfully, though she still relished the feeling of his hand holding hers. Michael might be able to bounce back from their imaginary involvement unharmed, but Anna was starting to think she was very much falling in love with Michael Tyler.

*****

Before Michael could follow the directions Jake sent his phone, he needed to stop at a store to pick up the small list of items his friend needed.

"Tell me again why we're doing his grocery shopping?" Anna looked perplexed as Michael brought the truck to a stop in front of the minimart.

"My guess is it's for the very reason *you* shouldn't be back in this area. People might recognize him." Michael gave her a pointed look before adding, "Stay put. Keep your head down. I'll be quick."

She gave him a perturbed look in return, but he didn't care. She had been spotted *twice* in the short time they had been in Skennan Cove... two very awkward and unpleasant situations. Though Michael had to admit pretending to be her boyfriend was surprisingly enjoyable.

Anna's hair smelled sweet like cinnamon and vanilla. He might've lingered there a little longer than he had intended. Something about holding her close felt right... and Michael did not like it one bit. He had resolved to stay unhindered from any relationship, but in the brief moments that he had held her hand Michael could see himself quite content to do it again.

Several months prior, Michael told Sean that holding hands was the woman's way of tethering a guy down. His brother had just laughed and told him, "*If it's the right person, you want to be tethered.*" Maybe for the first time, it started to make sense to Michael. It scared him to death. And he had to admit... hearing Jonathan plead for Anna to return back to him terrified him as well.

"What are we looking for?" Anna asked coming up beside him, startling him in the canned food aisle.

"What are you... Did you not hear me say to stay in the truck?" He responded harsher than he meant to and instantly regretted it.

Anna's chin rose and he sighed, bracing for her inevitable spicy response.

"Oh, I'm sorry. Did I *disobey* you?"

"Alright. Alright. I'm sorry. That was a jerk thing to say," he apologized.

"Yeah it was." Anna agreed readily.

"It's just that the more we're here, the more I'm realizing this might have been a big mistake."

"Well, it's too late now and I had to use the bathroom," she pointed out. "By the way, if you need to use the restroom ... hold it in."

Anna's face broke his resolve and a smile tilted the edges of his mouth. She was starting to garner a reputation regarding public facilities.

"Noted."

"So, what's on the list? Maybe we can divide and conquer?" Anna looked over Michael's shoulder to the list and the scent of cinnamon wafted to his nose once more.

"Cinnamon sugar." Michael thought he said the words in his mind, but Anna looked up at him confused.

"What? Why does he need that?"

"I mean dog food. It's over here." Michael quickly moved away and grabbed the brand Jake specified. *Dan and Sean can never know about this or they will never give me peace.*

Moments later, everything had been purchased and they followed the directions Jake had texted. The truck turned down a few country roads until they came to a cemetery.

"I think you took a wrong turn," Anna said looking around at the headstones.

"This is the location he sent." Michael scanned the perimeter until he noticed a truck parked further inside the cemetery. "I see his truck."

"I don't like cemeteries," Anna said under her breath, clutching the manilla envelope containing the pictures.

"I think they're peaceful. It was smart thinking to have us meet him here." Michael drove down the narrow winding road to a small parking area and pulled in next to Jake's truck.

Jake wasn't inside. The windows were rolled down and Goose stuck his head out of the front passenger window. Anna, drawn like a moth to a flame, went towards the dog.

"Anna... Goose is not the petting type," Michael warned, but of course she didn't heed him. *Why is she so blasted stubborn?*

"Oh… my… word!!! Look at your sweet face! Aren't you so handsome," she gushed in a baby talk.

"Anna, really! You don't want to touch…"

But it was too late. She held out her hand and just as she reached out for the dog, he barked loudly and aggressively in rapid fire succession. Anna flew backwards in fear, crashing into Michael and pushing him into the side mirror of his own truck.

"Goose, *halt*." An authoritative voice sounded from among the headstones and trees. Instantly the dog sat back on his haunches, but his eyes remained on Anna.

Anna was still standing on Michael's feet and still leaning against him, afraid to move. He slid her to his side before pulling his back out from his now folded in mirror.

"I tried to tell you. Goose is *not* Bentley."

"Why is he so angry?" Anna asked in shock.

"Come on. I think Jake wants us to follow." Michael tugged on her arm and walked in the direction of where his friend stood.

Jake's scowl was unmistakable.

"Before you yell at me for bringing Anna back to Skennan Cove," Michael began, "We got the things you needed. It's all in my truck."

Jake's expression softened slightly. Then he turned to Anna.

"Are those the pictures?" he asked nodding at the envelope clutched tightly in her hands.

"Yes. I had a friend blow them up." Anna handed him the packet. "The guy in the hoodie was there the night your friend ran into me. The other guy is…"

Jake sighed as he looked at the images. "Nick. I suspected as much."

There was a moment of uncomfortable silence as Jake looked at the pictures in his hands before he turned his attention back to Anna.

"Do you have any idea how dangerous this was, Anna? I know you're trying to help, but I'm trying to keep the bad guys from finding their way to you. You coming here…" Jake shook his head in disgust. Then he leveled Michael with a look as well. "And you… Why would you offer to drive her here after I told you to make sure she stays put where she was?"

"She was coming anyway. Regardless of whether I came or not," Michael pointed out. Clearly, Jake had no clue the extent of Anna's stubbornness. "And… I might add … no one has heard from you in days… weeks. I was worried about you, Cory."

Jake sighed. "I appreciate that, Tyler. This was still stupid."

"Yeah… I can see that now."

His friend must've picked up on something in his tone. "What happened? Did someone recognize you?"

"Well…" Anna sounded like a child trying to hide something from a parent.

"Who?" Jake demanded.

"Just my former brother-in-law and my ex-fiancé."

"*Just*? Oh, is that all?" Jake rubbed his temples and sighed loudly. "Come with me, Anna. I want to show you something."

Anna looked over at Michael in uncertainty, but moved to where Jake led her. They stopped at a freshly packed grave. There was a small marker, but a stone hadn't been placed yet. The name on the marker read Lewis Sparks. Anna's eyes filled with tears at the sight and Michael resisted the urge to reach out for her.

"He knew *less* about this situation than you do," Jake said quietly. "Do you think they'll just leave you alone?"

"So it wasn't a …"

"It wasn't a suicide." Jake shook his head. "I found duct tape at the scene and he had ligature marks on his wrists and residue over his mouth."

"Why are they saying it's suicide then?"

Jake grunted. "The duct tape I had the technician bag at the scene mysteriously disappeared. The coroner's report conveniently left out the residue even after he had told me what he found. We're not just dealing with street thugs, Anna. There are people in positions that can find you and hurt you. Understand what I am saying?"

Anna swallowed hard and nodded slowly as she stared at her friend's name and the dying flowers laying on top of the mound of dirt.

"Is Martin still working or did he retire?" Jake turned to Michael, referring to Detective Luke Martin, a longtime friend of the Tyler family.

"He retired last year."

"He might have people he still trusts at the department. Anna, talk to Luke and let him know what's going on, but no one else." Jake waited until she looked him in the eyes. "I'm hoping you don't take any unwanted attention home with you today. You'll need someone looking out for you on that end."

"What about you, Jake? Are you going to be okay?" Michael asked.

"I'll be fine. Goose and I are laying low until Branson takes out the trash at the office." Jake smirked. "Did I hear you were in the ER, Anna? What happened?"

Anna looked uncomfortable. "Bee sting."

"Bee sting? I thought it was something serious." Jake looked confused.

"I'm highly allergic. I guess I put the Anna in anaphylaxis." Anna let out an adorable snort in her laugh and immediately looked mortified.

For the first time in a long while, Michael saw Jake smile. It was good to see. Hopefully, the danger would blow over quickly and everyone could go back to their normal, boring routines. *Then again*, Michael thought to himself as he watched Anna step around every grave so as not to step on the deceased, *life with Anna Munson could never be boring*.

23

Sunday after church, Michael convinced Anna to sit down with Luke and tell him what was going on and to get his advice on who was trustworthy at the police department.

"Another one?" Luke had asked shaking his head and looking at Michael with an odd expression.

"Another one *what*?" Anna questioned.

"The Tylers seem to be attracted to ladies in danger."

Anna's eyes got wide and was about to tell Luke that he misunderstood her and Michael's relationship, but Michael spoke first.

"I'll remind you, Sir, that one of those women is your own adopted daughter." Michael smirked and Luke backed down. Anna looked at him wondering why he hadn't set Luke straight. Did she dare to hope that Michael was changing his thoughts?

"Well, if you're asking who I would trust in Deer Creek with this information, my old partner Cal is the first person that comes to mind. I'd trust him with my life. Do you want me to talk to him for you... off the record, of course?"

"Would you?" Anna felt instant relief. "I don't know how much to say... who to trust... I've never been in a situation like this."

"Does your father know about this? He's acting quite in control of his emotions for someone whose daughter can bring down an entire crime ring."

"Not exactly." Anna looked away from Luke, who crossed his arms against his chest. "I was looking for a moment when the kids weren't around, but..."

As if on cue, Sam came running to his aunt and handed her the coloring page he had done during Sunday school. Luke nodded then as if he understood. "Don't put off that conversation. No father wants to find out his daughter has been carrying something this big all alone."

Anna nodded and Luke gave her a gentle smile before adding in a whisper Sam couldn't hear, "Keep a low profile. I'll be in touch after I talk to Cal."

Luke tousled Sam's hair before taking his leave. "You're not carrying anything. What does Mr. Martin mean, Aunt Anna?" Sam asked with a quizzical expression on his face.

"Nothing, Little Dude. Let's go get some lunch, okay?" Anna gave Michael a side glance, noticing he hadn't dismissed himself yet.

"What's on the menu today?" he asked as he walked side by side with she and Sam.

"Oh no. I'm not falling for this again. I'll tell you what *I* made then you'll tell me what *Colleen* made… then you'll ditch me." Anna laughed.

To her surprise Michael didn't offer a joke or flippant comment. In fact, he looked rather serious. He continued to walk alongside her towards the house until she paused and turned to face him.

"I'm going to make a stir fry. Does that sound appealing to you?" Anna asked.

"That sounds great actually." A small smile formed, but not his usual buoyant grin.

"Really?" Anna resented the high pitch tone in her voice. "Okay. Cool. Stir fry it is then."

"Are you sure you don't mind me inviting myself to lunch?" Michael's smile grew amused, possibly picking up on her awkwardness. "Things feel weird at home since Jen got married."

"Not at all. Although, the house may be a little messy. My schedule has been busy and I haven't had a lot of time to straighten up for company." Images of the laundry pile on the couch and dishes in the sink sank her stomach.

"I'm not company. It's just me." Michael's smile took on a whole new life… tender… gentle… soft. What was happening? *Don't read into it, Anna.*

"Do you mind waiting here?" Anna asked as they got to the door of the parsonage.

He smirked and shrugged while Anna entered the house and went into lightning mode.

"Sam, grab those clothes on the couch and throw them on my bed. Ellie? Ellie, where are you?" Anna called until Ellie poked her head from her room. "Start working on the dishes. Michael is joining us for lunch."

"Michael is?" Both her father and Ellie said in unison.

Her father, who had walked over earlier with Ellie and Livi, had already changed into comfortable clothes. He smiled as he cleared the books from the table.

"Stop that please." Anna whispered in case Michael heard from his place on the other side of the door.

"What? I don't know what you're referring to?" Her father's eyes grew wide and innocent.

"Don't make this weird," Anna begged. "He's just a good friend."

"If you say so," Tim chuckled. "Are you going to let him in? Or shall I run a vacuum and paint the walls a fresh coat first?"

Anna put her hand on the doorknob and shot her father a warning look over her shoulder.

"Come on in," Anna invited.

Michael walked into the house and smiled warmly at his pastor, shaking his hand.

"This is a pleasant surprise, Michael. I thought you'd be spending as much time with Jen and Ben before they head out." Tim beamed.

"Well, I thought I might be able to convince Anna to let me read her work. And I do like a good stir fry." Michael spoke to Tim, but his eyes were on Anna as she started grabbing veggies from the refrigerator.

She froze mid step.

"What's this now? You want to read my..." she prattled. "It's not done. I told you that."

Did he *like* seeing her flustered? The grin on his face gave him away. She tried to ignore him and set about getting lunch ready. Ellie set the table hastily and mumbled an excuse to disappear into her room.

"You've been spending more time than usual in your room, Ellie. With only a week left of school I doubt you have that much homework," Tim observed.

"I...I'm working on something, Grandpa."

Anna looked up from the skillet. Something in Ellie's voice and demeanor seemed off. Since visiting her father, she had acted strangely. Almost secretive. Was this some type of emotional response to seeing Jared again?

"We have company." Tim's voice held an edge of sternness that Anna was well acquainted with.

"Fine." Ellie plopped down on the couch but she kept looking back towards her room.

Jared had given extravagant gifts to his kids during his visit. Sam received a video game console. Ellie was given perfume that cost more than a day of Anna's income at the school. He had also gotten her expensive ear buds that made Anna envious. If Jared had still been present when Anna and Michael arrived to collect the kids, she would've made him take the gifts back. Yet, the kids seemed so happy. Now Anna wondered, as she watched Sam zone out in front of the TV with a game controller and her niece acting even more reclusive, if she should have insisted the social worker give the gifts back to their father.

"Can I help?" Michael's voice from behind her caught her off guard. "I can throw together a pretty great salad."

"A salad sounds great." Anna smiled as he went into action.

Tim said something under his breath about there being an abundance of vegetables in the house, but Anna ignored him. Her father had shaved ten pounds off his overall weight since she returned home. Her mother would be pleased.

Soon everyone sat at their dining table as Tim blessed the food. Livi threw most of her food onto the floor. Sam chatted nonstop about his new game with Michael and managed to get him to commit to playing one round with him. Michael made comments and asked questions centered around the message Tim delivered during the church service. Tim, of course, responded with delight.

Ellie kept staring towards her bedroom. Anna nudged her niece.

"Aren't you hungry?"

"Not really. I think I may be coming down with something. Can I go lay down please?"

With a sigh, Tim nodded and Ellie disappeared behind her shut door.

"Me too. I don't think I can eat another bite." Sammy said dramatically.

"I'm sorry to hear that," Michael said with a smirk. "I was hoping to play that game with you, but if you're not feeling well..."

"Maybe it's just gas. Yup. That's all it was," Sam said emphatically before taking two large bites of his lunch.

Anna started clearing plates and sent Michael an appreciative smile.

"How about you get the game queued up while I help your Aunt Anna?"

"Okay," Sam answered Michael excitedly.

"Well, I guess since you are taking my chore of dish duty, I'll put Livi down for her nap." Tim winked at his daughter. "You are more than welcomed to come over anytime if it means I get out of doing dishes, Mike."

Anna groaned inwardly as she turned on the garbage disposal in the sink. Michael just smiled as he brought the remaining plates.

"You rinse and I'll load the dish washer. I know you and this machine have an interesting relationship," he teased as he pulled out the bottom compartment and neatly placed the dishes inside.

"You're funny." Anna pretended to grouse.

"Anything to speed things up. I'll play a game with Sam while you grab your laptop."

"My laptop? For what?"

"So I can read your story. I got a glance at your chapter outline. It looks awesome."

Anna turned to look at him.

"But it's not done… and it might not even be any good, Michael."

"Or it might be awesome," Michael shrugged. "But if you don't want me to see it …"

"You really want to read it?" Anna bit her bottom lip. "If you'd trust me with it… yes I really want to read it."

Anna smiled. She had gotten a little further in her story line, but wondered if she was making sense. It would be helpful to have another pair of eyes on it.

"Do you promise not to laugh or to make fun of it? It's kind of… *personal*."

"I promise."

She looked up into his face, scanning for even the slightest eye twitch or involuntary muscle movement near his mouth. Michael was the picture of sincerity. She couldn't believe she was even entertaining the notion of letting him read her work. This was *her* story. This was Anna in word form. What if he didn't like it?

As promised, Michael joined Sam in the living room. Anna listened to the funny competitive bantering as she held her laptop to her chest. Just a few months ago, she never would've considered letting Michael read her writing. But then again, she wouldn't have had any writing for him to read at all.

Nervously, she brought her laptop to the dinner table and put it down with her document pulled up and ready to go.

"You beat me, Sam. I give up," Michael told his little buddy before getting to his feet.

"Just one more game... please?"

"Maybe later, okay?"

Michael moved to sit down at the table in front of the laptop and all of the sudden Anna felt shy and self-conscious.

"Do you want some coffee while you read? An oatmeal raisin cookie? A banana?"

"I never turn down coffee," he said with a warm smile as he started looking at the laptop screen.

"Coffee. Got it." Anna turned to get the coffee started and caught her side on the corner of the kitchen island. She suppressed the words she wanted to say at the sudden pain and forced an awkward smile.

"You okay, Anna Banana?" her father called.

"Great." She gave her father a thumbs up.

"Do you call her Anna Banana because of her obsession with bananas?" Michael inquired with a laugh. "She's always got a banana handy."

Tim laughed before launching into a childhood tale of Anna's nickname.

"In kindergarten... before we moved here... Anna was the banana in the school play. She had to do this little dance in a banana costume that her mother made. It was way too long for her..."

"Would you like some coffee, Dad?" Anna interrupted and gave her father a glare.

"I'd love some. Thank you." He smiled before finishing his story. "Anyway, she danced too close to the edge of the stage and started to fall down the stairs. Thankfully, she was so well insulated in that costume she just kind of rolled down them."

Michael's laughter echoed through the house. "She landed right at our feet in the front row, looked up and said *I'm good.* She got up and waddled right back up on stage to finish her part." Tim looked highly pleased with himself. "And *that* is why she is my Anna Banana."

"I'm sure you needed to know all of that," Anna muttered as she put down a piping hot mug of coffee next to the laptop.

"That's adorable." Michael beamed at her. "So the whole *Anna's Law* thing started pretty early in life then?"

"Oh, you've heard about that?" Tim chuckled.

"Here's your coffee, Dad. I think Michael wanted to read. Don't you have to get ready for tonight?"

"No, I'm ready for the service." Tim got the hint and rose to his feet with his mug. "But if you'll excuse me... I think I might enjoy reading a good book myself."

A few moments later, Anna found herself nervously milling around the room, every so often watching Michael's face for his reaction to her story. A few times he grunted and then chuckled at one of her more humorous parts.

"Which part are you on?" she asked.

"Are you going to keep watching me read? It's very distracting, you know," he said with a smile, but never took his eyes off the screen.

Finally, he sighed and shut the laptop.

"Well? What do you think?" Anna asked carefully.

"You've got a great story so far. I can hear your voice in my head when I read it," Michael answered. "I can't wait to read more, *Anna Banana*."

"Stop…" Anna groaned. "I will take Petunia over that nickname any day."

"Really?" Michael looked intrigued.

The two stood staring at one another for a few moments when Michael finally looked away first.

"I should head home, but I will see you tonight at church."

"Yeah. I'm… I'm glad you could come over." Anna fidgeted with her hands as she followed Michael out the door. Just as he was about to walk down the driveway Anna stopped him. "Mike."

He turned and looked at her with a sweet smile.

"You really liked it? You're not just trying to spare my feelings?"

He moved back to stand in front of her and put his hands on both of her shoulders. "You are probably one of the most talented writers I have ever read. Don't stop. Finish it."

She smiled a watery smile and then Michael did the unexpected. He pressed a kiss to her forehead and left. Her heart thudded in her chest as she watched him walk to his truck and drive away.

"I was hoping to catch him before he left," Tim said coming up beside her and causing her to jump.

"Oh, I think you have said quite enough to Michael Tyler today, Dad."

"I hope you know I share those stories because they are precious to me. *You* are precious to me," Tim said softly. "I wanted him to know that you've always been that resilient girl… the one who lets God help her rise above it all. I think *he* sees that, too."

Anna turned teary-eyed towards her father, ready to crush him in a hug when she noticed a thick stack of papers in his hand.

"What's that?" she asked.

"Just a good book I was reading."

Her father held it up with a proud smile to show his daughter. The pages were yellowed with age and the picture scrawled on the cover was rudimentary indeed. However, the title transported Anna back to a long time ago when she was in fifth grade with her best friend sitting in the library. *Super Mike to the Rescue.*

*****

"Where are we in handling our little *nuisance*?" the deep growly voice questioned Nick late Sunday night.

"I think we're finally getting somewhere. Our informant gave us a location and I passed it on to the Broker's men. Now we wait for them to do their part."

"I have no confidence in Davidson's people. I feel our relationship is about to have an abrupt end."

Nick knew exactly what Damon was insinuating and hoped he'd get to play a part in that break up.

"And what about your partner? Any news on Cory?"

"No. He's in hiding, but he can't hide forever. He doesn't have that much time off accrued." Nick smirked. He never pegged Jake Cory as a coward, yet the facts didn't lie. He had all but disappeared from the face of the earth.

"You know, Nick, you're getting to the point where you're going to need to decide who you're loyal to."

"Excuse me?" Nick wasn't about to push Damon's buttons, but at the same time he felt he had gone above and beyond in the tasks he'd been given.

"That badge is holding you back. I think you know you make more money with me." Damon laughed.

"It's not about the money."

"Tell me it's about the sense of honor… You're hardly a boy scout, Spencer."

"It's personal. That's all you need to know."

Nick didn't shrink back at much, but Damon's laughing response gave him a moment of concern. He didn't want to do anything to get on the man's bad side. Damon had the power to not only end his career… both of them… but his life.

"I'll tell *you* how much I need to know. Understand?"

"Yes." Nick hissed.

"I didn't hear you."

"Yes." Nick answered a little louder and forcefully.

"Right now, I couldn't care less about your motivations for staying at the department, but when I say you're done… you're done. Understand?"

"I understand."

"Right now, your connections are handy, but eventually you'll be a liability if you stay. And I'd hate to lose you. You're a great *enforcer*."

Nick sighed. "What do you need me to do?"

"I'm sending you a location now."

His cellphone lit with the address Damon texted.

"It's quite a nice little cabin. Too bad it's gotta burn. Make sure the inhabitants go with it."

"And who are the inhabitants?" Nick asked.

"A mutual friend of ours. I want him burnt to ashes. Leave nothing behind."

24

Lance Davidson stared mindlessly into the flames in the fireplace. At any other time, the setting would've been cozy. A quaint cabin in the woods of Deer Creek. The crackling fire. The sound of crickets intermingled with other woodland wildlife. Kyra humming in the kitchen as she made his old fashioned on the rocks. However, this was no vacation.

Every so often the Broker looked down at his cell phone to see if the message he was waiting for came through. What was taking those fools so long? They had the address. They had the means. How hard would it be to take out one woman?

Damon would be waiting for confirmation that the girl was no longer a problem. Until he could text Damon the good news, there would be no rest for him. "Here you go, Sweetie." Kyra said bringing in the cocktail.

With one large gulp, Davidson drained the whiskey glass and fixated on the ice cubes clinking together.
"Are you going to tell me what's bothering you? You've been agitated the entire drive here." Kyra loomed above him with concern in her eyes. "I thought this getaway was supposed to be fun."
"You're not having fun? Why don't you go soak in the hot tub."
"Are you going to join me?" Her smile was suggestive. Any other night at any other time, he might've followed her out. This was not the night to let his guard down.
"You go on ahead. I'm waiting for a phone call."

Kyra muttered something under her breath and stormed away from him. He heard her go up the stairs to the loft of the rental cabin and begin unzipping her luggage. Most likely looking for her bathing suit. Hopefully she would distract herself so he could focus on the matter at hand. Anna Munson needed to be dead no later than eight o'clock that night. Those were the orders of Damon.

A glance at his phone showed there was only an hour left. What would happen if there was a minute or two delay? Did Damon and his enforcer have a plan in place? A chill ran down the Broker's spine at the thought. Somewhere along the way the predator became the hunted. It was a feeling he never wanted to experience again. *Rob and Keith better not mess this up.*

*****

Monday night found Anna in a rare moment of solitude. Her father was at a pastors' dinner with a few of the other local clergymen. Dan and Kate invited the kids to come along to a movie with them and Eli while Tessa and Sean entertained Livi. Anna found herself alone after a day of getting the library ready for the end of the school year.

She didn't expect to feel sad over collecting the library books from the students, but she realized she was going to miss the kids terribly. She felt the melancholy setting in so she decided to go for a run. Yes, she knew Michael would have a lot to say about her decision.

Anna hadn't yet filled her dad in on the events of the past months. If she had, undoubtedly, he would've added another layer of stifling protection.

"As long as I stay close by it'll be fine," Anna rationalized to Bentley as she put on her sneakers and grabbed her hydration belt with her epi pens tucked in the pouch.

Bentley tilted his head at her.

"Don't give me that look. I have a lot on my mind right now."

Bentley rested his head down on his bed with a little groan.

"You just hold down the fort, Bentley. I'll be right back." Anna bent down and kissed the dog on the top of his head and smiled when his tail swished in appreciation. "Good boy."

Putting her earbuds in and turning up the volume, Anna immediately got lost in the music. It was the perfect night for a run… not too warm and not too cool. A breeze blew through the leaves on the trees. The sunset promised to be stunning.

She was going to take the dirt trail that went along the church's property, but noticed a car parked there. It wasn't out of the ordinary for local fishermen to park along that road so they could fish the lake's edge. Still, she opted to stay on the roads surrounding the church.

A call came through on her smart watch and she spotted Michael's name. A small smile tugged her lips. A memory of the day before flickered into her mind. He had kissed her forehead. *Again*. And for no apparent reason other than to show her care. The question was: Did he care for her as a friend or as more? Anna accepted the call.

"How was your day?" he asked.

"Okay. It's sad saying goodbye to the students."

"Why does it sound like you're out of breath? Are you running?" Michael asked.

"Maybe."

"Are you at the gym... on a treadmill?"

Anna bit her lip.

"*Anna*..." His tone held a hint of warning.

"Don't start, Michael. I needed fresh air. We were cleaning the dusty library all day."

"There is no excuse for you to be out in the..."

"Oops. Sorry, Tyler. I think I'm losing you." Anna smirked. "Bad reception on this street."

"Anna. I'm not playing. Do you want me to call Jake?"

"What's he going to do from Skennan Cove? Do you know how ridiculous that just sounded?"

"Yeah... it sounded better in my head. Still though..."

Anna chuckled. "I'm not going to be out long. The kids are at a movie with your brother's family and dad is at a pastors' gathering. I just thought I'd get some time in before they got home."

"Promise me you'll wrap it up and head home now."

"Why, Michael Tyler, it almost sounds as if you care about me." Anna slowed her pace. She desperately wanted to hear him confirm that thought, but he stayed silent for far too long. She changed the direction of the conversation. "You could always put on some running shoes and join me."

"I would, but I'm at work..."

"Oh. Well, you'd slow me down anyway."

He laughed quietly into the phone.

"Just get home, Petunia. Text me as soon as you get there. If I don't hear from you in about twenty minutes, I'm going to call you."

"Fine. If it puts your mind at rest."

Anna made it to her driveway after her run and pulled her ear buds out, putting them back in their case. She'd text Michael, but first she needed to stretch. As was her usual routine, she put her foot up on the bumper of her Jeep to extend her hamstring. When Anna bent over her leg, she saw a trail of droplets on the pavement. Putting her foot securely on the ground, she moved in for a closer look at what resembled smatterings of blood.

Quietly, Anna scanned her surroundings. She saw a mound of golden fur lying at an odd angle near her mother's rose bush in the front yard and she ran to it. *Bentley*!

She was about to scream at the sight of her precious dog oozing blood from a wound to his temple when a sound came from the garage. The *open* garage. Anna knew that the house was shut up tight when she left. All of a sudden, Anna felt exposed and out in the open.

Darting to the side of the house she pressed her back flat against the wall as she heard voices talking to one another.

"She's not here."

"No... really? *Idiot*! Of course she's not here."

"We can't afford to mess this up, Rob."

"Shut up. We're going to wait until..."

Just then Anna's ringtone sounded. *Blasted, Michael*! Her heart nearly stopped as she quickly answered it.

"Call 911. They're here," she whimpered into the phone.

Michael yelled something, but Anna dropped her phone. She had to think and act quickly. Unzipping her hydration belt, she grabbed the only weapon she had at her disposal. Her Epi pens. With one in each hand, she flicked off the lids with her thumbs.

She inched her way to the corner of the house until she saw a man with his back to her, a gun poised to shoot. He eased backwards against the side of the house and Anna knew she had to move fast. If she tried to make a break for it she was as good as dead. She was surrounded by open fields and she didn't doubt they were good shots.

Sending up a quick prayer, Anna sprung from the corner of the house and pounced. With stamina she didn't know she possessed, she jabbed both pens into either side of the man's shoulders and held them in place while he screamed. As soon as his gun dropped she lunged for it while he stumbled around holding his chest with both hands.

"What did you... put in me?" He was unstable on his feet.

"Get down on the ground," Anna screamed as her shaky hands held the gun pointed directly at him. It was then that she realized this was only one of two men.

"My heart... what's happening to me?"

"Shut up!" Anna yelled.

"You stupid... my heart is going crazy. Is it meth? Heroin?"

"Where's your friend?" Anna demanded.

The man acted as though he were dying, clutching his chest. Anna wasn't going to tip him off that he'd be fine after a few minutes.

"*Keith*. I need you, Man."

Sirens filled the air after what felt like an eternity and soon flashing lights emerged from behind the trees bordering the property. In the distance she saw the other man running in the field going towards the direction of the car that had been parked on the dirt path. One of the police officers must've seen him as well because a squad car zoomed in that direction followed by loud screams and yelling.

"Put the gun down... slowly," A voice came from behind her.

"Gladly," her voice quivered as she released the gun to the safe keeping of an officer. "They broke in and shot my dog. He was here when I got back from a run."

"She injected me with something. She tried to kill me. Arrest *her*," the man on the ground said trying to clutch his chest despite the officer pulling his arms behind him.

The cop handcuffing the man looked back at Anna with a raised brow.

"Two Epi-pens. In his shoulders," Anna confessed.

"Medic, over here." The cop called out and an EMT breezed by her to the man on the ground.

"Anna," she felt a hand on her shaking elbow and turned to see Michael. Without hesitation, she buried her face in his chest breathing the scent of stale smoke from his coat. A moment later, Anna felt his arms encircle her and one of his hands gently pressed her head firmly to his heart.

"You know her, Tyler?" the police man asked joining them after handing off the suspect to EMT's and another officer.

"Yes," Michael choked the word out. "This is her house."

They ushered her to a bench in the yard and Michael sat down next to her.

"They shot Bentley," Anna wept, pointing to her beloved friend still lying in the rose bush.

Michael turned to look and his shoulders slumped as he watched the police take pictures of Bentley's body.

"Am I... going to go... to jail for stabbing him?" Her question came out in sobs as she looked up at the officer in front of her. "I didn't know what else to do."

"Try to breathe normally, Petunia," Michael soothed.

"We're just assessing the situation until we get a clear picture of what happened here, Miss," the officer said kindly, but sternly. "Did you really jab him with your Epi-Pens? And then take his gun?"

Michael's face held a little bit of what looked like admiration and pride... and then terror as reality set in. "If I ran away they would've shot me. There was nowhere to hide."

The officer looked around the area at the fields and nodded, hopefully seeing how accurate that statement was.

"Remind me not to get on your bad side." Michael attempted a weak smile.

"He's going to be okay right? Am I in trouble?"

Michael grunted. "The Epinephrine will wear off. He should be fine."

A man in a suit walked up to them and cleared his throat. Recognition registered on Michael's and the other officer's face and they moved to give the man access to Anna.

"Miss Munson? I'm Cal Jenson. I'm assuming this has something to do with the situation Luke was filling me in on earlier." The man took the seat Michael vacated.

There was something about the lines at the corner of his eyes that told her he laughed often. The warmth in his smile made her relax as he waited for her to respond. Just as she was about to speak, Michael's radio sounded off, calling all available first responders to another location.

"I have to go." His tone and expression conveyed his regret and reluctancy to leave Anna.

"It's okay. I'll be okay."

Cal spoke up. "I promise I won't let anything happen to her. Go on, Tyler."

"I'll check in on you later, okay?" Michael squeezed her hand in his to reassure her before leaving.

Anna nodded. Yet as she watched him walk briskly to the fire rescue truck alongside his coworker, she felt the keen absence of his presence and wished she could still be safely tucked in his arms.

*****

"Be advised. The rental office said there are *two* occupants. One male. One female," the dispatcher's voice came over their radios.

Michael listened to the run down as they approached what used to be a luxury cabin. A wooden structure fully engulfed. A small narrow road unable to support the necessary rescue vehicles. By the looks of things, the wired in alarm system did little to get help there quickly enough. Michael's stomach sank. Chances of finding the occupants alive looked grim.

By the time they arrived on scene, another unit had already started drafting water from the nearby lake. The first responders worked hard to contain the blaze before it spread. A tanker truck was enroute. Meanwhile, Michael and Scooter were given the task of scouting the perimeter, looking for places the flames could spread to the trees or brush. Thankfully, the trees surrounding the cabin stood a good distance away from the fire.

Movement off to the side caught Michael's attention. The closer he got, he noticed a streak of crimson in the grass leading to an area of overgrowth. The badly burned legs of a female trembled under the branches of an evergreen tree.

"Scooter, I have a victim," Michael spoke into his radio and his friend moved to his location. "We need EMS… west end. A female… badly burned. With a…"

Michael froze in terror at the sight. A large gaping hole in the upper part of her chest- one of the only places she wasn't burnt - poured out blood over the remnants of what looked to be a bathing suit.

"We have a gunshot victim. Burned on the right half of her body. Thready pulse." Michael struggled to put the words together.

Maybe it was because his heart was still racing from Anna's close call, but for a split second he saw Anna's face right there on the victim… gasping for air. He wanted to vomit.

Anna's words from earlier echoed in his head. *Why, Michael Tyler, it almost sounds as if you care about me.* She had no idea just how much he *did* care. Even Michael hadn't realized how much. That is, until he grasped how close he had come to losing Anna at the hands of those intruders. And it scared him. Losing Anna scared him. Losing *himself* scared him as well and he felt that happening the more he allowed himself to care for Anna Munson.

Kneeling next to the frightened woman, Michael tried to calm her. Surely it was more than an odd coincidence that there was a suspicious fire and a gunshot victim on the same day as Anna's attack. Her eyes weren't looking at anything in particular, but her lips were moving as if she was trying to speak. He pulled off his helmet and leaned in close to hear her.

"Can you hear me? Help is coming," he said loud enough to get her eyes to move in his direction. "Stay with me. Can you tell me your name?"

"Kyra," she choked out.

He recognized the sound of the death rattle settling in. He knew there was no way she would walk away from this alive. Her fading eyes met his and she mustered what remaining strength she had to say one name over and over until her voice fell silent forever. *"Lance. Lance. Lance."*

25

Anna lay on her back staring up at the ceiling as the events of that day replayed over and over in her mind. She had to call her father in the middle of his gathering and inform him of what had happened. Then, when he had rushed home, Anna had the displeasure of filling him in all of the horrible details she had managed to keep secret. The kids stayed a little longer at the Tylers' home until Bentley's body had been removed as evidence. It was gut wrenching to hear her father tell the kids that Bentley was gone followed by their sobs. *This is my fault.*

Swiping at her tears, Anna sat up and looked at her phone. Michael had said he would check on her after his shift, but it was two hours past. Maybe he was exhausted after the call. Or maybe he forgot about her all together. *Don't sulk, Anna. It's not Michael's job to make you feel better. Only God can give peace.*

For the hundredth time that evening, Anna prayed for comfort and the ability to fall asleep. It was after she rolled over and put the pillow over her head that she heard the *ding* from her phone. She lifted the pillow off of her face just enough to read the text.
"Are you still up?"

And sometimes God uses people to accomplish His purposes.
"Yes." Anna texted back.

She watched as the dots went across her screen indicating he was typing a response. Finally, it came.
"Can you come outside?"
"Right now?"
"Please," was his short response.

"Give me a minute."

Anna got up quickly and put on the clothes she had been wearing earlier that day. They were still draped over her desk chair. She ran to the bathroom and wet her hair down, scrunching her curls into place. The house was eerily quiet. Normally, Bentley would get up from his bed and pad across the floor to see who was up. His bed remained empty and cold. A fresh wave of tears threatened to fall, but Anna pushed forward to the side door.

Flipping the outside light on she saw him. He stood still in her driveway, hands in his pockets as he awkwardly kicked a piece of gravel. There was something about his countenance. Sad. Sullen. Shoulders slumped.

"Hey," Anna said quietly as she slipped out of the house. "Are you okay?"

He lifted his head up and Anna could've sworn she saw moisture on his cheeks.

"I couldn't save her. She died in my arms." The words were etched with pain.

"Oh, Mike." Anna rushed to stand in front of him, but paused not knowing what to do. She wanted to hug him and offer comfort, but at the same time she was painfully aware it might not be appropriate. "I'm so sorry."

He reached out and grabbed her, pulling her into an embrace. She could hear his sniffle as he nuzzled the side of her head. Anna's heart leapt and longed to stay right there forever in his arms… in his smoke scented hug. However, he released her and she backed away. He moved to sit on the bench in front of their house and she followed.

"She was charred all over and... and was shot in her chest," he said with his head in his hands. His voice was slightly muffled and Anna thought maybe she had misheard him.

"*Shot*? Who was she?"

He raised his head to look at her. "Her name was Kyra. She was Davidson's girlfriend. They checked the registration of the car in front of the cabin. It belonged to Lance Davidson, Anna. His remains... what they believe to be his remains... were found inside."

"He's... *dead*?" Anna's mind went in a million different directions, uncertain of what that meant for her situation.

"Cal was on the scene. You should probably expect a call from him tomorrow." Michael stared out into the dark night. "She was so scared. I've seen people die before, but the terror in her eyes... There was nothing I could do for her but talk to her. I don't even know if she heard me."

A tear fell to the grass below and Anna put a hand on his arm, giving it a slight squeeze.

"Mike, I know you want to save the world... to keep all of us safe from harm," Anna soothed. "But you're *not* God. You're an amazing, sweet, funny man. But you are just a man. You didn't fail her. You did what you could. You did what God wanted you to do for her and that is more than enough."

He turned to look at her then. Her cheeks flushed as his eyes wandered down towards her lips. If he kissed her... impulsively and without real meaning... Well, she didn't think she'd be able to bounce back from another broken heart. Not from Michael Tyler.

"Stay here. I have something for you," Anna said abruptly and got to her feet.

At first, she didn't know if her legs might give out on her as she briskly walked back into the house. Anna froze as she saw her groggy looking father looking at her with a concerned expression.

"What's going on, Anna? Who's out there?" he asked.

"It's Michael, Dad. He lost a victim at the fire. I want to give him this," Anna said quietly so as not to wake the kids. She held up the book she had written all those years ago when they were children. "I'll be back in a minute."

Her father cleared his throat. "I'll wait here."

Anna nodded with a smile and went back outside. Michael was not sitting on the bench anymore but standing by his truck, looking just as tortured as before. "Dad found this." Anna held it out to Michael and at first he stared at it blankly. Then realization dawned.

"*Super Mike to the Rescue.*" He read the title out loud and started flipping through the juvenile tale of heroic antics.

"You've always wanted to be a super hero, Michael Tyler." Anna smiled. "But you're a hero when you are just... *you*."

His eyes met hers and the two stood motionless for several moments until Michael held up the book. "Mind if I take this with me?"

"Sure. I mean, it's yours." Anna smiled nervously and felt her hands starting to shake.

"Thanks." He started to turn away, but paused. "I saw *your* face tonight."

"What? What do you mean?"

"When I looked down at Kyra... I saw you. That could've been you today."

Anna shuddered. "But it wasn't."

"Anna... I don't know what is going on with me. I think about you way too much." Michael shook his head. The words sounded positive to Anna, but his expression was grim. "I was distracted tonight because all I could think about was you. Were you safe? Were you okay after everything that happened? There's a reason I made the choice not to look for a relationship."

She didn't know if she was supposed to respond, so Anna remained silent and stared at the man that had managed to somehow capture her heart.

"I don't want to hurt you... I would never forgive myself if I hurt you like Jonathan did." Michael looked remorseful as if he already had. "I think I need to distance myself a little. I don't know what this is. It's scaring me."

Those weren't the words she wanted to hear. Surely he wasn't serious. He couldn't be serious. The way he had looked at her and held her didn't match what he was saying. *Don't react. Stand tall, Anna.*

"Okay, Mike. If you say so."

Was that hurt on his face? What was he doing to her? Did he want her to cry and beg him to love her? She wouldn't. It didn't work with Jonathan and she would never beg anyone else to care for her again when they clearly did not. Obviously, Anna had just seen what she wanted to see all those times he acted as though there was more going on than friendship.

"I should go back inside. My dad is waiting. Get some rest," Anna said softly as she turned her back.

She heard the door to his truck open and the ignition start as she put her hand on the handle of the screen door. She glanced back in time to see his red tail lights leaving the parking lot. Her throat felt constricted and she tried to stifle the tears.

"Is he okay?" Tim asked a little more awake than before. "I thought I was going to have to come out and chaperone you two for a minute."

Her father smiled and Anna forced herself to smile as well so she wouldn't worry him. She allowed Tim to pull her into a hug as a tear slipped free. "No. We're just friends. That's all we'll ever be."

*****

"Gentlemen, I'd like to introduce you to my new Broker," Damon announced with a beer in his hand as Nick entered the room.

"*Him*?" a man in a nice suit asked. "I recognize him. He's a *cop*."

The murmuring at the table picked up as people shifted uncomfortably, but Nick just stood quietly with his arms crossed at his chest and a smile on his lips.

"Correction," Damon called out loudly, commanding the attention of all in the room. "He *was* a cop. Nick here was given an option to choose his loyalties and he chose well."

"I don't know, Damon," another man spoke up.

"Well, I *do* know. Nick has been my right hand man now for quite some time. He hasn't let me down yet. In fact, he's been key in handling the mistakes of his predecessor."

"What if the Broker's men are willing to talk to get their sentences reduced?" A man that Nick recognized as a high profile politician's advisor asked. "What's being done about them?"

Nick took a seat next to Damon arrogantly, and spoke up. "That's not going to happen."

Another man, that Nick was pretty sure he had arrested once in the past, started laughing mockingly. "You're going to have to elaborate, Cop. It's going to take more than your word to gain my trust."

"By this time tomorrow night, Davidson's men will all be silenced. That's all you need to know," Nick said in an even tone. He didn't take his eyes off the other man's stare until the other fellow looked away.

"Damon said it himself… You're a great *enforcer*. A killer at best. But do you have the same resources Davidson had?" another man in a suit piped up. "He had connections to get shipments through customs. What do you have?"

"He has *me!*" Damon banged his hand down on the table. "*I* appointed him. He has *my* resources and connections. Davidson was nobody. A dressed up puppet with my hand up his backside. Don't forget that."

The room went silent and Nick's smile grew.

"Now, Gentlemen, any other questions?" Nick asked.

"Yeah… I have one. What's this I hear about a woman that has information on all of us. I don't exactly feel like engaging in business if I'm going to see my face on the news tomorrow night."

"She is under control. I have someone watching her. At the right time, she'll be taken care of," Nick assured.

"Why not right now? Get her out of the way."
"She's being protected by some of my old friends, but don't worry. As soon as they let their guard down… our little pest will be exterminated."

*****

The prison guard checked his watch. Sweat beaded on his forehead as he reached into his pocket and felt the sharpened blade of a shiv. He approached a cell and dropped the shiv between the bars as he pretended to lean against the wall.

"You know your target?"

"I don't know… was the money deposited into my account?" came the surly response.

The guard reached for his phone and showed the screenshot Nick sent him. "It hit ten minutes ago."

"Then yes… I know my target."

Less than fifteen minutes later, the yard was bustling with inmates getting their hour of rec time. The armed inmate walked up to Keith and spoke low enough that only he could hear.

"Your friend Rob wants to see you by the north corner. It's about Davidson."

He waited until Keith nodded and moved on to find his next target. Rob was easy to find… acting like an idiot in front of some lifers. He probably thought he was making an alliance.

"You Rob?" he asked in between animated tales that were most likely made up.

"Yeah. Who wants to know?"

"Come here. I have info on Davidson."

It couldn't have been any easier. Rob moved away from the group who stared after him in irritation.

"What do you know?" Rob asked falling into step alongside the inmate.

"He's not dead, Man. He escaped. And word got out to him that Keith is about to talk. He wants *you* to take him out. He wants to know if he can trust you?"

"He's alive? How? Everyone in here is saying he was burnt beyond recognition."

"Quit talking. Can he trust you to do it?" the inmate repeated, annoyed.

"Of course. Sure, but what's in it for me?"

"You know Davidson's connections. He's going to get you out."

Rob nodded, a smile flickering on his lips. "But what do I do it with?"

"Give me your hand. Don't draw attention." The man slipped the shiv up Rob's sleeve as they walked where Keith stood anxiously waiting.

Keith looked up and saw the two approaching. "This is about Davidson? What's going on?"

With impressive speed and accuracy, Rob lunged and stuck the blade up and under Keith's rib cage. Initially, the third inmate stood blocking the view from onlookers, trusting the guard was also doing his part to distract the authorities from the north corner.

When he caught the eye of the guard the inmate yelled at the top of his lungs and pointed at Rob. "Help! Help! Shiv! He killed him!"

"What's going on, Man? What are you doing?" Rob asked stunned, trying to wipe the blood from his hands.

In a matter of moments, chaos broke out and Rob was buried under several guards. He was escorted to solitary confinement. The inmate continued to play his part as a shocked observer as Rob screamed expletives at him along with threats that the inmate knew he'd never be able to carry out. Dead men don't kill.

It was later that night, after everyone had gone to bed and the lights out call was issued, the guard made his way to the cell containing a battered man. Rob had been heavily sedated in the infirmary by yet another of Nick's men, making the guard's task much easier to accomplish.

He entered the cell, finding Rob on his cot sleeping in a medicated stupor. He needed to move quickly. The shift would change and those in on the plan would leave as if nothing had ever happened. The guard began removing Rob's jumpsuit. Using the legs of the clothing, he fastened them into a noose and put it around the motionless man's neck, constricting it and tying the remainder of the jumpsuit tightly to the bed.

Rob squirmed a bit but gave the guard no trouble as the life drained from his face. The low life should be grateful that his death wasn't as painful as the one afflicted on Keith hours earlier. Sticking his fingers in the man's neck, he was content to discover there was no pulse. Just to be sure, he tightened the noose a little more for good measure. Pulling out his phone, he sent a picture to Nick with the words, "Problem solved."

Moments later, a return text appeared. "Transfer complete." Checking his banking app, the guard smiled when he saw his account balance. This new Broker would work out just fine.

26

Torture. It was absolute torture. Anna forced herself to get up, shower, dress, and get the kids to school... all without letting anyone know how crushed she felt inside. Anna woke up expecting to feel Bentley's snout resting on her leg, waiting for her to take him for a walk. But Bentley did not jump up on her bed or wake her that morning.

Her first thought had been to text Michael, to tell him how sad and lonely she felt. Then she realized she couldn't do that after the conversation they ended on the night before. Her loneliness increased tenfold. *In Him I have my being,* Anna reminded herself of the verse that had become her daily encouragement and reminder. *Not in Michael. In Him. In God.*

The reminder was enough to get Anna to pull out her Bible, read a few Scriptures, and get her focus where it needed to be. Yet, sometime around mid-afternoon her mind started feeling sorrowful again.

"Anna, go on ahead to lunch. I hear the PTO brought in all kinds of food to celebrate the elementary and Jr. High staff," Mrs. Erbe insisted.

"What about you? If you wait too long it may disappear. I once caught Mrs. Hanly putting extra food in her purse to save for later." Anna managed a quirky smile.

Mrs. Erbe laughed. "I have what I need right here. The doctor has me on a special diet anyway. You go. Enjoy."

Anna didn't need to be told again. She grabbed her phone, sneaking a peek at the screen as she slipped into the teacher's lounge. No new notifications since the last time she had checked... ten minutes prior.

"So do you think you'll be back again with us next year, Anna?" Mr. Tenner, the fifth grade teacher asked, waving her into the food line ahead of him.

"Yes. That's the plan." Anna smiled graciously.

After compiling a nice looking plate, she carefully navigated the teacher's lounge. With her food in one hand and her phone in the other, she sought out a place to sit further away from the other people. Her best option was at the table where Ellie's teacher sat. Hopefully, Miss Ballard wouldn't feel chatty that day. "Is it okay if I sit here with you, Miss Ballard?" Anna asked.

"Call me Kelly and of course. I actually wanted to discuss something with you... it's about Ellie."

Anna sighed. "Oh, no. Is everything okay?"

"Well..."

Just then, Anna's phone lit up. Excitement pulsed through her as she expected to see Michael's name pop up on the screen. However, it was Detective Jenson's name.

"Excuse me for a moment. I need to answer this, Kelly." Anna excused herself and found an empty corridor to talk in.

"Anna? How are you holding up?" Cal asked right off the bat.

"How about I just say *fine* even though we both know I'm not."

Cal sighed. "I understand. There's a lot to fill you in on. Do you have a moment?"

"I'm on my lunch break. I can talk." Anna looked back in the direction of the teacher's lounge wistfully knowing her plate of food was getting cold.

The next few minutes consisted of Cal telling Anna that not only was the Broker dead, but also his two cronies ... the men responsible for killing Lewis and Bentley. Their deaths were labeled as murder-suicide. "We're looking into their deaths as well, but according to an inmate they had gotten into a fight while behind bars after news started spreading about Davidson's death."

"What does this mean for me? I don't want to sound selfish. I know people died, but..." Anna wasn't sure how she was supposed to feel. It seemed wrong to be relieved that someone had died, yet she wanted to be safe. She wanted to move on with her life.

"The immediate threat is gone. Unless you know of any other people who want you out of the way?" Anna couldn't tell if Cal was teasing or not.

There was Jake's old partner that had been consorting with the Broker, but would he have Anna in his sight?

"Have you talked to Jake yet? Does he think I'm okay?" Anna wasn't sure how much if anything Cal knew about that end of the issue. She figured it was best not to mention Nick, though she wondered if maybe she should be concerned.

"I was going to try to call him next. He's tricky to catch," Cal said. "For the most part, Anna, I think you are in the clear. Maybe things will get better from here on out."

Anna sighed. "I hope so."

The conversation ended. On the surface level, the news was positive. Anna could proceed with a summer full of plans without looking over her shoulder. Yet, she wondered if that was really the case.

"Is everything okay?" Kelly asked once Anna sat down again at the table.

"An ... *acquaintance*... passed away."

"Oh, I'm so sorry." Kelly's face was sympathetic.

Anna cleared her throat. "What was it you wanted to talk to me about?"

Kelly scooted closer and Anna dreaded what was about to be said. She wasn't a parent, but she felt like she was going to be given news only parents knew how to handle.

"A parent reached out to me this morning. Apparently, her son received a pretty forward text from Ellie's phone," Miss Ballard spoke softly. "I know you and Mr. Munson have very good rules for Ellie and..."

"Did you say Ellie sent a boy a *text*?" Anna's brow furrowed. "That's not even possible. My niece doesn't own a phone."

"I don't know what to say," she said before pulling out her phone and showing Anna screenshots of the supposed texts that were forwarded to her from the boy's offended parents. "Could she be using a friend's phone?"

Anna read the texts. There wasn't anything shocking or explicit, but they were definitely pushy. The numerous texts asked the boy if they could be boyfriend and girlfriend.

"What if someone is sending texts pretending to be my niece?" Anna asked.

"That could be." Kelly conceded. "Though when I brought this up to Ellie she didn't seem surprised."

Anna shook her head as she tried to figure out what to do about the situation. "I will talk to her when we get home. Do the screenshots show a cellphone number so I can do a little digging on my own before I confront Ellie?"

"I'll forward these to your phone. I think the number is on the top of this image."

"Thank you, Miss Ballard. I'll see if I can figure out what is going on." Anna got to her feet then, taking her untouched plate with her back to the library.

There was a reason God started parenthood with a sweet, cuddly baby and not a twelve-year-old pre-teen girl. Once again, Anna harbored resentment for her sister. Alexis should've been the one dealing with Ellie's teachers, not Anna. Anna barely knew how to handle herself at the moment, let alone an angsty pre-teen.

The rest of the day passed uneventfully. Before school, Anna had promised to take the kids to get ice cream to try to ease the pain of Bentley's death. She debated whether to go through with it under the circumstances. However, Sam did nothing wrong. Anna couldn't confront Ellie in front of Sam so the conversation about phones and texts was put on hold until after they got home for the evening.

Anna honored her promise and stopped at the small ice cream shop, but spoke very little. She found herself observing her niece, wondering if Ellie truly sent that boy those messages and wondered how she could have.

She was deep in thought as she stood in line waiting to put their order in when she heard Sam call out to someone enthusiastically.

"Mike! Eli!" the little boy yelled and ran from Anna's side.

As if in slow motion, Anna turned her head to see Michael getting his nephew down from the back seat of his truck. Seeing him there both perked her up and tore her down. With a quick gulp, Anna turned away and pretended not to notice his arrival despite her nephew heralding him as if he were royalty.

"Aunt Anna, look it's Michael," Ellie whispered with a smile and nudged Anna's arm.

"Mmm hmm. I'm sure he just wants to spend time with his nephew. Let's leave them alone."

Ellie gave her Aunt a puzzled expression, but dropped the subject.

"Sam, come back here. It's time to order. What do you want?" Anna called out.

The little boy returned to her side instantly.

"Look! Michael and Eli!" Sam said excitedly.

"Yes. I saw. What would you like? The lady is waiting."

Sam spouted out his flavor of choice and Ellie followed with hers. Anna lost her appetite for ice cream. After she paid, she stepped to the side so the next person in line could order. The kids buzzed around Michael and Eli while they waited for their turn at the window, but Anna did her best to appear uninterested. She had her phone out and scrolled through social media mindlessly.

A few moments later, Anna heard their order announced at the pick-up window.

"Kids, come on. Before it melts," Anna called as she collected both cones and several napkins.

"Can we eat here with Mike and Eli?" Sam asked as he took his cone from Anna.

"Yeah, can we please?" Ellie asked. "You don't want us getting melted ice cream in your Jeep anyway."

Eli grabbed Sam's hand and pulled him to a picnic table before Anna could even answer. Ellie smiled at her aunt and followed behind them, leaving Anna and Michael awkwardly standing in silence.

"Kate had her baby. A little girl. Lydia." Michael blurted out. "That's why I have Eli today. Just being the fun uncle. Keeping him occupied."

He attempted a smile, but it fizzled out.

"That's great… you know, for Kate and Dan. Very exciting." Anna hated how monotone she sounded.

"Yeah."

Michael's turn came and he placed Eli's ice cream order.

"I'll just go wait with the kids at the table," Anna spoke quietly as she turned to go. However, Michael caught her arm, ceasing her escape.

"Did you hear from Cal?" he asked.

"Yes. Sounds like my life can go back to normal." Did he feel the icy edge in her voice? She kind of hoped so.

"Really? Did he say that? You're safe?" Michael sounded hopeful almost pleased.

"Anna! What a pleasant surprise!" Another voice sounded from the edge of the parking lot. "You just saved me a trip back to the church!"

Anna and Michael turned to see Bonnie, the church secretary.

"I got a notice from the post office that they had tried to drop off this package," Bonnie said before opening the door to her back seat and climbing halfway in to retrieve a box. "I went to pick it up and it turns out it was addressed to you. Whoever mailed it, used the church's address and not the parsonage's. What providence that I decided to stop in for a hot dog!"

Bonnie reappeared with a box and handed it to Anna. It had some weight to it. No return address was used.

"Thank you, Ms. Bonnie."

"Of course, Dear." Bonnie looked between Anna and Michael with amused pleasure. "You two enjoy your day now."

With that, Bonnie got in line leaving Anna and Michael in uncomfortable silence once again. The pick up window called out Michael's order and Anna used that time to join the kids, placing the box onto the table.

"What's in it? What's in it?" Sam asked excitedly as if he assumed it would hold some great treasure for himself.

"I don't know. It's probably nothing." Even as she said the words, however, Anna's curiosity grew as well.

"Open it, Aunt Anna," Ellie urged.

Michael reappeared behind her and handed Eli his bowl of ice cream. She could feel his eyes on her as she pulled at the tape. She opened the flaps and saw a card on top of packaging peanuts. Anna pulled the card from the envelope and almost choked on her own breath. It was from Jonathan.

"I know you thought I didn't care, but I never stopped. Please call me."

While Anna had been reading and re-reading the card, Sam plunged into the packaging materials and pulled out a large white binder.

"Whoa. What's this? It's heavy?" her nephew said as the binder landed on the table with a thud.

"Our wedding plans. Jonathan must've gone back for them after I left that night," Anna thought out loud.

"*Jonathan* sent you this?" Michael asked in disgust.

A storm cloud crossed Michael's face and Anna was brought back to reality. The kids were flipping through pages of dress swatches, pictures of floral arrangements, and honeymoon ideas. Dreams that would never come to life. In a surge of heightened emotion, Anna grabbed the binder, threw it back in the box, and lugged it towards the Jeep.

"Time to go, Kids."

"But why? I haven't finished my ice cream," Sam whined.

"Because I feel like I need a little distance," Anna spat out.

She didn't need to turn around to know she had Michael's eyes boring through the back of her head. The kids followed behind her spouting out questions that went unanswered. Her little outburst felt good in the moment, but as she pulled the Jeep out from its parking spot she felt a moment of regret. Michael's head hung, much like it had the night prior. *If he wants distance, I'll give him distance.*

*****

It was early Thursday, that Jake got a call from Sargeant Terry Branson. The call did not begin with a "*Hello, how are you doing?*" Rather…

"Did you hear what happened, Cory?"

"About Davidson and his idiots? Yeah, I heard. Very odd they should be found dead with all that is going on, don't you agree, Sir?" Jake asked.

The man laughed. "Undoubtedly. But that's not what I'm referring to."

Jake's brow furrowed as he tried to think of what his sergeant could mean.

"Nick is gone." The words were spoken so plainly, so matter of fact.

"I'm sorry... *gone*?" Jake sat up a little straighter.

"Yes, gone. Handed in his resignation. Word got out he was being looked at for mishandling evidence. Turns out Lewis Spark's family is fighting to reopen the case."

"Good for them."

"I had someone go by his place to bring him in for questioning. His house is empty. The neighbor said he packed up and moved out days ago. We've got units on the lookout for him."

"What does this mean, Sir?" Jake was pretty sure he knew the answer.

"It's time to come back. Unless you are actually enjoying your vacation." There was an edge of humor in his tone. "I want you to take on the Lewis Sparks case."

"What about the others on the force, Sir?"

"You mean Nick's lackies? I think we'll find they aren't as well hidden as they once thought. There's a sweep going on. Several departments are being audited. Cases are getting the once over treatment. We'll flush them out."

A moment passed as Jake digested all of this new information. Finally, Terry asked him point blank.

"You understand. This doesn't remove you from danger. Nick is still out there," the sergeant reminded him. "But are you ready to get to work, Cory?"

A smile touched Jake's lips.

"Yes, Sir. I'm ready."

27

"I was trying to protect her. To keep her safe from getting her heart broken again." Michael vented to Jake who had stopped in to check in on his friend. "But she's acting like I've done the unpardonable sin."

Jake sat at Michael's kitchen table with a smirk on his face as his friend ranted and paced back and forth. Occasionally, Jake took a sip of his soda and pet Goose's head while he waited for Michael to take a breath. The pizza he brought with him was getting cold, but clearly his friend needed a listening ear. Or a stern talking to. Jake wasn't sure which one at that moment, but he was leaning more towards the latter.

"And I *told* her from day one that I didn't want to be in a relationship. I was perfectly happy not being in a relationship."

Michael finally collapsed into his chair at the table and took a frustrated bite from his slice.

"*Was*?" Jake asked.

"Was what?" Michael looked at him confused.

"You said *I was perfectly happy not being in a relationship* … not I *am*. You said *didn't* … not I *do not*," Jake pointed out. "Did that change, Mike? Because it kind of sounds like it changed."

Michael sat back against the chair and stared at his friend in disbelief. "Are you even listening to what I'm saying? You're getting lost in my grammar and not listening to what I'm trying to say."

"Oh… I am listening alright. For the last hour I've been listening to a man so emotional about someone who he swears he can't get emotional over." Jake leveled Michael with a look. "What are you afraid of, Man?"

Jake watched as his friend wracked his brain for an answer.

"*You* injected yourself into her life… made it *your* job to watch over her. Don't you see it? It's too late to say you're not falling in love," Jake stated emphatically with a laugh. "You're already there. And apparently you bought her ugly flipflops as a memento."

"How did you know about the flipflops?" Michael didn't deny anything.

Jake smiled. "I stopped at Anna's place earlier to check on her before heading here. She was wearing the brightest pair of flip flops I have ever seen. She told me the whole story."

Michael couldn't hide his smile. "She was wearing them?"

Jake nodded.

"The *whole* story?" Michael asked.

"The whole weird story." Jake leaned forward and looked at Michael with all seriousness. "And you know what else? I recognized the look in her eyes when she talked about you. It's a mix of wanting to be mad at you, but also the confusion that comes with being in the early stages of love sickness. I remember it well."

"Love sickness." Michael tried to laugh it off. "I never thought of you as a romantic, Jake."

"Why? Because I'm a loner? It wasn't that long ago I had Beth with me. I know a thing or two about love."

Michael's expression was one of instant regret.

"I'm sorry, Man. I didn't mean anything by…"

"And *that* is why I think you're stupid," Jake spat out.

"Wait… what?"

"You heard me. Stupid."

Jake got up and started putting on his jacket, before turning back to his friend and laying it all on the line. "You are seriously going to let Anna slip through your fingers because of… what? Because you are scared of losing yourself? Scared of growing up?"

Michael snapped his gaping mouth shut.

"Don't you know that God uses the people we love to make us more who He intends us to be?" Jake softened his expression. "Mike, Beth changed me for the better. Before her I was selfish and thought I could do anything on my own. I didn't need anyone. I'd like to think she saw some positive changes in herself too from her time with me."

Jake felt the emotions threaten to come to the forefront. Emotions he didn't let show very often. He buried his hand in Goose's fur for comfort and the German Shepherd looked up at him with soulful eyes. "I miss her. I would give anything to have had more time with my wife."

Michael sat in thoughtful silence.

"If you don't love Anna… that's one thing. But if you *do* love her… and you're just holding out because you think what you have now is somehow better than what it would be with her by your side… Well, I just feel sorry for you, Man. I don't wish the loneliness I feel on anyone."

*****

Michael sighed as he rolled over in bed willing sleep to come. He had to be awake in a few short hours to see his sister and Ben off. Dan and Kate had gotten home earlier that evening with baby Lydia. The day was going to be emotionally charged, meeting his new niece and saying goodbye to Jenna.

Jake's words kept replaying in his mind like a broken record. His friend always did speak his mind. *He's not wrong though,* Michael finally concluded. *I'm scared. What if I fail her, God? What if I'm not good enough? Dan and Sean have the husband thing down pat. It's like they were made for that life. But me... I'm a cut up. A screw up.*

He reached for his phone to see if he had any texts from anyone. His dentist sent him an appointment reminder. Other than that, there was nothing. Michael missed Anna's texts. He scrolled through their past conversations and laughed at a picture she had sent him a while back. It was a picture of her burnt toast. She thought maybe she could see the image of Abraham Lincoln.

The two of them had texted each other quite a lot. More than he had even realized. And then there were the random calls while he was bored during his overnight shifts. Michael remembered one of the last phone conversations they had before that fateful Monday night.

"I think my dad is upset with me," Anna had said out of the blue.

"Why? What did you do now?"

"I don't want to go see my sister. She sent a letter asking for me... but I just don't want to go."

"Hmm. And your dad thinks you should be more forgiving?" Michael had asked.

"Something like that." *Anna had sounded wistful.* *"I think I can see his point, but I haven't talked to her in forever. I just remember how shocked I was to see how she had let herself go. Her missing teeth. She was skin and bones. She was shaking... probably from withdrawal."*

Michael kept quiet as Anna processed her thoughts. "I don't know if I could hold myself together seeing her again if..."

"If what?"

"What if she's worse? I know she says this is the real deal this time, but she's said that before," *Anna sniffed. "And that's what I told Dad. I told him I think it's a waste of time."*

"And he was mad at you?" *Michael tried to envision his pastor angry. "He can't be that mad at you. I can't imagine Pastor Tim angry with anyone let alone his precious Anna Banana."*

"Ha! Do you remember the time that I got feisty at old Mr. Dunquist for heckling my dad about ending his sermons before noon so he could get to the restaurant on time?"

Michael laughed and spat out his drink. "What? No! When was that?"

"I think I was fourteen. He had been saying mean things for a while and I guess I had had enough that day. So, I told Mr. Dunquist that when he started acting like a Christian he could try to preach a sermon himself and see if he could end on time."

"Annalise Munson. I am shocked." *Michael's cheeks hurt from smiling.*

"So was my father. Needless to say, I had to apologize to Mr. Dunquist and then my dad made me write out the whole book of Ephesians."

"I doubt your father is as mad as that day."

"It's worse. You know how our parents do that whole, I'm not mad, I'm disappointed thing? I don't think there's anything worse than disappointing him."

Michael heard Anna yawn.

"Are you tired? Do you want to hang up?" he had asked.

"No. I'm okay."

"I'm going to give you some Michael wisdom…"

"Uh oh. You don't have a bunch to spare."

"Funny," Michael smirked. *"After this whole mess is over, maybe pray about visiting your sister. You've been on this journey of rediscovering yourself and who God wants you to be. Maybe she needs to remember who she is, too."*

A soft snore sounded.

"Anna? Are you sleeping?"

No answer. Michael smiled and whispered *"Goodnight, Petunia"* before ending the call.

At some point Michael had fallen asleep remembering his conversation with Anna. The alarm on his phone stirred him and he readied himself for the early morning farewell breakfast. With a sigh he threw off the covers and did what he had to do as a good brother and son.

By the time he made it to the house, everyone was already downstairs. Jenna held Kate and Dan's baby, Lydia, in her arms and cried ugly tears on the poor kid's blanket.

"I feel like I'm going to miss so much," Jenna hiccupped. Ben stood next to her lovingly and pressed a kiss to his wife's head.

"I'll text pictures every day. I promise," Kate said as her own tears fell in torrents down her cheek.

Off to the side Tessa tried to hide the fact she was also crying. Sean handed her a tissue discreetly.

"These stupid hormones," she muttered.

"Yes, it's all our hormones' fault," Kate chuckled despite the tears. "Or maybe it's just because we're really sad to say goodbye to the baby of the family."

"Breakfast is ready," Colleen said. She looked as though she had never stopped crying since the day she found out Jenna was leaving.

The whole thing made Michael rather uncomfortable. Even his father looked on the verge of misting up. Looking to Dan and Sean for some type of normalcy, Michael only felt the crushing realization that his brothers were drawing strength from their wives. For the first time, Michael realized he wanted that too… no… he *needed* that type of relationship. And not just with anyone, but with Anna.

"Are you going to sit down, Son?" his father asked from his place at the head of the table.

After everyone took their seats, the food was blessed and stacks of pancakes were passed along with every other breakfast food Colleen could think of.

"Are you still planning on stopping and seeing some of the sights on the way down?" Colleen asked Ben and Jenna.

"Well… we *were*, but hotels are too expensive. We're thinking of just driving straight through," Jenna said.

"What if money weren't an issue? When do you need to report, Ben?" John Tyler asked.

"I technically don't need to report until next week, Sir," Ben answered.

Michael smiled as his father pulled an envelope from his shirt pocket and slid it to the younger man.

"This is from all of us. Take your time getting to North Carolina. There should be plenty of money for you to stay a few nights and do some silly touristy things on the way down." John smiled at his son-in-law and daughter.

Jenna and Ben opened the envelope and gasped.

"Daddy! This is too generous."

"Stop it now," John laughed. "You saved us the expense of the wedding your mother was planning. The least we could do was chip in to make sure you have a good nest egg to go back home with."

Colleen cleared her throat and gave her husband a put out look.

"Thank you, Sir," Ben said sincerely and squeezed Jenna's hand in his.

"And you…" John shook his head. "Stop calling me Sir. I'm your father-in-law, not your commanding officer, Ben."

"Yes, Sir… I mean Dad."

"Mom, I'm sorry we didn't get to have the big wedding you dreamed of." Jenna put her head on her mother's shoulder like she did when she was little.

"You're happy. That's all that matters to me," Colleen whispered as she rested her head on top of Jenna's.

"Maybe Michael will finally get serious with Anna and you can throw that big wedding here for them," Jenna gave her brother a mischievous smile while still hugging her mother.

All eyes landed on him. In the past, the notion would have caused him to make an over the top joke to deflect the attention. Or maybe he would've even gotten snarly with his sister for such a comment. For some reason, all he could do was sigh and shrug.

"Weirder things have happened," he said, getting the attention of everyone at the table.

Sean and Dan exchanged smirks. Michael would let them have their little victory. The way he left things with Anna, it wouldn't matter if Michael had a change of heart if they weren't even talking to one another.

Soon breakfast was done and the time had come to say good-bye. Michael held little Lydia while Dan and Kate hugged Jenna and Ben. He stayed on the outskirts of all the emotion until it was his turn. Kate took her baby back and Michael was forced to accept that his baby sister was leaving.

"I don't like this. I can't protect you when you're way down there," he said as he hugged her.

"Pfft. Like you protected me when I lived *here*," Jenna said playfully. "I only remember you putting me in danger... not keeping me from it."

"What? Like when?"

"Uhh, the time you made me climb on top of the tall monkey bars promising to catch me if I fell and then you ran off leaving me stranded." Jenna quirked one eye brow at her brother. "Or how about the time you convinced me to eat twenty radishes as an initiation to your secret club... that didn't even exist."

Michael laughed. "Oh yeah. Those were good times."

Jenna laughed.

"But I hope you always knew- even when I was being stupid- that I love you," Michael said truthfully. "And I will always be here. If you need me, call."

"I know. I love you too, Michael." Jenna's eyes glistened with tears and Michael cleared his throat.

Michael even hugged Ben, whispering a warning that he had better take good care of his sister. And then they were off. Jenna Tyler… now Jenna Clark… was the first of the Tyler siblings to leave Deer Creek. Michael felt incomplete and he pulled out his phone. He had to call Anna.

*****

Anna had been up for a while. Early morning Wednesday found her sitting crisscross on her bed, leafing through the wedding binder. She knew better than opening it. In fact, she had intended to throw it in the garbage dumpster as soon as they came home from the ice cream place. Yet, when she got to the house she just wanted to disappear into her room, forgetting the conversation she was supposed to have with Ellie about Miss Ballard's concerns.

Sometime around four in the morning, Anna rolled over and spotted the binder sitting on her desk. She hesitated at first, but when it was obvious she wasn't going to sleep she figured she'd look at it one last time. She'd throw it away before leaving for work.

She forgot how detailed she had been in her planning. It would've been an amazing wedding. Everything from the peony bouquets to the three tier wedding cake. All she had to show for it was a wedding dress hanging in a garment bag in the closet and several lost deposits from the various vendors she had to cancel. Anna tried to push the familiar feeling of resentment away at the fact Jonathan was not out anything on his end. He had never even booked their honeymoon... his one job.

Yet, if she were to plan a new wedding, Anna realized it would look drastically different. Had she changed that much? Or had most of the wedding plans been what she thought others wanted to see. As she thought about it, Anna had taken so many suggestions from people like Kirstyn and her other friends that she realized very few decisions had actually been hers.

Jonathan wanted a sleek wedding dress to show off how much weight she had lost. Kirstyn chose the sage green bridal party color scheme as well as the dresses. Even the music she had given to the DJ had been a compilation of requests from friends. *If there's a next time, things will be different. I know who I am now. Please let there be a next time, Lord.*

It was while she was looking at the menu she had planned for the reception that her phone lit up. The sun was barely casting light outside. Who would be calling her that early? *Michael.* She saw his name and a thrill shot through her followed by extreme hurt. She sent it to voicemail.

Jake had stopped by to check on her. Maybe he had reported back to Michael that she was a mess. Why had she felt the need to tell him so much when he questioned her on the stupid flip flops she was wearing?

"Are you up? I know this is about when you get ready to go for a run." He texted.

Go away, Michael. Anna answered in her mind.

"I just saw Jenna and Ben off," the next text said. "We had an early breakfast farewell party so they could get on the road."

And? So what?

"I met my new niece this morning." This text came a moment later after she hadn't responded.

I'm not taking the bait. Move on, Mike. I refuse. Yet, she picked up her phone and held it in her hands as she read his words.

"I really need to talk to you. Do you think we can have dinner together before church tonight?"

Church. Youth group. It's Wednesday. Ugh. I guess I'm still a volunteer. Anna resolved to call Sean later and back out of her commitments. After everything that had happened over the past week, surely Sean would understand why Anna needed to step away.

The sound of her father and the kids moving around in the living room as they readied for the day snapped her out of her thoughts. Anna shut off her phone and pulled herself off the bed. That day had all the makings of being long and exhausting. The last thing she needed was to add *emotional* to the mix. Michael Tyler would have to wait.

28

When Anna saw Miss Ballard in the school parking lot that day at school, she had tried to blend in with the students and avoid eye contact. Now that she was home with the kids, she had to address the uncomfortable topic of how or *if* Ellie was able to text the boy from her class. Walking down the hall that led to the bedrooms, Anna heard a muffled conversation and furrowed her brow.

"It's been scary. Aunt Anna told us that men tried to break into the house and that they shot Bentley." It sounded as if Ellie sniffled back tears. Who was she talking to? "I didn't get to say goodbye to him. We came home and he was already gone."

Anna paused at the door and in one frightening moment thought she heard a male voice respond, though she couldn't make out words.

"I can't wait to be with you again," Ellie said. "I really miss you."

Trying the doorknob, Anna realized it was locked. She knocked firmly on the door and heard a frenzy of whispering and scuffling. When the door opened, Ellie stood before her, wide eyed and guilty.

"Who were you talking to?" Anna demanded as she walked into the room and scanned every inch.

Ellie stayed silent, but tears filled her eyes.

"Ellie, who were you talking to?" Anna asked again.

"Daddy."

"Your father? *Jared*? How?"

Hesitantly, Ellie pulled a small phone from behind her back. "Please don't take it away from me, Aunt

Anna. He gave it to me so we can talk when he can't come see us."

"Ellie…" Anna stared in shock at the phone in her niece's hands.

"Don't take it from me," Ellie said louder and more emphatically.

"You're not supposed to have a phone. I know your grandfather made that clear to you." Anna tried to reason with her. "Your teacher approached me with screenshots of texts. She said you sent them. Is it true?"

Ellie set her jaw, simply staring at her aunt. Then Anna knew she had lost her. "Hand me the phone, Ellie."

"No!"

"*Ellie!*"

"Who do you think you are? You're not my mom. *You* moved in with *us*. I was here first."

"Eleanor Ann Hadley! Give me the phone," Anna asserted as she felt her insides quiver. She had not signed up for this.

"No! Get out of my room!"

Then came a loud booming voice that caused both to stand at attention. "Ellie! Give it to her… *NOW*."

Anna turned to see that her father had entered the house and was standing at the doorway, face red and flushed.

"Now, Ellie!" he reiterated, less angry.

Ellie threw the phone at her aunt. "I hate you! I wish you never came back here!"

Anna caught the phone, handed it to her father, and walked out of the room. The door slammed behind her and she heard her father scolding Ellie in a much gentler tone than he used with her as a young teen, she concluded. Anna went into her room, changed clothes and headed to the door.

"Where are you going, Aunt Anna?" Sam asked, puzzled from his place on the couch. Livi sat next to him also confused.

"I'm going for a run."

"Can we come? Please?" His eyes were filled with tears and Anna remembered how hard it had been for her to listen to her parents scolding Alexis during one of her many rebellious streaks.

Anna wanted solitude. This wasn't supposed to be her life. She was going to be a successful journalist with respect. Not Anna the terrible and hated aunt. Not Anna the lonely librarian assistant with the penchant for getting into fixes. *Think beyond yourself, Anna.*

The words hit their target. Anna's expression softened and motioned for the kids to come to her. She gave them a quick hug.

"Why don't we load the stroller and go walk the trail with the ducks," Anna suggested and Sam nodded.

They turned to leave the house when Anna felt a hand in hers.

"I don't care what Ellie said. I'm glad you're here, Aunt Anna."

"Thanks, Sam," Anna sighed and tried to muster a smile. Ellie's voice raised louder as she tried to argue her case. "Let's go, Kids."

It was while Anna was trying to lug the stroller free from a pile of clutter in the garage that she heard Sam talking pleasantly to someone.

"Ellie is acting crazy so we're going out. Aunt Anna is taking us to the duck pond. You should come with us," he said excitedly to some unknown person.

Anna quickly wheeled the stroller towards her car and saw *who* it was her nephew was talking to. Michael. The man wasn't even out of the driver's seat of his truck and Sam was chatting his ear off.

"Uh, Sam. Please stop," Anna gasped the words out as she saw Michael emerge from his truck.

"We're going to feed the ducks these bread crumbs. I have plenty for us to share." Sam held out the bag of stale leftover bread that Anna had grabbed from the counter on their way out of the house.

"Those are going to be some happy ducks." Michael smiled softly at the little boy before lifting his eyes to Anna. Her heart stopped and then fluttered back to life again. She really needed to stop allowing him to affect her like that.

"What are you doing here?" Her voice sounded choked, almost hoarse, even to her own ears.

"I tried calling you earlier," he said quietly.

"I saw that."

"And then I texted."

"Mmm, hmm. Saw those, too. It was a busy day."

Michael nodded and looked at his feet. "Ah, I thought maybe you were just avoiding me."

His eyes came up and he looked at her then. There was something different there... something that unnerved her more than normal.

"We... we need to go. I promised the kids," Anna said absent-mindedly.

"Mind if I come along?"

"Uhh... I don't... it's probably not a.." Anna stuttered.

"Can we take your truck instead of Aunt Anna's Jeep? It smells funny in there," Sam spoke up, cutting his off his Aunt.

"Sam! I'm sure Mr. Mike is busy." Anna leveled her nephew with a glare, hoping he'd get the hint with her stern look. "And my Jeep does *not* smell."

"Yes, it does. Smells like sour milk," Sam stated before turning to Michael. "You're not busy, are you?"

Michael was trying not to laugh.

"I'm not busy... and I do like ducks," Michael said. Then he put his hand on Sam's shoulder and said thoughtfully, "But I don't want to invite myself either, Buddy. Let's not make things hard on your Aunt. We'll get together another time. I promise."

Anna looked at him, desperately wanting to be mad at him, but he looked like a wounded puppy.

"Please, Aunt Anna. Can he come?" Sam begged.

Michael's bottom lip jetted out in a playful pout and he clasped his hands together as if pleading. Anna tried to hang on to her icy exterior but she felt the smile start at one end of her mouth and work its way over.

"Fine, but it needs to be a quick trip. There's church tonight."

"Are you sure you're okay with me coming along?" he asked looking hopeful.

"I'm too tired to argue and I just want to get away from here so..."

Judging by his expression, it probably wasn't the answer he wanted to hear, but he helped her get the stroller loaded onto the truck and moved to get Livi's car seat from her Jeep.

"Ha. Found the source of the smell." Michael's face contorted as he held up a container of her homemade yogurt. "Running a science experiment?"

"Oh. I wondered where that went." Anna smirked and took it from him, throwing it into the dumpster. She caught a glimpse of her wedding planner that she had thrown in earlier that morning. She only paused a moment before throwing the container on top of it and joined Michael and the kids in his truck.

Anna stayed quiet the entire trip to the trail, letting Sam have Michael's full attention. It wasn't until they were well onto the trail and at the banks of the pond that Michael probed. The kids were happily throwing breadcrumbs at the ducks and geese.

"So... what happened?" he asked.

"What do you mean *what happened*?" Was he referring to what happened between *them* or what happened to make her upset at that particular moment? She had no idea where to even begin discussing either topic.

"You said you needed to get away from the house."

"Oh. That." She couldn't help but notice his head dip in what she would've liked to think was guilt and shame. "Apparently Jared gave Ellie a phone and we didn't know it. She's been talking to him this entire time... telling him who knows what. And texting a boy from her class in a way that made him uncomfortable."

"Whoa... Ellie? That's crazy."

"And I am the evil Aunt for calling her out," Anna sighed. "She said she wished I had never come back."

"She didn't mean it, Anna. She loves you," Michael tried to comfort.

Anna laughed out loud. "Oh, she definitely meant it in that moment."

"Maybe, but we all say things we don't mean sometimes… especially when we're feeling things that scare us."

Something told Anna they weren't talking about Ellie anymore. She chanced a glance in his direction and found him looking at her intently.

"We should probably get back. I need to feed the kids before church tonight," Anna said, hastily getting up from the bench she sat on.

"Anna… please." Michael put a hand on her arm. "I was an idiot the other night. What I said…"

"It's okay, Mike."

"No, it's not."

"I don't want to talk in front of the kids," Anna lowered her voice and watched as her niece ran away from a hungry duck.

"When *can* we talk?"

"I don't know. Maybe tomorrow after school? It's the last day and my mind will be less cluttered," Anna suggested. "Although, Mr. Turner from church is letting us use his cabin for the week. Maybe I can meet you before we head over."

"Do you promise?" Michael asked hopefully.

"I promise." Anna mustered a smile before pulling herself away and walking to the edge of the pond where the kids were. "We should head home, Kids."

"But we still have bread crumbs and the ducks out there haven't gotten theirs yet," Sam said pointing to a few stragglers that were slowly floating their way over to the banks.

"Sam, if they really wanted it they would move faster. We need to get home so I can feed you ducklings."

Livi laughed. "I not a duck."

"You're right. You're a silly goose," Anna chuckled and tickled her niece's belly.

"Can you throw the other ducks some bread, Aunt Anna? Can you throw that far? I don't want to leave them hungry." Sam looked genuinely concerned and Anna sighed.

"I can try." Anna grabbed the bag with the few remaining breadcrumbs and eyed the distance to the slow ducks. There was a large rock that protruded further out into the water. Taking a careful step onto it, Anna inched closer and closer to the edge.

"This isn't a good idea, Petunia," Michael said with a shake of his head.

"Oh you of little faith. I'll let you know I have a pretty decent throwing arm," Anna said without looking at him. She got the ducks in her sight and reached into the bag, pulling out a handful of pieces.

"Anna, please be careful." Michael was close by now, unnerving her.

"Ribbit, ribbit." This came from Livi, but Anna paid no mind.

That is, Anna paid no mind to her niece until a fat toad jumped high into the air and landed on her arm. She shrieked. The ducks dispersed. The kids laughed. And Michael instantly held her other arm to keep her from falling.

"Froggy! Ribbit! Ribbit!" Livi gushed with glee.

"Get it off!" Anna screamed and started flailing her arms, realizing the rock she stood on was actually pretty slippery.

"It's just a frog." Michael laughed as he shooed the big bulbus bullfrog away.

"Is it gone? Please tell me it's gone." Anna flapped her arms wildly, dropping the bread. However, in doing so she felt her foot slip. It was like everything happened in slow motion as she braced for her water landing. Instead, she felt a pair of arms twirling her down from the rock and back onto stable ground. The ground may have been steady, but her heart and balance were not as she looked up into Michael's face. It seemed like hours, not mere seconds, until Sam piped up.

"Ew. Are you going to kiss Aunt Anna?" he asked incredulously.

Michael sighed but didn't move away. His expression didn't look disgusted by the notion. In fact, he looked quite the opposite. He looked very much like he actually *wanted* to kiss her. Anna swallowed hard, realizing the idea didn't scare her so much after all.

As if feeling the eyes of the children on them, Michael dropped his hands and stepped back, though his face still held tenderness in his expression.

"Another frog!" Livi exclaimed and clapped her hands together. She began running towards another amphibian and Anna forced herself to move from Michael's gaze.

"No. No more frogs." Anna found herself giggling awkwardly. She tried to casually sneak a glance in Michael's direction as they made their way to the truck. He held a hint of a smile on his lips. *What just happened? What does that smile mean? Would he have kissed me if the kids weren't here?*

"So about tomorrow… we'll get home from school at noon since it's a half day," Anna said in a higher pitch than what was normal for her. "How about lunch?"

"I'd like that. I have to go in for a little while to cover for Scooter in the morning, but I should be done by lunch."

They made it back to the truck and though there was little conversation, their bashful smiles spoke volumes.

*****

Some things never change. She's still as klutzy as she's always been, Jared thought to himself as he watched the entire pond exchange from a safe distance. Hatred rose up inside of him. The Munsons were the bane of his existence. He was more than happy to oblige when Nick offered him a bonus to lead him straight to Anna. Leave it to her to cross paths with the likes of Damon.

All that mattered was that now Jared had a way to finally claim his kids. For years, the Munsons kept him from Sam and Ellie. It was stupid to make him have supervised custody. They were *his* kids. If they wanted someone to blame, they should've looked at their drugged out daughter. It was Alexis' fault that he had to go to jail in the first place. Meanwhile the Munson family vilified *him*. Well, he'd give them reason to hate him. He was taking back what was his… Sam and Ellie.

It had been a long time since he had been in *Dad mode*. Surely it would come back to him. It wouldn't be so hard. Back then, the kids were in diapers. Ellie was intelligent and feisty. Sam seemed smart and wanted to learn all kinds of things. A new start as a family in the south would be good for all of them. Ellie could cook, keep the house, and look after Sam while he found some type of job.

They'd have to get used to answering to their new names. Ellie was now Darcy and Sam was going to be Kyle... according to their new birth certificates and documents he had managed to obtain for their big move.

His phone vibrated and he answered it quickly.

"Where are we with the plan?" Nick asked.

"Hello to you, too. Everything is going just as expected." *Almost.* Jared hadn't banked on Anna finding out he had snuck Ellie a phone to keep tabs on the family and their whereabouts. It didn't matter. *After tomorrow, I'll have my kids and we'll be headed south.*

"And what exactly *is* your plan? So far I've only heard lip service from you," Nick said in a steely tone. "I don't have a lot of patience for screw ups."

"Ellie told me they plan on heading to some cabin out in the boonies after school. I convinced her to get me the location so that I could sneak up and visit her. She's supposed to ask her aunt to take her and her brother on a hike. That's when I'll grab my kids and you take out Anna," Jared relayed the plan, pleased with himself.

"And if your daughter doesn't follow through?"

"She will. She misses me. I know she'll give us what we want." Jared felt his pulse quicken and tried to push away his uncertainty. What if his father-in-law planted seeds of doubt in Ellie's mind? What if she told him everything after Anna caught her talking on the phone? He hadn't heard anything from his daughter since their conversation ended abruptly. Good thing he had a backup plan for tracking them. As long as Sam took his game to the cabin it would be fine.

Nick didn't need to know any of this, however, and Jared decided to cling to hope. He'd have what was his and Alex could rot in the gutter where she belonged.

"Your reunion with your kids is not my priority. Understand that." Nick spoke, void of emotion. "The only concern I have is making sure that Anna Munson is finally dead."

29

"My client wants full assurance that he will be moved to another facility within the day after he shares the information he has." The lawyer looked expectantly at Jake across the table Thursday late morning. Next to him sat a jittery prisoner, still in cuffs.

"I'll see what we can do, but I have to say… a lot depends on what he's about to tell me. It better be something I don't already know. You're pulling me away from my coffee." Jake watched as the scrawny man looked him in the eye and a jagged toothy smile spread across his face.

"It's good stuff, Man. If you don't listen to me, someone's going to die."

It took a lot to make Jake shudder. Something in this shady character's confidence unnerved him, but he couldn't let that show.

"Oh yeah? Let's hear it then."

"I want to hear the words… say it in front of my lawyer." The convict shifted in his seat excitedly like a man holding a winning deck. "I want a sentence reduction and to be moved… *today*."

Jake forced a sardonic laugh. "You better start talking or I'm walking out of this room. And if I do… you're going right back to your cell. I think…" Jake paused his sentence to look at the clock on the wall for dramatic effect. "…you'd be just in time for Rec in the yard. I'm sure your buddies miss you."

"Don't send me back. They'll kill me if they know I'm talking."

Jake shrugged and started moving to the door. His hand was on the knob when the inmate blurted out, "If you leave, some lady is going to die."

"What lady?" Jake paused.

"I don't know her name, but she's like a librarian or something. It's going down at some cabin in Deer Creek."

The man's lawyer put a hand on his client's arm to quiet him. "Does he have a deal, Detective?"

"You know that's not up to me, but I will put in a good word if what he's telling me is true," Jake promised.

The lawyer nodded and the man started talking.

"My buddy Jared has a new friend. I think it's someone you know."

Jake's impatience was going to come to a head if the inmate didn't start talking faster.

"This guy... he's a cop. I happen to know that he paid people off to get rid of the two new guys that were brought in. Then Jared told me that he's paying him crazy money to get him close to this librarian chick so he can kill her. Which Jared didn't mind, because she's like his ex-sister-in-law or something. But apparently this woman knows stuff. *Big* stuff."

Jake sat down in the chair across from the inmate and tried to compose his thoughts. "Do you know a timeline?"

"Jared snuck his kid a phone– I guess she lives with the sister-in-law – and has been keeping track of her schedule for weeks now. He was excited because he's gonna get his kids back and run away."

"*When*? When is this supposed to happen?"

"Today, Man. Jared had me reach out to my contacts to get him and his kids new birth certificates and ID's. He got them yesterday. My man Jared's not wasting any time."

"And the name of this cop?" Jake's heart pounded.

"Nick something, but they say he's calling himself the new *Broker*. Works for a real bad son of a…"

"Who does he work for? I want a name!" Jake cut the man off.

"His name is Damon. I don't want on his radar. He's a real bad dude."

Jake got to his feet and handed the man a pad of paper.

"Write it all down. I want names, dates, times… I want it all." Jake knew there wasn't a moment to lose as he pulled out his cell phone to fill in Cal Jenson on what he just heard. He had to get to Anna before it was too late.

*****

Not only was it the last day of school, but also an early dismissal. The school emptied out quickly. Michael was supposed come over to talk over lunch so Anna was pleased to be able to leave the school quickly with her niece and nephew. As soon as she got home, Anna changed her clothes and helped her father pack the cars with camping gear in the on and off rain that fell from the sky. When Michael still hadn't showed up or called, she eventually forced herself to eat lunch with the kids. Maybe he ended up staying at the station longer than expected. No, he still would've texted to tell her he couldn't come, right?

Anna checked the hour on her phone for the tenth time since getting home after school let out. Surprisingly, she wasn't mad at *him*. Anna was, however, mad at *herself*. How stupid was she? Michael had made it clear from day one he had no desire or intent to be in a relationship. How could she blame him for that when he had been honest about it from the start?

Clearly, he only wanted to clear the air so things wouldn't be awkward between them anymore... so they could continue being friends. That's it. She obviously had read too much into his expressions and looks. *But it felt genuine... warm. Real! Why am I such a bad judge of reality?*

"Uh oh. That is the face of my daughter overthinking something," Tim commented as he walked by Anna staring mindlessly at her Jeep's open back hatch.

"What do you mean?"

"Either you are thinking about a certain person or you're getting ready to repack everything we just packed inside your Jeep. I kind of hope it's the first part, because I don't want to repack everything we stuffed in there." Tim smirked.

"Stop trying to read my thoughts, Dad." Anna smiled back at her father.

"This trip will be good. I think we could all use a distraction." Tim nudged Anna with his arm. "Maybe you'll get some writing time in. Go for a hike. There's that trail that goes up high above the waterfall. Maybe we can walk that together like we used to when you were little."

Her father paused and watched her face for some type of reaction. Anna forced a smile. Walking the old trail to the waterfall *did* sound delightful despite the fact the rain wasn't dissipating. Mr. Turner let the pastor's family - and several others in the church - use the cabin for an escape every summer since Anna could remember.

"Now that I think about it," her father cut through her thoughts. "...with your track record of *Anna's Law* moments lately maybe a walk along the ledge to the waterfall wouldn't be a good idea."

"Ha, ha, ha. Funny, Dad." Anna rolled her eyes at his playful teasing. "Part pastor, part comedian."

"Seriously though... this will be a good trip. I need a rest and hopefully it will help absorb the kids' hurt that Jared cancelled his visit this weekend." Tim sighed.

"I imagine he knows you're not too happy about the phone thing." Anna turned to look back at the house to make sure Ellie wasn't within earshot.

Tim shrugged. "I doubt my feelings on the issue phased him at all, but I do hate it for the kids."

"I just hope Ellie can move past this. She's been ... different... since I found her on that phone." Anna sighed. The last thing she wanted was to be stuck in a cabin on a rainy weekend with a cranky pre-teen.

"She'll be fine," her dad assured her. "And what about you, Sweetheart? Will *you* be fine?"

"Pfft. Yeah. Sure." Anna shrugged and tried to play as if nothing was bothering her. "Why wouldn't I be?"

"I haven't forgotten what this weekend was supposed to be." His tone was gentle and Anna almost lost her composure.

"Jon wasn't who God wanted for me, that's all."

The kids came out of the house at that moment with their bags and Anna was grateful to drop the subject. Tim came alongside Ellie and took the backpack from her shoulder after noticing how heavy it was. Her shoulder was slumping under the weight.

"Goodness, Girl. What is in this thing?" he asked good humoredly.

"Nothing," was her quick response. "I want to make sure I have a lot of things to do, that's all. I can carry it, Grandpa."

"Yes, you *can* carry your own bags. You're a strong independent young woman. *But* you shouldn't have to." Tim pressed a kiss to his granddaughter's forehead and squished the heavy bag into the last open spot in the back of his car. "I want you to find a gentleman someday, Ellie. Don't expect any less from any man. Do you hear me?"

"You really are amazing, Grandpa. I love you. I will always love you," Ellie said out of the blue.

Anna cocked her eyebrow at her niece, but decided against asking why she was being so kind. Her father beamed under the compliment and Anna didn't want to take that from him. Maybe they had made peace when Anna wasn't looking.

"I thought Mike was coming today." Sam looked genuinely disappointed.

"Yeah… I thought so too," Anna muttered. "Things must've gotten busy at the station, Little Man."

"Aunt Anna," Ellie came up on her other side and spoke softly.

Anna looked down at Ellie. There was moisture in her eyes.

"Do you think maybe you could take Sam and I for a walk on the trail after Livi takes her nap?"

There was something in the way Ellie asked the question. Anna couldn't quite put her finger on it. Normally in the past Ellie would ask her with excitement... eagerness. It almost felt like she was asking to do something she really didn't want to do... like take out the trash.

"I don't know. Are you sure you want to be with me? We haven't really talked about yesterday..." Anna watched the young girl's face go through a wide array of emotions. Over exaggerated happiness, which Anna saw instantly as fake. Shame. Guilt. *Fear*? "Listen, Ellie. I want you to know that I love you. I know you miss your father and that you feel we took away the only chance you have to speak with him... we're just trying to protect you. It may seem like we're being... *mean*... but we love you."

Tears surfaced in the girl's eyes and she slid her arms around Anna's waist. "I know you love me. I love you, too. I'm sorry... about what I said. I'm glad you're here. Grandpa and Livi need you."

Anna wished she could enjoy the hug, but her niece's words felt off. *Just Grandpa and Livi? Not Ellie or Sam?*

"Enough schmaltzy stuff. Let's get this vacation started," Tim called from his car after buckling the baby in her car seat.

Ellie smiled at her aunt lovingly before running to the front seat of her grandfather's car.

"You have the directions, right?" Her father leaned his head out of his window to talk to his daughter. "You'll follow right behind us?"

"Uh, yeah. I'll be behind you. I just want to double check to make sure the house is locked tight," Anna told her father. "You go on ahead. I know the way."

With that, her father pulled down the drive and headed to the cabin for some summer fun. Anna sighed and went back into the house to grab her laptop bag and make sure everything was secured.

Her heart sank once again looking at the empty dog bed. Bentley loved the cabin. He would splash in the river and collect all kinds of sticks to bring back to the porch. This would be the first year Bentley wouldn't be there with the family.

That fateful day popped into her mind and Anna shuddered. Moving through the house, she checked windows and doors, nearly jumping out of her skin when her phone rang out from her pocket. It broke the eerie silence that permeated the house. It was Michael. "Anna, I am so sorry. Am I too late?" Michael sounded frantic. *Good.*

"Too late for what exactly? Lunch or to talk?" *Maybe I should lay off the snarky attitude a little*, she thought to herself. *Then again, maybe not.* "I'm getting ready to leave for the cabin, Michael. Is there something I can help you with?"

"Anna, please. Scooter didn't come back when he said he would and we got called out to a massive barn fire. I'm sorry. Please."

Anna weighed her options. She could make him grovel a little longer. She could be kind and forgive him. Hadn't she concluded earlier it was her own fault for letting her heart get all tangled up in Michael Tyler? She'd err on the side of mercy.

"It's fine, Mike." Anna sighed.

"No, it's not. We need to talk. It's all I thought about all day." He sounded truly tortured. "Then when I had a moment to text you after we got back to the station, I realized I had forgotten to put my phone on the charger."

Anna stood in the dining room, clutching the handle of her laptop bag. He hadn't forgotten her! A slight thrill resonated through her heart, but she forced herself to calm down. This roller coaster ride was too much on her heart.

"Anna? Are you still there?"

"Yes. I'm still here," Anna said in a rush of air.

"Good. I thought you gave up on me for a minute there." He sounded relieved and Anna felt a glimmer of a smile touch her lips. "Can I meet you at the cabin? I know we'll have the kids and your dad around, but I'll take whatever time I can get with you."

Anna's mouth gaped open and she tried to formulate coherent words to string together. None came to her.

"I can bring s'mores fixings," he rushed to suggest when she didn't answer right away. "Everyone likes s'mores, right?"

"I like s'mores. Burnt marshmallows are my favorite."

You're a writer and that's what you come up with, Annalise Munson?

Michael chuckled. "Burnt? Nah… lightly toasted over a longer period of time is best so the insides get gooey."

Her insides were gooey.

"I guess we'll just have to agree to disagree, Mr. Tyler." Anna smiled. "Do you know how to get to Mr. Turner's cabin?"

"Yeah. I know where it is. We had a men's retreat there last spring. Give me time to go to the store to get some supplies and I'll see you there."

"Are you sure, Michael?"

"Am I sure about what? S'mores?"

"Are you sure you don't want distance still?" Why had she blurted the question out like that? Yet, she needed to know... and sooner than later.

"Yeah... about that... That didn't work out so well for me, Petunia." Michael's tone turned soft. "But we'll talk later."

"I'll see you there," Anna said as she ended the call.

In a burst of excitement, Anna broke out into a happy dance on the way to her loaded down Jeep. She quickly recovered and looked around to make sure no one saw the silly act. Maybe this trip wouldn't be so bad after all.

*****

If that fool calls or texts me one more time. Nick was losing his patience with Jared.

"What is it now?" Nick answered the call on the cell phone as he lifted his binoculars up to see the church property and the little house.

"Where are you?" Jared asked nervously. "I'm trying to keep a safe distance from the kids, but what if Anna catches up to me? Has she even left the house yet?"

"How about I just text you when she pulls out like we planned earlier?" Nick seethed. This is why he worked alone. Others were liabilities and Jared was a huge one. Somehow the idiot got it into his head that they were now partners.

Nick did not need Jared to accomplish his job. Yes, he would be the one to take the fall for the woman's murder, but ultimately it was Jared that needed Nick. There was no way he'd be able to get his children away from Anna without Nick taking her out first. Little did Jared know that Nick had already planted ammo and spent casings in the man's car for when Jared got caught. And he *would* get caught. It was a part of the plan that he hadn't divulged to his *partner*.

"Text me as soon as she pulls out."

Who was this loser to think he called the shots? Nick found out the location the day earlier by piecing together the scant information Jared had divulged. He had already preplanned where he would park. He already knew the best perches to set up his gear and be able to tear down quickly after he had killed the target. Nick was a pro. Seven years in the military as a marine sniper and five years as a cop afforded him some respect. Who was Jared? Yet, he would play along until he got what he needed from the guy.

"Sounds good. I'll be in touch." Nick rolled his eyes as he threw his phone onto the seat next to him.

Movement caught his eye and he raised the binoculars once more. A curly haired redhead exited the house. So that was Annalise Munson… the cause of all his clients' anxiety. She didn't look so intimidating at all. In fact, she had a rather petite stature.

All of the sudden the woman broke out into a dance. Her arms swung what looked to be a laptop case as she twirled and moved in a very uncoordinated manner. He dropped the binoculars slightly and furrowed his brow as he looked in the direction of the house in confusion. *What in the...*

Then she stopped and looked around. He dropped the binoculars into his lap and sunk low in his seat as her eyes scanned directly in his location. A moment later, her Jeep began pulling down the driveway and onto the street ahead of him. Too bad she had to die. In another place and another time, he might've thought she was cute. Grabbing his phone he sent the promised text.

"She's moving. It's a go."

30

Michael made a mad dash to his apartment to get a shower. In an attempt to save time, he decided to raid his mother's pantry for items to make s'mores rather than waste precious moments at the store. He found everything he needed except for skewers, but the Munsons were camping. They could *rough it* and use sticks from the trees.

Michael managed to dodge his family's questions and curious looks. The farm was a hub of activity that day since it was the last day of school. It felt like every family or school group used *The Tyler Family Farm and Fun Spot* as a means of celebration that day. Normally, he would have been thrilled to help his family entertain the masses. However, Anna was waiting for him. He was almost in his truck when someone pulled in behind him.

"Come on," he grumbled and threw his hands up in frustration, thinking it was another patron of the farm. It was then he realized who it was.

"Anna's not answering her phone," Jake slid down from his truck and approached Michael with a worried expression. "Do you know where she is? She's not at her house."

"What's going on?"

"I don't have time to explain. Is she here?" Jake questioned.

"No. She's at a cabin with her family. I was just heading there."

"You know where she is?" Jake pulled on his friend's arm. "Good. Get in and tell me where to go."

Michael complied, leaving the s'mores ingredients behind on the seat of his truck. The frenzied look on Jake's face and the growing panic Michael felt rising in his gut told him s'mores were no longer that important.

"Are you going to tell me what's going on?" Michael asked, gripping onto the side of the truck as his friend ran a stop sign.

"You got your phone? Keep calling Anna until she answers. Tell her to get everyone inside the cabin. Lock the door. Close the blinds and curtains and find a room to hide in."

Michael didn't ask for clarification. He started dialing and redialing… no answer. Meanwhile, Jake talked to Cal on his phone.

"We need the witness secured and her family brought in immediately. Yes, my source is reliable. Persons of interest are Jared Hadley and Detective Nick Spencer. Consider them armed and dangerous."

Jared? The kids' father? He was working with Nick? As the whole bleak situation dawned on Michael, he felt his throat constrict. If only he hadn't gone in for Scooter… He could've been there with Anna… keeping her safe. He failed her.

"Keep calling. Don't stop," Jake ordered. "Don't you dare give up, Mike."

"She's not answering. I doubt she has cell service out there." Michael thought out loud. Then a horrible thought struck him. "That cabin fire… was that Nick? What if he does that again with Anna and her family inside?"

"Don't think that way," Jake warned. "Let's just get there."

Anna's words floated into his mind from the night he found the poor burnt woman struggling to live… the night he stupidly told Anna he needed distance. *Mike, I know you want to save the world… to keep all of us safe from harm. But you're not God. You're an amazing, sweet, funny man. But you are just a man.*

Sweet Anna. She was right. She was always right. Michael was just a man… a man who needed God to step in and save the woman he loved.

*****

"Why don't we play checkers until it stops raining? I know you want to go on the trail and we will. I promise. It's just too wet right now." Anna tried to comfort her agitated niece.

"It's okay. I'm … not sure I want to go anyway," Ellie said softly as she sat at the checkerboard already set up on the wooden kitchen table.

"Well, that's dramatic." Anna chuckled. "The rain won't last forever. Give it an hour or so."

Ellie didn't respond. She stared at the pieces on the gameboard absently. *What have I done?* Ellie asked herself as she felt her heart rate pick up as the reality of what was about to happen hit home. Her father didn't exactly have the best track record when it came to carrying through with promises. Maybe he would forget? Oh, she how she hoped he had forgotten!

Looking around the cabin, Ellie felt deep regret and remorse. Her grandfather sat on the floor playing cars with Livi and Sam. Aunt Anna waited patiently for her to make the first move at checkers. If only she knew that she *had* made a move… a very bad, horrific move.

When her father had given her that phone she had been thrilled. She could talk to him about her day, the guy she had a crush on in her class, about how funny Aunt Anna acted around Michael Tyler. At first, it was great. He laughed at her jokes. He let her talk about anything and everything. He seemed like he really understood her.

Then he said he wanted her and Sam to come live with him. At the time, that sounded amazing. They were going to move to Florida. Her father made promises of beaches and palm trees. However, as they continued talking over the days leading up to her Aunt Anna finding the phone, it had gotten kind of scary. Her father wanted to know weird things like when Anna woke up and when she went running. After Anna found the phone Ellie had wanted to tell her dad that she had changed her mind... that she and Sam would stay with their grandfather. But there was no way to get him the message.

Now it was too late. If she told on her father... he'd get in trouble and she'd never see him again. In fact, they'd put him in jail. That was what her father told her would happen. But Ellie didn't want to leave. What if she never saw her grandpa or Anna again? What about Livi? What if Sam didn't want to go? Would her father force him? She didn't want to go without Sam.

"Hey..." Anna reached over and placed a soft hand on Ellie's arm. "Are you okay?"

"Do you remember when you gave that testimony at church for Youth Sunday, Aunt Anna? You said that at the retreat God changed how you saw things that day at the gazebo."

"Wow, you were actually listening." Anna smiled proudly at her. "I remember. What about it?"

"What if God changes how you see things… but it's still too late?"

"I don't think it's ever too late to change paths. The only time it's too late is when we're dead. As long as you have breath in your lungs it is never too late."

Ellie swallowed hard. She hoped that was true. "Do you think God can save us from stupid things we do? What if we do bad things and then it's too late to stop something from happening?"

Anna looked at her with concern. Maybe she had said too much. She opened her mouth to say something, but Sam cut through.

"Hey, I thought you said you packed my video game, Ellie. It's not in my bag," Sammy whined.

"That's because *I* took it out of your bag." Tim laughed. "We're at a beautiful cabin in the woods to enjoy nature… not to play video games, Kiddo. Don't worry it's safe at home."

Sam groaned and plopped himself down on the couch with a disgruntled thud. Ellie, however, felt relief. Her father had said he would use her phone and Sam's game to track their location somehow. Their grandfather had removed both her phone and now Sam's game. *Problem solved. Maybe I don't have anything to worry about. He can't find us now.*

"I think I know of something to make you feel better, Sammy," Anna said cheerfully. "Guess who's coming over with stuff to make s'mores?"

"Who?" Sam poked his head up off the couch cushion he had laid on. "Mike?"

Anna nodded and Sam bounced up happy again.

"Michael Tyler is coming *here*?" Tim asked with piqued curiosity.

Ellie realized then just how close she had come to really messing up a good thing. *Sam is actually happy with Grandpa and Aunt Anna. And so am I.*

"Back to our conversation, Ellie," Anna said lovingly to her niece. "What has you worried?"

"Nothing." Ellie smiled and ran to her Aunt, throwing her arms around her neck. "I'm never going to mess up again, Aunt Anna. I promise."

*****

Jared waited where Nick told him to wait. Good thing he hadn't relied solely on tracking the kids' electronic devices. Even if Sam had his game on, there was no cell phone service on Jared's phone to pick them up. Admittedly his plan was hinging on Ellie doing *her* part.

Somewhere up further on the trail - in one of a thousand trees - Nick was hiding and waiting. A shudder racked Jared's body. *What if Ellie backed out? What if she didn't carry through with her part of the plan? She could be sending her own father to the grave if things went sideways.*

The sound of a door opening snapped him to attention.

"See? I told you the rain would stop eventually." It was Anna's voice. "Let's make this a quick walk. Michael will be here soon. Hopefully the firewood stayed dry enough under that tarp for our fire pit. I'm craving s'mores."

Jared shifted ever so slightly in his hiding spot to see who she was speaking to. His kids were right on her heels. Sam had his hand in hers. Ellie looked around nervously… almost fearfully. That wasn't a good sign. He needed her willingness if his plan was going to work without causing his kids unnecessary trauma. He needed to get them away from Anna *before* the shot rang out.

He reached for his phone before remembering there was no signal to contact Nick. The man would have to figure it out for himself that his target was getting ready to take the trail. Surely, Nick would wait until after his kids were cleared away, right?

Jared had to get Ellie's attention without getting Anna's. He tried to move stealthily through the forest so as not to alert anyone to his presence prematurely. When he was within twenty feet of his daughter, he threw a stone. It landed near her shoe. He watched as she looked down at the pebble and then to where it had come from. They made eye contact and he gave a nervous wave before putting his finger to his lips to warn her to keep silent.

What he had not banked on was his daughter turning to her aunt and saying, "Can we go back to the cabin? Like *right* now?"

"Why? I thought you wanted to see the waterfall?" Anna looked surprised.

His stomach sank when he heard his daughter utter the words, "My dad is here. He's going to try to take us. I'm so sorry, Aunt Anna."

So much for keeping the kids from trauma. Now he had to get them to safety and away from a sniper's gun. Jared emerged from the trees.

*****

"Please don't let him take us," Ellie cried and tried to hide behind her aunt as Jared strategically blocked the way back to the cabin.

Anna's mind raced. He inched closer to them and pulled a knife from his pocket.
"This doesn't have to go badly, Anna. Just let them come with me," he said.
"Stay back, Jared."
"Daddy, what are you doing?" Sam asked confused.

Think, Anna! Think! When she and Alexis were kids, they explored every inch of that forest. That was a long time ago. *Wait! Where's that old trail? The one Alexis used to sneak up to the road to meet up with her friends?* Anna spotted the path off to the side of the main trail. It was mostly covered up now with brush, but she could still make it out. If she could get the kids to the road maybe they could get phone reception to call the police or wave down a car. It was a risk, but they had no choice as far as she could see. To continue in the direction they were heading would just take them further away from civilization.
"Run." Anna grabbed each of their hands and took off towards the overgrown trail.

They had done well getting out of Jared's sight initially. Adrenaline kicked in. They were all in better shape than Jared, but it was a matter of time before he caught up. Sam was struggling to maneuver the tree roots and bumpy terrain. They were dodging branches and getting whipped repeatedly by the boughs as they ran. Anna knew what she needed to do. Stopping abruptly, she reached for her cellphone.

"Take this. Keep following the path. Call 911 when you get to the road, Ellie. Don't stop."

Ellie shook her head no and started to protest.

"Go! Now!" Anna hissed when she heard movement below them on the path.

Ellie reluctantly nodded through tears as she grabbed her brother's hand and forced him to press on up the incline. Anna moved behind the camouflage of a tree as she watched until the kids were out of sight. *Protect them, God.*

Jared's heavy breathing and grunting sounded nearby. Anna grabbed the tree limb in front of her and pulled it back as far as she could. She didn't know how long she could hold it taut. Willing herself not to make a sound, she timed the release perfectly. Just as Jared approached she let go and watched as the force of the large branch hit him square in his chest, knocking him off balance. He tumbled back down the hill.

At first he didn't move, but Anna knew she only had moments to plan her next steps. She started taking off in the same direction as the children when a loud cracking noise echoed through the air. The bark of the tree just two feet from her splintered and exploded.

Anna sobbed as she realized she was being shot at. If she was going to die, she was going to die running towards freedom. She set her eyes on a distant mark up ahead on the path and set her pace.

*****

Nick cursed under his breath as his shot missed. He hadn't expected Anna to be as fast as she was. He wouldn't miss next time. He came up on Jared.

"You're on your own now," Nick seethed as he took off in the direction of the gazelle he chased. A small thrill coursed through him. It had been a long time since he had gone hunting.

Nick moved through the forest quickly, occasionally pausing to listen and observe the branches and limbs for breakage. He spotted Jared climbing up the trail behind him. After a moment's temptation to shoot the fool, he refrained. Jared needed to be the scapegoat for Anna's death. The police would find the sniper's rifle somewhere easy to spot in the forest which would match the ammo Nick had already put in Jared's car. But first, he needed to shoot his prey.

About thirty feet ahead of him, a rush of birds flew into the air as if their peace had been disrupted. That's when he caught sight of the red hair in between the branches. He set off in her direction, gun poised and ready to fire.

*****

Michael and Jake jumped out of the truck as fast as they could, taking the steps to the cabin two at a time. They swung the door open to find Tim quietly reading in a chair, a look of perplexed shock on his face as they entered the cabin.

"What in the…"

"Where's Anna and the kids?" Michael asked immediately. He'd apologize later for the abruptness with his Pastor.

"She took them for a walk on the trail. Livi is asleep. I'd like it to stay that way so if you'd please lower your voice, Son."

Outside, sirens filled the air and Michael could see the moment the reality dawned on Tim Munson's face. "What's going on? What's happening?" the older man asked as all of the color drained from him.

"We need to find Anna and the kids. Which direction did she go, Mr. Munson?" Jake asked calmly.

"Down... down the trail to the waterfall."

All of the sudden the door burst open and two sobbing children ran into the arms of their grandfather. They were followed into the cabin by Cal. Jake looked to the detective for an explanation.

"I found these two on the side of the road waving down cars as we were heading here." Cal scanned the room quickly before turning back to Jake. "They said their Aunt sent them up to the street alone. Their father is still out there."

"Jared? Jared was *here*?" Tim questioned.

"It's my fault. This is all my fault," Ellie repeated over and over, burying her face into her grandfather's side.

"Any sign of the other suspect?" Cal asked, increasing Anna's father's concern.

Jake shook his head.

"Any sign of *who*? *Another* suspect?" Tim asked, his panic growing. "Will someone please tell me.."

"Sir, we're going to need you and the kids to stay here with our officers," Cal stated in an even tone. "I promise we're doing everything to locate Anna safe and sound. The best thing you can do for your daughter right now is to remain here and comfort these two kids. Okay? Do you have a piece of clothing of Anna's? The canine handlers are outside. The dogs will be able to get her scent."

"That's Anna's suitcase there." Tim pointed to an unzipped bag, laying open on the floor.

One of the officers grabbed a shirt and headed out the door.

"Do you know these trails, Tyler?" Jake turned to Michael.

"Yes. Let's go." Michael ran out the door with Jake right behind him.

"Whoa. I get it. You want to find her fast," Jake said pulling Michael's arm. Then he grabbed the bullet proof vests that another officer handed him. "But you're not a cop and you are not armed. Put this on. Stay behind me."

It was all he could do to respect his friend's authority and not forge ahead. Michael watched anxiously as the dogs sniffed Anna's shirt. He fastened the vest on and followed Jake down the trail, praying they would get to Anna in time.

31

She couldn't run anymore. Anna was used to running on the roads… level ground… treadmills… not uphill and definitely not for her life. In her exhaustion she must've gotten off the trail at some point because she didn't see the path clearly anymore. She found herself near the wall of a massive rock.

Anna smiled. It struck her funny how random memories could pop into her head at the most inopportune times. Then again, maybe it was right on time. *Thank you, God, for reminding me.* Alexis and Anna used to play in an old cave every time they went to the cabin as kids. They loved that cave because it sat high above all of the trails and they could see the rapids of the river below. It was their secret. Mostly because if their parents knew how dangerous it was to get to, they'd never let their daughters return to it.

Anna pressed her back against the rocks and tried to listen over the wild beating of her heart. She could hear it… the low thunderous roar of the water below. Slowly feeling her way along the rock's edge, she saw the tiny opening.

How old had she been back then? Six? Maybe seven? She remembered the entrance being a lot larger than what she was looking at. And the drop didn't seem as terrifying back then. Now it petrified Anna to consider skirting the edge of the narrow rock wall.

"You can do it. You've got this. Be brave." She cheered herself on as she took the first step onto the slim outcropping.

Rain started falling in big heavy drops. She closed her eyes and put her face upwards to feel the downpour rush over the open cuts she received while running through the brush and brambles. The cold rain was welcomed as it soothed her worn out and enflamed muscles. It did, however, make maneuvering the small rocky ledge tricky and slippery. Anna had managed to ignore the pain in her legs up to that point, but there was no way she could possibly go any further. Her best chance of survival was getting inside that cave.

Holding on to a piece of the rock that jetted out with one hand, she cleared the entrance of the opening with her other. Her sneaker slipped with a terrifying squeak, but she regained her balance. Now was not the time for *Anna's Law* to kick in.

"Thank you, God," Anna whispered as she crawled into the small crevice. "Please let the kids be safe."

She scooted as far into the space as she could and sat sideways so she could lean her back against the rock. Anna stifled her moan when she straightened out her legs and felt her hamstrings constrict. After a race, she soaked in ice. At the very least she would put cold packs on her aching legs. *No such luxury here.*

"God, You've been teaching me that it's in You that I have my being. Well, *My being* is in a lot of trouble right now. Help me, Lord."

It was while she rested her head back against the stone wall of the cave, verses from the Bible flooded her mind... verses that spoke of God as a mighty fortress, a solid rock. She began whispering them under her breath to keep her mind from the pain in her legs and the danger lurking outside in the woods.

"Psalm 18:2… The Lord is my rock, my fortress, and my deliverer… in Him I take refuge." This was the last thing Anna uttered before allowing her eyes to shut and succumbing to her exhaustion.

*****

"Be advised… suspect apprehended trying to get into his car," the words came over the radio.

"Which suspect?" Michael asked Jake.

"I'm guessing Jared. Nick is too good at what he does to get caught."

The K9 officer shifted further uphill as his dog hit on something and pulled against his lead.

"Whoa. Whoa." The handler spoke to his dog. Then he noticed the split bark on the tree they were passing. "Detective, I have a bullet here."

Earlier, the officers had fanned out to cover more territory. Cal took some men along the trail that went below them to the waterfall. Jake followed the dog with a handful of officers to what looked like a steep overgrown path uphill. It looked like a promising trajectory for where Anna would've gone considering the visible broken and bent branches. Sure enough a large caliber bullet was lodged in the wood of the tree next to the officer.

"Is it recent? Do you know if it's Nick's?" Michael asked taking in the rather large bullet protruding from the tree.

"I know enough to know it's not good," Jake muttered under his breath and looked up ahead of them towards a rocky ledge. "Keep moving, Tyler."

*****

The forest was swarming with cops, some who were very familiar to Nick Spencer. He weighed his options. He could ditch the gun and still let Jared take the fall for *attempted* murder. Nick didn't think Anna had seen who had shot at her. She may believe it was Jared. But could he go back to Damon and say he failed? That was suicide.

Below him, Nick heard a commotion. Through the branches he spotted a K9 officer and a very large dog that would undoubtedly lead them to his location. Movement behind the handler caught his attention. *Well, looky here. It's my old friend. Hello, Jake.*

Nick slid the rifle's strap to his side and began climbing a tree. The branches were spaced just right so that he could conceivably climb to a rocky ledge well above the approaching officers. It was a better option than sitting and waiting for them to find him.

He had to distract that dog. Reaching for his rifle, he sought the K9 officer in his scope. He wouldn't kill him... just keep him off his scent. Nick squeezed the trigger.

****

The shot rang out. Chaos erupted all around Michael. The man standing just feet ahead of him fell backwards onto the ground writhing in pain. The dog howled and barked.

"Get down, Tyler." Jake ordered, drawing his gun and moving behind a tree. "Collin, you okay?"

"Just my arm," the wounded officer said through gritted teeth.

Michael moved into action, doing what he knew he had to do. The dog lunged forward protectively, but thankfully the officer still held the lead in his other hand. He said the right words to soothe the dog and Michael gently pulled the man to safe coverage under the trees.

"Rubber gloves are in my right pocket," Collin choked out.

Michael found the gloves and began ripping the officer's shirt sleeve away. He balled up the fabric he had torn and started packing the wound.

"I need a tourniquet," Michael stated. "Are you carrying one?"

"Left side pocket."

Thankfully it was standard practice for officers to carry them in their tactical pants. Michael found what he needed and tightened it against the wound. The man breathed in sharply, but nodded a thank you to Michael.

"Jake," Michael called to his friend but soon realized Jake was nowhere to be seen.

*****

Anna jolted awake at the sound of the gun shot. Instinctively, she felt her chest and was relieved when she didn't find an open gash. How long had she been asleep? She knew she would hear it from Michael if and when he ever found her. He would probably say something like, *Leave it to you, Petunia, to fall asleep in the middle of danger.* Had she dreamed the gun shot? Everything seemed calm. Eerily quiet. As if nothing had happened at all.

Then came the raised, angry voices calling to one another from multiple directions. She debated whether to stay put or to look outside the mouth of the cave. Curiosity won out and she slid over just to the opening. She saw a man with a rifle strapped around his neck and shoulder. He clung to branches of a tree below her and moved effortlessly as he attempted to climb higher and higher. Soon he'd be at her level. Was he an officer?

It was when he had turned his body to reach for the next tree limb that she got a glimpse of his face. Jake's partner. The one she had seen in the photos. Her heart plunged. She looked around the cave to see if there was anything she could use to defend herself should he spot her. There was nothing. Absolutely nothing.

Anna slid back against the wall and clenched her eyes shut. When she was a kid she used to think if she couldn't see the monster in the closet, he couldn't see her. Well, this was the updated adult version. If anything, at least she wouldn't see her death coming.

Bang!

The reverberation of the gun shot vibrated in her ears. Her eyes flew open just in time to see Nick fall from the branch he had grabbed. Anna moved to the opening, dragging her stiff legs along in the dirt. She looked over the ledge to see he had landed onto the trail below… very close to the edge of a steep drop off to the river below.

"Don't move, Nick. Hands where I can see them," A loud familiar voice shouted.

"You still have horrible aim, Cory." The wounded man laughed.

"If I wanted you dead… you'd be dead. Don't make me shoot you again." It was Jake. *Thank you, God!*

Nick laughed and started getting to his feet despite the bleeding wound in his leg.

"Stay down. Last warning." Anna saw Jake inching closer up the trail, gun drawn and trained on Nick.

"You see, that's the difference between you and I, Jake." Nick reached for a smaller gun hidden in his belt. "You're slow to act. Maybe if you weren't so slow Beth would still be …"

Another shot rang out. Anna gasped as she watched the events transpire. It was as if they were happening in slow motion. Nick was hit in his chest, but the man ran… *actually ran*… to the edge of the drop off and *jumped*. She screamed. Jake looked up and spotted her leaning over the side of the rocky ledge.

"Anna… stay there!" He called to her and ran to the edge of the trail to confirm that Nick was dead. He holstered his weapon and radioed in. "Be advised… the second suspect is deceased."

*****

"How did she even get up there? I don't even see a path." Jake squinted to the opening of the cave high above where he and Michael stood in bewilderment.

"Are the kids safe?" Anna called down.

"Everyone is safe and accounted for," Michael called up. He could see her visibly relax even from the distance between them.

Cal joined them to let them know Collin had been taken by ambulance to the hospital and was in good spirits.

"Have they found Nick's body?" Jake asked.

"Not yet. With those rapids… he could've been pulled under or pushed downstream further than we thought. They won't give up until he's found, don't worry."

"I'm not worried. I *know* I hit him squarely in the chest." Jake's words were confident, but Michael knew his friend wouldn't be content until it was confirmed that the threat was finally over.

It was then that Cal looked up to see what they kept looking at. "How in the world did she…"

Both men just shrugged.

Michael looked above the cave entrance and pointed. "That's the main road above her. We can drop down and get to her that way."

"Oh… we're just going to *drop down*? What are you? Part spider?" Jake looked at his friend partially amused.

"You did your part, Cory. Now let me do what I do best." Michael thumped his friend on the chest with a broad smile. Anna was alive. Michael could fly at that moment… rappelling would be nothing.

"So, Petunia…" He called up to her and she scooted to the edge once again, looking down. "You okay up there? Think you can wait a little longer?"

She responded with a thumbs up.

Leaving her under the watch of an officer, Michael and Jake ran down the trail back to Mr. Turner's cabin. There was a shed full of gear that would come in handy for the task at hand. The ride back to the drop zone after retrieving the gear felt like it took hours rather than minutes. Michael comforted himself with the knowledge that she was alive and safe.

The sun was setting and the police officers started to illuminate the area with spot lights and flash lights. As he got the gear from Jake's truck, Michael called down to Anna.

"You still there, Anna?"

He heard shifting and moving around. "Where would I go exactly? Please tell me you have a plan that doesn't involve me climbing down a tree."

Michael smiled as he fastened his harness. "Good news. You do not have to climb down a tree."

"You wouldn't happen to have some fancy fire man machine to drop down and get me, would you?"

Securing his line to the back of Jake's truck Michael moved carefully to the edge. "Well, I wouldn't call it *fancy* necessarily."

He heard shuffling followed by, "Michael Tyler, what are you doing?"

"I'm coming to you, Petunia."

He started descending, giving his rope enough slack to drop down little by little.

"Um. Now might be a good time to tell you," Anna said nervously. "I have a real fear of dangling by a string above a scary drop."

"You were brave enough to get this high up and find this cool hiding spot... I think you're brave enough to do a little rock climbing with me." Michael was just above her now. "Scoot back into your cave for a minute so I can rappel down a little further, Anna."

She complied and he dropped to just a little below the ledge and opening of the cave. It was then he noticed the thin, rocky path she must've taken. He knew better than to do it, but he looked down and his heart nearly stopped. If she had fallen…

"Okay. Ready? Do you think you can slip this on for me?" He pulled a pen light out of his pocket to shine on Anna to assess her condition.

"What even *is* that? It's just rope." Anna shook her head and pushed it away.

"Hey, Jake. Have EMT on standby please," he called up after noticing the cuts and bruises on her face, arms, and hands.

"I'm fine. I just want this day over with."

"Mm hmm. Bring your legs over this way and let me help you slip this on."

"I don't think so, Sir." Anna looked highly offended.

"Anna… the alternative is much worse, believe me."

"But… I don't want to fall."

"You won't. Trust me."

Anna swallowed hard and looked past him to the trees below.

"Nope. Don't do that." He lifted her chin gently with one of his fingers. "Look at my face, my forehead, or above us. Got it?"

She nodded and let him put the harness on her, clipping her to his own harness with a heavy duty carabiner. Terror. Her expression was one of pure terror when he told her to put her arms around his neck and let herself slip off the ledge. Yet, she did it. Now, he needed to distract her.

"I have to apologize to you, Anna," he said as he gave the signal for the men above them to start pulling.

"Why? Did you forget the s'mores stuff?" she asked

nervously, clenching her eyes shut as they began to move upwards.

"I kind of rewrote our story."

She opened one eye and looked up at him. "What?"

"*Super Mike and Super Anna*... I want it rewritten."

"Wh... what's wrong with it?" She sounded indignant.

"Let me see if I can retell it for you..." Michael glanced down at her before continuing. "Once upon a time there was a guy named Super Mike. He wore a cape and was bullet proof. His job was saving people. There was one person in particular he seemed to save a lot. Her name was Petunia..."

"Wait a minute. I'll have you know..."

"Shh. Don't interrupt," he whispered in her ear before continuing. "Now there was this other girl that Michael knew really well. Her name was Super Anna. This girl was amazing. She ran faster than light. And, Man, she could shoot fire from her eyes... especially when she was feeling snarky."

Anna cleared her throat.

"One day... Petunia had gotten herself into a fix, but something happened that she didn't expect."

"What? What happened?" Anna asked after he paused for too long.

Michael looked up and saw that they were getting closer to the top.

"Well..." he started up again. "Petunia was reminded by God one day that she *wasn't* weak... she was amazing and brilliantly creative. Beautiful, too. But people had made her feel like she was nothing. And she believed them for *far* too long."

Anna swallowed audibly and Michael cleared his throat before finishing the story.

"And that's when it happened." Michael reached up and grabbed a rock that jetted out to keep Anna's head from hitting it.

"What happened?"

"Petunia remembered that *all* super heroes have secret identities. Petunia was a secret identity... for Super Anna. Petunia was Super Anna all along... she just forgot who she was."

Anna's mouth dropped open just as Michael took a hold of Jake's hand extended to him, pulling the two up to solid ground. As soon as they were safe, Michael undid the clip to Anna's harness.

"You're safe, Petunia." He winked at her and smiled gently, desperately wanting to pull her back into his arms.

Anna didn't speak and Michael grew concerned.

"Are you okay? Are you hurt?" He noticed she was clinging to his arms for dear life. "Is it your legs?"

"That was..." her voice sounded watery and he leaned down to her ear.

"There's more to this story, but I'll tell you later," Michael smiled.

"There's more?" Anna's balance was off.

"Yup. I'll tell you the ending... after you go get checked at the hospital." He waved his coworkers over and they began helping her onto a gurney. Surprisingly, she didn't fight or complain.

He was about to join her in the ambulance when Jake came up next to him.

"Super Mike? Super Anna? Do I even *want* to know what you were talking about down there?"

"Just taking *your* advice, Cory." Michael laughed and slapped his friend on the back before jumping inside the ambulance alongside the woman who held his heart.

32

The hours that followed the whole horrible incident at the cabin were a blur. By the time Anna was released from the emergency room with a clean bill of health it was early the next morning. She and Michael had very little opportunity to speak any more though she desperately wanted to know the ending of the story. Her father refused to leave her side.

Tim had driven his daughter home and made sure the house stayed quiet so Anna could get much needed sleep. Ellie and Sam went to the Tyler farm and Colleen distracted them both with fun activities. Everyone decided the boat had sailed on the cabin. It would take a long time to be able to enjoy it again… if ever. Especially for Ellie, who continued blaming herself for falling for her father's manipulation.

Of course, an event involving a shady cop and a potential list of corrupt authority figures got the attention of the news stations. While no one spoke directly to the reporters, except for a vague statement delivered by Cal Jenkins, word got to Alexis in rehab. Anna could hear her sister sobbing on the other end of phone when Alex talked with their father. The kids spoke to their mother to calm her fears. And then she asked to speak to Anna. At the time, it was too much. Anna didn't have it in her to comfort her sister when she was still trying to heal from the episode herself.

Anna was kept busy talking to Cal Jenkins, making a formal statement. The DA had heavy charges to bring down on many people, including Jared who faced attempted kidnapping, assault, and weapon charges.

"But what about the people on that list?" Anna asked as Cal walked her safely to her car early Friday evening. "J.T. and Lewis died for that information."

The detective just sighed and his shoulders slumped. "I wish I knew how to answer you, Anna. It's not fair that some are going to face charges and others aren't. All I know is what I was told. Sometimes it's safer to let a few get away with some bad things than to risk stirring up a bee hive that can threaten the safety of many people."

"That's the dumbest thing I have ever heard," Anna said plainly.

"Yeah. I know." Cal sighed and opened her car door for her. "Be safe, Anna. Call me if you need anything, okay?"

Anna stewed over the injustice for the rest of Friday, occasionally sending Michael a rant via text while he was on shift. He sent her funny pictures and quips to lighten her mood. And for the most part, it worked. However, what really helped Anna get through the initial anxiety and emotions pertaining to everything she had been through was her writing.

Flicking on the desk lamp and lighting her favorite scented candle, she spun a story on her laptop well into the early hours of Saturday. The fiction novel mirrored her own life and experiences. Some of it brought laughter and some of it brought tears. While she recounted tales of her childhood and beyond, Alexis' face kept popping into Anna's mind.

God had given Anna a new view of her identity. Could he do it for Alexis as well? That fateful day at the cabin came to Anna's mind. Ellie had asked if it was ever too late to change... could God still step in?

She remembered her response to her niece. *I don't think it's ever too late to change paths. The only time it's too late is when we're dead. As long as you have breath in your lungs it is never too late.* Did Anna truly believe that? Would she be willing to hold out the same hope to Alexis? To potentially help her sister find her identity in God… so that she could find her being in Him like Anna had?

After sleeping in for a bit, Anna dressed and quietly whispered to her father where she was headed. His look was one of pure love and he whispered, "Tell her daddy loves her." With that, Anna drove the two hours to New Hope Rehabilitation Facility.

She had to check in her purse due to the tight security. Anna allowed herself to be searched prior to being led to Alexis' room. Walking the halls of the building and seeing people in varying stages of addiction and healing caused a lump to grow in her throat.

"Alexis, you have a visitor," the attendant said as she opened her sister's door, revealing Alexis sitting cross legged on her bed reading.

There was a look of pure shock on Alexis' face when Anna entered.

"Annalise?"

"Hey, Alex."

An uncomfortable silence filled the room as the two stared at each other awkwardly for several moments. Then a tear slid down Alexis' cheek, followed by several more.

"You came. I never thought you'd come."

Anna nodded and moved further into the room, sitting on the edge of the bed. She scanned the small bedroom. There wasn't much there by way of décor or furniture, but one thing got Anna's attention. On top of a side table was a frame that held many pictures. The kids' most recent school pictures. An old family picture. Then there was one of her and Alex that Anna didn't remember. They were young... definitely pre-teens.

"When was this taken?" Anna asked as she took the frame down and examined it closer.

Alex smiled a mostly toothless smile. "Don't you remember?"

"I really don't," Anna smiled at the image. Her sister had always been so beautiful, but in that image... Alex was glowing. She was happy.

"That was my twelfth birthday. Remember we went to the movies and shopping at the mall?"

"Oh, my word! Yes! I remember it now. We bought matching bracelets."

Alexis nodded with a reminiscent smile. "I kept that bracelet forever. Until this last time... I couldn't go back for it. They wouldn't let me."

"Who wouldn't?" Anna asked feeling her heart melt.

"The police. We were all forced out of the house and they boarded it up. They condemned it."

Silence filled the room again and Anna wasn't sure where to start saying all of the things she wanted to say to her sister. Alexis spoke up first.

"That was the last time I remember feeling happy."

"The last time? Alex what happened? How did you..." Anna paused.

"What? How did I get this way?" Alex blurted out and cackled. "I wish I knew. I lost myself somewhere."

"Do you want to find you again? This you?" Anna asked as she held up the picture.

"Oh, Girl. That Alexis is long gone."

"What if you can find a *new* you? There's always hope, Alex. God hasn't given up on you… and neither will I."

The next hour was spent talking, crying, and laughing. Anna shared what God had done in her own life. Whether Alexis understood completely would remain to be seen. Visiting time was soon over, but Anna promised to return.

"You promise for real?" Alexis got up off the bed as Anna rose to go.

"I promise." Anna said and embraced her sister. Alexis felt so bony and slight in her arms that Anna didn't want to squeeze too hard.

Anna was about to let go, but Alexis held on tighter and leaned close to her sister's ear. "Thank you for protecting my babies. They told me what you did. Thank you for doing what I can't do right now."

"You're welcome." Anna gulped back the emotion and released her sister. "I'll keep them safe until you're ready to do it yourself."

On the way home, Anna decided to drive through Skennan Cove since it wasn't far out of her way. There was a cute boutique that Anna used to frequent that sold various things, including jewelry. Alexis' birthday would be coming up in a month and Anna wanted to find a pair of matching bracelets. She settled on a pair of thin gold chains with hearts in the center.

It was when Anna was back on the road and driving through town that she spotted the venue where she and

Jonathan were supposed to have had their reception… on that *very* day. What possessed her to park across the street and watch a bridal couple pose for pictures, she didn't know. They looked so happy and he couldn't take his eyes off his bride. Their friends flittered around them playfully, smiling and brimming with joy. *That was supposed to be me. I was supposed to be the bride today, God.*

Anna shook her head as if clearing her mind of faulty thinking. She and Jonathan wouldn't have been like that happy couple, she realized. He would have criticized every little thing she did. Kirstyn would've been looking longingly at Anna's groom. No. Things happened how they needed to happen. In truth, Anna didn't even miss Jonathan… just the *idea* of him.

She let herself have a moment to mourn, but turned the car around and headed home where she belonged. It was when she pulled into her driveway that she saw Michael. His arms were crossed at his chest and he smiled as she put her Jeep in park.

"Look what I brought," he said with a cheesy smile, holding up a bag of marshmallows.

"For s'mores?" Anna gushed.

"Yup. Your dad helped me get the fire pit going in your back yard."

"What fire pit? We don't have one," Anna questioned.

"The one I hauled from Mom and Dad's house in the back of my truck."

Anna just stood staring at him in wonder.

"Come on." He took her hand and led her to the backyard. "I'll charbroil you a marshmallow."

She giggled. "You remembered."

"Of course I did." He smiled. "I also remembered that I need to finish telling you the ending to the revised story."

"Tell me Super Anna doesn't take up trail running, because I think I have had enough of that." Anna smirked. Then she noticed they were alone. "Hey, where are the kids? I bet they'd like a s'more, too."

"Yeah, I convinced your dad to keep them inside for a bit. Just until we finish talking." Michael motioned for her to take a seat on the bench near the fire as he put a marshmallow on a skewer.

Anna smiled and bit her lower lip. What was happening right now?

"So where were we…" he asked reflectively as he set her marshmallow on fire. "Oh yes. Petunia and Super Anna are one and the same."

She watched as he wedged the blackened marshmallow between the graham crackers and chocolate before handing it to her. She took a bite as he put a new marshmallow on the skewer.

"Nice plot twist. Go on. I'm listening." Anna said with a mouth full of delicious marshmallow.

"Turns out Super Mike found himself in quite an unpleasant spot, however," he began.

"Oh?"

"Yeah. He fell under this weird spell that had him believing he wanted to be alone forever. He saw people around him happy in love with some pretty great people. Yet, poor Super Mike thought that wasn't for him." Michael paused to put his lightly toasted marshmallow on a graham cracker and he took a long bite, building the suspense in Anna.

"That sounds lonely. So, what happened?" Anna urged him on.

"Well, he met Petunia – also known as Super Anna – and found himself really confused. And *scared,* to be honest with you," Michael said thoughtfully, putting the s'more down on a plate next to him. "She made him want the things he saw his other Super friends having. And somehow through some weird magic… I think they call it *Anna's Law*… Super Mike fell in love with Super Anna."

He turned to face her then with all vulnerability and sweetness. "Do you think you might possibly feel the same, Petunia?"

In that moment, Anna wondered if this is what it felt like to have a heart so full that it might burst. She had heard people describe such moments, but she had never experienced one herself. That is, until now.

Michael cleared his throat and looked at her with nervous anticipation

"I might." The words came out like an embarrassingly high pitched squeal of glee. *Somewhere down the street a dog just lifted his head in confusion…*

"You… *might?*"

"I do." *Wait, that sounds like a marriage vow. Too dramatic, Anna. Try again.* Anna sighed self-consciously. "I mean… I do feel the same. Very much so. Yes."

Why couldn't she stop her mouth from speaking? Michael was going to change his mind and leave her holding the bag of marshmallows.

He laughed softly, apparently not put off by her quirks. "Anna, I love you."

"I love you, too. More than I can verbalize."

Michael smiled sweetly and she noticed his eyes went to her lips, just as they had in the past. "Do you mind if I kiss you?"

"I… I don't think I would mind at all," Anna stuttered.

He moved in closer. She moved in closer. They both moved in closer until… they bumped noses and foreheads awkwardly.

"Oops. Sorry," Anna whispered.

"How about you turn that way and I go this way," he suggested tilting his head in the opposite direction.

Anna had always wondered what it would be like to kiss Michael Tyler, even as a young smitten pre-teen girl. Whatever she had imagined it would be like… it didn't compare to the reality of being in his arms. He kissed her so tenderly and it ended way too soon. The back door opened and Sam came running out with Livi hot on his heels.

"S'mores! S'more time!" they called out.

Ellie quietly sat down next to Anna on the other side of the bench with a knowing smile. Then her father sat down in the lawn chair right across from them. He smiled at his daughter and then leveled Michael with a look.

"So how about we go over the rules for dating *my* Super Anna," Tim began. Michael laughed nervously and reached over, taking Anna's hand in his. "Rule one… if you break her heart I am fully prepared to perform your funeral."

Michael laughed out loud and then realized the Pastor was not. "He's kidding, right?"

Anna just shrugged with a huge smile that she didn't think would ever fade away.

*****

"Let's see. Do I have a volunteer willing to model all of the equipment that firemen have to wear during an active fire?" Michael asked the massive group of students and teachers in the school parking lot.

Anna sighed. She knew very well what was coming. Even Mrs. Erbe knew what was about to happen and began giggling before Anna's name was even called.

"Miss Munson, you did such an excellent job when we went over this last year. Why don't you come up and help us out again?" His smile was incorrigible.

"Go on, Dear. He's waiting," Mrs. Erbe urged.

Anna forced herself forward and gave Michael a warning look. "Just remember we're playing dodgeball with the family tonight. Paybacks are tough, Tyler."

He smirked before beginning his spiel. "Let's start with the overalls. Do you know how many layers of heavy fabric make up these special pants?"

Once again Scooter held out the pants and Anna stepped inside, pulling the suspenders to her shoulders. And so it went much as it had before with Michael explaining each and every piece of equipment leading up to the heavy helmet. She did her part as his supportive girlfriend even when he placed the awkward helmet on her head and pulled the visor down.

Her claustrophobia was about at its peak when she heard him say, "Ah, I forgot an important piece of hardware."

"What are you talking about?" Anna couldn't imagine what he could've possibly left out. She was hot and weighed down.

"Scooter, could you kindly remove the helmet from our volunteer please?" Michael asked.

The helmet was lifted from her head and Anna looked over at Michael in confusion. He held a small little jewelry box. Her breath caught in her throat as it registered what was happening.

Michael got down on one knee. Anna looked out at the sea of faces and noticed her father and the entire Tyler family, minus Jenna and Ben, had appeared. Had they been hiding somewhere? Colleen recorded the moment with her phone, most likely to send it to Jenna in North Carolina. Tessa and Sean held Evie. Kate and Dan wrangled little Eli and Lydia. Sam jumped up and down excitedly. Ellie held Livi up so she could see everything that was happening. Her father looked teary, but happy.

"Annalise Munson, will you marry me?" Michael looked up at her with all the love he felt showing in his eyes.

"Yes. Yes, I will marry you!" she said enthusiastically. Realizing that the glove on her hand hindered proper engagement ring placement, she attempted to shake it off of her. However, in her attempts to free herself from Michael's huge glove she hit the ring right out of his grasp as he was coming close to put it on her hand.

A collective gasp sounded through the crowd as it flew into the air and rolled under the wheel of the massive firetruck. Anna moved to help retrieve it, but Michael leaned down and kissed the top of her head.

"Stay put," he said. A moment later, it was found and safely tucked in his palm. "Let's try this again."

Anna smiled innocently up into Michael's face and whispered, "Are you sure it's me that you want? I can be…"

"You're exactly who God made you to be and that is who I want, Petunia." Michael spoke in a low voice for her ears only as he slid the sparkling diamond onto her ring finger.

The crowd cheered and surrounded them in a circle of love. Even Scooter threw on the sirens for good measure.

Later that evening after dinner had been served, eaten, and cleared away Anna decided to spring a surprise of her own. Reaching into her bag she pulled out a brand new book. Hugging Michael from behind while he sat at the dinner table, she slid the book in front of him.

"Look what came today," she whispered in his ear.

"Anna… is this…"

"Mm hmm. Read the dedication page."

He flipped the cover open and read out loud, "*To Super Mike, whose love and encouragement made this book happen. You have my heart forever and for always.*"

"I'm so proud of you, Petunia." He stood, pulling her into his arms.

"*Anna's Law* by Annalise Munson," her father read the title proudly and held it up for everyone in the room to see. "My girl wrote this!"

"Way to go, Anna!" Sean smiled. Everyone else followed with affirmations of love and encouragement.

"Can I see it?" Ellie opened the cover and read the first few lines out loud. *"Anna Lawson stuck her earbuds in and set out at a steady pace down the street leaving her apartment far behind her. The pounding music vibrated off of her eardrums and matched the thudding of her heart in her chest..."*

Dear Reader,

Thank you for reading book three of the Deer Creek Chronicles! I'm not sure who derives the most pleasure from these stories... you or me.

If you are enjoying these books, keep your eyes peeled for the fourth and final installment coming soon in 2025!

Be blessed and I'll see you around in Deer Creek.

With much love,
D. Emily Smith